charcuterie girl

JA WRIGHT

ISBN (979-8-9915393-1-9)

Printed and bound in the United States of America. First printing May 2025. First edition.

Publisher: Saint Johns Creek Publishing, LLC, United States
For more information, visit: www.jawrightauthor.com

All Persons Fictitious Disclaimer Notice

This is a work of fiction, as the characters, events, and places have been rearranged to suit the convenience of the story. Unless otherwise indicated, all of the characters, story, names, and incidents portrayed in this production are completely fictitious, either being a product of the author's vivid imagination or have been used in a fictitious manner. No identification with actual persons (living or deceased), places, buildings, and products, is intended or should be inferred. Any resemblance to actual persons, living or dead, or actual events is purely coincidental.

Special Thanks and Acknowledgments

I'd like to acknowledge the hard work and dedication of the following individuals and/or companies who also helped bring this novel into reality.

Illustrations: Gemma Rakia
Book Cover Artist: Kebbie Soleo
Formatting and Page Design: Marie Stirk

Contents

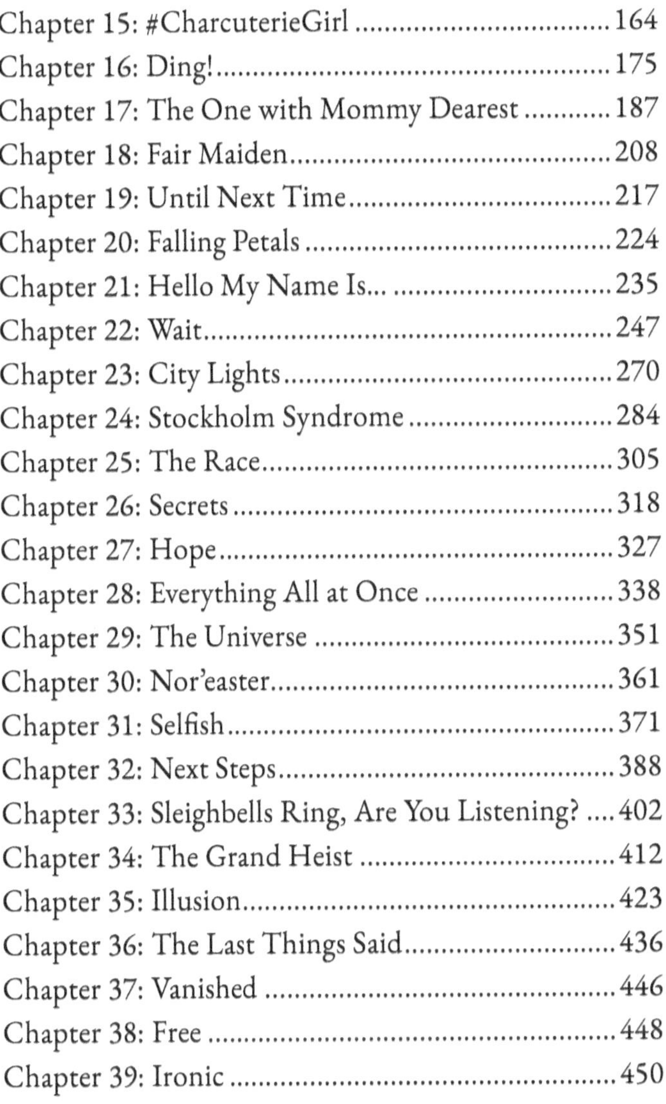

Prologue

Internet Search: Nervous Breakdown Symptoms 3,498,112 results. *I see I'm not alone in this.* Google results:

- Feeling anxious, depressed, or tearful
- Intense distress and nervousness
- Shaking, dizziness, or nausea
- Neglecting personal hygiene, unhealthy eating, or not exercising
- Overwhelming desire to punch someone or something

However, Google failed to mention:

- Having a total meltdown in a packed McDonald's restaurant at 2:00 p.m. on a Saturday in the snooty, judgmental town of

Belmont, New York, right in front of a group of uptight soccer moms hungry for fresh gossip.

- Or that those same cliquish Belmont women would ensure I never heard the end of it.

I now know that if a nervous breakdown is inevitable, one should try and wait to do it in the comfort of one's own home, a therapist's chair, or even alone in one's car, with Adele blasting at full volume. That's how it's meant to be done.

But I guess nervous breakdowns don't exactly wait for an invitation; they show up unannounced, driven by a brain on the edge.

Driven by a relentless hunger.

CHAPTER 1

The Fry-Sis I Didn't See Coming

I circled the Belmont McDonald's restaurant parking lot four times, questioning whether I should go in. At first, the drive-through had been a long, slow-moving line of cars, but it had finally shortened—mocking me.

My little darlings, five-year-old Myla and seven-year-old Austin, sat in the car's back seat, debating like a couple of oily-haired, strung-out gamblers in Vegas, placing their final bets on the exact moment I would cave. They thought I couldn't hear them.

"No, we're not actually getting lunch. She just wants to drive around and smell the food."

"It's not our fault she's fat. Do you think we'll get to eat? I bet no. She always does this."

"Be quiet! And don't say she's fat. She'll hear you."

"No, you be quiet."

Smack!

"Why did you hit me? Mommy, Austin hit me!"

"No fighting, or we're going home," I squeaked in an exasperated voice. Did they hear *me*? I wasn't sure. No one seemed to listen anymore.

"I knew it," Austin muttered under his breath as he stared hopelessly out the car window.

Myla sank back into her seat, arms crossed in utter frustration. Long, curly tendrils of chestnut brown hair had loosened from her ponytail and tumbled across her round cheeks. With a long breath, she blew the hair out of her eyes with a huff. She scowled.

I circled the building again as my stomach rumbled at the aroma of cheeseburgers and grease wafting through the car's air vents.

Don't do it, Emma. Drive away. You'll regret it later if you don't.

But...*french fries.*

Willpower gone, I turned the wheel and entered the drive-through line. Moments later, bags of food and money changed hands through the little window, and I handed the kid's meals over to the backseat gamblers. As I rolled my SUV forward, I put my hand in my bag and lifted a french fry to my mouth.

A soggy, cold, salt-free fry.

I slammed the brakes, and my SUV screeched to a halt. My eyelids fluttered ever-so-slightly, my breath quickened, and a few muscles twitched. I *needed* those fries. Needed them hot. Crispy. *Salty.*

The finale had come and gone: a disappointing climax in my twisted love-and-hate affair with food.

The car behind me honked, and I pulled my SUV into a parking space with a squeal. "Come on, kids!" I said as I marched the three of us into the crowded restaurant.

Pushing aside a brood of soccer moms, I slammed my fries on the counter. "These fries suck."

Astrid, a twiggy teenager sporting black winged eyeliner and a studded nose ring, stood behind the register and placed a fist firmly on each hip. She leaned into me. "What do you want me to do about it?"

"I want some new fries. Hot ones—with salt."

Astrid rolled her eyes and shrugged. "You got people ahead of you, lady. You're gonna have to wait." She eyed me up and down. "Besides, you don't look like you've missed too many meals."

The soccer mom next to me covered her mouth to suppress a laugh, and then audibly snickered. The other women exchanged looks. I narrowed my eyes at Astrid.

"What did you just say to me?" I said, voice low and tight, as a slow burn crept up my neck and into my cheeks.

The woman next to me scurried away and instinctively gathered her children into a protective huddle to keep them away from the mad woman clutching the bag of wilted fries.

A voice piped up behind me. "She said you could stand to skip the fries. Get to the back of the line."

People all around us murmured in agreement. I overheard the fry cook in the kitchen drop a tray of frozen fries into the sizzling oil. He shook his head and sighed loudly, griping, "Fat people are so damn sensitive."

A voice in the kitchen echoed his sentiment, "And crazy."

Astrid laughed out loud.

I spun around, realizing that *everyone* in the restaurant was laughing—at me. A chaotic, unstoppable feeling of exasperation overcame me. My stomach twisted, my cheeks burned, and frustration surged so quickly into anger that I barely had time to brace myself. I clenched my jaw.

Enough.

"Crazy? You want to see fucking crazy?"

I snatched a tray of salt and pepper shakers off the

counter and started flinging them into the crowded restaurant like I was Oprah giving out cars. "You get a shaker! And you get a shaker! You all get a fucking shaker!"

The McDonald's patrons dodged and ducked as the shakers went airborne, crashing into the floor and shattering as they created a black and white atomic bomb dust storm.

Snatching up two ketchup bottles, I squeezed with reckless abandon and watched a fountain of red rain down like a condiment apocalypse. People dodged behind booths and ran for the doors.

Leaning over the counter, I grabbed the drive-through mic, and shouted, "Clean up on aisle seven—fat girl gone wild!"

The drive-through window attendant backed away from me slowly, eyes darting as he planned an escape route.

I turned just in time to catch Astrid staring at me in disbelief, her hand clamped over her mouth to smother a laugh. I grabbed her brown, polyester, unpressed uniform by the collar and shook her back and forth with all my might as the days, weeks, and months of frustration poured out of me. Her lightly fastened hair came undone from its bun, beads of spit flew from her wide-open mouth, and her eyes rolled in her head.

"Listen to me, bitch," I growled, still shaking her,

"I've got seven extra Healthy Horizons weight loss points left to use this weekend. Seven! For this entire weekend. And I'm not wasting them on some soggy, unsalted, pathetic excuse for french fries that your dumb ass is too lazy to cook. Give me some fucking hot fries right now, or this place goes down!"

Looking back, I don't recall the exact moment when Astrid's punch landed me sideways on the floor. I was later told I convulsed slightly and even smiled before losing consciousness.

As I lay unmoving and still, I floated into a dark, comforting abyss. I dreamed I was sinking my teeth into a decadent burger, the succulent meat, and rich, savory cheese igniting my senses—a sublime explosion of flavor. Then, like a sputtering bulb, my mind flickered back to awareness.

"Is she breathing?" I heard a voice say. My eyes peeked open. An elderly man covered in salt and pepper dust fanned my face with a grease-stained McDonald's paper napkin while his wife peered over his shoulder, brows furrowed.

Darkness again. Silence. Then—

"Josh called an ambulance. Should we try to move her?"

"Just wait until the PTA hears about this."

"Scandalous."

Twilight. Another flicker of awareness. The fry cook

hovered over me, shaking his head. "I can't pick her up. I mean, come on—I'm strong but not that strong."

My eyes jolted open.

"Bright light!" was all I could muster. And then back into the abyss.

When I finally came to, I was lying in a booth across from a skinny, twenty-something, redheaded man named Josh wearing a short-sleeved Oxford shirt and maroon tie. His name tag hung onto a safety pin, which dangled beneath the cursive embroidered title of Assistant Manager on his shirt. He clutched a clipboard holding a Customer Incident Form and looked at me, quite flustered.

A paramedic stood behind Josh. He held up my cell phone and shook his head.

"No one is answering," he reported to Josh. "I've tried calling her SOS number three times."

The paramedic had found my cell phone in my purse and tried to call Jack, my estranged husband. Jack was my next of kin and emergency contact, a paradox in my phone list because he had become my anti-family without my consent. He never even answered the call.

The paramedic shot a worried glance. "Ma'am? Are you okay?"

Whomp. Whomp. Whomp. My head thumped with a steady rhythm at the spot where Astrid punched me. He held up his hand and made a peace sign at me.

"How many fingers am I holding up?"

I squinted in double vision as two fuzzy sets of his fingers swayed before my eyes.

"Two? Four? No, two." I held up a peace sign with my two fingers and waved them back at him.

"Do you know who you are?"

"Emma Davis."

"Do you know where you are?

"Bloomingdales?"

Then, as the fog dissipated, reality settled in. My face flushed hot with embarrassment as I realized where I was—and that everyone in the restaurant was watching me. Through bleary eyes, I scanned my surroundings.

Red lights from the ambulance outside danced swirly patterns on the dining room walls. A group of minivan moms observed from a distance, whispering and snickering amongst themselves. Nearby, a ketchup-covered toddler clung to his mother's leg, pointing at me as he wailed. Astrid winced in pain, holding her hand while glaring at me from behind the register. The fry guy stood behind her, filming the scene with his cell phone. Myla and Austin were crouched behind a booth a few feet away, eyes wide, their heads stacked like a couple of cartoon spies.

Josh lowered the clipboard and frowned. "What can I get you, Ms. Davis?"

Two words, guttural and deep, rose from my throat. "Hot fries," I croaked.

My tears threatened to spill, but I held them back, knowing it wasn't the fries I craved. What I desperately wanted was to stop loathing myself so much. *Rotten mother. Horrible at relationships. Pathetic career. Fat. Alone. And just plain scared.*

Inside me, far below the oversized sweatshirt and the jeans that dug into my sides, I remembered her and missed her—the old me. The confident, tech-savvy entrepreneur and strong athlete I once was looking at this scene, shaking her head and scoffing. *What the heck, Emma? You need to pull yourself together. Like right now.*

Ten years ago, I had been everything; I had followed my dreams. Then, I met Jack, and the successful life I had built crumbled.

Josh beckoned an employee over, exchanged a few words, and then returned to the clipboard. He began methodically asking questions from the form and writing down answers. At the same time, the paramedic shoved a blood pressure sleeve up my arm, trapping me in the tiny booth. The force from the instrument squeezed my flabby arm into a balloon-like appendage. A pre-teen girl stared at my billowed arm and giggled with her friend.

My children watched from a few feet away, ostensibly embarrassed and looking as if they prayed no one knew we were related. That was when I saw it, felt it, and will never forget it: rock bottom.

Someone set a tray of hot fries down in front of me, reaching over my shoulder. I looked around at the mess I had made in the restaurant, then stared at the food as big, wet tears finally let loose and fell onto the platter. I no longer felt hungry. The paramedic removed the blood pressure sleeve, and as my arm deflated, so did my soul.

"Ma'am, would you like to go in for observation?"

"No," I sniffed. "I'm going home."

I pushed the fries away, gathered my children, lowered my head, and walked to my car.

"Mommy's sorry. *Again.*"

"You can't help it if you're hungry. I don't need much lunch, Mommy. I'll share mine with you," said Myla, reaching out and placing her small hand in mine.

And rock bottom fell deeper still.

No wonder Jack left me.

CHAPTER 2

Triggers

The Belmont Healthy Horizons weekend weight loss group met on Saturday afternoons at the Our Lady of Mass Consumption church on Pratt Street. My cohorts and I shuffled in like the dutiful worshippers we were and filled the forgiving pews, which gave hope to the wide-bottomed and well-endowed.

Normally, we were a somewhat cheerful group, chatting and gossiping with one another about the prior week's mundane events, like PTA meetings, kids' birthdays, and club sports. *Normally*. However, on the Saturday following the McDonald's incident, the church was especially quiet. A few people coughed uncomfortably, and one or two even excused them-selves to the restroom when I entered.

I supposed this was because in Belmont, a small, affluent commuter suburb tucked away on the out-skirts of New York City, everybody knows everybody. Where parents put their infants on waiting lists for the good schools and pay hefty deposits to hold their place. Where domestic CEOs hire live-in nannies to do the child rearing. Where bored homemakers fester in gossip and drama because most have left their cushy ex-ecutive jobs for the 24-hour rat race of Mommy hood. In towns like Belmont, news travels fast, especially among the heavy set.

I sat in the back and pretended to leaf through the latest Healthy Horizons brochure until Sandy arrived. Sandy Meyers, our perky and skinny role model, led our group. A five-foot-three brunette with big brown eyes, Sandy had weighed 250 pounds following the birth of twins who had been spawned through the aid of the local fertility clinic. Two years later—and 120 pounds lighter—Sandy was living proof that pregnancy hor-mones and binge eating were no match for a woman with a slight case of OCD counting points with her calculator.

But today, Sandy was late, and I was starting to sweat. The room was too quiet. A tragedy occurred in the world of fat people this past week, and I was the leading news story: *Depressed Divorcee Attacks McDonald's Worker.*

"Ladies!" Sandy bounced in wearing cute yoga pants and a skintight T-shirt, showing off her skinny waist and fabulous bosoms, which she had acquired from two years of nursing her fertility twins. Her ponytail bobbed back and forth as she scanned the room, searching. Her eyes finally settled on me, and her voice lowered to a more serious tone when she spoke again.

"Ladies, er—and gentleman, I am delighted you all made it today."

Roy, our token male, shifted uncomfortably in his seat and nodded at Sandy.

Sandy continued, "Today, before we go around the room and talk about our successes, which is, *of course*, the reason we are all here, I'd like to take a few moments to talk about the dark side of weight loss. We won't call these failures"—she popped a set of air quotes by her head—"because we have no losers in this room. We call them setbacks. And they happen to all of us from time to time."

I looked up and caught Sandy staring straight at me. My face flushed warm with embarrassment as everyone turned to follow her gaze. I wanted to leap across the pews and smack the perky smile off her skinny cheeks.

"Show of hands, friends. How many of us become grumpy when we don't get enough to eat?"

A murmur spread across the room as hands raised half-heartedly in agreement.

"Yes, this is normal," Sandy said, nodding. "Okay, who among us becomes very angry when we're hungry? *Hangry*." She practically growled the word.

There were more murmurs but no hand raising.

"Well," Sandy continued, "hunger-infused rage can be very common if you factor in all the things that contribute to it." She started counting off on her fingers. "Low blood sugar. Dehydration if you aren't drinking enough water—"

"Lack of sex because your estranged husband is a cheating asshole," I muttered to myself.

A loud laugh erupted behind me, echoing against the stained-glass windows lining Our Lady of Mass Consumption's walls.

"Excuse me?" Sandy looked around.

All eyes fell on the person behind me, whose chuckle had morphed into a belly laugh. I turned to see a slightly heavy-set brunette woman convulsing in silent, suppressed joy. Sandy cleared her throat and readdressed the room.

"I assure you all, there is nothing funny about the physical effects that food withdrawal can have on our bodies. This is a very real condition, ladies and gentlemen, and one we must all be prepared to address through our weight loss journey."

"Journey," I muttered again. "What a fucking crock of sh—"

The woman behind me cackled again, and I slithered down in my seat, grateful that Sandy's attention was no longer focused on me. The other meeting attendees broke out into confused whispers as Sandy straightened herself and walked to the whiteboard.

"Triggers!" Sandy said loudly. "Let's talk about what they are."

"Stress," A voice from the front pitched in confidently.

"Yes, stress is a major trigger of weight loss rage. What else?"

"Kids." This contribution came from Marilyn Feinstein in the front row. She had obviously just left the salon, rocking a perfect blowout and freshly manicured nails. She waved her hands in the air as if in despair, flashing a two-carat diamond, and looked around the room for confirmation as if to ask, "Am I right?"

No one confirmed that she was right.

Marilyn and I were friends when the kids were toddlers. We would meet at Jumpy Land and watch them play on the indoor trampolines while we gossiped about the neighbors. That was before the Great Separation when she decided to join Team Jack instead of staying loyal to me, as most of our friends had done.

On either side of Marilyn sat the two Jessicas. Married to oil tycoon Mortimer Wentworth, Jessica Wentworth hailed from a world of old money. On her other side was Jessica Pemberton, a former beauty queen who wed an aging Wall Street broker with thinning hair and liver-spotted skin. Both Jessicas followed the lead of their husbands, longtime friends of Jack, and distanced themselves from me the moment they learned of our split. All of them—*money-grubbing traitors.*

"What else might trigger weight loss rage?" Sandy asked, scanning the room.

"Exhaustion." This one came from Roy on the sidelines. I felt bad for Roy. It had to be hard being the only guy in Belmont counting points and getting in touch with his inner skinny chick. He began nodding off in his chair.

"Absolutely," Sandy said in a reassuring voice. She wrote 'Exhaustion' on the board in big letters. "Any other ideas?"

The room buzzed, but no one spoke.

"Come on, friends," Sandy cajoled. "There must be *something* else..." She looked right at me.

Annoyed, I pierced my lips and held her gaze. *You want to make an example of me? Fine. I'm going to set these people straight.* I abruptly stood from the wooden pew, cleared my throat, and addressed the room.

"There *is* something else, Sandy. How about when your husband leaves you for the waitress he met at Fun

Fridays family restaurant, sticking you with two confused kids and a sizable mortgage on a six-bedroom Colonial bought when all things seemed possible? How about wallowing in your misery by spending endless nights with your fat ass parked on the sofa as you devour wine, snack cakes, and bags of cheese puffs? Or better yet, let's talk about the joy of being in a room full of women who get to return to husbands who actually care about them, where their kids are growing up in normal, stable households. Look around you. The collective problem in this room isn't stress, dehydration, or exhaustion. *Hell no.* It's too much time on your hands, too many mommy cocktail hours, and too much goddamn fun that those of us who must work to support our kids will never know!"

Sandy gasped. Roy woke from his gentle slumber, and the group looked on in disbelief.

I nervously shifted from one foot to the other, twisting the Healthy Horizons pamphlet in my hands. Then, summoning the last bit of dignity I could muster, I stood tall, looked around the room and said, "Now fuck off."

"Good for you," the voice behind me whispered.

"I'm going home." I gathered up my coat and brochures and, head held high, marched slowly down the church's center aisle like a jilted bride.

Marilyn Feinstein gave me a side-eye and whispered

loudly to one of the Jessicas, "This confirms it. She's gone completely crazy. No wonder Jack left her."

Jessica, eyes wide, nodded in agreement.

The cackler who had been sitting behind me followed me up the aisle. She addressed the room. "I have to leave, too. I need to get her a candy bar. Must be low blood sugar."

"We have many low-point candy bar alternatives in the Healthy Horizons store!" Sandy yelled as I burst out of the church and into the cold, early spring air. I marched to my car.

"Wait. Wait up!" I turned to see the cackler sprinting towards me. When she caught up, panting and breathless, she said, "You're a rock star."

I looked around to see who she was talking to. Me? A rock star? *You've got the wrong fat girl.* I shook my head in denial, but she kept talking.

"I mean, I sat in that room looking around at the perfectly put-together women in their Lululemon leggings and Hermes handbags and thought I'd just landed in a Target commercial full of chubby Stepford Wives. But you're a real person."

I sighed. "You certainly read that room right."

She smiled. "I'm Evelyn Hanover. Evy. I just moved here from Washington, DC. Are the Healthy Horizons meetings here always so brutal?"

"I'm Emma Davis. And no, not normally, but I got

punched in the face by a McDonald's employee last week, which has caused some dissent amongst the fat population here in Belmont."

"What happened?"

"I only had seven points left for the weekend, and my fries were cold. We had an altercation."

"Who swung first?"

"Me?" I shrugged.

"See that?" Evy grinned. "Rock star!"

"I think I need a candy bar."

Evy paused, studying me momentarily, and replied, "I think what you need is a drink."

She extended her hand, and I shook it.

Hello, friendship.

CHAPTER 3

Tequila, Tacos and Therapy

Evy and I wandered into a bar called The Repub, located a block away from Our Lady of Mass Consumption and down the street from the University of Belmont. A large bar sat in the center, surrounded by tables and booths. Outdated red velour and gold wallpaper covered the walls, along with sports memorabilia from the university. Towards the back, two college kids set up sound equipment and a karaoke machine on a small stage.

We settled into a booth, and Evy motioned the waiter. A college student with a scarcely grown goatee and a Tweety-bird tattoo on his left forearm approached the table. He pulled a pencil from behind his ear and held up his notepad.

"What can I get you ladies? The bar is running a special tonight. Buy-one, get-one margaritas and pitchers of beer. Half-price tacos."

My mind started mentally calculating those points, somewhere in the range of *don't even think about it.* I began to decline, but Evy spoke up.

"Sounds great," Evy smiled. "Two margaritas and two pitchers of beer!"

"Are you crazy?" I whispered over the table to her. "That's an entire week's worth of flex points!"

She looked at me and laughed. "I declare it No-Points Saturday. Your cheat meal! Today, we toast the seven-point punch that apparently landed you in the Belmont Fat Girl Hall of Fame. Besides...*half-price tacos...*"

I lifted my hand to the spot where Tonya punched me. *Yeah, I could use a drink.* And tacos were basically my love language. I nodded in agreement. The waiter wrote down our order and walked away.

I studied Evy. She had a slightly heavy build, straight brown hair that fell to her shoulders, striking high cheekbones, a nearly perfect nose, and wide, expressive green eyes. When she talked, her face animated, and her laugh sounded genuine. She seemed like the kind of girl everyone would have been friends with during high school, the one who effortlessly fit in with every group. She starkly contrasted me, with my thick, wiry, sandy-blonde hair, steely gray eyes that never shined blue, and timid smile. She had the kind of confidence I'd let go of years ago.

"So," she leaned forward. "I'm new here. What's your story? What do you do? You don't seem to be anything like the women in that meeting. You don't look like the well-off, kept woman, stay-at-home mom type."

"I was," I mused. I stared down at the table, my finger tracing the edges of my napkin, not wanting to look up. "I mean, I was until my husband left me."

Evy reached over, put her hand on mine, and squeezed it. "Yeah, I kind of figured. That was quite the speech back there."

We were silent for a moment, but then I perked up. "Before that, though, I owned a successful technology company."

She looked up, surprised. "You *owned* the company?"

The waiter returned with our drinks. Evy poured beer into the plastic cups and handed one to me. "Now I'm intrigued. Spill."

I told Evy my story, which started with an idea I came up with during my senior year of college as a computer science major. I went to a state university in a small mountain town in Maryland with only one community bank. I worked as a bartender at a bar that sold ten-cent beer drafts to college students. My tips were small and usually metal rather than the paper variety.

Once a week, I took my bag of change to the bank and deposited it into my account. One day, I struck up a conversation with the bank teller and asked how to get an online account to access my money when I went home on weekends. The teller said she didn't know what I meant.

So, I explained it to her: "The big national banks all offer a way to manage your money through your computer. For example, you could log into your home computer and check your balance or transfer money."

I air-typed to show her what I meant.

"You need to speak with the bank manager," she said, shaking her head. "I don't know how to help you."

The clerk led me to a small, dingy office in the back where Frank, the bank's manager, sat hunched over a pile of paperwork. He looked up, startled, his face full, reddish, and blotchy. The room smelled like stale whiskey and Old Spice cologne. Pictures of fat Elvis hung on the wood-paneled walls.

"Frank," she said, waving her hand at me, "This girl has a question. How do we get her an online banking account?"

Frank looked at me and shook his head slowly. "We don't. This is a community bank, honey. Community banks don't offer that type of thing."

"But the big banks—"

Frank abruptly cut me off. "That's just it. The *big* banks. They can afford to do it. But they don't set up shop in small towns like this. And we do things the old-fashioned way. Face-to-face service. It is so much better, don't ya think? Like the two of us right here talking. You can't get that kind of personal service from a computer."

I smiled at Evy as I recalled standing before Frank, still clutching my plastic shopping bag filled with quarters and dimes, my thoughts racing.

"That was when the idea came to me," I told her. "A simple yet completely doable solution. The idea for OneBank was born."

Evy took a large swig of her beer and leaned across the table. "What is OneBank?"

"OneBank. One Solution for Community Banks."

Just saying the name immediately took me back. I remembered sprinting back to my dorm room, still clutching my bag of coins, as ideas and possibilities raced through my head.

I explained, "I realized that most small, community banks probably couldn't afford to offer the types of services, such as online banking, that the big banks were offering. But what if they had a plug-and-play option? Online banking software that they could buy with all the code already in place to handle financial transactions? But customizable. Their logo. Their photos.

Their marketing message sitting on top of standardized software that they could adapt to fit their business needs in a matter of days or weeks."

Evy sat back in her chair, visibly impressed. "Awesome! What happened next?"

"I went to the college library that day and researched online. No one had created anything like it yet. It was a true niche waiting to be tapped. I convinced my parents to let me stay at college another semester so I could take some business classes. During that time, I planned, plotted, and coded. By the time I graduated, I had a degree in computer science, a business plan, and a prototype of my software."

"So, you were an overnight success story," Evy said as she noisily slurped the last of her margarita through her straw and refilled my beer cup.

I scoffed. "Not really. OneBank took some time to get started. A group of computer science friends and I played around with it, testing the software for bugs. Another friend, a graphic design major, helped me make a logo and design the site layout. Within a few months, I was ready to go. I tried to get a small business loan, but everyone turned me down, saying I had no experience and there was no guarantee it would sell."

"You needed to prove the concept," Evy stated, matter of fact. I nodded.

At the stage, one of the kids began a mic test on the

karaoke machine. "Check one. Check one." The room filled with a loud, piercing squeal, and we winced.

"I tried to prove the concept, but it wasn't easy. I traveled to small towns, visiting with community bank owners to sell the idea. They liked it, but they were hesitant. Finally, the owner of a bank in Pennsylvania— The Community Bank of Pottstown—offered to try it out on the condition that I let him use the software for free. He had only three bank branches. I had nothing to lose at that point, so I agreed."

I recounted to Evy how, in two months, I had the online version of the Community Bank of Pottstown up and running. Within six months, eighty percent of their customers had moved to online banking. I captured data on the time they saved by banking online. I gathered feedback from users about the convenience. The owner wrote me a glowing testimonial about how his customer base had doubled. And then, I reapplied for a business loan, this time with a successful pilot.

"That's when my success story began."

Evy squealed so loud that everyone in the bar stopped what they were doing and looked at her. "Sorry," she whispered. "You are so impressive. Well done!"

Those. Words. I hadn't heard them in years. A big lump rose in my throat, rendering me temporarily speechless. I grabbed my cup of beer and took a big swig, swallowing hard.

"So where did OneBank end up?" Evy asked, eyes curious.

"Everywhere. At community banks across the country. You've probably used it but didn't even know it. My company started small. Just me, another developer, a graphic designer, and a marketing person. We worked in a cramped office space over a donut shop. I still remember working at the office, sometimes well into the small hours of the morning, when the sweet smell of fresh-baked crullers would waft up through the air vents."

Breathing in, I was transported back to that amazing time, remembering that scent. "They started baking at about 3 a.m., and our tiny workspace would smell like Dunkin'. Now, when I smell donuts, I think back to when it all seemed possible. I had a concept for convenient community banking and donuts. Everything felt right with my world."

I shrugged and continued, "Of course, I could eat all the donuts I wanted back then. I had been a collegiate competitive long-distance runner. Now I'm just a fat software developer." *And a virtual nobody these days.*

Evy frowned. "Stop."

"It's true. When I sold the company, OneBank was worth millions of dollars. My husband, Jack, encouraged me to let him invest the money. So, I did."

Evy plunked her cup down on the table and leaned forward. "Why? Why would you do that? I mean, how did you even meet him?"

"As my company grew, I spent a lot of time traveling and going to trade shows. I met Jack at one of them. He visited my booth several times, picking up brochures and talking to my team. At one point, I remember him standing in the corner, watching me give demonstrations of the OneBank software to the conference attendees. Then, on the last day, just before the conference ended, he returned to my booth and introduced himself. He was the Chief Executive Officer of a large string of community banks nationwide. He was young, successful, and *hot as hell*. I'll never forget that first moment he and I talked. I couldn't stop staring at his gorgeous face."

That Jack. Tall with an athletic build, dark brown curls, and an irresistible smile.

Evy chewed on her straw and leaned back in her chair, eyeing me suspiciously. "You slept with the hot bank CEO?"

"What can I say? He had me at, 'I want to buy your software.' I felt smitten." I shrugged.

"I'm sure. Funny how things change. I came across one of those silly memes online the other day. It said something like, 'All good things come to an end, but bad things drag on forever.'"

I gave a knowing nod. "Yeah, exactly. He went straight into the arms of a waitress named Kiki—and probably straight into a divorce."

"Ugh, what a shit. I'm so sorry, Emma." She finished off her beer. "It sounds like you had it all. What happened to your money?"

I looked away, hating this part of my story. I had achieved so much, only to lose it all instantly. It left me feeling utterly foolish.

"Jack had a business partner who convinced him to 'invest' the money in a community banking startup in underserved nations. Turns out you can't open a bank where people don't even have enough money to buy food. The First Community Bank of Uganda was the last I saw of my money."

I sank back into my chair, feeling deflated. Evy frowned and pursed her lips. The server passed by our table, and she grabbed his arm.

"We need Fireball shots. Right now!"

Her look of urgency sent him scrambling to the bar. And then she turned to me. "Why didn't you speak up? Why didn't you stop him?"

The waiter returned with two shot glasses filled to the brim, along with the bottle. I took a shot and winced. *That burns.* I cleared my throat. *And now for the rest of the story: enter 1950s housewife, stage left.*

"Well, new friend of mine, at that point, I was several

months pregnant and on the verge of being a stay-at-home mom. That was the other thing Jack convinced me to do. Give up OneBank to raise our family. He had a way of making all his bad ideas sound like great ones. And in the end, I love my kids. I wouldn't trade them for anything. But I sure as hell miss the adventure of it all."

I wistfully recalled the excitement of growing my business. I had traveled and explored new cities, spoke at industry conventions, and was respected in my field. I remember standing on podiums in front of large crowds, feeling fearless. *Back before, my world became so small.*

"The most exciting thing about my days now is waiting for the kids to go to bed so I can binge streaming services on TV with a cheesecake and a bag of chips."

"Well, I'm sorry," Evy sighed, "but that's just fucked up. Where do you work now?"

"I'm a software developer for the federal government."

I looked away, suddenly feeling embarrassed at my own predicament. I had gone from being the owner of a thriving technology company to a government-paid coder.

Sensing my frustration, Evy poured another shot and pushed it across the table towards me. I gulped it down, feeling the warmth of the drink spread through my body. I didn't usually drink much, but tonight, I made an exception because it was the first time in months that I had socialized with another adult, and I realized how much I had missed it. Pushing the empty shot glass aside, I explained how I ended up at my dreary job to Evy.

"By the time I tried to return to the workforce, all my software development skills were outdated. No one would hire me, even though I had once built a successful technology company. But the government—they'll take anybody, especially if you know how to code the outdated software that was around when I first started working. Now, I work at the Federal Center for Fiscal Enforcement. You know when the IRS flags tax returns for audits?"

Evy nodded.

"Those tax returns end up at the Center for processing. That agency's software is old, and they needed someone to support it. None of the kids coming out of college these days know how to code it. Anyway, a guy named Larry hired me. He stared at my tits during the entire interview. Still does. Can't have a conversation without him looking here the whole time." I pointed to my boobs.

Evy snorted. "Well, in his defense, you do have good tits."

"Ha! Thanks." I grabbed the Fireball bottle and

clumsily splashed some into both our glasses. Raising my shot glass toward Evy, we clinked and downed the drinks together.

"Larry needs to show me some respect!" I shouted at Evy to be heard over the growing din as the bar filled with students from the university down the street. "Do you know what happened last week when I told him I wanted him to include me in the management meetings? He told me it was a cute idea but get back to work and code something. And to get him some coffee. Might as well have smacked me on the ass!"

Evy shook her head. "Fuck him. Your story is not over."

"Wait a minute," I replied. "Your turn. What's *your* story? Why are you in Belmont?"

She looked down and was silent for a moment. "My husband died nine months ago. I didn't know where else to go."

Before me, she visibly deflated. I looked at my new friend in disbelief. Her shoulders drooped, sagging like the world's weight had settled upon them.

"Car accident. Just like that, he was just gone. I kissed him goodbye one morning, but he never came back. I couldn't stay in our house without him, so I sold it and searched for a new place to live. Did you know that Forbes magazine named Belmont, New

York, one of *The Best Small Towns No One Knows About*? I thought this might be a good place to reset. I'm going to teach Creative Writing at the university next semester."

I wanted to reach out and hug her. She became a widow way too young.

Just then, the DJ yelled into the mic, "Karaoke! Retro night!"

A tall, dark-haired girl wearing a University of Belmont hoodie and skinny jeans stumbled onto the stage as the DJ queued, *I Will Survive* by Donna Summers. The girl swayed back and forth. She sang loud and off-key. "This is for you, Anthony."

Below her, a small group of girls had gathered near the stage, shouting, "Woooooo! Sing it, Sara! Fuck Anthony! You can do better!"

On the other side of the bar, a table of boys who were in the middle of playing a drinking game stopped and looked up. One of them shouted, "Heck yeah, girl! Anthony sucks!" And then the whole bar broke into song, crooning along with Sara.

Somewhere in town, a boy named Anthony sat in his dorm room, blithely unaware that he was the subject of a loud karaoke rendition of Sara's unrequited love. Yet across from me sat Evy, whose husband had just died. I stared at her, unsure of what to say.

Evy gave me a small, thoughtful smile and said, "The

funny thing is, you lost all your money, and suddenly, I have more than I know what to do with. My husband left me a huge insurance policy and all his stock options. Poor rich girl, huh? But I'm not feeling sorry for myself. Your life is way worse than mine."

I scoffed but then nodded. *She had a point.*

She waved her hand as if dismissing her inescapable plight and refilled our shot glasses. "Drink!"

We threw back the shots, and she looked around the room. "Where's that server? We need tacos."

The DJ called out, "Up next...the 90s."

Evy gripped the table's edge and leaned towards me, her eyes suddenly bright.

"You. This is *all* you. Let's go."

She grabbed my wrist and dragged me onto the small stage. While she discussed song choice with the DJ, I looked out at a room full of college kids staring back at me. I knew what they were thinking. *Why is someone's fat mom on the stage?*

I turned away to avoid their stares and noticed the drinking game had resumed. Then, out of the corner of my eye, I saw Evy, mic in hand, pointing at me. Over the noise of the crowded bar, Evy bolted out the lyrics to *You Oughta Know* by Alanis Morrissette.

The girl group shouted, "Alanis!" and joined the chorus.

I could feel my cell phone vibrating repeatedly from

the back pocket of my jeans. I left the stage on wobbly legs. The room seemed to spin as the lights from the bar swirled around me. *How much of that Fireball did I drink?*

I pulled my phone from my pocket. Jack had left several text messages.

JACK

> Where are you? Myla is throwing up everywhere. You need to come and get her.

The next one read,

> You really are a horrible mother. Selfish. Useless. Get over here and get our daughter. I don't care if it's my weekend to have the kids. I'm not dealing with this!

The crowd cheered, and I turned around to see Evy, still on the stage and singing, surrounded by college students. This woman had just lost it all but bravely stepped back into life. Alone. *And so fearless.* She sang as if her world hadn't just crashed around her.

I read the following text from Jack.

> Are you coming to get her or not?

And then a final one:

> I'm talking to my lawyer tomorrow.
> I'm taking these kids from you.
> You're a worthless person.

I stared at my phone in disbelief, my hand suddenly shaking. *He's going to take the kids from me.*

The crowd applauded. On stage, Evy bowed to a standing ovation.

CHAPTER 4

Miss Kiki

'**I** *am a beautiful princesss... standing by the seaaaa. The fish and the dolphins are singing, "Come and swim with meee." ... I'm a beautiful princesss... The mermaid inside me knows... The enchanted sea awaits me... the mystical water flows...'* Mommy! Wake up! Do I have a beautiful singing voice like the fairy princess?"

I opened one eye to see Myla dancing in circles around the family room, clutching a bag of gummy bears, and periodically stopping to watch a children's movie playing on the TV.

My head was in a vice grip–pounding. I tasted Fireball whiskey and nacho cheese.

"Mommy, do you like my singing? Watch me dance!"

Myla twirled three more times, let out a long, loud burp, and projectile-vomited a rainbow of undigested sugar onto the carpet.

I opened the other eye. "Who gave you those gummy bears?"

"Miss Kiki. She said I could have them for being so good and not throwing up in the new car Daddy bought her. Did you know she has earrings on her belly button *and* nose, Mommy? And also, in a place she said only Daddy could see. How come Daddy can see, but I can't?"

"Where is Daddy?" I asked, looking around, my head throbbing.

"He brought me here and said I could watch the princess movie until you wake up. But it's no fair cause Austin got to go to the mall with him. *'Wretched, fat excuse for a mother.'* He said that when he left. What does 'wretched' mean?"

Myla began twirling again, oblivious to the big, wet pile of undigested, dismembered gummy bears on the floor and the sweet and sour stench of vomit permeating the room. I winced at the smell.

My cell phone blinked on the coffee table. Three missed voice messages.

Larry from work: *"I can't do the Monday management team meeting tomorrow. I have a golf game with our department head. I need you to go to the meeting in* my place, type the minutes, and send them to me. Make sure there's coffee and bagels. And clean the conference room afterward."

Austin's second-grade teacher, Ms. Williams: "*Emma! Just checking in! Will you still be bringing a charcuterie board to our sock drive for the underprivileged at the school on Thursday? Oh, my goodness, I just realized we still need a name for it. Socks for City Blocks? I mean, even the non-gentrified need cozy feet, right? Warm Feet on the Street? Now that has a ring to it!*

Anyway, please omit all olives and nuts from the charcuterie board because we have allergies in the class. Also, the crackers need to be gluten-free. We need a dairy-free cheese alternative because of the lactose-intolerant children. I read about an almond milk cheese substitute, although the environmental implications are very concerning. All those crushed almonds—too much water wasted and too many trees to replant! Wait, but then we're dealing with the nut allergies again.

Please remember that some of our kids don't eat pork. One of the moms complained when you brought in pork hotdogs for spring field day last year. So, really, just omit all pork products. And no beef, either. I'm so looking forward to seeing you at the sock drive!

Oh, and Emma, we need to talk. Austin is failing gym. I'm concerned about his academic future."

Jack: "*Check your email. My lawyer said he sent*

another notice to you. You can't keep ignoring them, Emma. You'd better respond to him. I'm not messing around anymore!"

A text message from Evy:

EVY

Emm! It's me, Evy! You left your jacket in the taxi. Call me! I can take you to get your car.

I looked up from my cell phone to see Myla staring at me inquisitively, head cocked to one side. "Mommy, what's a Coochie?"

I sat straight up. "Where did you hear that word?"

"From Miss Kiki. She said that's where her special earring is—on her Coochie. She said it's a *wonderful* place. Can I get one, too?"

Myla began twirling again, singing loudly, "Coochie! Coochie! Coochie! I want a wonderful Coochie!"

Miss Kiki. I recalled that night last year when Jack and I were at Family Night at the Belmont Fun Fridays casual dining restaurant. As I helped Austin with a puzzle on his paper placemat, I looked up and there she stood before us. Tall and thin with large breasts spilling out of her green and white striped polo shirt. Warm olive skin. Full, red lips. Long, thick hair and eyes so dark they were almost black. She looked exotic. Jack stared at her in awe.

"Visualize Whirled Peas," he said, smiling at her. "That's very clever."

She smiled back shyly and fumbled with the *Visualize Whirled Peas* pin clinging to her rainbow suspenders below the pin that read *OK Boomer.*

"My name is Kiki, and I'll be your server tonight. What can I get you?"

She placed her hand on Jack's arm, leaned into him, and then looked at me, his fat wife clutching a purple crayon and his two young children staring on. She turned back to him. "I'll bet you could use a beer."

In truth, Jack had aged gracefully; the hot young CEO I had met years ago transformed into a distinguished and handsome older man. Women stared at him when we went places. He carried himself with confidence. They immediately sensed the stature and the money.

Kiki caught his gaze for a few more moments and then turned to me and gave me a once-over.

"Diet soda for you?"

Jack spent the remainder of the dinner watching her move around the restaurant, only half-listening to Austin talk about his video games and not responding to Myla's repeated requests for a Shirley Temple drink with seven cherries. He barely looked at me. Towards the end of our meal, Kiki's other tables had cleared, so she lingered close by, circling the outskirts of us.

"Are you ready for your check?" she cooed, staring directly into Jack's eyes.

He pulled his gaze away momentarily, turned to me, and handed me the car keys. "Here. Go ahead and get the kids to the car. I'll take care of the check."

They both stopped and watched me. After a moment, I hastily gathered up the kids and their coats. Feeling flustered, I headed for the door. When I looked back, I saw Kiki leaning over the table, talking with Jack. They were laughing. I couldn't look back again.

Goodbye, marriage.

᠁

Myla stopped twirling and stared at the TV, singing along with the cartoon princess. *"The sea water prince is callinggg...he wants to play by the shore...I am the magical mermaid...a beautiful princess no more..."* She did a curtsy.

I lifted my head as my stomach growled in protest. Memories from last night flashed by—margaritas, pitchers of beer, and way too much Fireball whiskey. Tacos. We stayed until the last call. By the end of it, Evy and I tumbled into the back seat of a taxi.

"Home, please." She instructed the driver.

"I need to know where lady."

She looked at me and asked, "Where is home?"

"421 Browncroft Boulevard."

He put the address into his GPS, and we sped off. Beside me, I noticed Evy leaning in and squinting at the lacquered placard on the back of the driver's seat, which had his name and license information. She got closer and then whispered, "Come here. Come here!"

I scooted over and read the placard. We looked at each other and simultaneously burst into laughter. Evy laughed so hard she wheezed. She could barely get the words out.

"His name is Harold...Balz. Harry Balz!"

Saying it out loud set us into a fit of hysterics. We crumpled over in the backseat, stealing each other as we laughed, trying to catch our breath. The driver glared at us through the rearview mirror and turned up the radio.

When Harry Balz approached my house, Evy gave me a fierce hug and said, "I love you, my new friend. Your story isn't over yet."

She fumbled with her phone, squinting as she sloppily typed in my number, then gave me another hug and shoved me out of the car.

"Mr. Balz, take me to 27 East Main Street. Stat! I need to pee!"

I watched the car speed away and then looked at my

dark six-bedroom McMansion—no life or lights inside, just shadows of a life that had been. I wandered up to the front door and unlocked it. Inside, I gently laid my head on the family room sectional that Jack and I had purchased together just the previous year. Spooked by the silence, I wrapped a blanket snugly around myself and drifted off to sleep.

CHAPTER 5

Charcuterie

After I told my new friend Evy about The Bolton Academy's upcoming sock drive for the under-privileged, she informed me that it was her civic duty to assist. She and I walked into Belmont's bustling Urban Orchard organic grocery store, where the smell of eucalyptus, tea tree oil, and peppermint wafted through the front entrance vents, beckoning us.

An Avett Brothers indie rock song piped softly through the store's intercom system as a young mother brushed past us, oblivious to her wailing infant in its stroller. She mindlessly scanned the shelves as she sang along with the music. Her baby let out an ear-piercing screech.

"So let me get this straight," Evy said. "You need to

make a charcuterie board, but it can't have meat, cheese or olives?"

"Or nuts, unlike Harry Balz. Where shall we start?"

I steered the shopping cart over to the dairy aisle. Two men stood in it, blocking the cheese display. They were bickering over which brand of feta to buy.

A woman with a perfectly coiffed A-line bob, wearing an expensive suit and sensible jewelry, stared at them sternly. She tapped her stiletto heel. They were clearly making her late for something.

One of the men paused, glanced at her briefly, rolled his eyes, and turned back to his partner. He squeezed his partner's arm firmly but lovingly. "Babe. You bought that brand last time. We need the *melty* kind for feta puff pastry."

The woman let out a loud huff, turned on her heels, and clicked away, almost knocking over the stocking clerk busily topping off the burrata cheese balls.

"Bitch," the stocking clerk mumbled under his breath.

"You got that right, honey," said one of the two men, and they giggled.

I turned my attention back to Evy, who was intently examining the dairy display case.

"Okay, check this out," she said. She held up a package that looked like one of Myla's green slime projects from last year's summer camp and tossed it into the shopping cart. "Zucchini cheese. Unless your son's classmates are allergic to green."

I paused for a moment, thinking that might be a possibility.

Evy wandered off, leaving me to study cheeses. I rounded the next corner into the meat aisle—and then stopped in my tracks.

Oh my.

I saw Evy conversing with an attractive guy sporting a backward baseball cap. He stood tall and lanky but solidly built. He looked like he was in his thirties, with a youthful, clean-shaven face and gentle brown eyes. Long, curly, brownish-blonde hair spilled out from under his baseball cap onto a faded Duke University hoodie. He immersed himself in a deep discussion with Evy.

With a serious tone, he explained, "So, you have options for substituting meat: seitan, a plant-based protein derived from vital wheat gluten, is ideal for creating vegan sausages and ribs. Hearty vegetables such as eggplant, jackfruit, or finely chopped cauliflower can effectively replace meat in various recipes. Seasoned legumes, when prepared properly, are another excellent choice."

Evy pulled out her cell phone and started taking notes. I hadn't known her for long, but I discovered she could strike up a conversation with just about anyone. I missed the days when I had that much confidence.

She saw me and waved me over. "Emm, Andy here says we need seitan."

The man turned to me, and for a brief second, his gaze flickered with a hint of recognition. I locked eyes with him. *Do I know you?* He looked at me inquisitively as if trying to place me. We momentarily held each other's stare before his lips curved into a small, wistful smile. Then, as if snapping out of it, he shifted his attention back to Evy.

"Well, good luck with your *non*-charcuterie board," he said, turning and heading toward the snack aisle. He glanced back and smiled. I gripped the shopping cart tighter, my breath catching as I watched him walk away. *What just happened?*

"I think he was just checking you out." Evy smacked my arm. "Go get yourself some gluten-free cheese puffs!"

"Nope. Impossible. Nobody has checked me out in years."

I glanced back in the direction of the snack food aisle again. *Who was that guy?*

We continued through Urban Orchard, piling food into the cart. Tofu meatballs. Pork-flavored tempeh cubes. Seitan sticks. Not-so-nutty almond substitute bars. Chickpea pops.

"You know, I've been thinking," Evy said as we loaded our bounty onto the conveyor belt at check out. "Maybe it's time for you to get back out there. I mean, clearly, nothing is holding Jack back. He's running around Belmont with someone almost half his age."

I shook my head. "I don't know. I just don't feel right doing it. The kids are young, and I don't want to confuse them."

Evy narrowed her eyes at me. "You mean more confusing than Kiki the Wonder Coochie?"

The cashier who was ringing up my groceries raised one eyebrow and sighed.

I shrugged. "Seriously, I wouldn't even know where to start."

The cashier stopped bagging my groceries, looked at me, and said, "I don't know what this 'Wonder Coochie' is all about. I don't want to know. But someone your age? You need to start online. Definitely MatchUp. com. Or Seasoned Singles. You need to stay away from Winder, though, or you'll swipe yourself right into the arms of a balding pedophile with a foot fetish."

He held up a package of chicken breasts and sighed again. "What should I do with your meat?"

Evy glanced back and forth between the two of us, suppressing a smile. "How do you want your meat handled, Emm?"

I hadn't had my meat touched in such a long time; I didn't even know how to respond. Behind us, the backward ballcap guy had entered the checkout line and watched us in amusement.

Evy turned to him. "You. Duke University. Take a look at my friend here. Date worthy?"

He shrugged, a small smile curling onto his lips as he responded, "Definitely *not* unfortunate looking. Your friend has beautiful blue eyes and a fantastic smile."

Heat rushed to my face, and I felt myself flush. He locked eyes with mine again. Just then, a woman walked up to him, looped her arm into his, and looked at all of us, confused. I quickly looked away. *Damn.*

Behind us, bitchy business suit-woman joined the checkout party, looking irritated that we had stopped hurrying through the business of grocery shopping. She had somewhere to be.

In the next checkout line over, the feta cheese guys argued over bags of frozen wontons. "You're being ridiculous. You don't even like shrimp. Take those back to the frozen aisle right now before they thaw out and they make us pay for them. I don't even know what to do with you sometimes!"

Business suit clicked her stiletto heel loudly.

"Matchup.com," the grocery clerk instructed me and said, "Next?"

Business suit shoved everyone aside and placed her prepackaged sushi on the conveyor belt. She glanced at her watch and glared impatiently at all of us.

We've made her late.

Somewhere in the produce aisle, a baby wailed.

CHAPTER 6

Time Stamp

The Federal Center for Fiscal Enforcement occupied an old building on Edgewood Street, near an industrial complex at the edge of Belmont. During World War II, the building served as a makeshift warehouse before its conversion into federal government office space. An odd smell of mildew and commercial-strength cleaner permeated every corner. The floors creaked underfoot, covered with stained, cheaply made carpet. Asbestos had once lined the walls until the facilities manager temporarily shut the building down and brought in a hazmat team to clear it away.

Florescent lighting flickered obnoxiously over the windowless Cube Land that I called work. The management team tucked the software developers here—away and out of sight. I hunched over my desk in my cubicle, eyes scanning the long list of software change requests that needed to be implemented. My boss, Larry, hovered in the hallway, talking to our department head about his golf game.

"That last birdie I played was insane. Right on the heels of your double bogey. Did you check out that new chick at the clubhouse? Yeah, I'd like to play her." He chuckled.

Another day in the life of corporate misogyny.

I sighed loud enough for Larry to hear me, hoping it would shut him up. He rounded the corner and peered down on me. Larry, a tall man, had a perpetually bright red face and a thick crop of shocking white hair on his head. He sported bushy white eyebrows that resembled two caterpillars perched on his forehead. His voice boomed deeply when he spoke.

"Emma! Did you get my message? I need you to schedule that appointment with the Cloud vendor. Did you take care of that? And Steve told me that the printer is on the fritz. You'll need to get that fixed."

I looked up from my work to see Larry staring at my chest. *Up here, buddy. My face is up here.*

I retorted, "No, Larry, I didn't. Because you see, I've been busy trying to work with this antiquated software. It needs to be rewritten in a newer language because the one I'm working with now is full of bugs that I don't think can be fixed. I've sent you several emails about this. We should start looking at commercial-off-the-shelf products and work with industry to recreate this. I have the old requirements document that I can rewrite. I can spearhead this—"

Larry waved his hand in the air and abruptly cut me off, "Whoa, whoa, there, Emma. Don't get too ahead of yourself. Or rather, I should say, get *over* yourself. This software does the job just fine. We are having budget cuts, and the last thing they are going to do is pony up money to buy some expensive, new, fancy software. That's why we hired *you*. To keep it running. If you don't think you're up for the challenge, well—"

His eyes wandered south again. *Stop staring at my tits, you buffoon.* I snapped my fingers to get his attention. He abruptly looked back up at my face.

"Larry, this software is running on the ByteLynks XP operating system. It's full of defects. It needs to be upgraded to a newer operating system and reprogrammed in something safer to mitigate security issues. I got a call from the cybersecurity manager because we're not following the government's Risk Management Monitoring guidelines. But it's fixable. Our team could very easily accomplish this—"

He cut me off again. "So anyway, as I was saying. Broken printer. Take care of that. Also, today is Jerry's birthday. There's cake in the kitchen, although I'm sure you're on a diet."

Before I could respond, he turned the corner and walked away. I stared at my computer, seething. *I once owned a software company, you idiot.* I pierced my lips and blew out a loud sigh of frustration. *Vile man.*

I could hear Larry further down the hallway, regaling someone else with his golfing antics. "Bogey. Par. Par. Yeah, it was awesome! Did you get some cake?"

Needing a distraction, I turned to my computer and typed "online dating sites" into the search engine.

Whoa, there were a lot of them. Matchup.com. InHarmony. Winder. Seasoned Singles. My life had come to this: potentially pimping myself out to the digital world. I wasn't ready for that yet. Evy came up with the idea anyway.

Ah, yes—Evy. I realized that I knew little about her besides what she told me. I typed "Evelyn Hanover, Washington DC" into the search engine.

Facebook
Evelyn Hanover is on Facebook.
Join Facebook to connect with **Evelyn Hanover** and others you may know.

LinkedIn
Evelyn Hanover – Teacher –
District of Columbia Public Schools

Instagram
<u>Evelyn.hanover.98</u>
200 Followers, **108** Following, **400** Posts –
See Instagram photos and videos from
Evelyn Hanover (<u>@evelyn.hanover.98</u>)

I clicked on the Facebook link, and Evy's page popped up; most of her settings were set to public view. *Risky. I will talk to her about that.* She hadn't posted in a while—her last post was from almost eight months ago. Condolences from friends filled her Facebook page.

> Evy, our thoughts and prayers are with you right now. Ben was a light that filled every room he entered. We will miss his dog dad jokes. Hug Benny for us. Please reach out if you need anything from your friends at Golden Paws Animal Rescue.

> The finance world lost a true genius. And we lost our leader. Condolences from all of us at Hanover, Davis and Associates. Ben was one of a kind.

> We lost our beloved son, but you will always be a daughter to us.

A picture showed a younger Evy standing beside Ben and his parents at their wedding.

> Ms. Hanover! We are so sorry about Mr. Ben. All your students are here for you!

I continued reading through Evy's feed, watching her story unfold. Her page went on and on with an outpouring of support: kind words from friends and family, pictures posted with her husband from happier times, and then the abrupt upheaval of her world.

Social media is really just an omniscient time stamp. Anyone can see extracts from a person's life and then scroll back to that moment *before*. The day before, a person's world changed in a blink. The life story that was carrying on oblivious to the plot twist about to happen. I scrolled to that moment. Evy appeared in a photo with Ben at a wine festival the day before his accident. Her post read, "*Vino with the love of my life!*" The two smiled happily at each other, toasting with glasses of wine. Looking at that picture, a wave of sadness passed over me. She had no idea what was coming.

I continued scrolling through her page, going back through months of her life. Birthdays and holidays. Family gatherings. All of them were filled with pictures of a happy Evy with Ben and her golden retriever at her side.

She posted about school events. "*My students are my world!*" Evy was in one picture standing with a group of her students on a field trip to see a Shakespeare play. Another with Evy working with her kids to build a homecoming float.

Further back, Evy posted links to fundraisers. "*Lymphoma Cancer Support. A Silent Killer. Please donate!*"

"The Golden Paws Rescue League of Washington, DC needs your support. Please donate and help our furry friends!"

She even volunteered at a women's shelter. Evy's life seemed so complete. But oddly, she went silent for an extended period about two years ago. *Had something happened?*

I looked up her old address and found her house on the real estate sites. She and Ben had lived in an expensive brownstone in northeast Washington, DC. It was listed as sold four months ago for $1.2 million. She now lived in a small, rented condo in downtown Belmont.

Next, I searched for the name "Benjamin Hanover".

The Washington Chronicle Obituaries

Benjamin David Hanover, Jr.

Benjamin "Ben" David Hanover, Jr., a long-time resident of Washington, DC, passed away suddenly on June 7, 2024. Ben was 32 years old.

Ben was born on March 3, 1992, to Benjamin Hanover, Sr., and Karen Hanover (Lory) in Boston, Massachusetts. He is survived by his wife, Evelyn Hanover,

---

of Washington, DC; his parents; his brother, David Hanover, and wife, Elizabeth Hanover of Gloucester, Massachusetts; and sister, Patricia Brown; and husband, Jacob Brown, of Danvers, Massachusetts. He was also a loving uncle to two nieces, Kayla and Alison Brown. Ben leaves behind a golden retriever named Benny, lovingly named after his human dad.

A 2009 graduate of Northwood High School, Ben obtained a bachelor's degree in finance from the University of Maryland, followed by a master's degree in accounting from George Washington University. Following graduation, Ben enjoyed a successful career as the Chief Financial Advisor to several large political organizations in the Washington, DC metropolitan area before co-founding his financial management firm, Hanover, Davis & Associates. Ben was an avid golfer and runner, having just recently completed the Marine Corps marathon. He also enjoyed photography, especially still-life photos of nature. His favorite pastime was traveling with his partner in crime, Evelyn.

Funeral arrangements were entrusted

to Mattingly Funeral Home, Washington, DC. Visitation will take place on June 9 and June 10 from 4:00 p.m. to 8:00 p.m. A funeral mass will take place at 11:00 a.m. on June 11 at Holy Trinity Church at 4712 G Street, NW, Washington, DC. Burial will immediately follow at Heaven's Garden Cemetery.

In lieu of flowers, donations can be made to the Golden Paws Animal Rescue in Washington, DC.

The Herald Journal

June 8, 2024

A 32-year-old Washington, DC, man was killed yesterday morning when his car collided with a dump truck at the intersection of Thompson Street and Lindbergh Avenue, SE.

Benjamin David Hanover, Jr. of 241 F Street, NW, died at 11:00 a.m. at Immaculate Mary Hospital, where he had been taken following the accident. He was pronounced dead upon arrival. The driver of the dump truck, Randall Simmons, was not seriously injured and is expected to survive.

Police said the accident occurred as Hanover crossed through the intersection of Thompson and Lindbergh. Simmons did not stop for the red light and entered the intersection at a high speed, striking Hanover's car on the driver's side.

Police are requesting witnesses contact Sgt. Dean Harris at the Metropolitan Police Department at (202) 555-8746. This accident is still under investigation.

Oof. It was just as Evy had said. He left for work one morning and never came back. That must have been devastating. Evy was so much fun, the comic relief to my spiraling life. I remember asking her that night at the bar how she could have so much optimism when she had faced so much loss.

She responded, "When you come so close to losing it all, you see the hope in everything. Perspective is *everything.*" What else had happened to her to make her think that way? Scrolling through her social media, I saw she seemed to have a perfect life.

Larry returned to my cubicle and peered down on me again. "I see you're working hard."

I closed the screen and said, "I'm allowed to take breaks, Larry."

"Get the printer fixed," he grumbled, then paused to stare at my chest again before turning and walking away. I hurled a pencil at him, only to have it rebound off my cubicle wall and land on the floor with a solid 'thunk.' *Someday, I will tell that man where he can shove the printer.*

After work, I picked up Myla and Austin from after-school daycare. Myla ran up to me and handed me a picture she had drawn at school. Her teacher was doing a unit on family. In careful kindergarten penmanship, Myla illustrated three people. One large, round person was in the center labeled "Mommy," and two smaller people labeled "Myla" and "Awstin". She wore a skirt, and Austin wore a baseball cap. The picture also included a picture of a vertical rectangle with a small circle on it.

"This is amazing, Myla, but I think you forgot someone." She looked at the picture and shook her head, 'No.'

"Where's Daddy?"

She pointed to the rectangle and said, "Behind that door. In the bedroom with Miss Kiki."

Myla's daycare teacher, Miss Jane, looked at me, eyebrows raised.

I quickly took the picture from Myla and folded it in two, slipping it into my purse. I shrugged and explained, "She has no filter. We're working on that."

I turned back to Myla. "Well, maybe you can bring him out of the bedroom and draw him into the picture when we get home."

As I arrived home, I noticed a truck on the street in front of the house. A man sat waiting inside, watching us. We climbed out of my SUV, and I approached the vehicle.

"Can I help you?"

He abruptly got out of the vehicle and walked toward me. He held a large manila envelope in his hands.

"Mrs. Emma Davis?" he asked.

"Yes, can I help you?"

"I'm here from the law office of James P. Fortney on behalf of your husband, Jack Davis. Your husband has filed for divorce. Please consider yourself officially served."

I stared at him. *What?* He shoved the envelope at me, got into his truck, and drove away.

I clutched the envelope, shaking. *This is finally it.*

Austin gave me a hurtful look before bolting towards the house.

I can't believe Jack would do this in front of the kids.

Speechless, I glanced down at Myla. She was innocently unaware of what was happening.

"What does that mean, Mommy?"

I kneeled beside her, put her hand in mine, paused, and said softly, "It means that Mommy and Daddy won't be married anymore."

She pondered that momentarily, crossed her arms, scowled, and stated defiantly, "Well, if that's the case, if you think I'm drawing Daddy back into this picture, you've got another think coming!"

She snatched the picture from my purse and marched angrily towards the house, yelling behind her, "He can stay in the bedroom with Miss Kiki for all I care! I'm drawing a lock on that door!" She shook her tiny fist in insurrection as she disappeared through the front door.

I stood in my driveway and looked down at the envelope in my hands, realizing my new reality. I guess I could have ignored the emails and voice messages from his lawyer for only so long. I needed help. *Legal help.*

From inside the house, something crashed. Myla stormed.

"Goddamn it! *Where are my crayons?*"

The Shark

The morning of the sock drive arrived, and I was running late. The day had gotten off to a rough start. That morning, Austin came down for breakfast and slid into the seat across from me at the kitchen table. He quietly moved his food around his plate, not eating. When he finally looked up, his eyes were puffy and red—like he'd been crying.

"What's wrong, bud? Are you feeling okay?"

The news of the divorce must have hit him hard. I struggled with what to say next. I knew I would need to sit down with the kids and talk through the impending divorce—as soon as I could come to grips with it myself. Austin was older than Myla, and a little more tuned in to what was happening. He must be so angry with Jack.

He dropped his fork and shrugged. "I'm not going to school today,"

"Of course you are. I'm driving you. Today is the sock drive. Warm Feet on the Street." I pointed to the overflowing bag of new socks sitting by the front door.

He shook his head. "I'm not going. I can't go there anymore."

"Why not?" I asked, reaching over to touch his hand. He abruptly pulled it away.

"Jason Stone said he can't sit with me at lunch anymore. His mom said you are crazy. He said some other parents are saying it too. And everybody likes Jason. If he doesn't want to be my friend, nobody will like me. So, I have to find a new school to go to." He sighed deeply. "Can we please not go to McDonald's anymore?"

Oh. He's angry with *me.*

He stared at his food but wouldn't look up. He reached for his fork again but barely moved it, the prongs nudging the eggs around his plate.

Myla stopped shoving Fruity Puffs cereal into her mouth long enough to protest. "No fair! I like McDonald's!"

"Maybe I should just go and live with Dad. And Miss Kiki," Austin muttered under his breath.

"You mean Dad?"

He shook his head, still not looking at me. "No, Dad said Miss Kiki is going to live there too. And they don't know my friend's moms, so if I live with them, I can still play with my friends."

Pushing his plate away, he ran up the stairs and slammed his bedroom door. I stared at his uneaten breakfast in disbelief.

Kiki is moving in with him. So soon?

Myla gently placed her hand on my arm, looking concerned. "Well, this isn't good, Mommy." She was thoughtful for a moment and added, "Maybe we should get him a wonderful Coochie. It might cheer him up."

As I pulled up to the front of The Bolton Academy, Belmont's premier college preparatory school, I saw Ms. Williams waving a handful of socks at me from the school's front door. Behind me, a bag of fluffy wool socks had spilled over and tumbled across the car floor under Austin's feet. Oblivious, he stared into his gaming console. He still wasn't speaking to me.

"Mrs. Davis! Do hurry! We need those snacks!"

I glanced over at the charcuterie board on the seat next to me. The zucchini cheese had started to melt, forming a green lake that was dangerously edging toward the tower of tofu.

Myla opened her car door and yelled, "Bye, Mommy!" before racing up the school stairs, never looking back.

Austin grabbed his backpack and marched into the school without me. I gathered up the bag of socks and steadied the charcuterie board with my other hand. The zucchini cheese was now a swirling river of goo.

The Bolton Academy's sock drive was underway, and the gymnasium had transformed into a scene from *The Lord of the Flies*. Children in plaid uniforms ran wild, chasing each other and throwing socks, now strewn all over the bleachers.

I looked up to see that Naryan Patel had climbed the thirty-foot exercise rope and was dangling twenty feet in the air, legs kicking wildly. Ethan Brown and Teddy Howard stood under him, debating how to help.

"One good yank should get him down," said Ethan.

Teddy furrowed his brow at the prospect of yanking poor Naryan to his death.

"Or maybe we should call the fire department," Ethan suggested.

Teddy nodded and walked away.

A loud whine came from the other corner of the gym. Someone had tied Olivia Pemberton's hands behind her back with her scarf and stuffed a glittery rainbow-colored sock into her mouth. It sparkled in the sunlight.

Ms. Williams surveyed the scene and clapped her hands loudly.

"Children!" she spoke into a microphone. "Children!

Put down those socks and find your seats immediately! I am counting to three! One... Two... Three..."

I looked around for Austin and saw him sitting alone on the bleachers. As I approached him, he shook his head, 'No,' and looked away.

A group of parents congregated by the food table. I overheard one of the Jessicas say, "What *is* that?"

The charcuterie board had morphed into something reminiscent of a Picasso painting. The chickpea pops bobbed buoyantly along the river of slime and rolled onto the floor.

Jason Stone's mother whispered loudly, "She can't even get a charcuterie board right. Look at that mess."

The second Jessica nodded in agreement.

A loud, piercing siren suddenly rang out through the gym. The fire alarm had been set off. Teddy Howard peered on from the hallway, smiling.

"Fire!" one of the children screamed and then panic ensued as Austin's third-grade class ran in circles and tumbled over each other, making a mad dash for the door.

Naryan Patel cried out, "Someone get me dooooown!"

Jason Stone's mother ran to his aid, slipped in the puddle of zucchini cheese on the floor, and fell. Just then, Naryan lost his grip, slid down the rope, and landed on top of her.

Perfect. Mess with my kid, will you, Mrs. Stone? *Thank you, karma.*

Back in the day, Jack and I would have laughed at all of this. He used to say, "Our Bolton dollars at work," every time one of the kids would come home to tell us about something amusing at school. We knew we were paying a ridiculous amount for elementary school, but Jack wanted only the best for his family. Back when his family mattered. But now? *She is moving in with him.*

My cell phone beeped.

APPOINTMENT REMINDER:
L. Livingston, 10:00 a.m. The
Coventry Building.

The time of reckoning loomed before me. I scanned the gymnasium for Austin to say goodbye, but Ms. Williams had already ushered him outside. Naryan Patel lay splayed on the floor on top of Jason Stone's mother, holding his arm and crying. A fire truck siren howled in the distance.

I headed off to my appointment to see Lauren C. Livingston, Esquire. Evy had done extensive research, mostly on social media, and learned that Lauren came highly recommended as a defender of women whose wealthy husbands left them in a lurch. Now, I had to explain my lurch to a total stranger.

"She's a shark, Emma. A *shark*. That's what you need. Someone who won't put up with Jack's bullshit."

I took her recommendation and arranged an appointment, knowing she was right. A shark by the name of Kiki had closed in on my life, and I needed another shark to finish the fight.

I entered The Coventry Building, Suite 2B, and was greeted by the receptionist. The office looked like something out of *Town and Country* magazine. The décor featured understated hues of white and beige, with plush sofas and lavish chairs. A sparkling chandelier hung in the center. I was afraid to sit down. Lauren C. Livingston's office reeked of elegance, influence, and power. *This is going to cost me.* The receptionist waved me over.

"Please have a seat, Ms. Davis. Lauren will be with you shortly."

Minutes later, I heard the unmistakable clicking of stiletto heels coming down the hallway, all no-nonsense and matter-of-fact. The door opened. Bitchy Business Suit Woman from Urban Orchard stared back at me.

She gave me a once-over, turned in a huff, and said,

"This way," clicking loudly all the way back down the hall to her office.

I followed her and settled into an overstuffed white chair in her office, scanning the walls. On one wall a picture hung of Lauren standing on a boat next to a famous celebrity. Another photo showed a younger version of her next to a Supreme Court justice. I saw a scattering of pictures of Lauren posing with senators and politicians—several college degrees and certifications decorated the wall behind her desk.

I glanced up to find her watching me with impatience. She drummed her perfectly manicured nails on the desk. She was studying me, debating if I was worth her time.

"What brings you here today, Ms. Davis?"

I blurted out quickly, "It's Emma, please. My husband left me for a waitress. He moved out and is now having an affair with her. His lawyer has been trying to contact me for weeks, but I've been ignoring him. I was served papers last week. Now I need help." *Whew.*

Lauren peered over her glasses at me. "I see. And are there children involved?"

"Yes, two. My oldest, Austin, is seven, and my daughter, Myla, is five."

"Do they know about her?"

"Yes, they do. They even spend time with her."

Just saying those words made my heart hurt. I never

thought I would be sharing my kids with another woman, especially not one like Kiki. Lauren typed notes into her tablet.

"And will you be contesting the divorce?"

That question gave me pause. Despite everything that had happened, I still loved Jack. We made a family together. Agreeing with the divorce felt like a betrayal on my part, as if I was an active participant in the severing of my kid's worlds. Yet the idea of him being with Kiki made me simultaneously sad and angry. I felt torn. I reflected on Evy, who had also lost everything without her consent, yet she persevered. I needed her bravery. I needed to carry on, too.

"I'm not happy about it. I don't know. There might be a considerable amount of money involved."

Lauren stopped typing, raised one eyebrow, and leaned forward. *"Realllly?"* she said. "Keep talking."

From the beginning, I told Lauren my story—my success with OneBank and the years I spent building my company, meeting Jack and the whirlwind romance that left me breathless. I recalled the years after that when we traveled and worked on our careers, putting off any discussion of children. We had it all, and I did not want that to change.

Then, one day, he came home from work and said we needed to talk. His colleague was building a company and needed start-up capital. He said he had also been thinking about us and decided that we needed to start trying to have kids.

"You're running out of time, Emma. You're in your twenties. Wouldn't selling OneBank to focus on the family make sense?" I told him he was crazy. There was no way I was selling my company.

His campaign continued for weeks. He started bringing home flowers and taking me out to expensive dinners. It was as if we were reliving our honeymoon. I believed the discussion about having children had dropped until he brought home a tiny box and put it on the kitchen table one day. The tag on it said, "Open me."

Pulling the top off the box, I found a tiny pair of athletic shoes inside, with another note saying, "For your future running partner. The next member of Team Davis."

He dropped to his knees, put his head in my lap, and said, "Please, Emm. Please make a family with me."

OneBank went up for sale the following week. After it was sold, Jack went into a partnership with his colleague.

My name was nowhere on the agreement.

Lauren stared at me in disbelief. "Why? Why would you do that?"

I was beginning to think I'd spend a lifetime trying to answer that question.

I retorted, "Because even the smartest and most

accomplished women can be roped into the belief that to be a complete woman, you must also be a wife and mother. I was newly pregnant with Austin."

She shook her head at me and said, "But the business. What's it worth now?" *Here comes the shark.*

"I should know that answer, right? I don't. They originally tried to start a community banking concept overseas but failed. I don't know how much money is left."

Lauren's eyes narrowed. "That's what he *told* you, but we will get to the bottom of this. That money you gave him might be considered separate from marital property. New York State law recognizes both separate property and marital property. Separate property includes assets that one spouse owned before the marriage. Marital property, on the other hand, includes any assets that were acquired during the marriage. We are going to contest his motion and counter on the grounds of adultery. There are processes! There are ways to find out *everything*. Tell me about his business."

Lauren typed into her tablet as I spoke. She then picked up her phone and called her paralegal.

"Rocco, I just sent you an email. I need you to research something. The details are in the email. And get to work. Time is of the essence."

She turned back to me. "New York State Divorce Law, under DRL 170 (4), states that the commission of an act of adultery is a punishable crime. It also changes the rules on how property can be distributed. It buys you some leveraging power. At the very least, you are entitled to half or more of that company and your marital assets. We are going after every cent."

The look on her face sent a chill down my spine. I could now see why she was the go-to lawyer for women left in a lurch. Lauren C. Livingston, Esquire was not one to be reckoned with.

"And are you employed now?"

"Yes, I work for the federal government."

She nodded. "A civil servant. I'm assuming you don't make much money. That will fare well for you. Now tell me more about this waitress."

I told Lauren the story of Kiki and that night at the restaurant. Jack started acting differently after that encounter. He began lifting weights again in our basement gym. New clothes appeared in the laundry. He worked more hours and started taking long trips.

Then he came home late one night and headed straight upstairs to shower. He must have forgotten and accidentally left his cell phone on the family room's TV stand. His phone suddenly beeped; I picked it up to see a text message,

KIKI

Baby, come back over. I know you want more of this.

An image popped up of a naked Kiki, followed by a kissy-face emoji and three hearts. Jack stood in the doorway, mouth hung open.

"I can explain," he said. Except he couldn't. He moved out a week later.

Lauren stopped typing and shook her head.

"Ridiculous. I have seen more of these cases than you can imagine. I assure you, he will not get away with this. My assistant, Rocco, will do some research to document the adultery case and see what he can find out about his business. Your husband's financial information will be disclosed in court. We need to make sure we get all of it. People are very good at hiding things. I'll reach out to your husband's attorney. There is also the issue of my retainer. I'll need $10,000 to get started."

Ouch. I cringed.

Lauren continued, "I will draft and send you an Engagement Agreement by tomorrow. Once I have the retainer payment and countersigned copy, I will enter my appearance on your behalf, and we will get started."

She turned to a stack of documents on the credenza behind her desk, rummaged around for a minute, and said, "Aha!" She slid a small stack of documents across the desk.

"These are Interrogatories, Requests for Production of Documents, and a Statement of Net Worth. It's called 'discovery'; both parties must complete them in a contested divorce. What you are seeing is a very basic boilerplate set. We can customize the documents as we see fit. Given the fact that there is a business involved, we will also seek disclosure of the business's financials as well."

I scanned the documents and saw that Jack would need to provide copies of his personal financial statements, tax returns, bank accounts, and other documents related to his assets, investments, and liabilities. He would also have to answer many questions about his personal living situation.

"What does this mean?" I asked.

A sharp light flickered in Lauren's narrowed eyes—calculating—as if she could already see Jack's downfall unfolding.

"It means we are going to find every last penny. It also means we can prove our grounds for adultery. Your husband's lawyer will also prepare a set of these documents for you to answer. Rocco and I will help you with that, but I cannot stress enough the importance of complete and utter honesty and transparency in your responses. I just found your case listed on the docket. The case has been assigned to Judge John Hawkins. He's been around for a long time, and nothing gets past him. There's a good reason why we call him 'The Hawk.' Don't worry, Emma. We will prevail. We'll be suing for my attorney's fees and so much more. $10,000 will feel like chump change by the time I'm done with him."

I shook Lauren's ice-cold hand.
This shark smelled blood.

Later that evening, I got busy with putting the kids to bed. After tucking Myla in and giving her four kisses on her nose (our nightly routine), I crept into Austin's room, hoping he would talk to me. He sat quietly at dinner, but his mood seemed to have improved.

"Hey, bud. How did everything go after I left the school today?"

His face lit up. "It was awesome, Mom! The fire department showed up, and Naryan and Jason's mom were taken away in ambulances! Naryan came back to school later with the coolest cast. He broke his arm, and they let him pick any color that he wanted. I was the first to sign it. He said nobody had ever paid attention to him before. Now he's really popular because he almost died. He asked me to be his best friend, and now everybody wants to sit with us at lunch."

A look of relief spread across his face.

"Austin, I just wanted to say I'm sorry about what happened at McDonald's that day. I am *not* crazy. I was having a terrible day, and I was hungry and grumpy. I haven't been feeling very good about myself lately."

Austin looked at me thoughtfully. "Then why don't

you do something about it? Our gym teacher, Mr. Fielding, tells us moving is improving. He said if you are feeling down, sometimes it helps to get up and go for a walk. Maybe you just need to move some?"

I swallowed hard, thinking back to my days as a distance runner. The feeling of joy and exhaustion after finishing those ten-mile runs. *That runner's high.* These days, I could barely get up two flights of stairs without losing my breath.

"It's not bad advice," I told him as I tucked him in. "I'm glad your day got better. So, what happened with Jason Stone's mom?"

Austin shrugged and said, "She's expected to survive."

When I settled into bed, I opened my email to see a message from The Bolton Academy front office.

From: Catherine Hunt, Headmistress

Subject: Unfortunate Incident

Dear Bolton Academy Community,

I am writing to clarify a matter, as I hear rumors circulating throughout The Bolton Academy community about an incident at our school today during the Warm Feet on the Street sock drive. First, I commend

Ms. Williams, our third-grade children, and their parents for coming to the aid of the non-gentrified in our community with an outpouring of socks. Unfortunately, no good deed goes unpunished.

During the event, one of our children had an ill-fated incident with the exercise rope in the gymnasium, resulting in a broken arm. A second child nearly swallowed a sock. To complicate matters further, one of our parents slipped on an unknown substance originating from something liquid on the snack table and suffered an injured tailbone and concussion. A concerned child pulled the fire alarm, which alerted the Bolton Fire Department to dispatch several trucks and an ambulance.

Please understand that your children's safety and emotional well-being are of the utmost concern. I encourage you to make me aware immediately if your child or children have experienced any emotional suffering resulting from this incident. A therapist will be on hand tomorrow in the library to hold a group counseling session on school-place stress. In the gymnasium, Mr. Fielding will later demonstrate how to descend the exercise rope safely.

To dispel any rumors you may be hearing, there was no fire, the injured parent is not in intensive care, and one of our parents did not purposely bring a hazardous substance to the event with the intent of harming others.

Get well cards will be on display in the front office if you would like to stop by and leave a kind word for those who were injured. As a community, I encourage us all to uplift one another and come together. We Are Bolton Strong.

Next, I read my text message from Evy:

EVY

How'd it go today? Did you meet with the lawyer?

Me:

Yes, and she's a tough one. You were right. *Shark.*

Evy:

EVY

> Perfect. Meet me for lunch tomorrow at the Mexican place. I want to hear all about it.

I turned out the lights and closed my eyes. For the first time in months, I felt a sense of peace again. That night, I dreamed of running down a long road. The sky was a brilliant blue, and the sun felt warm on my face. My strong legs carried me for miles. I turned my head. Evy ran by my side.

Soulmates

Monday, 7:30 a.m., Text to Evy:

> I'm taking your advice. I'm not covering for Larry at the management meetings anymore. I've come up with an idea for a new coding project. I'll tell you about it at lunch.

Monday, 10:15 a.m., Text to Evy:

> Never mind. I have to cancel our lunch plans. I'm so sorry! The school called, and Austin is sick. Raincheck later this week, okay?

Monday, 9:00 p.m. Text to Evy:

> Haven't heard from you today!
> I'm sorry again about lunch. How
> was the orientation for new
> instructors at the university? Are
> you ready for your first day?

Tuesday, 10:15 a.m. Text to Evy:

> Larry called me into his office to
> say he was disappointed in my
> attitude because I wouldn't take his
> meeting minutes. He also said I'm
> taking too much time off because
> of the kids and need to fix my
> work/life balance. What is this, the
> 1950s? Do I look like June Fucking
> Cleaver? I need to find another job!

Tuesday, 1:15 p.m. Email from RoccoMaroni@lcliv-ingstonlaw.com.

"Ms. Davis, I have attached an Engagement Agreement from Lauren C. Livingston regarding her representation of you in the matter of Davis v. Davis in the Supreme Court of the State of New York. Please sign page five where indicated and return the

> *countersigned copy as soon as possible.*
> *As you are aware, time is of the essence. It*
> *is firm policy that we do not commence*
> *work on your case until we receive both*
> *the signed Engagement Agreement and*
> *receipt of your retainer payment. You*
> *may wire the funds to our office (wiring*
> *instructions attached) or hand deliver*
> *both to our offices. We accept cash, checks,*
> *and all major credit cards. Our office*
> *hours are Monday-Friday, 8:30 am-5:00*
> *pm. We look forward to working with you*
> *and are grateful for your trust in our firm.*
> *Best, Rocco."*

Wednesday, silence.

Thursday, 8:30 a.m. Text to Evy:

> Evy? Are you mad at me?

Thursday, 11:30 a.m. Text to Evy:

> Evy?

Thursday, 2:45 p.m. Phone call to Evy. Voicemail: *"Hi! You've reached Evy Hanover. Please leave a message!"*

Four days had passed, and I had not heard back from Evy. She always replied to my messages and contacted me several times daily, always with a cheerful voice message or a text. But now, there was nothing but radio silence.

I left work and drove straight to her condo on East Main Street. I arrived to discover that all the lights were off, and the blinds hung closed. I rushed to the door and knocked loudly, but no one answered.

"Evy! It's me, Emma!"

I could hear her golden retriever, Benny, barking from inside the condo. I knocked louder.

"Evy! Are you in there?"

There was more barking but no movement. I tried the door handle and turned it, surprised to find it unlocked.

When I opened the door, an overwhelming stench of raw garbage and trash overwhelmed me. The condo was dark inside, so I flipped on a light switch. Piles of dirty dishes littered the kitchen counters and sink, and the trashcan overflowed. Clothes and papers lay scattered across the living room. Unpacked moving boxes lined a wall. *How long has this mess been here?*

Benny barked from behind a door. When I opened it, he rushed out, jumping on me and licking my face. I saw Evy curled up in the bed.

"Ev!" I rushed over to her and found her covered in sweat. "Oh my God! Are you okay?"

She sat up, and the look on her face made my heart sink. Her eyes were red and puffy, her hair greasy and messy, and her pajamas stained. I stood in front of her, speechless. *What was happening?*

Almost as if she had read my mind, Evy exclaimed, "I don't feel well. And I miss Ben." Her expression crumpled, and she broke down into tears.

In the few months I had known her, I had only seen the strong, confident, optimistic version of Evy. I sometimes wondered how she could always keep it all together despite everything that had happened to her. Seeing her like this now, I realized how insidious grief could be. It acted like a dark shadow that crept into the crevices of your life, waiting until you faced it and gave it homage. Grief spared no one and was front and center right now, not backing down. Evy's shoulders heaved with sobs. Benny jumped up on the bed and licked her face.

I climbed into the bed next to her, wrapped my arms around her, and hugged her, echoing the words she had said to me in the taxi that night. "I love you, my friend. Your story is not over yet."

She sobbed louder as I wrapped her in a blanket, Benny circling and trying to help.

"Talk to me."

Through tears, Evy recounted their journey to me. I learned that she and Ben had been a true love story. They met before her sophomore year of college. She studied English Literature, and he pursued a degree in Finance. A mutual friend introduced them to each other over the summer at a party on a warm July night.

He immediately commented on her rusty, beat-up old Honda Accord sitting in the driveway, laughing and saying, "I hope you don't try to wash that thing. It will disintegrate."

She countered with a retort about his boat shoes and polo shirt. "Seriously, dude, nobody wears those anymore."

The exchange went back and forth all night, the two roasting each other. She made fun of his Boston accent. "It's a *car*, not a CAH."

He made fun of her choice of a college degree. "Your parents are paying good money for that? You're studying your own native language."

She quoted her favorite poetry. She liked Yeats. He talked about the value of compound interest. They drank keg beer out of red plastic cups and talked into the small hours of the morning. He kissed her at dawn.

She said she couldn't explain her feelings that night, but it was as if she had discovered something had been missing her whole life. When they met, that gap became filled. They parted ways with a promise to keep in touch, but they did not. She lived three hours away and returned to her lifeguard job for the rest of the summer. He went back to work as an intern at a bank.

She didn't see him again until one morning in the fall as she walked up a hill to attend university class. He sped by in a convertible, slowed the car down, and put it in reverse.

He flashed a big smile at her. "Need a ride?"

"Oh," she replied. "You want me to get into your CAH?"

He stopped the car in the middle of the road. Cars beeped loudly as he blocked traffic.

"Come on," he said. "You're causing a traffic jam."

She made her way to the passenger's side and got in.

"Finally," he said as if he had been waiting a long time for her to be sitting there. "That's your seat now."

And it was. They dated for three years and then married after college. Ben went on to build a successful financial management company, and Evy taught high school.

She said they tried for several years to have children, but she had too many medical issues. She remembered the day her doctor told them it would probably never happen. She became depressed, worried that Ben would leave her if they couldn't have a family.

"He must have sensed it," she told me, "Because one day he came home from work and announced, 'Evy, I would like you to meet our new child, Benjamin David Hanover, III. We will call him Benny for short.'"

A small, fluffy golden retriever puppy bounced

through the front door and into Evy's lap. Ben wasn't going anywhere.

An ache of sadness overcame me as she told me their story. She had nothing to offer Ben, yet he never left her side. I had given Jack everything I had, and now he was gone. That was the difference between saying the word love and actually showing it.

A now much bigger Benny snuggled up next to her and lay in the crook of her arm, wagging his tail happily every time she spoke.

"This one became my baby," she said as she took a tissue from the bedside table and blotted away the last of her tears.

She looked at me with mascara-smudged eyes and asked earnestly, "Do you think you only get one soul-mate? As if the universe pegged another soul for just you, and you are destined to keep traversing time to find each other? I feel like I've known Ben over and over. And losing him felt like a crack in time that opened until we could reconnect. I know that we will, though."

"A crack in time?" I asked.

A sadness flickered in her eyes, as if she were reliving the moment she got the call about Ben's accident. She turned to me, her expression heavy.

"Actually, yeah. It was almost as if I could hear it," she said softly. "It was quiet, and then it wasn't. Just a low, distant crack—like thunder without the storm."

I sat with her, unsure of what to say next. I had never felt a love so deep I'd traverse time to hold onto it. I had loved Jack, but it was on a more surface level, like we were good domestic partners, but nothing deeper. Yet, she had known it. Maybe experiencing that kind of love gave her the courage to keep going. And also, why the fractures of grief could dig so deep. Some people never do recover from a broken heart. I leaned in and hugged her.

"You will find him again," I assured her. "Right now, you need to get better," I said. "Stay here."

Evy settled back on the pillow and gave me a small smile. "Thanks, Emm."

I took Benny for a quick walk and then set out to scavenge Evy's kitchen for some food. Benny circled underfoot, so I refilled his bowl with kibble and refreshed his water.

"Now, let's take care of your mom." He wagged his tail as I got to work.

I slid a frozen lasagna into the oven, then tackled the mess around me—unloading Evy's dishwasher, loading it with a week's worth of dirty dishes, tossing trash, and wiping down the countertops. After tidying up the living room, I gathered some dirty laundry and started a wash cycle. Finally, I found a cinnamon-scented candle and lit it.

Evy emerged from the bedroom. She looked flushed,

so I put my hand on her forehead. "I think you have a fever. Where do you keep your medicine?"

She pointed to the corner cabinet. When I opened it, prescription pill bottles spilled onto the counter. I located some medicine and handed it to her.

"I probably just have a touch of something. I think the flu is going around. But I am starving. Thank you so much." She sat down and devoured the food.

"I'm sorry I didn't respond to you," she said as I cleaned the dishes. "Everything came crashing down on me. I haven't been feeling well. Tomorrow is my wedding anniversary, and the first one I will spend without Ben. I think I just need something to pull myself out of this funk I'm in."

I had an idea: "Somebody wise recently told me that moving is improving. Do you want to start exercising with me? Maybe just start with walking? Every day, rain or shine, until we both start to feel better."

Evy nodded. "Walking. I could do that."

She was thoughtful for a moment and continued, "Speaking of feeling better, I have been thinking about what we discussed at Urban Orchard that day. I still think you should try dating again. You can't spend all your time just working and taking care of your kids. I started poking around on the online dating sites. You can create accounts for free."

I pondered the idea for a moment. What I wouldn't

give to have someone come into my world again and whisk me off my feet. Someone to have dinner out with me. Go on excursions. *Sex.* But no. I refused to try to love anyone else again until I figured out how to love myself first.

"Someday. For now, we walk before we run. I get off work tomorrow at five, and Jack has the kids. Meet you here." I kissed her forehead, smelled her hair, and said, "You need a shower."

She laughed. At least she was smiling again. I headed home.

Tuesday, 5:15 p.m., Voice message from Livingston Legal: *"Good afternoon, Ms. Davis. This is Rocco Maroni, Lauren Livingston's paralegal. Thank you for returning the Engagement Agreement and your credit card payment. Can you please call me in the morning? I have some important questions about your husband's business. The business I found seems small compared to the one you described. Certainly not in the millions that you said you gave him. We obviously haven't yet gotten to the discovery phase of your trial when additional details will be forthcoming. Still, I did find some information online that we should discuss as soon as possible."*

The shark was circling again.

What didn't I know?

CHAPTER 9

Lobotomy

Life with the kids fell into a routine. We developed a steady schedule since I was handling most of the parenting on my own. I was always up before dawn, preparing myself for work before waking them. After breakfast together each morning, we headed to the bus stop at the end of our street.

After watching the bus pull away, I returned to the house. My cell phone blinked on the kitchen counter—five missed calls from Rocco. The doorbell rang as I grabbed my things to leave for the office. Two police officers stood at the door. Startled, I took a step back.

"Can I help you? Is everything okay?"

Scenarios raced through my mind. A horrific accident involving the school bus. Something had happened to my parents. Was Evy okay? Was I being arrested? *Why were two police officers standing in my doorway at 8:00 in the morning?*

"Emma Davis?"

"Yes, I'm Emma. What's going on? Are my children okay?"

"Your children will be entrusted in the care of your husband for the time being—"

I cut him off. "Wait. What are you talking about? I just put them on the bus."

"Ma'am, we're here to escort you to Belmont General Hospital for your court-ordered psychiatric evaluation. Your attorney should have notified you. Your husband has retained custody of your children until you have been deemed fit to care for them. He will pick them up from school today." *He did what?*

Flustered, I ushered them in. "Please come inside. I need to call my attorney."

After listening to my voice messages, I discovered Rocco had desperately tried to contact me while I was at the bus stop. He said Jack had requested a psychological evaluation because of the McDonald's incident, and the police were on their way to escort me. Jack wasn't happy about my refusal to agree to his terms for the divorce, and now he was coming after me.

I called Rocco back, but his phone went to voicemail. My voice pitched higher in panic as I spoke into the phone. *"Rocco! It's Emma Davis. The police are here. Please have someone meet me at the Belmont General Hospital. I need help!"*

I attempted to reach Evy next. Voicemail. I quickly left a message and filled her in on what was happening. *"Help me, Evy! Jack is having me sent to the psych ward!"*

With my head hung in shame, I followed the officers to their police cruiser. The neighbors peered out of the windows and doors of their McMansions as the scene played out. Nothing like this ever happened on Browncroft Boulevard. *Breaking Morning News! Depressed Divorcee Sent to Psych Ward Prison.* I reluctantly climbed into the back of the police cruiser, and we sped off.

⁊⁊⁊

When we arrived at Belmont General Hospital, I was greeted by Delores, a social worker wearing dark blue scrubs and matching clogs. Delores had a kind face, with mocha brown skin, gentle wrinkles framing her eyes, and short, gray curly hair. She carried a clipboard and a folder with my name on it.

"Follow me, Ms. Davis." She turned to the police officers and said, "I've got her now. You can go."

I followed Delores down a long hall. She took me into a large windowless room painted a sterile light green, scattered with a sagging black sofa and several gray metal chairs. A poster on the wall showed a cat clinging to a tree branch over an inscription that read *Hang in There.* Another poster showed a picture of dancing cartoon tacos with a caption that read *It's Okay to Fall Apart Sometimes. Tacos Do and We Still Love Them.* A third poster read *Be Kind to Your Mind* with a picture of a beer bottle, a prescription pill bottle, and a marijuana leaf crossed out.

"I'll need your things," Delores said gently.

"But I need my purse. And my cell phone! What if something happens to my kids and the school can't reach me?" Panic began rising in my throat as my heart pounded in my chest.

"I'm sorry, Emma. You will not have contact with anyone until Dr. Friedman has assessed you." She took my purse and jacket.

I took a step back. "Well, how long is that going to take?"

"You'll probably get in to see him tomorrow. He's got a full schedule this week. The protocol is to keep you for 72 hours unless the doctor deems you fit for release."

72 hours? I had to spend the night here?

"I assure you, this is a mistake," I told her. "My husband did this. He's angry at me because I won't agree to his divorce terms. This is *revenge* because I've hired an attorney. I don't belong here!" My voice reached a high-pitched yelp, and I started hyperventilating. Delores handed me a piece of paper.

"On a scale of one to ten, where are we right now?"

Where are *we?*

MENTAL HEALTH PAIN SCALE

MILD ☺

1 – Nothing wrong at all! I'm doing fine.
2 – Doing pretty good but having some trouble sleeping.
3 – To be honest, I have a bit of a headache. I'm a little stressed.

MODERATE ☹

4 – I'm having a bad day. I've had a few recently. And I kind of feel sad.
5 – I'm feeling nervous and irritated. Go away!
6 – I'm losing motivation to do the things I like to do. I'm very anxious.

SEVERE ☹

7 – I just want to be left alone all the time now. And I'm sleeping a lot.
8 – I can't sleep, eat, or work. I feel like it's all falling apart at once.
9 – I can't function. I feel like I'm about to have a nervous breakdown.
10 – I don't want to go on.

"I'd give us a 10, Delores, considering I'm supposed to be at work right now, not assessing my mental health with numbers!"

She patted my arm and said, "Let's see if we can't get you something to make you feel better. I'll call Dr. Friedman."

Delores led me to a small, padded room, locked the door behind her, and left me alone with nothing but my thoughts. *What if the kids find out?* Austin already thinks I'm crazy. *What about work?* I'll never hear the end of it. *How was Jack even able to put me here?* I will never forgive him for this.

Delores returned with a small paper cup containing two pills, a second cup filled with water, and a clipboard with a stack of papers.

"This should help your anxiety," she said, handing me the pills and water. "And I'm going to need you to fill these out. Please provide the names of people you interact with daily. There are also some questions about how you've been feeling lately. You must be truthful. Otherwise, it could negatively affect your assessment. You also give us consent to contact anyone listed."

She handed me a black crayon.

"What is this?" I asked, holding it up and examining it.

"You'll need it to fill out the form. No pens or pencils allowed."

I thought about Myla's family unit drawing, which was now hanging on the refrigerator at home. She had drawn a big black X over the picture of the door, perpetually locking Jack and Kiki into the crayon bedroom forever.

Begrudgingly, I took the crayon from her and sat down to complete the paperwork. Emergency contact? I put down Evy's information. Work point of contact? There is only Larry. *Ugh.* Family physician? Any allergies? Was I taking any medications? Had I had surgery in the last ten years? *No, but right now, I wish someone would give me a lobotomy.*

Delores returned twenty minutes later. "All finished?"

I nodded. Suddenly, all I wanted to do was nap, lie down, and sleep all this away. She took me to my room, which contained nothing more than a twin-sized bed under a window with bars.

"The women's restroom is down the hallway, and meals are served in the dining area at 8 a.m., noon, and 5 p.m. Someone will be stopping by at regular intervals to check on you. You're not allowed to leave this floor. There are security guards at all the entrances."

She turned and left the room. I looked at the clock in the hallway. It said eleven o'clock. The kids would now be at lunch at school, oblivious to all of this. *What will they think when I'm not there to pick them up today?* I lay down on the bed and drifted into a deep sleep.

Delores took me to my appointment to see Dr. Friedman the following afternoon, leading me to an office on the other side of the hospital floor. Old wooden furniture and a faded leather chair cluttered Dr. Friedman's office. Along one wall, cheap pressed wood bookshelves bowed under the weight of outdated psychology journals. Several drought-stricken plants lined the windowsill. Like the intake room, hokey posters lined the walls, giving hope to the hopeless.

Storms Don't Last Forever.

When You're at the End of Your Rope, Tie a Knot and Hold on.

When Things Go Wrong, Don't Go with Them.

Dr. Friedman's college degrees hung on the wall behind his desk. He studied at SUNY Farmingdale College for his undergraduate degree and completed his medical residency in Puerto Rico. Lauren C. Livington's posh office stood in stark contrast to this one. Image truly was *everything*.

The door opened, and an older, grandfatherly-looking man walked in. He wore a short-sleeved plaid shirt and khaki pants that stretched over his rounded belly, tucking under his armpits. Rather than accept the inevitable fate of his baldness, he had styled his graying hair into a comb-over. He huffed slightly when he walked. As he settled into his chair, he picked up the folder with my name on it and smiled at me.

"Good afternoon, Ms. Davis. I'm Dr. Friedman. Delores provided your file to me this morning, and I've read your response to the assessment. Thank you for being open and honest with your answers. How are we feeling today?"

We again.

I responded, "*We* are very anxious to go home."

He peered over his glasses and studied me briefly. "Yes, of course, and our goal is to get you there. Nothing seemed too out of the ordinary on your written assessment, but I was wondering if I could ask you a few more questions?"

"Yes, of course. Fire away!" I tried to sound light-hearted and giddy, but it came out more like a squeak.

Dr. Friedman opened his laptop and began typing.

"Do you fantasize or have thoughts about harming yourself or others?" *That was a loaded question. I fantasized about harming Jack every day.*

I gave Dr. Friedman a reassuring smile. "No, I don't have thoughts like that."

"Do you have unusual experiences, such as hearing voices other people cannot hear? Or seeing things that other people cannot see?"

"What? No, of course not!"

"Do you have unusual ideas, such as feeling that the TV or radio has special messages just for you?"

I stared blankly at Dr. Friedman. "No, neither the TV nor the radio has spoken to me. However, Alexa is another story. I can't get her to shut up."

Dr. Friedman raised his eyebrows at me. "Sarcasm will not get you home any faster, Ms. Davis. Now tell me, do you have unusual ideas, such as the feeling that you have special powers that no one else has?"

Yes, I have the power to endure these bullshit questions.

"No, nothing like that."

"Do you find that you can be feeling okay, then suddenly feel angry, or you can be feeling okay and suddenly feel sad? Does this happen a lot during the course of a day?"

Only when I'm locked up against my will while my husband is banging Kiki the Wonder Coochie.

I needed to play along. I shook my head 'no'.

"Do you often experience periods of rage?"

"What? No! I am not an angry person!"

"But you assaulted a teenage fast-food worker." His face turned serious.

"I ran out of Healthy Horizons points! The fries were cold, and I only had seven points left for the entire weekend. Seven!"

"Your husband said he found you drunk and passed

out in your living room the following week, unwilling to care for your sick child."

"I made a new friend. It was buy-one, get-one!"

"He states that you have purposely ignored correspondence from his attorney to work out a separation agreement."

"The terms of that agreement are ridiculous!"

"And I checked on your performance at work. I spoke with someone named Larry, who said you are sometimes belligerent and seem to have difficulty staying focused and taking direction. He said you seem obsessed with rewriting perfectly good code but are excellent at fetching coffee."

"But that code has bugs in it!" I blurted out. "Larry is a complete moron! And I don't get coffee!"

Dr. Friedman typed notes into his laptop.

"What are you writing? Stop writing! I need you...I need *someone* rational to listen to me when I say that my husband...my *estranged* husband, always gets what he wants. He stops at nothing to go after whatever serves his agenda. And the person currently serving that agenda is a twenty-four-year-old college dropout by the name of Kiki! He is having an affair, and he's angry that I'm not making it easy for him. If I'm certified as crazy, he can then justify having left me for a younger woman. *That* is why I am here today."

Dr. Friedman stopped writing and looked at me.

"He said that you pushed him away. Withheld sex. Stopped worrying about his needs."

I reflected on all those nights I tried to seduce Jack, only to be met with a turned back and a complaint that he was tired. I probably looked ridiculous in the sexy lingerie I had bought. It barely covered my fat body. He wanted nothing to do with *me.*

I stared at the doctor, unsure of what to say. I saw scenes from the last ten years of my life flash through my mind as if I were watching a movie. The younger me in that community bank at college when I knew I was on to something great. Jack standing in my tradeshow booth, carefully assessing my worth. The year when my business took off. Tiny running shoes in a box with a promise of a family and growing old together. The crushing feeling I felt the day that Jack told me that my business had been sold to a company from China. Long, lonely days and nights at home alone with crying babies while Jack was off jet-setting and building his business. Kiki circling my family, the image of her perfect naked body still imprinted on my brain. Larry squashing my career in his good old boy bureaucracy.

And now this. *This.* Jack boldly challenging my mental health. On the Mental Health Pain Scale, I was at atomic bomb level rage. I wanted to explode into a brilliant, flowering bloom of wrath.

But I calmed, centered, and remembered what someone once told me about getting through tough times: Sometimes, you have to fake it until you make it. I was being assessed, and I needed to play along. I cleared my throat, straightened myself in my seat, and looked Dr. Friedman squarely in the eye.

"I understand my behavior may seem a bit irrational. I also understand there could be some concerns about my ability to care for my young children in the face of a looming divorce and all the stress that goes with it. But I assure you that I am a hardworking single mother who puts my children first and foremost in my life. My life is literally a cycle of 'Kids. Work. Sleep. Repeat.' I haven't even been on a date since Jack left. One drunken night in a bar does not make me an unfit mother. I was blowing off some steam, and it was his weekend to watch them. The McDonald's incident was just that. An *incident*. I don't belong here and just want to go home and hug my kids."

"Well, fortunately for you, I also contacted Ms. Evelyn Hanover, whom you listed as your emergency point of contact. Ms. Hanover seemed very pleasant and described you just as you said. Loving. Hardworking. Selfless. And also, perfectly sane in light of the events going on in your life right now. I would tend to agree."

I breathed out a loud sigh of relief. *I don't know what I would do without my best friend.*

"She also put me in touch with someone named Sandy Meyers, who seemed quite well-versed on the physical effects of food withdrawal on our bodies. She explained the Healthy Horizons points system in great detail. Who knew that most fruits and vegetables individually had zero points, but if you blend them into a smoothie, you must count them? It's mind-boggling. In any event, I am clearing you to leave here on the condition that you try to work with your husband. I'm sure this is a trying time for both of you."

Work with him? This was now an all-out war. *Fake it until you make it.*

I smiled at Dr. Friedman and said in the most reassuring voice I could muster, "Don't you worry. Everything is going to be just fine."

"Wonderful," he said. "Delores will do your out-processing. Ms. Hanover will be called to pick you up."

I never wanted to see anyone so badly in my whole life. *Come and get me, Evy. Spring me free!*

After Delores finished my paperwork, she escorted me out and rode down the elevator with me. When the doors opened, I saw Evy sitting in a chair near the hospital's entrance. She smiled and waved.

"That's Evy. Can I go now?"

"Of course, Emma. Good luck with everything." Delores quickly hugged me before stepping back into the elevator.

"Ev! I'm so unbelievably happy to see you!"

"Come on," she said. "Let's get you out of here. You still owe me a walk." She pointed to her walking shoes.

"Are you sure? You still don't look well." Her complexion was still washed out, and she looked tired.

"Moving is improving," she shrugged. "Plus, I want to hear about your night in Belmont General. Someone named Dr. Friedman called me. He asked me if you talked to your TV."

I laughed for the first time in days.

"Okay, but I need to go home first. I've been wearing the same underwear since Thursday."

꩜

After cleaning myself up and grabbing my walking shoes at home, Evy and I set out on our first walk together. We circled the Browncroft Boulevard block four times. I could barely talk to her and walk simultaneously without getting winded.

"This is pathetic," I said through labored breathing. "I once ran a full marathon, barely breaking a sweat. Now I can't make it around the block four times."

My feet started to hurt. Evy kept my pace but also struggled. She sat on a bench and announced, "I'm done." She didn't look well, and I wasn't going to argue with her.

"Me too. We just have to keep at this. Four laps every day this week. Next week, we'll strive for five. Thanks again for rescuing me today."

"I think that's what we do. We rescue each other." She patted the bench next to her, beckoning me over.

I sat down, trying to slow my breathing. "I can't believe he had me sent to the psych ward. I had to fill out my paperwork with a crayon! When I asked the intern for clean underwear, he gave me a pair of men's underclothing!"

"Tidy whities or airy briefs?"

"Airy briefs. It's the only kind my fat ass would fit into. I declined." Evy nodded as if she understood the predicament.

"Well," she said, "Jack is just starting to show his true colors. You've always backed down to him. For the first time, you're standing your ground. Being a bully is a lot easier when someone is one hundred percent dependent on you. He took everything you had. Ben never would have treated me the way Jack treats you. It's hard to witness it, but I'm so happy you are standing up to him."

"It helps when you have Lauren C. Livingston on your side."

"Whatever it takes. Women need to have each other's backs. Our mothers and grandmothers fought hard during the feminist movement, but we live with the residual cleanup. Sometimes, I'm okay with the fact that I didn't have kids...a *daughter*. How do you build up a girl's self-esteem in a world where a woman's worth is *still* measured by whether or not she can fit into size two jeans? They promote science, technology, engineering, and math programs in college, but women rarely make it to the top of their fields in STEM. You're the most inspirational woman I've ever met. Look at what one man has done to you." She sighed and squeezed my hand. "I just want to see you fight back."

And there was my strong-willed and outspoken Mighty Myla. I never wanted her to lose that spirit. There would be no more of poor Mommy stuffing away feelings with food and no more holding in all the frustration and anger to the point where I felt like I wanted to explode. I had to mirror what she needed me to be.

"I will. With everything I've got," I replied. I pulled her up from the bench. "Let's head back."

✐

Later that day, Jack pulled up to the front of the house with the kids. He didn't come to the door. Rather, he just sat there, half-hidden behind the wheel, like the coward that he was. Myla rushed in and hugged me.

"Mommy! Where were you yesterday and today?

You weren't there when I got out of daycare, and you weren't there to tuck me in last night! Daddy had to work late, so Miss Kiki made us fried baloney sandwiches with ketchup for dinner and macaroni and cheese with the wrong kind of cheese in it." She made a gagging sound.

Austin brushed past her, sat on the family room sofa, and turned on the TV. "Forget what I said about moving in with Dad. I'm not eating that crap again."

"Austin! Language!"

He shook his head at me and said, "I just call it as I see it." Sometimes, he showed the world the old soul that he was.

I turned back to Myla. "I'm sorry, Myla. I had something to do, and I forgot my cell phone to call you. I'll be there to tuck you in from now on. Every night! Who wants McDonald's for dinner?"

"Me! Me!" Myla said, jumping up and down.

Austin grimaced. "Fine, but only if we don't go in."

That evening, as I climbed into bed, I opened my work email to catch up on what I'd missed during my two days away.

From: Liam Taylor, Department Head, Security

Sent: Thursday, 9:30 a.m.

To: Federal Center for Fiscal Enforcement
Software Development Team

Subject: Risk Management Monitoring
Security Protocols

Please be advised that we will immediately begin enforcing Risk Management Monitoring (RMM) security protocols for all existing government-off-the-shelf and commercial-off-the-shelf software running at the Center per Department of Defense policy guidelines. Please ensure your software code is up-to-date with the latest security scans. My office will begin creating assessment reports for the leadership team. Please reach out if you have questions.

From: Larry Steward

Sent: Thursday, 4:32 p.m.

To: Emma Davis

Subject: Meet & Greet

Emma,

I need you to stop by my office tomorrow. I've scheduled a meeting for 9:00 a.m., and don't be late.

Larry

Text message from Evy:

> Oh my God! My feet are killing me!
> But back at it tomorrow. I'll meet
> you at your house after work.

Same, girl. Same. My feet were on fire.

The MBA

When I arrived at work the next day, I found a small group of junior developers huddled in the hallway outside of Larry's office, whispering amongst themselves.

"Hey guys! What's up?"

One of them rolled his eyes, snorted, and said, "You're about to find out." He motioned towards Larry's closed office door. They walked away.

Ugh. What did Larry and Dr. Friedman talk about?

I knocked on the door before pushing it open. Larry was seated behind his desk, focused on his laptop. As I stepped inside, he gestured for me to take a seat. His face was so red today that it looked like a middle-aged carrot.

A younger guy sat across from him. His hair was styled in a mid-fade short crop, and his goatee was perfectly shaved. He wore a tailored Oxford shirt paired with dark jeans and a belt. Light brown wingtips adorned his feet. He reminded me of a younger version of Jack.

"Emma! Come in! I'd like you to meet Bradley."

Bradley didn't bother to move from his chair. Instead, he gave me a once-over and coolly extended his hand. I shook it and sat down next to him.

"Bradley, Emma manages the Center's workflow software."

Bradley smiled smugly. "Come on, Larry. It's Bradley, *MBA*."

Larry chuckled. "Of course. Emma, Bradley just graduated from the University of Belmont with a master's degree in business administration. All ready to take on the world!"

"Damn right, I am!" Bradley jumped up, gave Larry a high-five, and then settled back into his chair.

"Bradley is your new boss."

My new *what?* This kid looked like he just traded his backpack for a briefcase.

"Wait a minute," I said, looking back and forth between the two of them, confused. "I don't understand. Is there a reorg going on I don't know about?" Larry's gaze lingered on my chest.

"No, nothing like that. It's just that I figured it might be a good idea to add another level of management and oversight to the team. You will report to Bradley. And he will report to me. This gives me more time to focus on bigger projects."

Oh. *Like your golf game?*

Bradley leaned back in his chair. "Oh yeah, I have all kinds of ideas on how to shake things up around here."

Larry continued, "And anyway, after receiving that concerning call yesterday from Dr. Friedman, I figured it might help you to have another supervisor oversee your work. A little stressed, are we?" He chuckled again. *Vile man.*

Oblivious, Bradley pulled out his cell phone and began scrolling through his newsfeed. He pointed to the screen and laughed.

"I'm sure you'll help Bradley assimilate. Maybe provide a little training. I'll be taking him to lunch with the department heads. Please meet with him afterward to get him up to speed on our software development efforts. You can go now."

As I left the office, I overheard Bradley say, "Check this out! This guy trained his dog to sing!"

I returned to my cubicle and opened my laptop, preparing to scan code. *Somebody* needed to do some actual work around here.

I met with Bradley later that day in the conference room. When I walked in, he had his feet propped up on the conference room table, still staring into his cell phone.

"Oh hey, Amanda," he said without looking up. "Have a seat."

"It's Emma." I sighed and sat down across from him.

"Oh, right. Right. It will take me a little while to learn all the names. I'm trying to get to know everyone. Tell me what you do." *Larry already told you.*

"I manage the workflow software for The Center."

Bradley looked perplexed. "What is workflow software?"

This guy was brought in to manage a team of software developers? This was basic stuff. I peeled back the onion of stupidity a little further.

"You know what The Center does, right?"

Bradley shrugged. "Something to do with taxes?"

I cleared my throat. *Okay.* I explained, "When the IRS receives tax returns, some are flagged for audits. Those audits come here for processing. They go through a whole series of reviews. Multiple people look at them to determine if further action is needed. The audit is called a 'package', and that package 'workflows' or moves from one person to the next electronically. And sometimes back. Decisions are made based on the research each team does. All the information is stored in databases and in the Cloud. And that information gets reported to the IRS. That's why we are called The Federal Center for Fiscal Enforcement. We ensure people pay their taxes when they are supposed to."

"So cool," Bradley said. "We're like the IRS cops! Pew! Pew! Pew!" He fired imaginary guns in the air with his fingers.

Yes, exactly like that.

I waited until he was done pewing, then I began interviewing him. "Do you have any experience in software development?"

"What? No, Larry brought me in to *manage*."

"What do you have experience *managing*?"

"Well, I mean, I went straight into my MBA program out of undergrad. But I did have a really cool internship! The company I worked for let me shadow a Chief Executive Officer. I was even 'CEO for a Day.' I put out some memos. I gave that guy some awesome tips. It was cutting-edge stuff. Yeah, I was good at that. Larry told me you're really good at taking meeting minutes and fetching coffee. It would be great if you could do that for me, too."

"Bradley, I'm a software developer. I sit in a poorly lit cubicle, and I code all day. I don't take meeting minutes, and I don't get coffee for anyone. If you're going to be managing this department, I have something I need to discuss. The software I work with is old and needs to be updated. In fact, we just got an email from the head of security about following RMM protocols. We need to make that a priority..."

"RMM, what?"

"Risk Management Monitoring. It's something we have to do."

"Right. Um, I'll have to run that past Larry. See what he says. I mean, I'm the new guy. What do I know?" He laughed to himself. *Apparently nothing.*

Bradley leaned back in his chair, studying me. "So, until I can get a better feel for what you do, I want you to put together a daily list of what you've worked on and email it to me. It might be a good idea for you to email me when you check in every morning. And maybe one when you check out."

Yeah, I won't be doing that.

"Well," he said. "Gotta run. I've got an important meeting."

Larry popped his head into the conference room. "Ready to go, sport?"

"You know it!" Bradley jumped up and headed for the door without looking back.

"The caddy is teed up and waiting for us."

"Awesome!" Bradley said as he walked out. "Oh,

Uncle Larry, before I forget to tell you. Mom said the cookout starts at 3:00 on Saturday." *Uncle* Larry?

I stared at The Center's decaying conference room walls—the building slowly falling apart around us. At my old office space at OneBank, we worked on one floor of a new building in the city. I purposely designed it for openness and teamwork, with office walls made of glass. Work centers were created with sofas and chairs arranged in a living room style to encourage people to come together and collaborate. I wanted think tanks for improving the product we offered banks nationwide. We operated under a model free of hierarchy, which encouraged my team to be creative and independent thinkers.

I always wondered what happened when the Chinese company took over. They kept the company name and logo and stayed in the same location. I sometimes drove past the building on my way home from The Center, imagining what was happening inside.

Text message:

ROCCO

Good afternoon, Ms. Davis. It's Rocco. Can you come by the office tomorrow? Lauren wants to discuss something. She has some concerns. And I have some research to cover with you. She's free at 11:30.

I returned the message:

> I'll be there.

I headed home to meet Evy for our walk.

CHAPTER 11

Skeletons

I arrived at the Coventry Building at 11:30. When I entered Lauren's office, I saw her reading an email intently as she chewed on her pen. She looked up when I entered her office, her lips pursed.

"Emma," she said evenly. "Please have a seat." A frown etched across her face.

"Morning!" I replied, trying to sound cheerful.

"It would have been helpful for you to tell me that you assaulted a teenager at the local McDonald's. And that a police report was filed." She looked at me, waiting for me to respond. Her eyes cut through me.

"I may have overlooked it," I said, averting her stare. I played with the zipper on my jacket, waiting for the moment to pass. I knew I should have told her, but I was hoping that day could be forever buried in the past. Jack's attorney thought otherwise.

"If you want me to represent you, you must be truthful about everything. What other skeletons do you have hidden in your closet?"

"No more skeletons," I sighed. "How was he able to do that? Can anyone just send the police to your front door, and have you sent away for a psychological evaluation?"

"In cases like this, yes. And if you have any hope of keeping custody of your kids, I advise you to keep your outbursts in check. Fortunately for you, someone named Dr. Friedman deemed you fit to keep them. I've seen cases where a parent is reduced to supervised visits or no custody at all."

That one felt like a dagger through my chest. The thought of Jack raising those kids alone with Kiki was enough to put me on permanent best behavior. *Fried baloney sandwiches for dinner. Not on my watch.* A gentle knock sounded at the door.

"Come in!" Lauren instructed.

Oh my. A tall man stepped through the doorway, dark hair tousled just enough to look effortless. His features were chiseled, like a model straight out of *GQ* magazine. He clutched a stack of papers in his hands and settled into the seat next to mine.

"Emma, I'd like you to meet Rocco."

Of course, she has a hot paralegal. That's how Lauren rolls.

He extended his hand. "Emma! So nice to finally meet you in person. My apologies for your surprise visit from the police. We received notification from your husband's attorney first thing that morning, and I couldn't track you down in time to give you advance notice. I really tried. Awful what they did to you."

He smiled at me warmly. He was the kind-hearted ying to Lauren's cold-hearted yang. My face flushed. *I will not have a crush on the too-young-for-me paralegal.*

Lauren cleared her throat, pulling my attention away from the Greek God sitting before me. This was serious business, and we all needed to *be* serious.

Lauren snapped at him. "I was just telling Emma we need full transparency. No more surprises. Now, tell us what you have found so far."

Rocco shuffled through the papers. "From what I can gather, your husband did make a sizeable invest-ment in a joint venture with someone named Robert Blankenship right around the time you sold your com-pany. Unfortunately, I'm having trouble finding out any information about it. I can only find the amount initially invested and a listing that is registered to Jack Davis and Robert Blankenship. It's as if he found a way to hide the actual financial accounts related to the business, as well as any detailed corporate information other than the small amount of data I've been able to find online. It is a local company called J&B Enterprises, and they only had a revenue of $250,000 last year. They are listed on Dun and Bradstreet as a consulting company, but not much more."

Lauren clucked and narrowed her eyes. "I knew it," she said. "And he will try to hide all of this during discovery."

She turned to me. "I need you to think. I know he kept you out of the business, but did he ever say anything extraordinary that may have given you pause? Did he leave any paperwork at your house that might give us some insight?"

I shook my head. "Nothing. He was very tight-lipped about all of it. And to be honest, I wasn't really paying attention. We had a joint checking account to pay for bills and things for the kids. There was always plenty of money in it. I just ran the household."

I suddenly felt like it was 1955, and I was the dutiful housewife trained never to question her husband's transgressions. I guess I played that role well. *God, I missed the old me.*

"We have time," she reassured me. "And Rocco is good at his job."

I'm sure he is. I could feel my face flush again.

"In the meantime, I need you to stay on your best behavior."

"Of course," I nodded, perplexed.

Why did he hide the business information from me? He had me sent to the psych ward to make me seem crazy, and now this.

I continued, "I will do anything I can to assist." *That man is going down.*

Back at the office, my thoughts raced, reaching back as I tried to remember any conversations I may have had with Jack over the years, any indication of anything out of the ordinary. I drew a blank. How could I have been so naïve?

I opened my laptop.

Email from Security:

From: Liam Taylor, Department Head, Security

Sent: Wednesday, 3:34 p.m.

To: Federal Center for Fiscal Enforcement Software Development Team

Subject: Second Reminder/Risk Management Monitoring Security Protocols

The need to complete RMM scans has been escalated in preparation for the next data push from the IRS. As a reminder, we are required to enforce RMM security protocols for all existing and new government-off-the-shelf and commercial-off-the-shelf software running at the Center per Department of Defense policy guidelines. Please ensure your software code is up-to-date with the latest security scans. If you haven't started to run scans, please do so immediately.

Email from Bradley:

From: Bradley Baker, MBA, FCFE Software Division Branch Head

Sent: Wednesday, 4:15 p.m.

To: FCFE Technical Group

Subject: Team Building Event

Team,

I am excited to inform you about an upcoming event next week. We will be

> holding FCFE's First Annual Fun Fest at
> Wicomico Park. This will be the perfect
> opportunity to get to know your co-workers
> (and me). The event starts at 10 a.m. Buses
> will be in front of the building beginning
> at 9:30. Please see the attached flyer for
> details. And one more thing, attendance is
> mandatory. Go Team FCFE!

Bradley stood in the doorway of my cubicle, watching me. "Emma! You're back. I didn't know you were going to be leaving for an appointment. Please tell me when you leave the building. I always need to know all my people's whereabouts. That is good management. So, I'm forming a social committee to help with corporate events. Did you see my email? Fun Fest at the park next week? Yeah, it is going to be awesome! I need volunteers to organize it." *Am I being voluntold?*

"Bradley, your Fun Fest sounds awesome, but I am currently swamped with software change requests and trying to run security scans. I'm just finishing up a sprint."

He looked perplexed. "A sprint? What's a software change request?" *Why is this guy in charge? Find your calm voice. Lauren said no more trouble.*

"Well, it's pretty straightforward, Bradley. We code

in something called sprints. Think of it like running a long race, only you break it up into a bunch of smaller, connected races. Each little race, or sprint, is made up of code that needs to be changed with the software to make it run better, or maybe because there's a need for it to function differently. We *sprint* through each little race for short periods of time and then stop at the end to test it and make sure it was coded correctly. If all is good, we will start the following sprint again with new changes. Software change requests are what need to be fixed in each race."

Blank stare. Then, the lightbulb flickered on. His face lit up like a kid on Christmas morning. "Like a relay race? Yeah, I get it! Pass that baton, girl!"

"So anyway, Bradley, I would love to be on your committee, but I have some serious deadlines. Speaking of which, the security director sent out another email to the group. Did you get a chance to talk to Larry about upgrading the workflow software? I sent you some emails about it. I could oversee the junior developers who work with those programming languages every day. I've managed big conversion projects like this before—"

Bradley cut me off.

"Do you think it would be cool to have a clown at the Fun Fest? To make those funny animal shapes out of balloons? Or maybe one of those dunking booths? Ha! I could nail Unc...I mean Larry. I will definitely talk to the committee about that! Well, good luck with your sprinting. Don't run too fast. Heh. Heh. And don't forget that check-out email."

He turned and walked away. I fired air guns at him. *Pew. Pew. Pew.*

Just then, Larry walked past, paused, and said, "Now, now, there's no room for workplace violence. You must still be stressed. Good thing I hired Bradley. Pew. Pew." He fired air guns back at me, chuckled to himself, and kept walking.

After work, I met Evy for our daily walk before picking up the kids from after-school daycare. She looked visibly better. A college session had started, and she told me about her new students.

"I'm teaching two sessions," she began. "My first class is composed of freshmen students. They look so young. *Babies.* I told them their first assignment was to write a story, putting themselves as the main character and describing an event that defines who they are. So, I could get to know them. One student raised his hand and said, 'You mean like I like to skateboard, so write about a skateboard? Like life from the eyes of the board?' I said, 'No, write about *you* on the skateboard. What do *you*, as the main character, do?' He stared at me blankly and said, 'Duh. I skateboard. No offense, but this assignment is stupid.' Another student asked if she should do an existential interpretation of the alter ego she felt she should be. She said it would be her quantum self, reflecting on her other self. I can't make this stuff up."

"What about the other class?"

We rounded the block, both struggling to breathe. *When will these walks get easier?*

"Seniors who need an English credit to graduate. It's going to be a long semester." Evy sighed.

I told her about what Rocco had discovered about Jack.

"I knew it," she gaffed. "That whole underserved nation community bank concept was bullshit. I wonder where your money actually went."

"I'm not sure. Lauren said to lie low. I need to try to play nice with Jack while they keep digging for information. He's paying half of the mortgage and for the kid's school right now. I'm making just enough to cover the rest of my bills. Unfortunately, I still need his financial support."

Evy shook her head. "It won't be like that forever. That money is somewhere. *Nothing* is undiscoverable. Until then, at least be happy you're free of the jerk."

We rounded the block again. Maintaining a decent walking pace remained difficult, but I kept going. A muscular woman in tight running pants and a tank top ran by us. Her stride was effortless.

That will be me again someday.

My quantum self, reflecting back on my other self. Evy and I rounded another block and headed home.

CHAPTER 12

Box of Truth

"It's going to be a hot one today, friends. Unseasonably hot for New York this time of the year."

News 4 meteorologist Chuck Byron turned to his co-anchor and pretended to wipe sweat from his brow.

"That's right, Chuck," said Mindy Mossberger, the Barbie-doll-looking cohort sitting to his left. "And you know I like it hot."

She winked at him, and Chuck winked back and wiped his brow again. I mentally pictured the two of them going at it in a passionate love tryst on the news desk, with the breaking story about the triple homicide and the 'News 4 for You' investigative consumer alert scripts buried in a pile of papers beneath their naked, sweaty bodies.

I turned off the news, second-guessing the outfit I had planned for the Federal Center for Fiscal Enforcement Fun Fest. Jeans and a sweatshirt were out. Reaching into the back of my closet, I grabbed a pair of denim shorts with a stretchy elastic waistband and an oversized t-shirt for the win.

I packed a salad and put some fruit into my lunch cooler. Earlier in the week, I heard Bradley in the hallway at work bragging about the immense food buffet he was planning for the event. Evy and I started tracking points again, hoping that Healthy Horizons and the walking would bring us some success. It helped me to attend the meetings together and to have a friend keep me accountable. When I wanted to reach for the salty cheese puffs in the evening, I texted Evy instead.

EVY

Put them away, Thiamin Mononitrate and Orange #3 are not your friends. It's processed food, not love. 5 points! Have some fruit.

I arrived at work and found three yellow school buses near the Federal Center for Fiscal Enforcement entrance. *They couldn't pay for air-conditioned buses?* The day ahead promised to be long. True to Chuck's prediction, the temperature had begun to rise quickly. I grabbed my lunch and climbed onto the bus in front of the line. It smelled like the sweaty armpit of a hormonal tween.

Several software development coworkers sat at the back of the bus, discussing the upcoming data surge we expected. The IRS released audits quarterly in batches and our team always scrambled each quarter in preparation for them. Surprisingly, Bradley scheduled the mandatory Fun Fest just before our next data push, occurring in just one day.

I joined my coworkers for the twenty-minute ride to Wicomico Park, one of Belmont's nicer recreational areas. The park had pavilions scattered throughout, with playground equipment, playing fields, and a lake at the edge. Our bus stopped at the pavilion by the lake.

A clown greeted us as we exited the bus. He had a big, Joker-like smile painted on his face with thick red and white makeup—yet he didn't actually *look* happy. His face contorted into a grimace as the makeup began to melt. Drenched in sweat, he looked ready to dissolve inside the heavy, oversized clown suit he wore. A fake red nose, precariously perched on his face, threatened to fall off.

"Welcome, staffers!" He made a strange noise that

was supposed to be a funny high-jink laugh, but sounded more like a hyena in heat. "I'm Henry the Happy Clown. Come with me and set off for a fun-filled day of teambuilding and camaraderie. Follow the red balloon."

Thinking back to one of my favorite horror story authors, I pictured that red balloon dancing gingerly in the wind, protruding from a storm drain somewhere, with Henry lurking beneath.

We followed Henry to the pavilion. Bradley and the rest of the entertainment committee were already there, setting up team-building stations. Bradley assembled a large dunking booth at the far end of the adjacent field. On another corner of the field, at the top of a hill, other committee members set out sumo wrestling suits.

Inside the pavilion, picnic tables were arranged cafeteria-style. A podium with a microphone had been placed in the front. Next to it stood a large box labeled "Box of Truth." Outside the pavilion, several buffet tables stood by the tree line, covered with large aluminum containers filled with food. I put my lunch into one of the beer and soda coolers and found a seat. At 10:30 a.m., the temperature approached ninety degrees.

The buses unloaded, and everyone streamed in and found a seat in the pavilion. Larry stood next to Bradley at the podium. In this heat, Larry's face turned a deep purple. Henry the Happy Clown lay slumped in a corner, looking as if he would pass out any moment. A loud squeal rang out across the pavilion as Bradley spoke into the microphone.

"Welcome, team, to the first annual Federal Center for Fiscal Enforcement Fun Fest! If you haven't met me yet, I'm Bradley Baker, Larry's number two. As a recent MBA graduate, I come to you with ideas on how we can cultivate The Center into one of the nation's best federal institutions. Imagine, if you will, a client-focused Center where customers become *more* than customers. They become friends."

Steven from the Audit Team raised his hand.

"Steven! My man!" Bradley said. "Do you have something to add?"

"Yeah. We process IRS audits. You are aware that people actually *hide* from us?"

Bradley laughed nervously. "Right, well, what I meant was, we become their go-to for all things taxes. Like trusted advisors. Nothing like making friends with your enemies. Heh Heh."

Kenny from Accounting piped in. "That makes no sense. We put people in jail."

Janiece from the Help Desk concurred. "Sometimes for life."

Bradley was losing his audience. Around the pavilion, people stared into their cell phones and held sidebar conversations. Henry the Happy Clown stood at the beer cooler, downing his second pale ale.

"In any event," Bradley continued, "Today isn't about you or me. It's all about getting to know each other. There is no 'I' in teamwork!"

He laughed into the microphone, which squealed loudly again. The pavilion became silent.

He continued, "I mean, what do you really know about the person sitting next to you?"

We all looked around, but no one spoke up.

"We've set up teambuilding stations and an *awesome* buffet. But before we dive into lunch, we're going to do an exercise that gives you the opportunity to let people know what you really think."

Steven from the Audit Team started handing out beer from the coolers. Kenny from Accounting followed, and a few others helped. Within minutes, the entire pavilion looked like a middle-aged frat party.

Two tables over, the team from Human Resources started stacking beer cans into a pyramid. Henry the Happy Clown joined them. He was beginning to look happier.

I held on to my water bottle and passed back the beer that someone handed me. I could hear Sandy Myers in my head, "Liquid calories. The kind that sneak up on you. Seven points! Have some water."

Bradley continued to address the crowd. "You will notice slips of paper and pens on the table before you. Here in front of me is a box labeled the "Box of Truth." In this exercise, you will write down something you don't like about a coworker. Hearing these truths gives us the opportunity for self-improvement and growth. And *that* is how we grow as a team. Pretty cool stuff, huh? I learned about this in one of my MBA classes. So go ahead, start writing! Don't be shy! Help your teammates with their self-growth. Once you are finished, put your responses in the box."

Silence settled over the room. Everyone looked around, hoping someone else had the answer. No one did.

I picked up a pen. *Is this anonymous? Do I really get to say whatever I want?* I wrote, "Larry is a sexist pig who stifles women's professional growth and stares at their tits."

I smiled at the piece of paper and nodded. Writing that felt amazing. I looked around, and people were now writing and downing beers. We hadn't even had lunch yet. Bradley walked around with the box, and people dropped their slips of paper into it. Once everyone finished, he returned to the podium.

"We will now take the moments of truth out of the Box of Truth."

He read the first slip of paper. "*What is up with*

Karen Feldman's wardrobe? I've seen salad that dresses better than her. Tell her the 90s are over!"

The pavilion erupted in laughter and clapping. Karen Feldman looked down at her outfit, confused, and started crying.

"Anthony Siebert is such an idiot; if he had a thought, it would have died of loneliness."

More laughter. Anthony stood up quickly from the HR table and knocked over one of the pyramids. Beer cans clattered onto the floor and rolled into the aisle.

"I want to know who said that! I'll kick your ass!"

Bradley continued reading slips of paper.

"Please tell Cynthia Bonner no one cares about her kid's Tae Kwon Do tournaments. Stop posting that shit on Instagram."

The clapping and laughter continued.

"Elisa Connolly is the worst gossip. If she ran like her mouth, she'd be in amazing shape."

"You've got that right!" someone yelled out.

"TeamFit. Blah. Blah. Blah. Workout of the Day. Blah. Blah. Blah. Nobody cares about your ab workout, David Kelly."

"Yeah, we all know you live at the gym!" another voice shouted.

Bradley pulled another slip from the box: *"Larry is a sexist pig who stifles women's professional growth and stares at their tits."*

The pavilion went silent, except for Henry the Happy Clown, who laughed like a hyena again. He blew up a balloon so hard it popped. I slithered down into my seat.

A moment later, someone clapped. Others followed. Soon, there was a standing ovation. I stood up and clapped, too, not wanting to out myself. Teambuilding *was* fun! Henry the Happy Clown stood up and took a bow.

Larry looked around the room, eyeing everyone suspiciously. Bradley intervened.

"Yes, well, maybe now is a good time to have lunch before the activities. Please make your way to the buffet."

The demeanor in the pavilion changed. Karen Feldman ran back to the bus, still crying. Anthony Siebert pounded his fist on the picnic table, looking around the room for the perpetrator who called him stupid. David Kelly flexed his biceps and stared at his muscles in self-admiration.

A small group of women congregated, comparing notes. "Yeah," one of them said, "He stares at my tits too."

I wandered over to the buffet and peered at the food spread. Bradley's awesome buffet was nothing more than flat, gray hamburger patties that looked like hockey pucks. Greasy chicken tenders. Limp hot dogs. A tray of pulled pork. Trays of coleslaw and potato salad sat at the other end. Deviled eggs. Mixed fruit. I grabbed my lunch from the cooler and sat down, grateful I planned ahead.

An hour later, people exited the pavilion and headed to the activity stations. I walked up the hill to where Bradley was busy helping Larry into a sumo wrestling suit. The suit was a big, yellow, round plastic blow-up contraption with a Styrofoam safety bumper around the middle and a cushiony black helmet. An air hose stuck out of the back of it, which Bradley used to pump air into the suit.

Within moments, Larry transformed into a big round ball, his face turning beet red beneath his mop of white hair and puffy white eyebrows. He looked like an Oompa Loompa from *Charlie and the Chocolate Factory*. Across from him, Andrea Fisher from the Audit Team also suited up.

In the center, Bradley laid out a round, flat wrestling mat with a bullseye in the center and several outer circles with points assigned to each circle. A large, bronze, flat, circular metal disk and a mallet stood to the side.

Bradley picked up the mallet and raised it high into the air like a mighty warrior, as if giving homage to the sumo Gods. He smacked the mallet against the gong, letting out a loud crashing sound. A crowd gathered and looked on at the scene. Someone queued ancient Japanese music on a portable speaker.

"I bring to you the Gong of Gamesmanship! When I strike the gong, you will commence wrestling. The goal is to knock your opponent out of the circle. If you knock them over inside the circle, you will collect the points assigned to that inner circle. The winner stays in the circle for the next round until he or she is defeated. Today's overall winner will have received the most points and have earned the distinction of Sumo Warrior!"

The crowd clapped as Bradley thwacked the gong and stepped back. Larry and Andrea walked onto the mat, bowed to each other, and then began circling each other. Larry looked angry.

"Are you the one who called me a sexist pig?"

Andrea looked confused. "Me? No!"

Larry charged at her as best he could. Bradley had blown the suit up too much, handicapping Larry's legs. All he could do was hop. He hopped over to Andrea and threw himself at her. She hobbled, rolled backward, and then rolled back up.

"Oh no, you don't! Although you do stifle women!" She sneered and charged back, throwing her body weight at him as he rolled into a ball to the corner of the mat. He righted himself just in time, and the two of them joined in a headlock. Larry shoved Andrea as hard as he could, and she bounced off the mat. The crowd cheered. Larry hopped a victory lap and asked, "Who's next?"

Anthony Siebert picked up his beer can, crunched it in his hand, and threw it to the ground. He hobbled onto the mat, his face bright red and sweaty. Bradley gonged the gong, and they bowed to each other. Anthony let out a loud roar.

"I want to know what M'fer called me an idiot. I think it was you, you son of a bitch!" Anthony bounced toward Larry and threw his body weight at him, toppling Larry over. Larry tried to get up but instead lay on the ground, feet kicking.

Anthony circled and shouted out, "Idiot this!" He jumped up and went airborne and landed squarely on top of Larry, who could only let out a loud, "Oooooof!"

Anthony then put Larry into a choke slam, grasping his neck, lifting him up, and slamming him down. This caused Larry to bounce like a basketball. He bobbed up into the air two times and then rolled off the mat and kept rolling. He neared the edge of the hill and then, with centripetal force, picked up speed and rolled down the hill. He looked like a big, yellow Oompa Loompa blur.

"Save me!" he yelled moments before bouncing off a log and crashing into the lake. The crowd cheered, and Anthony yelled out, "Hell, yeah! Who's next?"

A drunk Henry the Happy Clown had suited up and stepped onto the mat.

Bradley ran down the hill. "Uncle Larry! I'm coming!" He jumped into the lake and dragged Larry back to shore.

Behind me, someone made a retching sound. I turned to see Missy Drake from the front office sweating profusely and turning pale.

"I don't feel so well," she said and ran off to the woods and started vomiting. This caused Janiece from the help desk to retch.

"Me either," she said. She clutched her stomach and vomited into the middle circle of the mat.

Henry the Happy Clown yelled out, "Bullseye!" He cackled.

"Oh, my goodness, my stomach is gurgling!" said Cynthia Bonner. "Where are the bathrooms? I can't hold it in!"

She broke into a full sprint, clutching her bottom, and ran to the outdoor bathrooms. A crowd formed outside them. All around me, people fell ill. I walked back to the pavilion, where more people started getting sick. A few people from the entertainment committee had started cleaning up the buffet station but had abandoned the effort in search of bathrooms.

I blinked in disbelief at the buffet table. The trays of potato salad, coleslaw, and deviled eggs sat baking in the hot sun. No one had thought to put ice underneath them to keep them cold.

Bradley, looking ill and soaking wet, wandered into the pavilion.

"Bradley! How long have these trays been sitting out in the heat?"

He shrugged and said, "We put them out at 7 a.m."

The trays had been in the sun for five hours without anything to cool them. Bradley single-handedly gave food poisoning to the entire staff of the Federal Center for Fiscal Enforcement.

The only two who were not afflicted were Karen Feldman and me. She had marched off to the bus, crying, and never came back. When she emerged from the bus, she looked around at the scene, confused. The bus! Those old yellow school buses didn't have bathrooms on them, and it was a twenty-minute ride back to the office. I reached for my phone.

Evy answered. "Hey, Emm! What's up?"

"I need you to come and get me."

I explained the scene unfolding before my eyes.

"Oh, good God," she said. "Bad potato salad! Are you okay?"

"Yes, I packed my own lunch and brought it to save points."

"Good girl! I'm on my way!"

I turned to Karen Feldman. "Need a ride?"

Behind us, Henry the Happy Clown stumbled into the pavilion, still wearing a sumo suit. He downed another pale ale, hiccupped, and vomited into the *Box of Truth.* Then he let out another loud hyena laugh and rolled onto the floor.

The next day at work, Cube Land was like a ghost town. Everyone on the technical staff, including most of the software development team, had become ill with food poisoning. I heard a rumor that Larry had been sent off to the hospital in an ambulance. I could only imagine what the emergency room nurse thought when a soaking-wet Oompa Loompa rolled through the emergency room doors in a deflated sumo suit.

The timing couldn't have been worse. The third quarter IRS data push was about to begin, and we were severely understaffed. One of the developers who was out sick had not completed his security scans, so I opened my laptop and did them for him. Something wasn't right. The scan wouldn't complete. I manually pulled up the data and went through it line by line. I stopped cold.

"What the hell is this?" I said out loud. "How did this executable get into the code?"

I copied and pasted the executable code and ran a

search on it, then stared at my computer screen in disbelief. My stomach lurched as I realized what was happening. *This is bad.*

I immediately called Security. Liam Taylor answered.

"Hi, Emma. I see you also avoided the great plague at the picnic. So glad I didn't go," he said, laughing.

"Liam! Shut down everything running ByteLynks XP! Right now! I just discovered a Logic Bomb!"

His laughing abruptly stopped. "What are you talking about?"

"Just do it!" I yelled into the phone.

Within minutes, half of the Federal Center for Fiscal Enforcement's systems went down, putting it at a processing standstill. I rushed down two flights of stairs to Liam's office and flung his office door open with a loud bang.

He quickly stood when I entered. "Emma, what is going on?"

"I just found it in one of the other developer's code. It's a Logic Bomb. It's been there the whole time, hiding—a sequence of instructions set to attack and capture data from anything running on the ByteLynks XP operating system. The virus was scheduled to execute today because of the data push. They could have taken the data from all those tax returns, including people's social security numbers!"

Liam fell back into his chair and rubbed his eyes.

"We are going to have some explaining to do. Show me the code."

I repeatedly warned Larry about this and now it was actually happening. *I'm going to get fired.* Losing my job on top of everything else would be the icing on the cake. The last straw. The time to defend myself had come.

C H A P T E R   1 3

Proof

From: David Brown, FCFE Chairman

To: Emma Davis, Larry Steward, Bradley Baker

Date: Thursday, 7:42 p.m.

Subject: FCFE Data Breach

It has come to my attention that a near-catastrophic data breach was avoided this morning, preceding the scheduled quarterly data push from the IRS. I have also been informed that half of The Center's systems are currently locked down

until further notice, and we are at a work
stoppage. I have asked Liam Taylor and
his team to complete an investigation into
this matter ASAP to determine the root
cause and identify the necessary steps to
remediate the situation. Please be in my
office tomorrow morning at 9:00 a.m. to
discuss the situation further.

I met Evy for our afternoon walk and told her what
happened that morning at work.

"It was a Logic Bomb," I explained as we rounded
the first block of Browncroft Boulevard.

"A what?" she said. "Sounds made up."

"No, it's a real thing! It's when someone maliciously
inserts an executable code with the intention of stealing information. Whoever did it clearly understood
the quarterly data push from the IRS would be loaded with people's personal information. It was set to
'execute' when certain conditions were met—in this
case, the data push. It went undetected all this time.
I found it yesterday when I ran a scan. It could have
been disastrous!"

"So, you're a hero!" She patted me on the back.

I sighed, "Not exactly. The opposite of that. More
like they will point the finger at me because I manage

the software. Only its outdated software could have been easily infiltrated. Full of bugs. I have been warning Larry for months! I even tried to tell Bradley. No one would listen to me or give me funding to correct it."

"You need proof," Evy responded. She stopped walking and put her hands on her knees, out of breath. "Did you document anything? Can you prove that you tried to warn him?"

"Yes, I sent numerous emails to Larry. I even remember bringing it up in our weekly team group meetings. My concerns always fell on deaf ears."

"Okay, so now it's on you to prove your innocence. After we're done here, go home and fire up that printer with any paper trail you can find!"

I did just that.

The next morning, I walked into David Brown's office with my folder in hand. I arrived last. Bradley and Larry were sharing a story with David about their latest golf game.

Great. Golf buddies.

Unlike most of the offices at The Center, the executive team's offices were attractively decorated with newer furniture and higher-end computer equipment. A big flat-screen monitor hung on the wall, showing an executive dashboard with charts, graphs, and workflow statistics of audit packages.

Larry looked like he was still stricken with food poisoning. His normally bright red skin dulled to an undercooked pink. David straightened in his seat when I entered and motioned me to a chair.

"Have a seat, please," he said curtly. "Now that we're all here, I thought we could have a pre-meeting before I bring in Liam and the team to start the investigation. I need you all to help me understand what led up to the potential data breach and what we need to do now."

Bradley squirmed in his seat. "I'm new here! This is all news to me!" He laughed nervously and looked over to Larry. Larry gave him a reassuring nod and then looked directly at me.

"Well, this was bound to happen. I've been telling Emma for quite some time to work with the rest of the development team to update that software. We even tried to give her funding to do it." He flashed a smug, self-satisfied grin. Bradley nodded in agreement.

How dare they? Inside of me, atomic bomb-level rage blossomed. *Enough.* I stood up, knocking my chair out from under me. My hands shook in anger as I dropped my folder, spilling its contents on the floor.

"Now, you wait a minute! *I* have been telling *you* for months about the potential for a data breach! How dare you try to throw me under the bus like this!"

Larry smirked. "Well, now. I guess it's your word against mine."

He turned to David, "Don't worry, I'm on top of this. I won't let it happen again."

I reached down and grabbed the stack of paperwork, slamming it onto David's desk. I picked up the first piece of paper and read it aloud.

"August 15. Email to Larry Steward. '*Hi Larry. I know I'm new here and still becoming acclimated to the workflow software, but I have concerns about the operating system that it's running on. ByteLynks XP was sunsetted by its manufacturer last year and has been replaced by a newer version. I think we should work with the vendor to upgrade. There are some potential security risks if we don't.*' He ignored me."

I picked up the next piece of paper. "August 22. Email to Larry Steward. '*Hi again. Just following up on my last email to you. This is very important. I'll bring it up during our team meeting to see if others concur.*' We had that team meeting, and everyone else agreed with me. A few people on the team who were there said they would back me up on this."

I continued reading the timeline of emails, going through months of ignored requests. I looked at David straight in the eye.

"He ignored me. Every. Single. Time. This is the last one. March 25th. Email to Bradley Baker. '*Bradley,*

I'm following up for the third time to see if you talked to Larry about upgrading the software. We are coming up on a quarterly push. Now is the time to fix it if we're going to do it."

Bradley's face reddened, his eyes darting nervously back and forth between Larry and me. Larry glowered.

David cleared his throat. "I see," he said and turned to Larry. "Is this true?"

Larry shook his head 'no' and started to respond.

I pounded my fist on the desktop and shouted, "I've had enough! I'm done being second-guessed. These emails don't lie!"

I handed David the stack of papers. Larry sank into his chair, scowling.

"Well?" said David. "I'll ask you again. Is what she is saying true?"

Defeated, Larry nodded. He looked as if he might vomit at any moment, his face now a ghost white.

David cleared his throat again. "I'd like a word alone with Emma. Larry, Bradley, please leave my office. I'll follow up with you when I'm done."

Larry stood up and stormed out of David's office. As his dutiful number two, Bradley chased after him.

"Uncle Larry! Wait up! What does this mean? They can't fire me, can they? I have an MBA!"

I shut the office door and sat down. All the energy drained from my body. After nearly a year of putting up with Larry's condescending behavior, someone was finally listening to me this time. *Don't cry at work. Don't cry at work. No one takes women seriously when they cry at work.*

David read through the stack of papers and shook his head in disbelief.

"Emma, information doesn't always trickle up through the management chain. I had no idea any of this was going on. I wish you had contacted me if you couldn't get anywhere with your supervisor." He put the papers down and left his desk to sit down in the chair next to me.

"Look at me. I don't think you realize what you've just prevented. You averted a public relations disaster and legal crisis yesterday. The implications would have been so far-reaching that I don't even want to think about it. Thank you for your excellent work in mitigating a potential catastrophe." *Do not cry.*

He continued. "I had Human Resources send your resume to me this morning because I needed to know who I was dealing with. Before your stint at home caring for your kids, you had quite a career. Impressive. I've heard of OneBank. My brother is a bank manager and uses it."

My heart leaped inside my chest. I smiled and nodded. "Yes, OneBank. That was my company."

He stood up and paced the room.

"I need to ask you, is this thing fixable? We are at a standstill right now. Can you fix it? If so, how soon and what do you need? We need to get this resolved before anything gets leaked to the press."

I told David exactly what we needed to do to get The Center's systems back online. "I'll assemble a tiger team, and we'll work around the clock. All the junior developers know the newer operating systems and programming languages. I've led conversion projects like this before. I think I can have us back up in a matter of days." My mind raced thinking about the tight schedule and all we would need to do.

"Perfect. Please meet with me daily to keep me updated. Here is my cell phone number in case something urgent comes up." He handed me his business card. "I'll let Linda in Accounting know to purchase whatever software licenses we need. Anything you need, really. And I'm authorizing paid overtime for your team."

My team?

"Wait, but Larry usually has to authorize those things."

He shook his head, "Effective immediately, Larry will be reassigned. I would like you to take over as Software Division Head."

My jaw dropped. *Me? Software Division Head?*

"I have a lot of faith in you, Emma. I know you will see us through this crisis."

Overwhelmed with excitement, I felt like I did that

day so many years ago, clutching my bag of coins in the community bank at college. I would make great things happen again.

I shook David's hand. "I will not let you down."

Back at my desk, I called an emergency meeting. Most of the team was still recovering from food poisoning, but agreed to return when I told them they would get paid overtime. I had just one problem...daycare. There was no way I would ask Jack to cover for me. I called Evy and told her what happened.

"I am so proud of you for standing up for yourself! I'm packing a bag. Tell the kids that Aunt Evy will stay for a few days and bring Benny! I'll watch them while you get this all worked out."

I sighed into the phone. *Evy saves the day.* "I honestly don't know what I'd do without you."

"I rescue you. You rescue me. Now get to work, Software Division Head!"

The team and I congregated and set up a war room in the conference area, getting ready for a couple of all-nighters. We were going to update the software and bring The Center back online.

I could almost smell the donuts.

CHAPTER 14

Traverse

SIX MONTHS LATER...

Soon after the Logic Bomb incident, the Center was operational again, business as usual. After three days of working around the clock with my team, we were able to upgrade the software to bring everything back online. Word never got out that we almost had a data breach. Liam sent a memo to the organization explaining that we were doing routine maintenance on the systems and to expect them to be down for a couple of days. No one even questioned it.

Meanwhile, Larry cleaned out his office and moved to the basement of the building. David put him in charge of another team, and Bradley followed. I moved into Larry's office and filled the credenza behind my desk with pictures of my kids, as well as Myla's artwork and the Lego creations that Austin built for me.

My new workspace had a big window with a view of Belmont's skyline. In the mornings, warm sunlight streamed in and filled the room with light—a far cry from the flickering fluorescent lights over Cube Land.

I restructured the software development team and created Team Lead positions responsible for mentoring junior employees. We held weekly collaboration meetings, giving everyone the opportunity to share their ideas. I carried their concepts forward at the weekly management meetings to ensure the entire team had opportunities to make improvements and be recognized. Morale seemed to improve.

True to our promise to each other, Evy and I walked every day, rain or shine. Initially, we could only manage four blocks around Browncroft Boulevard, but soon four blocks became five, then six. Before long, we were exercising for an hour each day.

As we grew stronger, the walks became easier. With our routine and keeping each other accountable with food and tracking, we dropped several clothing sizes. Evy started to look like her younger version in the wedding photo on her Facebook page. I saw my cheekbones again for the first time in years.

One day, during one of our walks, I had an idea:

"Hey Evy, what do you think about running a half marathon with me? We already jog sometimes anyway."

She shrugged. "I don't think I'm ready for that yet."

I retorted, "But we're already up to a few miles each day anyway. We don't have to run the whole thing. We could run/walk it. I think we could do it. We've been at this for a while. Maybe challenge us?"

She was quiet for a minute and then said, "What the hell, I'm in. Catch me if you can!"

She quickly sprinted away. I ran after her, laughing.

CHAPTER 15

#CharcuterieGirl

"All right, let's do this."

Evy and I huddled over my laptop at a table at the local coffee house. We decided that it was finally time for the two of us to try online dating. Virtual self-pimping felt more like it. I would take charge of my romantic destiny. Become the Madam of my own brothel.

The barista shouted out, "Emma! Large unsweetened iced black tea."

Gone were my days of Velvet Caramel Frappé with a double shot of vanilla and whipped cream. That was three pants sizes ago. I grabbed my iced tea from the counter and returned to see Evy pulling up MatchUp.com.

"We need names. Not our real ones. Like a handle," she said. "Something that describes who we are in just a couple of words."

I sat down next to her and peered over her shoulder. A fake name. Coming up with one would be a challenge.

She looked at me thoughtfully. "You, for example. Maybe something about your job. But incorporate something trendy. #Tech_Tocker? #Computer Contessa? #Digital Dominatrix?"

I spit out my tea. "I don't even want to think about the response I'd get from that last one."

"What about something with the word 'Mom' in it? You might as well be honest about the fact that you have kids."

I shook my head. "Nope." The last thing I needed was a man with a Mommy fetish. I had a friend at work who told me a dating horror story about a blind date she recently went on. The guy intermittently sucked on a binky during dinner and later confessed he was wearing adult pull-ups. Curious, she hooked up with him anyway. At the end of the night, he asked her to read him a bedtime story. *Goodnight Moon.*

"This is harder than I thought it was going to be," I sighed. "We can't even come up with names."

"Okay," she said. "I'm going to just come up with something I like. Dogs. Benny is my favorite non-human. I'm going with #GoldenRescueMama. It's straightforward.

Maybe I'll meet a guy who also likes Goldens. It's something Ben would have responded to."

She frowned. I could tell she was thinking about Ben. I sat in the seat next to her and hugged her.

"It's a good name. Ben *would* have liked it. Maybe you can give Benny a step-dog sibling." That made her smile. She thought for a minute, and her face lit up.

"I've got it! You are #CharcuterieGirl! It connotes sophistication—a diverse woman who can expertly pair her cheese with her crackers. What guy doesn't want that? But in reality, your disastrous charcuterie board has been your single worst failure since I've known you. Kind of like a play on words!"

I reflected on the swirling river of zucchini cheese goo that landed Jason Stone's mom on the floor after her son bullied Austin. That was a great day. Why not? I sort of liked #CharcuterieGirl. It had a catchy vibe.

"#GoldenRescueMama and #Charcuterie Girl, it is! Now what?"

I looked over Evy's shoulder at the Matchup.com home page. On the right side, a vertical stream of pictures of incredibly attractive, mostly shirtless men scrolled up the page like a slot machine.

"Meet Your Forever Match!" flashed on the screen. Ding! Ding! Ding!

"We'll do you first," she said. "There are a bunch of questions that you need to answer. The first is, 'What type of relationship are you looking for?' The options are Any, Marriage, Serious Relationship, Friends with Benefits, Travel Buddy, Friends Only, and Other."

What did I want? I definitely did not want marriage again anytime soon—or ever. Travel was out of the question with two kids at home. Friends with Benefits sounded like drama waiting to happen. I wanted something more than just a friendship. I shrugged.

"Other, I guess?"

She clicked on *Other,* and a box popped up.

"You have to explain what the Other is."

"I guess I want something that starts out as friendship and *maybe* becomes more? How do you even describe that in a few words?"

Evy typed in "Open to Possibilities." Fair enough.

"Okay, next one. Tell us about the person of your dreams."

"That one is easy. Doesn't steal my hard-earned fortune. Doesn't bang the food service staff..."

"Those aren't options," she laughed. "Here, I'll list them. Age?"

"Definitely not a younger guy. That would make me as pathetic as Jack. How about 30-40?" Evy typed that in and continued.

"Has Kids?"

Oof. I hadn't even mentally gone there yet. *A mixed family?* I guess I was on a different playing field now, complete with other people's children. I nodded and sighed.

"Marital Status? Your options are Single, Separated, Divorced, Married, or It's Complicated."

"Single, separated or divorced. Wait, what do you think about separated? Do I want someone else's divorce drama? I'm going through my own."

"Misery loves company," Evy said. I guess I couldn't argue there.

"Body type?"

We exchanged a look, knowing it was a loaded question. Having both struggled with our weight, we were all too familiar with the self-loathing that comes from living in a society that prioritizes a slim figure over intelligence or a fun personality. Being overweight didn't make us flawed. Now that I was back in single-digit clothes, I noticed how differently people were treating me everywhere I went. Sadly, my self-love didn't even seem to manifest itself again until I started to shed the pounds. Life shouldn't be like that. I knew the battle and refused to judge another person by how much they tipped the scale.

"No preference," I said firmly.

The barista called out. "Kiki! Iced Brown Sugar Espresso!"

Evy's eyes grew huge. *"Holy shit,"* she said. "Is that her?"

I looked up to see Kiki, in all her perfection, staring icily at me from across the coffee house. She wore a skintight denim skirt with a cut-off tank top, exposing her perfectly toned waist and long, muscular legs. She looked as exotic as the first time I saw her. Her black eyes bore into me.

"Damn," said the barista a little too loudly.

Everyone in the restaurant stared at Kiki as she cat-walked over to the counter and took her drink. A smile curled up on her lips as she looked over at me before turning in a flourish and sauntering out of the coffee house.

The barista let out a low, "Shewwwww."

"What the fuck was that?" Evy asked.

"*That* destroyed my family."

A crushing feeling came over me. At that moment, the only thing I wanted was to be at home sitting on my sofa with a half-gallon of rocky road ice cream. I suddenly felt very hungry, but it wasn't hunger from a skipped meal. It was hunger from a broken heart.

"I can't even with that..." Evy started to talk but then saw the look on my face and stopped. She silently sat with me.

"Meet Your Forever Match!" flashed on my laptop screen again. I thought I already had.

After a moment, she squeezed my hand. "Do you want to keep going with this? We can pick this up another day. There's no need for you to rush into it."

Inside of me, anger took over self-pity. I was determined not to let that woman destroy another moment of my happiness.

"No, let's keep going," I said. "What's the next question?"

Evy gave me a quick hug and said, "That's the spirit."

She continued to rattle off questions until we had completed the questionnaire. I helped her complete hers next.

"We need pictures," she said.

"I need new clothes. I don't have anything to wear *for* pictures," I replied.

Nothing I owned fit anymore. I recently put off buying new clothes because paying for Lauren C. Livingston was expensive. The discovery phase started, and she had Rocco hard at work trying to track down information on Jack's business and my money. Every phone call and email with the two of them had a price tag associated with it that was draining the National Bank of Emma dry. Even though Evy was financially comfortable, she understood my plight and always delicately addressed anything related to money.

"I know a place," she said. "Let's go."

Evy took me to The Luxe Thrifter, an upscale thrift store located in the downtown shopping district. Belmont is a wealthy area, and The Luxe Thrifter was filled with gently used, barely worn, high-end clothing for a bargain price. Some items still had their original tags on them.

I skimmed through the small and medium racks while Evy lingered in the formal wear section, engrossed in conversation with someone decked out in a rhinestone-studded gown, a purple feather boa, towering four-inch heels, a vivid blonde wig, and dramatic false eyelashes. Their makeup was flawless.

"This would look cute on you," she said, holding up a red silk floor-length dress.

"Oh, honey! That would look *fabulous* in next week's show."

Beside Evy stood a gorgeous drag queen on the hunt for a bargain. The queen held the dress up to herself and did a twirl. "What do you think?"

Evy nodded and gave her a thumbs up. I wandered over as Evy tried to help her find shoes to match.

"Can I help?"

"This is my friend, Emma," Evy waved her hand towards me.

The queen held out her perfectly manicured hand, and I shook it.

"I'm Mona Lott," she replied. "I come here all the time. This place is so wonderful. Just last week, I scored a Dominic Castellani jumper. The retail price was $550, but I snagged that baby for $45! The others were so jealous." She hugged herself in excitement.

Evy looked impressed. "That is a steal! We're here to find clothes for a photo shoot."

Mona slapped her arm. "Stop it! Are you two models? You could be!"

I laughed and shook my head. "No, more like the lovelorn. *Single* lovelorn. We're setting up online dating profiles. We decided to revamp our wardrobes for a fresh start."

I pointed to Evy. "Widow."

Evy pointed to me. "Depressed divorcee."

Mona took a step back, looked at the two of us, and smiled warmly. "My favorite kind of friendship. One steeped in misery and comeuppance. Come on, ladies. Let's shop!"

We spent the remainder of the afternoon with Mona in The Luxe Thrifter, putting together outfits. Evy had a knack for fashion. She was one of those people who always looked perfectly put together. She paired tops, skirts, pants, and shoes for me that I never would have thought to combine. And Mona had a flair for, well, flair.

"You need polka dots," Mona instructed me. She searched through the racks and pulled out a blue chiffon low-cut blouse dotted with small white polka dots.

"White pants," she said next, and went through the racks until she located a cute pair of pixie pants. "I'm guessing you're a size six?"

"I don't think I'm quite there yet, but I'll try them on."

Evy and I walked into the dressing room. I tried on the shirt, and it honestly looked very cute on me. When I tried on the pants, I screamed.

"Are you being murdered over there?" Evy asked through the stall wall.

"No! Mona handed me a size six, and they *fit*."

We exited the small rooms and looked at each other. Evy wore a straight skirt and a tight cotton V-neck sweater. She looked so tiny.

"Wow! How much weight have you actually lost?" I was used to seeing her in bigger clothes. I had not noticed that she had lost so much.

"I don't know. I just go by how my clothes are fitting."

"They are fitting you great."

Mona met me outside of the dressing room with an armful of clothes to try on.

"I was right, wasn't I? Here you go, Six! Give these a try, too."

When we finished, the three of us had wardrobes fit for envy, even by *Vogue* magazine standards. Mona had picked out some outrageous outfits, explaining that she was going to be dancing in a drag show the following weekend. At the register, we parted ways.

"Come see me next week, ladies! Friday night at the Palladian Palace! It will be an extravaganza eleganza! 8:00

sharp!" Mona sauntered out of the thrift shop, leaving behind the lingering scent of a knock-off expensive perfume.

"Almost there," Evy said, looking at the pile of clothes on the conveyor belt. "Now we just need to take the pictures. Let's go for our run and figure out a place."

The next day, we took some pictures at a local park. Evy looked beautiful in her photos, and I could see why Ben fell in love with her so quickly. My photos also came out better than I had hoped. I was looking at the old me again. Hello, *you*.

Two days later, #GoldenRescueMama and #Charcuterie Girl went live.

C H A P T E R   1 6

Ding!

Ding! Ding! Ding!

I rolled over in bed and picked up my cell phone from its charger on the nightstand. My bedside clock glowed fluorescent, revealing the time: 3:30 a.m.

Ding! Ding! Ding!

"Damn robo callers!" I switched the sound off, rolled over, and went back to sleep.

A few hours later, I awoke to find forty-three message notifications from Matchup.com.

"#HarleyHogDog54 messaged you!"
"#ManofYourDreams sent you a wink!"
"#Inmate_2027 liked your profile picture!"

"#Jobless Junk messaged you!"
"#ArmyDangerRanger118 sent you a wink!"
"#SubmissiveSam messaged you!"

Message from Evy:

EVY

> I think our MatchUp.com accounts got approved. My phone won't stop dinging! Who are all these men?

I replied:

> Same! It started in the middle of the night. How many have you received?

Evy:

> I have 200 views, 24 likes, 38 winks, and 12 messages! Do you think these are real? Are these people vampires? It's 7:30 in the morning!

Me:

> No clue. One guy messaged me five times in a row with the same thing, 'Hey, hottie!' That's all it says. And he's only showing a closeup of himself unzipping his jeans. Nothing else.

Evy:

Ugh.

Me:

My friend at work does online dating. She said it would be like this in the beginning. She said it's like a big field full of weeds, and you have to keep yanking the bad ones out to find the good ones. I must get ready for work. We can compare notes later during our run. See you at 4:30. Happy yanking! 😊

My phone dinged constantly on the walk to the bus stop. Myla looked concerned.

"Mommy, I think your phone is broken. Your dinger won't stop."

I switched off my phone and didn't turn it back on again until I got to work. I shut my office door and pulled up my Matchup.com account. I had more new messages.

"**#AnytimeEddie** messaged you!"
"**#ImTheRealDeal** messaged you!"
"**#DaringDonny** liked your profile!"
"**#RhymingRob** messaged you!"

I scrolled through the pictures of the men. I had chosen the 30-40 age category, but most of the men looked like they either posted photos from their twenties or looked old enough to be a creepy older uncle.

I opened the message from #ImTheRealDeal.

> Hello, darling. I spent the whole night scrolling for the most beautiful girl on MatchUp.com, and then I found you. Amazing eyes. I have a thing about eyes. Yours are perfection. I'll bet you have cute feet, too. I feel like fate meant for us to be together. I'd love to get to know you more. Like why did you pick the name Charcuterie Girl? Is that what you're into? I bet you'd really like to see my meat. I'd like to put it on your crackers. ☺ Up for a hook-up?

Ugh. *Just no.* Block.

I next clicked on the message from #SubmissiveSam.

> Hello Charcuterie Girl. I haven't reached out to many women on here. I guess you could say that I'm not very bold. I looked at your pictures. You look like the kind of woman who likes to take charge and take control. My mother was a controlling woman. I like strong women. I like it when they bend me over and spank me when I've been bad. Will you do that for me?

What. The. Fuck. *Block*.

I read #RhymingRob's message next.

Charcuterie Girl, you're divine.

Someday, I should make you mine.

You're such a beautiful lass.

I'll bet you have a great ass.

And your breasts are simply sublime.

Sending you a big wink! ☺

Meet me for a drink?

I promise you'll have a great time.

What did Evy and I get ourselves into? There appeared to be an underground world of male trolls online who stayed up all hours of the night looking for a hookup. This is why women stayed in bad marriages. What was that old saying? Better the devil you know than the devil you don't?

Up next, #Inmate_2027.

> Hello there, gorgeous! If you don't
> mind my asking, what is charcuterie?
> I've been incarcerated since 2010
> and haven't heard that word. I
> asked my cellmate, and he said it
> had something to do with meat.
> My meat is amazing. Do you live
> close to the Belmont Penitentiary?
> If you're free on Sunday between
> the hours of 1:00 p.m. and 4:00
> p.m., I get conjugal visits.

Block.

With my last ounce of hope, I slid my thumb across the screen and opened the message from #JoblessJunk.

> Hi there, sweet lady! Would you
> consider dating a homeless man?

Slamming my laptop shut, I headed off to the management meeting. I had yanked enough weeds for the morning. Maybe Evy was having better luck.

♒

Later that day, I met Evy for our run. We were training for the Annual Belmont Half Marathon, which was only a few months away. We stepped up our training and were now mostly jogging with some walking. Those six months of working out significantly impacted our fitness levels. I became my old self again. And Evy was losing weight at a record pace.

"A guy messaged you from prison?"

"Yep, he wanted to show me his meat during a conjugal visit. I'm not sure #CharcuterieGirl was the best choice of a name."

"I didn't do much better. I had a guy ask me if I could meet him for a drink, but said it would have to be in the city because he didn't want his wife to find out."

"Well, it's like I said. Weed the garden. And we have other options. There is something called speed dating, where you get five minutes to interview men and then move on to the next person until you've met a room full of guys. There is also a thing called Single Adventures where single people meet to do fun things like take a cooking class or go hang gliding."

"Hang gliding! I'd be up for that!"

"The thing is, we just need to get out there. We won't meet men sitting in one another's living rooms researching low-fat recipes. What are you doing Friday night?"

Evy shrugged, "Nothing. Like usual. What do you have in mind?"

I grinned. "I'll grab a taxi and pick you up at 7:30. Wear something nice."

The Palladian Palace, an old movie theater, was once converted into a bar and live theater stage. Back in the 1950s and 1960s, people lined up outside to see classics like *Breakfast at Tiffany's* or *To Kill a Mockingbird*. Now, the building has been renamed The Palladian Palace: A Tavern for Tiaras. The feature show on the outside marquis read *A Very Drag Queen Holiday*.

"I can't believe we're doing this! Have you ever been to one of these?" Evy asked as the taxi pulled up to the front.

"No, but Mona seems like a lot of fun. Let's check it out."

When we entered, a short man wearing a blonde wig and a Santa's elf suit greeted us.

"Wow," Evy whispered. "That makeup is impeccable." I nodded in agreement.

"Welcome, ladies, to A Tavern for Tiaras!" he said. "I'm Jenny Talia. Tonight's show is all about the wonderful world of holidays. The best seats are down in front. What's your poison tonight?"

"Margaritas, please," Evy said. We made our way down to the front of the theater and took center seats. Behind the curtains, we heard noise and commotion.

The theater quickly filled with patrons, mostly

younger women. A bridal shower party sat to the right of us. The bride-to-be wore a sash that read "Wife of the Party" and a big white frilly veil. The entire group threw back tequila shots and noisily toasted her. I had a feeling this wasn't their first stop of the evening.

The lights went down, and the crowd cheered, "Wooooo!" The curtain opened, and a cadre of men in drag danced out, arm in arm, doing a rendition of the Rockettes' high kicks. They were all dressed in Santa outfits with wigs, long red hats, short skirts, fishnet stockings, and fluffy white and red jackets.

A disc jockey queued Mariah Carey's *All I Want for Christmas,* and the line of dancers split in the middle and parted, making way for a performer to be rolled out on a makeshift pile of snow fashioned together with papier mâché, white paint, and gold glitter.

Mona Lott sat high on the fake mountain. She looked stunning in a long white wig, skintight red catsuit, thick black belt, and faux fur lining her neck and wrists. She perfectly lip-synced the song. The crowd went wild as she expertly followed the choreography from the video. She exited the stage and descended into the audience.

The bridal party shoved "Wife of the Party" out into the aisle. Mona twirled the future bride and sang to her. The bridal party threw five- and ten-dollar bills at Mona as she continued to sing.

She moved through the room and then came back to the front and center. As she sang the song's last lyric, she looked down at Evy, and her face lit up when she realized who it was. Mona pulled Evy onto the stage, where she broke into a solo lip sync of George Michael's *Last Christmas.* The crowd went wild.

A Very Drag Queen Holiday focused on all the seasons. Men wearing Halloween costumes performed a cabaret dance. Another group acted out a skit involving leprechauns. A quintet held sparklers and sang and danced to *Yankee Doodle Dandy.*

The performers ended the show with a standing ovation. The queen dream team had put on an amazing performance. As we gathered our things to leave, Mona rushed out from backstage and threw her arms around us.

"I can't believe you came out to see me!"

"You were incredible!" Evy told her.

Mona beamed widely, "Oh, the flattery! Thank you, darling. Wait here for me. Let's go get a drink!"

Mona changed into an amber sequined dress accentuated by gangly gold bracelets and big hoop earrings. She greeted us at the entrance. We made our way to a bar, secured a table, and placed an order for a round of drinks.

There, we gained insight into Mona's life. Her other name was Steven Bostich. Steven was a tax accountant for a major accounting firm in the city. She said that no one at work knew about her drag queen persona, and she wanted to keep it that way.

"Unless I'm at work, I mostly cross-dress. I feel that I just relate better to Mona," she told us. "Anyway, it's a very conservative firm. The pay is excellent. What I do on my own time is none of their business."

Mona had no partner at the time but said she was happily raising two Afghan Hounds named Jimmy Chews and Bark Twain.

"How's the online dating going, ladies?" Mona asked. "I'm sure you two must have snagged some hot men by now."

"Disaster," I said, shaking my head.

"Just shoot me now," Evy sighed. "It's been a nightmare."

"Show me those men," Mona said. I pulled up my profile and handed her my phone.

"Oh my," she said, scrolling through my feed. Her face furrowed in concern. "You weren't exaggerating. Well, that's why you should be glad you've met *me.* Every straight girl needs a gay male friend—especially one with a knack for fashion. I'll help you navigate the treacherous world of dating. There are a few potentials on here. Don't give up hope. What are your next plans?"

"Speed dating, and we're considering joining a singles adventure club."

Mona's face lit up. "Can I come along?"

Evy and I looked at each other. "Why not?" we both said simultaneously.

"Thank you!" Mona beamed. "This is going to be so fun. Now give me that phone back. I'm sure there must be at least one man on this website who is worth your time."

If only Mona. If only.

I reflected on my life from several years ago and how dramatically it had changed since then. If someone had told me back then that I'd be sitting in a bar, sharing my online dating profile with my new best friend, Evy, and our new friend, Mona Lott, I would have never believed them. That I'd be preparing to run a half-marathon again. That I'd returned to work and even earned a promotion. That I had rediscovered a sense of hope.

"Here's to new adventures!" Mona cheered as we all clinked glasses.

Better the devil you know than the devil you don't?

Maybe not this time.

CHAPTER 17

The One with Mommy Dearest

After several months of filling out and exchanging paperwork with Jack's attorney, Lauren called me into her office to discuss our next steps. She was on the phone with Rocco when I entered, and she ushered me to take a seat.

"It's not adding up, and it doesn't make sense," Lauren said as she looked through a stack of documents on her desk. "There is no way J&B Enterprises is the only company, yet that is all that he has listed on the disposition of financial assets and liabilities. Keep looking."

She put down her cell phone and gave me a once-over.

"Good afternoon, Emma. I don't usually say this to another woman, but you look amazing. That divorce diet is serving you well."

Many people commented on my weight loss recently, but I wasn't expecting to receive a compliment from someone like Lauren.

"Thank you," I smiled at her, appreciative of the kind words. Maybe there was a kind side to her after all. *Was she being friendly?*

"Let's get to the point of why I called you in today." *Okay, maybe not.*

She continued, "We've received the Interrogatories, Request for Production of Documents, and Statement of Worth from Jack's attorney. I've reviewed everything, and he is claiming that he only made $250,000 last year. He claimed that J&B Enterprises is his only source of income. Does that sound right to you?"

I snorted. "Jack just bought his girlfriend a new $55,000 BMW. Our mortgage is over $6,000 a month. The Bolton Academy costs $20,000 each semester for each of our kids. He's currently paying their tuition. He has memberships in golf and sports clubs all over town. And he travels constantly. You do the math."

Lauren's brow furrowed. "That's what I thought. Rocco is still having a hard time uncovering any information. Have you had any luck?"

I shook my head. "Nothing. When he moved out, he completely cleared out the home office. There's nothing in that room now but office supplies. So, what happens next?"

"Jack's attorney will be filing a request for a preliminary conference with the court. At that time, you will both meet with the judge to determine what issues you agree to, including things such as the division of property, custody, and visitation of your children, and disposition of financial assets and liabilities. I can tell you right now that we will dispute the financial statements. In all divorce cases in the state of New York, all issues must be resolved before the judge will grant the divorce. This could drag on for years if Jack doesn't come clean about his businesses."

Ugh. I can't afford for this to drag on for years. I can barely afford for it to drag on another month.

"There is more," she continued. "If the custody and visitation issues haven't been resolved, the Family court will decide the issues, which is an additional process. I know you are asking for full custody, but judges are very lenient these days towards both parents. You can most likely expect 50/50 or some variation where you will each have a lot of time with your kids."

The reality of Austin and Myla being raised by Kiki made me physically ill. There would be years of school recitals, sporting events, and birthday parties with that woman ever present, hanging on Jack's arm like a coveted prize. Alternating holidays. Christmas mornings, when they would be the ones making the hot cocoa and opening the presents with the kids, while I woke up alone. Trick-or-treating at Halloween without me. *I hated every bit of this.*

Lauren softened again momentarily. "I know it sounds like the end of the world right now, but women do get through this. Many find out it was the best thing that ever happened to them. Look at you. You're already going through your own metamorphosis. You look fantastic. And your kids will adjust too. Kids are more resilient than we give them credit for."

She straightened in her seat. Back to business. "So, anyway, be prepared. If you and Jack don't agree on things, and I'm predicting you won't, a trial will be set, and the judge will decide. We can expect to be in court for the preliminary meeting within the next month or so. I'll have Rocco reach out to you with all the details. Until then, I encourage you to work with him. Sometimes, the clues are right there where we least expect to find them."

Later, at home, I opened my MatchUp.com account. The messages had lessened significantly. My friend at work told me this would happen. Once the creepers didn't get a response, they went on the hunt for the next victims of conjugal visits and Mommy spankings. When Mona looked through the pictures of the men who messaged me, she said there were at least a few worth considering. I scrolled through their profiles.

#NewYorkStateofMind claimed to be a widower living in the city. His profile read, "I don't have kids, but I don't mind if my partner does. I work a lot and don't even have time for pets. I think the right person could change all of that."

He was 35 years old, a tall man with slightly graying hair that he wore short, military-style. He was a self-professed foodie. His profile included pictures of him on a power boat in New York Harbor and a selfie outside *Moulin Rouge!* on Broadway. His interests included fine dining and playing pickleball.

Hmm...maybe. Theater buff. And who doesn't like a fellow foodie?

#DoctorsOrders' profile said that he was in the middle of a complicated divorce. He was a 40-year-old proctologist with two kids who lived with him part of the time. He liked Asian food and good sake. For fun, he said he liked to participate in Live-Action Role-Play and to compete in Quidditch.

"A doctor!" Mona had told me when she read through his profile. "You don't get too many of those on here!"

I wasn't sure how much I would have in common

with someone who intentionally administered colonos-copies for a living by day and vied for the Golden Snitch with broomsticks by night. *Assman.*

#GoodOldBoy said he enjoyed a good shindig with country music, cold beer, spicy barbeque, and sweet women. "Looking for that perfect cowgirl to ride off into the sunset with me."

He wore a wide-brimmed cowboy hat in his photos. In one, he proudly stood next to the five-point buck he had just assassinated with a bow and arrow. "Deer jerky makes for good eatin'," he wrote.

#NewYorkStateofMind messaged me the night before.

> Good evening, Charcuterie Girl! I'm intrigued by your user name. Are you a foodie like me? I spend a good amount of time checking out new restaurants in the city. My friends call me a food snob, but really, I just love a good meal. And I don't mind staying home to make one with the right person either. I read in your profile that you work in Information Technology. That's a lucrative field. I have a lot of friends in IT. I personally own my own consulting business, which keeps me very busy. Let me know if you would be interested in meeting for coffee or trying out a new restaurant with me. Hope to hear back from you. Regards, Brian.

Seems normal enough. I messaged back:

Hi Brian! Thank you for reaching out. My name is Emma. I just joined MatchUp.com a week or so ago, and it has been so overwhelming. Have you done a lot of online dating? Any advice for a newbie? You're honestly the first person I've messaged. I am an IT professional. My job, along with my two kids, keeps me very busy, too. What do you like to do for fun? My best friend and I are training for a half-marathon. Running doesn't sound like much fun to most people, but for me, it's a sanity saver. And yes, I also love food. What's your favorite type?

I hit send and then immediately second-guessed myself. *Ugh. I sounded stupid. Desperate. Anxious. Like an anti-social shut-in who never leaves the house and gets meals delivered to her door by kind-hearted churchgoers.*

Ding!

Oh! He messaged me right away. He must also be online.

> Hi, Emma! A runner! What's the furthest you've run? Running is also one of the things I like to do. Last year, I competed in an adventure relay race. It was a 200-mile relay with twelve people in my group, two vans, and no sleep. It took two days and one night to complete. We started at 6:00 a.m. and ran relay-style through the mountains of upstate New York all the way through the state overnight until we finally ended up in the city at 3:00 p.m. the following day. Ever tried to sleep in a van full of sweaty people? I wouldn't recommend it! Oh, and I like my food spicy.

A fellow runner! I messaged back.

> I've heard of those long-distance relay races! Sounds awful, but also amazing at the same time. I think I would do something like that if I had the opportunity. I'm honestly working my way back into running. It helps to have my best friend there with me to keep me accountable. I also love spicy food. Well, really, any kind of food! I'm not picky, but I do like trying new things. What's the most interesting restaurant you've been to in the city?

Food! I can definitely talk about food. I can do this. He replied instantly.

> That one is easy. I went to a Cambodian restaurant that served fried tarantula with a side of spicy mayo. It tasted like chicken. Doesn't everything when it's deep-fried?

I laughed out loud and messaged back.

> I don't think I'd be up for that, but maybe somewhere a little more tame that doesn't serve food with eight legs? Where should we meet?

Who is this Emma? Why did I type that? I just asked a stranger out! He's going to block me.

Ten minutes went by, and no response. I stared at the laptop, willing it to do something. *Do something!* I suck at this. I'll never date again. *Spinster Emma.*

Ding!

> Sounds fantastic. Free this weekend?

I'm okay. It's okay! A date!

Brian and I exchanged cell phone numbers and set a date for Saturday night. We planned to meet at The Cellar Restaurant on Canal Street in Lower Manhattan.

I was thankful to Evy and Mona for preparing me with a respectable wardrobe for The Cellar Restaurant. The online business review sites listed it as number three in the city for fine dining.

Brian messaged me,

> *No spider legs, I promise. Just good food and excellent wine.*

On the Thursday evening before our date, Evy sat on my bed as I tried on different outfits. We skipped our run because she said she hadn't been feeling well. She lay her head back on my headboard and closed her eyes. She looked tired.

"Are you feeling okay?"

She nodded without opening her eyes. "My doctor thinks I'm having an issue with my thyroid. I'm going to start taking medication. My energy level has been low lately."

Since we began our daily workouts, I had been buzzing with energy, but it seemed to have the opposite effect on her.

She sat up. "I like the black dress."

I rarely wore anything black, but I agreed with her that the dress was flattering.

"You don't think it's too funeral-ish?"

"No, not at all. Elegant. Tasteful. You look fantastic."

I felt fantastic. And nervous. I sat on the bed next to her.

"What if he's a total creep? People lie on their profiles all the time."

She nodded in agreement. "I've been thinking about this. We need a plan. I will be your wingman. I'm going to call you in the middle of your date, and if things are going badly, you can just use your safe word, and I'll come and get you. You can tell him it's the babysitter watching your kids, and one of them is sick. He doesn't need to know they will be with Jack this weekend."

"I don't have a safe word."

"Green," Evy said.

"Green?"

"Yes, you need something obscure that you can work into a conversation where I'll know what you mean, but no one else will. I researched safe words. A lot of people use the word *'Unicorn'*."

We made a quick video call with Mona to see what she thought of the outfit.

"Oh darling, you look fabulous!" she said into the screen. "Do a little spin for me?"

I spun around and then curtsied. She clapped and blew me a kiss. "Knock 'em dead, sweetie! You've got this! New York State of Mind should prepare to have his mind blown! Unless you don't do that on the first date." Mona laughed.

"Bye, Mona!" I said loudly and turned off my phone.

⁑

The Cellar Restaurant was everything the business review sites said it would be—classy, sophisticated, and elegant. I arrived early and told the hostess we had a reservation.

"Table for three?" she asked me.

"No, it will be just the two of us."

She led me to a table in the middle of the restaurant and instructed the busboy to remove one of the place settings. Teacup candles flickered on every table, casting a dim light over the room, while place settings large enough for five courses awaited the guests. A pianist gently played *Moonlight Sonata* on the piano in the corner of the room. The waiter handed me a menu.

"Care for a glass of wine while you wait for the rest of your party?"

I looked at the wine list. *$60 a glass? $450 a bottle?* And that was the least expensive wine on the menu. I pretended to peruse the menu and then smiled at the waiter.

"I'll have a glass of your Dom Perignon Rosé."

"Very good," he said and walked away.

My stomach began to hurt, and my palms grew sweaty. I nervously looked at the door. I hadn't been with anyone besides Jack in the last ten years. *Green, Evy! Green!*

I saw the hostess leading someone to my table. *Oh my.* He was better looking than his pictures. *Handsome.* I stood up as he approached the table, almost knocking my water glass over.

Hello, New York State of Mind.

"Emma?" he asked. He held out his hand and then leaned in for a quick hug. He smelled like heaven.

"Yes, hi Brian. So good to meet you in person."

We hastily sat down. After a moment of awkward silence, we spoke at the same time, talking over each other.

"You go first," I said. He laughed.

"Umm, I was just going to say that you are more beautiful than your pictures. I hope that doesn't sound corny, but you're stunning. You have such entrancing eyes."

I could feel my face blush. I think my whole body blushed. All of it all at once.

"I was going to say the same about you. Well, not stunning, *obviously.* Um, this restaurant seems nice." *And the Emmy Award for Eloquence goes to...not Emma!*

The waiter arrived with my glass of wine. "Dom

Perignon Rose," he said as he presented it to me. I looked over at another table and saw someone swirling their glass and sniffing the wine. I did the same.

"Very nice." I took a small sip, trying to hide my disdain. *What kind of pour is in this glass? Incompetent bartender!* The glass contained only a few ounces of wine. *For $60?*

On edge, I knew it would take more than a few sips to get me through my inaugural dip back into the dating pool. I think Brian read my mind.

"Great choice," he turned to the waiter and said, "Can you please just bring us a bottle?" He put his hand on mine. "Liquid courage." He winked at me.

His touch jolted me like a lightning bolt. It had been so long since I'd had any physical contact with a man, and I had forgotten what that felt like.

"So, I've been here before. Everything is excellent. Want to start with an appetizer?"

"Sounds great!" I said, a little too high-pitched than I would have liked. I took a sip of wine. It tasted delicious—dry, with notes of honeysuckle and vanilla. Much better than the mixed red boxed wine that Evy and I drank on our girls' nights when we stayed at home in our pajamas, ordered pizza, and binge-watched old *Friends* episodes. We always agreed that Rachel Green could not afford that apartment in the city on a waitress's salary. My stomach was in knots, and I inwardly wished I were sitting there with Evy right now, quoting our favorite Chandler-isms. Could I *be* any more nervous right now?

Brian gave the waiter our order. "We'll start with the goat cheese crostini with fig jam and prosciutto. And the roasted beet tartare." *Impressive.*

He turned to me. "So, what do you do in IT?"

"I work for the federal government. I'm the Software Division Head of an agency that processes tax return audits for the IRS. Prior to that, I owned a software company." I shared details with him about OneBank.

"What happened to your company? Why do you no longer run it?"

I held my hand up in protest. "I don't want to go there. We can save that conversation for another time. What about you? You said you own a consulting company?"

The waiter and his attendant set our appetizers on the table. I finished my first glass of wine, and he poured us another.

"Would you like to order your main course now?" the waiter asked.

"Not quite yet," Brian replied.

Am I not good enough to stick around for a second course?

He turned back to me. "I own an enterprise design and strategy firm. We work with small- to mid-sized companies that need to boost their businesses. We specialize in innovative marketing through creative product development and visualization." He went on to describe, at length, the work his firm does.

"Sounds interesting!" I took a bite of the crostini. It was divine, and it paired beautifully with the wine. I took another sip.

"It is, and it keeps me very busy. I was married, but my wife passed away. I think the business has helped me get through it. No kids. We had planned to, but..."

I frowned. "I'm sorry about your wife." I reflected on Evy. These two would have been perfect for each other. Perhaps sites like MatchUp.com were just a meeting place for broken souls with cracks and imperfections looking for their kindred spirits. And now we were part of that group.

"But you have kids?" He stared at me intently.

"Yes! Two. A boy and a girl. Each is a handful. I do love being their mom, though. It's probably the best job I've ever had."

His face softened when I said that. Maybe it was the ambiance in the room or that second glass of wine, but I instinctively reached over and held his hand. He didn't let go. He held my gaze. *There is no way first dates go like this.*

"There you are!"

I abruptly looked up to see an older woman wearing

modest clothing, sensible flats, and no makeup staring down at us. Her hair was wound into a bun so tight it seemed to tilt her eyes. A deep frown was etched onto her face, seemingly its perpetual expression.

"Mommy!" Brian's face lit up. I dropped his hand.

She gave me a once-over and a disapproving look.

"Where is my place setting?" She snapped at him and took a seat. "Fix this, Brian!"

Puzzle pieces fell into place in my head. There initially were three settings on the table. He didn't want to order dinner yet. He had been stalling. *He invited his mother to our first date?*

"Yes, Mommy, right away." He scurried away from the table and found the waiter. Mommy stared at me. I extended my hand.

"Hi, I'm Emma! Didn't realize there would be three of us tonight!" I laughed half-heartedly and nervously sipped my wine.

She narrowed her eyes. "And why not?" *Oh boy.*

Brian returned with the waiter, who was juggling plates and silverware. He put the place settings down on the table in front of her. I swallowed the rest of my glass of wine. She watched me.

"Are you an alcoholic?" she demanded.

"Of course not!" I put down my glass.

"Emma, this is my mother, Gwendolyn. I thought it would be good for her to meet you."

On our first date?

"Pleased, I'm sure." I gave her a small smile and refilled my glass. She glowered at me. I raised my glass and toasted, "Want some? It's delicious!"

"I don't drink," she said curtly. *Fine. More for me.* "And Brian, I don't like you having wine with dinner. Have you ordered yet?"

"No, Mommy, just the appetizers. I was waiting for you."

Stop calling her Mommy.

"Get the waiter." Brian motioned for the waiter, who returned with three menus.

"We'll just need one," she said, returning two to the waiter. She studied it.

"He will have the steak, rare, with a side of asparagus with no butter or oil. She will have the chicken and pasta dish. She's going to need carbohydrates to soak up all that alcohol. I will have the cod."

I took another swig. *Good stuff.*

Gwendolyn began drilling me with questions. Brian sat in his seat with his hands in his lap. I started looking for the exit signs.

"Do you have children?" she asked me.

Brian piped in. "Yes, two, Mommy! Isn't that great?"

"I'm asking *her*," she said, shooting him a withering look.

"Sorry, Mommy."

I smiled at her. "Yes, two."

"How old are you?"

"32."

"Not exactly a spring chicken. I was telling Brian to find a younger woman. One with young eggs and decent birthing hips. Are you planning to have more children?"

Swig. I was $225 into that $450 bottle of wine. *Delish.*

"I hadn't really thought about it. I suppose if the right person came along—"

"Well, you shouldn't. You're too old. What do you do for a living?"

"I'm in Information Technology. I work for the government."

She rolled her eyes. "Civil servant. Lovely." She waved her hand at Brian. "Brian owns a successful marketing firm. He needs to find someone who has more in common with him. Someone without a job who can organize his social events. Someone he can trust. He is inheriting a sizeable amount of money."

I scoffed, "Well, this is our first date. We're still trying to figure out what we do have in common. And I make my own money." I raised my glass to her again.

"Don't sass me, young lady!" She spoke so loudly that the entire room quieted.

I blew a raspberry and snickered. "Whatever you say, lady!" Mommy's frown turned into a deep scowl.

Just then, the food arrived. She took Brian's plate from him and cut his meat and asparagus into small pieces, separating them into two neat piles that didn't touch.

"Bring him some milk and ketchup," Mommy barked at the waiter.

My cell phone rang.

"What? Oh no, that's awful. Is he running a fever? Is he feeling *green?* Yes, of course. Can you come and get me?"

I observed Brian as he sat with his napkin neatly tucked under his chin, carefully chewing his steak and happily dipping it into a cup of ketchup.

So much for the sophisticated foodie.

"I'm so sorry, Brian, but my son isn't well, and I need to go home. Would you be offended if I took my meal to go?"

"That is for the best," his mother said. She snapped her fingers for the waiter. Brian nodded and kept eating.

"Nice meeting both of you," I said as I gathered my to-go bag and bee-lined for the door. When I looked back, Gwendolyn was wiping ketchup off Brian's chin with her napkin.

Evy pulled up. I couldn't get into the car fast enough.

"What happened?"

I told her how great the date was going until his mother arrived.

"He brought his mother on your first date?" she asked incredulously.

"Everything was good. And then Atila the Hun showed up. I had such high hopes. She was screening me because he has a sizeable inheritance, apparently. That man is in his thirties and kept calling her 'Mommy.' Can you please just take me home?"

ろうつ

Evy stopped on the ride home and grabbed a box of our favorite red wine blend. We snuggled up together on my sofa under blankets and watched *Friends* Season Eight, Episode Three: *The One Where Joey Dates Rachel.*

"Those two are definitely not a good match," I told Evy. "Monica and Chandler were a stretch. Rachel and Joey? Just no. They don't have chemistry." I sighed. "Sometimes I feel like we live in a *Friends* episode."

She was eating my dinner out of the to-go carton. Devouring it.

"*The One with Mommy Dearest,*" she said. "Oh my God, this food is so good."

I laughed and grabbed her fork. "Give me that! It's my dinner!"

Maybe it was a horrible first date night, but I ended up right where I wanted to be.

CHAPTER 18

Fair Maiden

Evy and I were only two weeks into launching #CharcuterieGirl and #GoldenRescueMama out into the digital universe, and we were already ready to shut down the accounts and commit to a life of dying single and alone.

"Spinsterhood wouldn't be so bad," she told me. "After your kids are grown, you, Mona, and I could get a place at the beach, recruit a few more women, and live like *The Golden Girls*. Anything is better than online dating. Let me tell you about this week's disaster."

Evy went out with a man by the handle of #BeachWalksLongTalks. They met at The Eccentric Grape, a trendy boho-style café and wine bar that served only farm-to-table menu items.

After my dinner disaster, she decided lunch dates were safer. She could make up an excuse about returning to work in case she didn't like the guy—no expectation of a three-course meal with drinks and dessert—a sandwich date.

She told me that #BeachWalksLongTalks, whose real name was Aaron, arrived at The Eccentric Grape right on time, and he looked just like his pictures.

"He was clean-cut, friendly, and told some decent jokes. He must have been a regular, though. It seemed like the whole waitstaff knew him."

He was also a teacher, so Evy thought they would have a lot in common. They ordered their food and talked about the bureaucracy of education and why so many teachers were quitting because of the lousy pay and demanding parents. She said she was having a great time talking to him until things took a turn.

"Our food arrived," she told me. "Just then, a woman walked in and sat at the bar. He looked at her, took two bites of his food, and then put his fork down, excusing himself to go to the restroom. He practically sprinted across the restaurant. I assumed he was having stomach issues. Ten minutes went by, and he never came back out. Then, twenty minutes passed. My food was cold, and I didn't know what to do, so I asked our waiter to check on him."

"Was he sick?" I asked.

She shook her head. "Nope, he was hiding. The waiter told me that it was his girlfriend at the bar. She didn't see him sitting at the table with me. Every time the bathroom door opened, he popped his head out, looked around, and then ducked back in. I decided to wait it out and see just how long he would stay there. After 45 minutes, I decided to leave. But before I did, I introduced myself to her."

"You did *what*? What did you say to her?"

"I told her she might want to check on her boyfriend because he'd been hiding in the bathroom for almost an hour. And please tell him we won't be going on another date. You should have seen the look on his face when she opened that bathroom door."

I sighed. "You've just confirmed what I am starting to believe. There are no good men left."

"At least that guy showed up. The last one stood me up. The last message I received from him the night before was, 'See you tomorrow.' And then nothing. He never showed. He left me sitting alone, eating a bowl of tortilla chips and salsa. At least the food was good." She shrugged.

"Well," I told her, "I'm supposed to meet a 40-year-old proctologist for drinks this Friday. We're meeting at The Repub, that place down the street from the university. Be on standby. I might need you."

"Safeword, *green*." Evy reminded me. "Maybe this one will be your prince charming."

I later phoned Mona to tell her I was going out on a date with the doctor.

"Oh, I'm so happy to hear this!" she said. "Wear that blue chiffon shirt with the white pants. It shows off your figure nicely. You've got this, girl! Here's to round two!"

I arrived at The Repub and sat at the bar on Friday night. The space gradually filled with college students. #DoctorsOrders, whose real name was Barry Weiner, was late. *Fifteen minutes. I'll wait fifteen minutes, and then if he doesn't show up, I'll be out of here.*

I slowly sipped my water and scrolled through social media. Although I had lost contact with most of our mutual friends after Jack and I split up, I remained friends with a few on Facebook. Marilyn Feinstein hosted a garden party the previous weekend and posted the photos on her page. She invited our usual old crowd of friends.

As I scrolled through her pictures, I stopped short. Jack was at the party with Kiki. Seeing her smiling and taking selfies with Marilyn and the Jessicas was unnerving. I tapped on the picture and scrolled in closer. *What is that on her finger?* Kiki wore a big shiny diamond on her left hand. *Are they engaged?* That thing was easily two carats. We were only separated for a year. How could he be engaged to get married again so soon? I couldn't even make it through a first date with a guy.

"Well, hello there, my fine lady," a deep voice boomed from behind me.

Startled, I jolted in my seat and turned to find a man dressed in skintight black pants, a white shirt with wide, puffy sleeves, a leather vest, and lace-up leather boots. A small sword rested in a holster across his chest, and a wide-brimmed hat with a large feather sat perched on his head. This guy was dressed head to toe in full Renaissance garb.

He bowed before me and said, "My apologies for being late. You must be the fair Emma. I am just back from a jousting tournament with the king himself! Hath thee partaken of the tavern's fine ale?"

He motioned for the bartender. "Innkeeper, kindly quench our thirst with two mules of your finest lager."

I picked up my phone and texted Emmy.

Green! Green! Green!

"Are you Barry?"

He laughed heartily and said, "I am Lord Weiner, at your service, my lady."

What the hell is happening? Where is the proctologist?

Then I remembered reading in his profile that he was into Live-Action Role-Play. My date showed up ready to play a Renaissance man intent on capturing the heart of the MatchUp.com maiden. He bowed again before me.

"So wonderful to meet thee," his deep voice boomed again. "You are more captivating than your pictures. A fine wench, if I may say so."

"You're Barry, the doctor?" I stuttered.

He chuckled. "Tonight, I am Lord Weiner, the great healer."

"But you're a proctologist? You administer colonoscopies?"

He retorted. "Fair maiden, I am but an apothecary and bloodletter. A learned man of medicine."

He took a big swig of beer and sat down. As he did, the sword that was strapped to his chest slipped downward out of the holster and plunged into his right thigh. He yelped. Blood seeped out of the open laceration.

"Oh, my goodness! You've cut yourself!"

Lord Weiner grimaced and grabbed a towel from the bar counter.

"Tis but a flesh wound," he countered. "A mere scrape." In a matter of minutes, the gushing blood seeped through the towel, turning it bright red.

He grabbed a menu. "Can I interest thee in some pottage? Or perhaps a turkey leg?"

Lord Weiner pressed harder on the cut on his leg, but

the blood flow continued. He was clearly in pain but refused to break out of character. He was a mighty Renaissance man, and mighty Renaissance men never let a severed artery stand in the way of courting the village wench.

Why is my life like this? Why do I have to be on a date with a bleeding LARPer?

Just then, my cell phone rang.

"Oh hey! She's what? Oh no, that's terrible. Is she running a fever? Oh my, she looks *green*? Yes, of course, I'll be right home."

I turned to Lord Weiner, who had now grabbed a pile of beverage napkins from the bar and used them to soak up blood.

"I'm sorry, Barry...er, Lord Weiner, but my babysitter just called. My daughter is sicketh. I'm going to have to cut this shorteth. It was very nice making acquaintance with thee."

He stood up to bow but then sat back down, wincing in pain. "Of course, my fine lady. Safe travels back to your village."

As I walked away, I heard Barry ask the bartender, "Do you have a first aid kit?"

I hurried to my car without looking back and drove straight to Evy's condo. When I knocked on the door, Benny bolted out as soon as I opened it, nearly knocking me over. I patted his head.

"Who's a good boy? Benny is the best boy!"

He licked my hand and followed me into Evy's room, wagging his tail. Evy was curled up in a big blanket, grading a pile of papers. She didn't look well.

"Are you okay?"

She shook her head. "I think I need to go back to the doctor. He gave me medicine for my thyroid, but I don't think it's working. I feel awful."

I made her a cup of tea and told her about Lord Weiner and the bleeding flesh wound.

"The dates with these men are getting more and more bizarre. Maybe we should just give up. Remember back in the day when people would just bump into each other on a train or cross paths somewhere? Their eyes would meet, and they would fall head over heels in love. Organic love. That's what we need."

"I regret to inform you that we promised Mona we would try Single Adventures with her. We're signed up for that next weekend. Until then, I'm taking a break from online dating. Lauren's paralegal, Rocco, called me, and we are due in court for a preliminary conference on Wednesday."

"Well, at least things are progressing," Evy said. "You're that much closer to being free of him. Do you feel like you're ready?"

"I guess so. We submitted the paperwork to the court. I'm asking for full custody, child support, and alimony.

Lauren doesn't know how successful we're going to be, though. His financial disclosures show nothing more than a small joint venture with another man that hasn't been very successful."

Evy rolled her eyes. "Then how can he afford his current lifestyle?" she asked.

"That, my friend, is the twenty-million-dollar question. The big mystery. We will see how it goes."

CHAPTER 19

Until Next Time

On Wednesday, I met Lauren and Rocco in the main hallway of the Manchester County Circuit Courthouse. Rocco pulled up his notes on his tablet. "According to the docket, we will be in courtroom 3C at 9:00 a.m.," he said.

An uneasiness came over me. I had not physically seen or been in Jack's presence for months. All hostage exchanges with the kids were done via drop-offs at our front doors or from cars, and all messaging occurred through text and email. That was our arrangement, and I was fine with it.

Rocco nudged me. "That man over there has been staring at you. Is that him?"

Jack stood at the other end of the hallway, his eyes locked on me. I made my way toward him.

"Jack," I said briskly.

He stood quietly for a moment. "You look a lot different."

"Divorce diet," Lauren muttered under her breath to Rocco. "The men say that every time."

"Yeah, took up running again. You look a lot different yourself."

What was that statistic of people gaining weight when they got comfortable with a new partner? I remember reading an article about it. *"Surveys show that people who are part of a couple may no longer feel pressure to look their best."* Jack must really be in love. He was easily thirty pounds heavier than the last time I saw him in person. *Funny.* He was gaining weight as I was losing it.

He leaned down to adjust his shoelace, and I saw a widening patch of baldness on the top of his head. He was also losing his hair. *Hello, karma, my old friend. I've come to talk with you again.*

"I almost didn't recognize you."

Lauren turned to him and shot a look that silenced him immediately. "We need to go find our seats," she said. "And if you want to correspond with my client, I'd suggest you do it through your attorney."

She grabbed my arm and steered me toward the

courtroom. Jack stood looking at us, speechless. The courtroom was almost full, so the three of us found seats toward the back and waited for the judge to arrive. Jack sat with his attorney, James P. Fortney, on the other side of the room.

"All rise!" A bailiff stood in the front of the room. "Superior Court of the state of New York, County of Manchester, Circuit Court Division, is now in session, the Honorable John Hawkins residing."

We all stood as an older man with a stern face entered and sat in the judge's seat. He narrowed his eyes, scanning the courtroom with a sharp stare. Lauren was spot on with her assessment—I could now see why they called him The Hawk.

"You may be seated," said the bailiff. He turned to Judge Hawkins and said, "Preliminary divorce hearings are on today's docket."

He took a seat and began calling out names. I watched as men and women were called to the podium with their attorneys. We waited for our turn.

"Davis vs. Davis!" the bailiff called out.

"Let's go," said Lauren. She grabbed a folder, stood up, and stiletto-clicked her way up to the podium while I trailed behind. Jack stood to our right with his attorney. Lauren spoke first.

"Your Honor, my name is Lauren Livingston, representing the defendant in this case, Ms. Emma Davis."

James P. Fortney stepped forward to introduce himself. The Hawk glanced over our paperwork.

"Plaintiff, state your case," he said.

"Your Honor, my client wishes to end this marriage based on mutually agreed upon irreconcilable differences. The parties have been separated and living apart for over a year. His request is for the defendant to waive all alimony and rights to his financial interests, including any retirement accounts. He is requesting 50/50 custody of the two minor children."

The Hawk studied Jack for a minute and then turned to Lauren.

"Defendant?"

Lauren leaned in. The shark fight was on.

"Your Honor, the plaintiff is clearly delusional in his request for the dissolution of the marriage based on irreconcilable differences! Mr. Davis has been involved in an adulterous affair for over a year with a 24-year-old waitress. In fact, he left Ms. Davis and moved out of their marital home when my client discovered this transgression. Since that time, the children have been in her care full-time, with the exception of alternating weekends. In response to his statement that he would like my client to waive alimony, we contest this due to the fact that my client put her career in information technology on hold to stay at home and raise their children. This has been a detriment to her career, one in which staying current with training and certifications in evolving technologies is essential."

Jack stared at her, wide-eyed with disbelief.

Lauren continued. "Further, upon review of Mr. Davis's disposition of financial assets and liabilities, we believe he is lying outright. My client entrusted Mr. Davis with millions of dollars when she sold her company, OneBank, under the falsehood that he would be reinvesting in a new venture in both of their names. After considerable research, we have been unable to trace this money anywhere. He is *hiding* something. In light of all of this, Ms. Davis is requesting alimony, full custody, and $3,000 per month in child support for the two children. She also requests the right to retain the marital home."

"Absolutely not!" Jack shouted. The Hawk gave Jack a look that made him wince. James P. Fortney intercepted.

"Your Honor, we understand the defendant is unhappy that my client left her. However, these allegations are far-fetched and unfounded. My client owns a small consulting company called J&B Enterprises that netted less than $250,000 in revenue last year. That is all. He is financially unable to meet these provisions."

Lauren straightened.

"Your Honor, I would like to make you aware that the plaintiff recently purchased a $55,000 BMW for the woman with whom he is having an affair. An *adulterous* affair. They just returned from an exotic trip to the Maldives. He spends $80,000 per year on the children's education at an elite school. My paralegal researched and discovered that he spends $10,000 per month to be a member of the Metropolitan Gentleman's Club. The condominium he purchased in the city was listed online as being sold for $1.4 million last year. His financial statement says that he brings home less than $7,000 every month after taxes. J&B Enterprises is jointly owned by another man named Robert Blankenship. He is sharing the revenue from that company with him. These numbers don't add up."

Jack looked at me, stunned. James P. Fortney appeared visibly flustered. *Good work, Rocco.*

"I see," said The Hawk. He leaned back in his seat and looked through the paperwork again. "For the time being, the children will remain in the care of Ms. Davis under the current arrangement. The plaintiff is ordered to pay $3,000 monthly in child support until further notice. I am requiring a full audit of Mr. Davis's financial statements, including a review of past tax returns, to be submitted to me prior to any additional ruling. Please see the bailiff for additional information."

Lauren beamed. Jack shot me a fierce glare, then turned and stormed out of the courtroom without a backward glance.

Lauren faced James P. Fortney, smiled, and said,

"Until next time." She turned and stiletto-clicked loudly out of the courtroom.

The bailiff called out, "Evans vs. Evans!"

At that moment, I reflected on a nursery rhyme that Myla often sang to me.

"Two little sharks went out to play down in a bay so far away. Then there was a shark attack. And only one little shark came back..."

Lauren C. Livingston was worth every penny.

CHAPTER 20

Falling Petals

vy, Mona, and I boarded a charter bus headed for Oneonta, New York, just a two-hour drive from Belmont. Evy sat next to me, and Mona took the seat behind us. I heard her reading an article on her cell phone, quoting statistics aloud as she went.

"This article says, 'Skydiving seems like a dangerous sport, but probably not as terrible as you imagine. How many people actually die from skydiving? According to the United States Parachute Association, there were just 0.28 fatalities per 100,000 jumps last year.' I suppose that's not that bad. But still..."

Mona nervously flipped through screens on her phone, looking for more information. When we signed up with the Single Adventures dating club, we had several activities to choose from. Mona wanted to do something more low-key, like a Wine and Paint class, but Evy talked her into trying skydiving. Evy said it was something she had always wanted to do, and now was a great time to knock another item off her bucket list.

"Life is short," Evy had told Mona.

"Yeah, it's going to be much shorter if I die free-falling to the earth. Splat! Pieces of Mona as far as the eye can see! It won't be pretty." Still, Mona bravely tagged along on our adventure. I didn't admit it to them, but I was nervous too. Terrified of heights, but also excited. I never would have done something like this with Jack.

The crowded bus was filled with single people out for the day, hoping to find a connection. Noisy, small talk and chatter filled the air.

"Ever skydived before?" The guy in the seat in front of us turned around and leaned over his seat to talk to Evy.

Evy shook her head and replied, "Nope, you?"

"Yeah, it's amazing. An adrenaline rush, for sure. I've been a few dozen times."

"Safe?" Evy asked him.

"For the most part. I only got my lines twisted once, and the parachute almost didn't open, but the tandem instructor fixed it just in time."

Mona gasped and muttered under her breath, "I knew it. I should have gone shopping today instead. The Luxe Thrifter is having a clearance sale."

Just then, Katie, our Single Adventures coordinator, walked down the aisle of the bus and handed out instruction sheets.

"Listen up, group!" she said. "Make sure you thoroughly read through what I'm handing out before we arrive at the skydiving center. We have a big party today, and they will want to get started right away."

Mona took the paper and read out loud, "You'll free-fall at roughly 120 miles per hour for about a minute. At around 6,000 feet, your instructor will deploy the parachute, and you'll glide under the canopy for about four minutes before landing in the field. *120 miles per hour? 6,000 feet?*"

"We'll be fine, Mona," Evy said, trying to reassure her.

Mona continued reading. "You'll be fitted with a special tandem harness during your jump. The harnesses are designed to provide maximum safety and comfort. Your tandem instructor will securely connect to you at four connection points. Two at the shoulders and two near the hips. You'll both face forward when connected. *Oh myyyyy.* Now I like the sound of that! I hope I get a hot one. Talk about the mile-high club!"

The bus pulled up to the front of the skydiving center. Two large hangars with airplanes inside stood next to a long landing strip. Katie led us to an intake center, where we put on our jumpsuits and sat through a twenty-minute instructional video. After that, one of the instructors walked to the front of the room to demonstrate how to harness. He asked for a volunteer. Mona waved her hand wildly.

"You," he said, pointing to Mona. Mona grinned and rushed to the front of the room. The instructor pulled out the harness, which consisted of several straps and buckles. He reached down and secured the straps around Mona's thighs. Mona's eyes grew huge. The instructor then secured the chest strap across Mona's chest and shoulders.

"As you can see, we are firmly strapped around our midsections, with the shoulder straps being a little looser. I will now do a series of final checks to ensure everything is secure and in the correct position."

He reached down between Mona's legs and tugged the harness. Mona looked up at Evy, smiled widely, and winked.

"She's a hot mess," Evy whispered. I nodded in agreement.

"Now, I cannot emphasize this enough," the instructor said. "Do not interfere when the instructors release the canopy. You might be tempted to want to try to help. We've had over 1,500 jumps, and I assure you, we know what we are doing. Your only job today is to enjoy yourself."

He unstrapped Mona, who returned to her seat next to us.

"Who knew skydiving could be so much fun?" she whispered.

Evy rolled her eyes.

Katie divided us into two groups. Our group followed her to the landing strip and boarded a military-style plane. The cabin interior was stripped down, with basic seating along the sides—definitely not what I had anticipated. Our instructors sat across from us.

The engine rumbled, and the plane pulled forward. The plane door, which was nothing more than a large round opening, sat propped open.

"Aren't they going to close that? We're not even wearing seatbelts." I yelled to Evy. She shrugged.

I leaned toward the open door, the deafening roar of the engines drowning out all other sounds as the plane surged forward. The ground began to fall away, and a blast of wind tore through the cabin, pushing me back into my seat. My fingers tightened around the edges of the seat, knuckles white, as I fought to steady myself.

There's nothing holding us in.

Terror filled me in that instant. I watched as the plane went higher while the ground below transformed into a distant quilt of brown and green patches of land. My stomach lurched, a sudden twist inside me that left me feeling weightless for a split second as if the ground had dropped out from under me. I pressed my feet firmly into the floor, wishing I could anchor them there for safety.

The instructors led the divers to the back of the plane and began preparing for the jumps. Mona seemed to have lost all fear and happily worked with her instructor. Evy glanced my way, worry written all over her face.

"You okay? You don't look okay."

I tried to answer her, but my throat felt tight, and I couldn't speak. My palms started to sweat. My head spun in dizziness. Out the plane door, I could see the patches of earth below growing smaller, now tiny squares.

That is such a long way down.

I gave her a nod. She frowned slightly, then turned to follow her instructor to get ready for tandem. I trailed behind, meeting up with mine. My heart thundered in my chest.

What the hell am I doing? I'm about to free-fall out of an airplane. It's so far down.

Fear surged through me. I grabbed Evy's hand.

"Evy! I can't do this! I can't. We're so high up! Did you see? It's too high. I don't want to die. I can't do this." The noise on the plane roared around us. *Could she hear me?*

My instructor yelled into my ear. "I've done hundreds of jumps. Trust me, you're in good hands. But if you're not up for it, just say the word."

I cast a pleading glance at Evy. She took my hand, looked me in the eye, and yelled over the engine roar. "You've got this. You're stronger than you think!" Evy squeezed my hand so hard I could feel my bones crunch in her grip. "You can do this. *We've* got this!"

Mona stood in the threshold of the doorway, looking back at us, her face full of excitement and fear. She gave us a small thumbs-up, and then she and her instructor stepped out of the plane and into the open air.

Evy's turn was next. She turned and looked back at me one more time. "You can do this. Be strong!" she yelled. She gave me a reassuring smile, and then she and her instructor stepped out of the plane.

"Yes, or no?" my instructor yelled.

He motioned for the pair behind us to go ahead. They jumped out of the plane and into the rushing air without a thought.

I needed to make a choice. I was frozen, unable to move. I could say no, unstrap myself from the instructor, and ride the plane down. That would be the safest thing. I knew the outcome of that decision. I would be unharmed and at home in a few hours, hugging my kids.

But what if I said yes?

I closed my eyes, unable to focus. At that moment, a memory flashed through my mind. I was sitting in the booth at the Belmont McDonald's, a plate of fries set down before me, as tears streamed down my face. I will never forget how I felt that day.

Rotten mother. Horrible at relationships. Pathetic career. Fat. Alone. And just plain scared.

No. Not anymore. I'm not that person anymore.

"Yes! I'm ready!" I shouted to my instructor.

"All right, let's go."

He led me to the door, and together, we stepped out of the plane. The world fell out below us. The earth beneath was a big, beautiful, vast canvas—an intricate piece of artwork that could only be understood by seeing it from this perspective. The horizon stretched on forever.

As the air rushed around me, I let go of my inhibitions and suddenly felt lighter than I ever had. Falling but free. Completely out of control.

This is what it feels like to be alive.

After a minute, the instructor reached up and released the parachute. We started drifting downward slowly. I watched as the small squares of earth grew larger and more distinct. Corn fields and forests. Zig-zagging roads. The other divers below me descended to the earth.

I remembered holding a dandelion as a little girl, blowing on the flower, and watching the soft white petals drift gently through the air. *We were all falling petals.*

The earth grew closer, and the instructor gave me the hand signal that it was time to prepare to land. I did exactly what we were instructed to do in the video. He and I reconnected with the earth.

"Great job!" he told me. He unhooked us from the parachute and then undid the tandem hooks. "What did you think? Are you okay?"

I lifted my hand to my face and wiped away tears. I hadn't noticed until then, but I had been sobbing the whole time.

"Yes, thank you. That was an experience of a lifetime."

"You're welcome. I think this is the best part of my job. Watching people overcome their fears. We hope you'll come back."

I walked away, feeling the firmness of the ground beneath my feet, gravity holding me solidly to the earth. Evy and Mona were further down the field. I walked slowly towards them, taking my time to reconnect with the planet and find my footing again.

Katie stood at the edge of the field and called out, "Team! Please come this way!" A group had formed, getting ready to head back to the skydiving center.

Evy walked up to me and slung her arm around my shoulder. "See that? Braver than you know. What do you think?"

"Amazing. Thank you for not letting me quit."

"Not a chance," she replied.

Mona put her arm around my other shoulder. "This is why I just love the two of you."

Just then, Katie approached us with a camera. "Care for a group shot before you change out of your jumpsuits? These will be available for sale when we get back to the center."

Evy, Mona, and I stood side by side with our arms

wrapped around each other as Katie snapped pictures.

"We also have some photos of you during your fall that we took from the plane. Be sure to stop by and check them out."

The Single Adventures group walked back to the center, talking and sharing stories about their jumps. When we got to the center, we changed back into our regular clothes and picked up our skydiving certificates. I purchased all the photos from the trip. This was a day I never wanted to forget.

Back on the bus to Belmont, Evy immediately fell asleep in her seat next to the window. Mona sat in the seat next to me.

"She gets tired easily," Mona observed.

"Yeah, I noticed that too. She's been seeing a doctor. She said it might be a thyroid issue."

Mona was quiet for a moment. "Well, so much for meeting men today," she sighed.

"Yeah, but who cares? We had a great time."

"So, now what? What's our next adventure?"

"Speed dating."

Her face lit up. "Oh, that's right! I forgot about that. You two are so much fun. I'm so lucky to have run into you at the thrift store that day. But I guess life is just like that. One day, you're out shopping for ball gowns, and then the next day, you're jumping out of airplanes with new friends."

I picked up Mona's hand and noticed red burn marks along the edges of her fingers, some of which had formed into scars.

"What happened here?"

"Glue-gun," she sighed again. "For putting on rhinestones. It's a labor of love to get those costumes just right."

She fell silent for a moment before finally saying, "It isn't always easy for me, you know. People don't always accept me for the way that I am. I mean, my dogs love me, but I can't always connect the same way with people. It can get lonely."

I knew the depths of loneliness; it was the most devastating of human afflictions. I turned to her. "The actor Robin Williams once said, 'I used to think the worst thing in life was to end up alone. It's not. The worst thing in life is to end up with people who make you feel alone.' You're not alone with us. We would never make you feel that way. And besides, I, for one, think you're pretty cool, Mona."

I held her scarred hand. She laid her head on my shoulder. We rode back to Belmont in silence.

CHAPTER 21

Hello My Name Is...

As the half marathon approached, Evy and I began incorporating weightlifting into our routine, using the equipment in my basement home gym. Sandy Myers recently presented awards to us at the Belmont Healthy Horizons meeting because we each achieved our goal weight. Evy continued to lose weight, though. She was on the floor mat doing sit-ups when I noticed her small body.

"Ev? I don't know how to say this, but I can count your ribs through your shirt. You're all skin and bones."

She stopped doing sit-ups and gave me a hurtful look.

I continued, "Don't get me wrong. You look *great,*

but I'm worried you may be getting a little too thin. Have you been eating?"

I instantly regretted asking her that question. I was the one who pushed the two of us hard these past weeks to get ready for the race, extending our training runs further each session. I gained a mentality of "all in or nothing." Thanks to my obsessiveness, I could see my best friend's ribs.

"I'm eating!" she protested. "A lot. Probably even more than before we started our diet together. You're killing me with all these training runs!"

Feeling self-conscious, she crossed the room and slipped on her oversized hoodie to hide her body from me. I was so focused on building up stamina that I didn't realize I might not have considered what was best for her, too. *Sometimes, I can be a rotten friend.*

I tried to sound cheerful. "Well, the race is close. Just a few weeks away! After that, we will cut back and work on finding that happy-medium sweet spot where we do just enough running. For now, we have speed dating to look forward to."

She nodded. "I think it will be fun, but I'm apprehensive. Online dating has been a disaster. Single Adventures didn't pan out. Why should speed dating be any better? It'll just be a room full of men to disappoint instead of a website full of creeps."

She spoke the truth. After several weeks on MatchUp.

com, the stream of men lessened, and it was just the same ones lurking out there. But we had to keep trying, and speed dating was our next option. Putting ourselves out there was better than not trying at all.

The speed dating event was held in a party room at a nearby restaurant. Mona was standing at the entrance when we arrived, waiting for us.

"Hello, beautiful ladies!" She ran to us and gave us each a hug. "I'm so excited and nervous!"

She was wearing one of the evening gowns she'd chosen from The Luxe Thrifter, paired with a long black wig, and her makeup was, as always, impeccable. Evy and I opted for business casual, figuring it was the safest choice—we didn't want to overdo it, especially since we had no idea what to expect.

A tall, red-haired woman greeted us when we entered the party room. She wore a *"Hello My Name Is... Megan"* sticker on her shirt. She was set to be our host and guide for tonight's event.

"Welcome to tonight's speed dating event! We're so happy you could join us!"

We signed up at the small table at the front. Megan handed each of us name tags and a piece of paper with a list of names.

"Now let me tell you how this works. The room is set up with individual tables. You ladies will find a seat and stay there for the duration of the evening. The men will rotate among the tables every five minutes. You have five minutes to find the love of your life! I'll ring a bell when it's time to switch. You'll start with an elevator pitch – a quick synopsis about who you are and what you're looking for. Then, the gentleman will have an opportunity to speak. If you're interested in the gentleman, simply indicate that by placing a checkmark next to his name on the paper. We will later update your speed dating online profile to let you know if there are any interests. You can then reach each other through the online portal. Here are some icebreaker topics you might want to try."

She gave each of us a second piece of paper. Evy and I exchanged a shrug while Mona clapped her hands with excitement.

We found three seats at adjacent tables and watched people enter the room. Women sat at tables, and men assembled at the back. At 7:30, Megan shut the doors and addressed the room, repeating the instructions for the late stragglers.

"Ready, friends?" Megan called out. "Let's go!" She rang a loud bell, and men dispersed to the tables.

"Hello, My Name Is...Danny" sat down in front of me. Clad in all black, Danny had a slender face with a pointed chin. Round spectacles sat perched at the

end of his long nose. He wore his dark hair slicked back with hair gel.

"Hello, Emma. How are you tonight?" he asked, deadpan.

"I'm doing well, Danny. How are you tonight?"

He shrugged and just stared at me. *Hmmm…okay. Time for my elevator pitch.*

"Yes, I'm Emma. I'm 32 years old. This is the first time I've tried speed dating. Currently going through a divorce. I have two young children with full custody of both. I work in information technology. For fun, I enjoy running and cooking. I love to travel, but haven't been able to do that much in recent years. What do you do for a living?"

"I'm a moirologist."

"Sorry, I'm not familiar with that term," I said. He just stared at me in response.

"A moirologist is a professional mourner."

"People pay you to mourn?"

He nodded. "I attend the funeral services of people who don't have any friends. I improve the deceased's reputation. I'm compensated to lament the loss of their lives and deliver eulogies to comfort the grieving family. The dead man's best friend. I'm *very* good at giving eulogies."

He stared at me, expressionless. I cleared my throat, unsure of what to say next.

"Well, that's very interesting. I've never heard of that profession. Do you have any questions for me?"

His face was stoic as he started firing questions at me in rapid sequence.

"Yes, given the choice, what floor of an apartment would you choose to live on?" *This is not on the ice-breaker sheet.*

"Whatever floor is available?"

"Wrong! The second floor. You can still safely jump if your building goes up in a blazing inferno. Last year, there were 81,252 apartment fires in the U.S. Eleven percent of those people *died*. They all lived on the top floors."

Why does this man know these statistics?

"Would you rather swim in a lake or the ocean?"

"The ocean?"

"Correct! The ocean has bloodthirsty sharks, but lakes have flesh-eating amoebas. Naegleria fowleri is a brain-eater and is the deadliest form known to man, killing roughly 97% of its victims."

I glanced at Evy, who appeared deep in conversation with a gentleman wearing a priest's collar. Mona sat on the other side of her, nervously biting her nails and looking around the room. The man across from her stared into his cell phone, ignoring her.

"Would you rather die from killer bees or be sucked into a toilet mid-flight on an airplane?"

OK, I've had just about enough. "I don't think that's really a thing," I replied.

"Oh, it is. Commercial airline toilets are some of the most powerful. Your vajajay isn't safe."

"You're telling me my vajajay could get sucked out of me?"

Danny dropped his head down in despair.

After another awkward pause, I continued, "You seem rather obsessed with dying."

"*You* are going to die. We are *all* going to die. It's just a matter of how. And when. It's just...inevitable. And that is what makes life beautiful." Danny's eyes softened as he reached for my hands. He started to speak again, but then a shimmer of tears welled in his eyes.

I pulled my hand away. "Are you okay?"

"Yes." He wiped away a tear. "I just mourn for your girl parts."

Riiiiing! Megan rang the bell. *Oh, thank God.*

"Hello, My Name Is...Leroy" sat down in front of me next. Leroy had just left Evy's table. His long dark hair lay piled on his head in a man bun. He wore faded jeans, a black button-down shirt, and a Roman collar. He carried a subtle hint of skunk. *Is this guy stoned?*

"Hello, Emma. I hope you are having a blessed day. I am Leroy."

I gave Leroy my pitch and said, "That's an interesting outfit. What do you do for a living?

"I'm a Dudeist Priest."

"A Dudeist what?"

"I am an ordained Dudeist Priest in the Church of the Latter-Day Dude."

"I don't think that's really a religion—" I started to protest, but Leroy cut me off.

"Peace, Emma. Let me explain. The Church of the Latter-Day Dude is a modern interpretation of Chinese Taoism. We also practice the Greek philosophy of going with the flow and taking it easy. I'm fully ordained and able to carry out religious ceremonies as a representative of the church. Just yesterday, I conducted a wedding ceremony. It was beautiful."

He smiled at me wistfully. I imagined him before a congregation toking up while the bride and groom exchanged their vows to Love, Honor, and Always Hold Each Other's Hookah Pipe. Dudeism? *I am researching that when I get home.*

"What can I say, Emma? Love was in the air." He waved his arm in a dramatic swoosh. *Whew.* That wasn't just skunk I smelled. Apparently, Dudeists also didn't believe in bathing.

"Do you trust in the power of love?" he asked.

"Well, I'm in the middle of a divorce, so..."

He patted my hand. "That's just the universe opening a door for you, Emma. When we don't follow our intended paths, the universe corrects us. I was once homeless and living in a tent on the streets of San Francisco when, one day, a vision appeared to me. Well, it was actually a pamphlet that blew into my path on the sidewalk. But still, a vision. The universe was speaking to me. It told me to go to the Church of the Latter-Day Dude. They sheltered me and welcomed me with open arms. And now, I am giving back to the Church. Walk through the door the universe has opened for you, Emma. Let the universe correct you."

The only door I'm walking through is that front door. How much longer do we have?

Ring!

"Hello My Name Is...Marty" was up next. After giving Marty my elevator pitch, he gave me his own.

"My name is Marty. No kids. I've been single for several years now. I really enjoy being outdoors. I love fresh air and wide-open spaces."

Marty seemed like a normal guy. Nicely dressed. Kind face. He continued.

"Well, single mostly because they just let me out. They cut five years off my sentence because of good behavior." He glanced nervously at the door. "The parole officer at my halfway house doesn't know that I'm here. I think I'm allowed to be here, but I'm not sure. Nice place, though. Don't you think?"

Parole officer? I couldn't think of anything to say. An awkward, silent minute passed. Marty became agitated.

"What? I don't care what the DNA showed. I did *not* kill my wife! Yes, that was my DNA at the murder scene, but it was planted there. I was set up!" Marty nervously looked back over at the door.

"And yes, it was just a coincidence that I had recently opened a two-million-dollar insurance policy on her. I mean, these things just happen sometimes. Who *knew* that she would end up being sucked into the log splitter?"

I'm out.

Ring!

Marty stomped off to the next table. I looked over at Evy, and she gave me a puzzled look and mouthed, "What just happened?"

I mouthed back, "Murderer." Her eyes grew huge.

Two tables over, Mona screamed at Danny. "Aaaaaugh! You leave my vajajay alone!"

Evy gave me a desperate look and said, "Let's go." I picked up my purse and coat before anyone else could sit down in the seat in front of me.

"Come on," I said. Evy grabbed Mona's hand, and the three of us rushed to the door.

Megan shouted after us as we exited the party room. "Ladies! We're not done yet! You still have more time! The party isn't over yet!" *Oh, that party is over.*

We stood outside on the sidewalk, looking at each other.

"What just happened?" Evy said.

"I don't know. But I'm not flying commercial anytime soon," Mona responded, looking nervously at the door. Evy squeezed her hand.

"Who's hungry? Pizza?" I asked. Mona clapped.

Cheese and pepperoni therapy was just what we needed. We went to Sharky's, Belmont's top-rated pizza joint, and ordered an extra-large pie.

"Well, so much for that," I said, lifting a large piece of ooey-gooey cheesy goodness to my mouth. "I'm officially off the market. Maybe I'll just focus on my kids for a while."

Mona concurred. "I've been neglecting Bark Twain and Jimmy Chews. We haven't been to the dog park in days. Work has been so busy."

Evy sat silently, listening to us.

"You okay, Ev?"

She smiled and reached out and grabbed both of our hands. I noticed she barely touched her food.

"Yeah, I just want both of you to know how much I appreciate your friendship. I'm realizing what a strange place the dating world has become. I may not have Ben anymore, but I know I have the two of you."

"Cheers to that!" Mona said, holding up her soda glass. We all clinked glasses. "Here's to friendship!"

Ding! A message alert appeared on my phone from MatchUp.com.

"Well, aren't you going to look?" Mona asked.

I shook my head. "No, I said I'm *done.*"

"Give me that phone," Mona said and snatched it from my hand.

"Blu_Devil messaged you! This one is charming!" I took the phone back and looked. He was very attractive and looked familiar.

"Never say never," Mona advised.

"Perhaps the universe is opening doors for you," Evy pitched in.

"You had that guy, too!" I laughed.

Evy and I simultaneously chanted, "Dude!"

And so, we ended the night with pizza and friendship. What more could a girl want? These were my people. I grabbed another slice.

Wait

"I want *pink,* and I need you to paint a flower on my big toe. A *daisy.* Just like Emily at school."

Myla's little legs dangled over the nail technician's chair and made a small splash as she plunged them into the swirling water below.

"Please and thank you," I reminded her.

"Sorry, miss. Please paint them pink with a daisy. Thank you so much."

Myla looked at me for approval, and I nodded to her. Sometimes she was a bossy thing and needed to be reminded that manners matter. The nail technician picked up her foot to scrub it with a brush. Myla squealed with laughter.

Mommy and Myla Day had arrived. Austin was off

at Cub Scout camp with Jack, who had recently shown a newfound interest in being more present in the kids' lives. Who knew how long that would last? Maybe his lawyer advised him to do so. After the divorce was finalized, I assumed he would revert to being an absent parent, gallivanting off to places with Kiki once more. Today, I was just thankful for the girl time with my daughter.

"Mommy, why do women paint their nails?"

I replied, "To look pretty."

"What if I don't care about being pretty? What if I want just to be smart instead?" She squirmed in her chair. "It's too much work." She sighed.

"You're capable of being both. Intelligent and attractive. It might require effort at times, but both are possible."

"Was it work to stop being fat?" She regarded me with curiosity. I guess I never really thought that Myla had been watching and observing me this past year. I didn't want her to think that getting healthy equated to something hard or negative that people wouldn't want to do. I turned to her and shook my head.

"Well, I wouldn't call it *work*, Myla. I started to exercise with Aunt Evy so I could be healthy again. So that I would have the energy to play with you and Austin. I wasn't feeling well, and I certainly didn't feel pretty."

"Yes, you were," she protested. "You were still pretty then, too, Mommy. *You* just didn't think so. That's why you got mad and shook the lady at McDonald's. I saw the whole thing. But why were you *so* angry?"

Oof. I wonder how long she had been thinking about that day and wanting to ask these questions.

"I was angry because I didn't like myself back then. I never should have done that. That was the wrong way to handle anger. The right way is to find somebody to talk to who can help you sort it out."

Myla nodded as if she understood. "Ms. Daniels says beauty comes from the inside and the outside. That's why we get in trouble at school for making fun of the way someone looks. You have to see all of their beauty. Being fat doesn't make you ugly."

My Bolton dollars at work.

And this kid. At times, it was hard for me to fathom that I was the one who brought her into this world. She saw things with an understanding I never could have grasped at her age. Precocious. And so sure of herself. Maybe I was doing something right.

She scolded the nail technician. "No, not *that* pink. The *other* one." She stopped for a second and added, "Please and thank you."

I sat in the chair beside her and picked up my phone while a technician applied a thick layer of warm lilac-scented paraffin to my legs and wrapped them in a hot towel. *Heaven.* I opened my MatchUp.com account. Evy swore off online dating and closed her account right after our speed dating misadventure, but I kept hearing Mona's voice saying, "Never say never."

I opened #Blu_Devil's message. His picture was maddening. *Where do I know this guy from?* I looked at his profile. He looked to be in his early thirties. He had short, sandy blonde, curly hair and a nice face.

> Hi Charcuterie Girl. That's a great name. I'll bet there's an interesting story behind it. I think we might have something in common. I'm writing a Vegan cookbook. There is a chapter called 'Entertaining Vegan' with recipes and ideas for hosting a party for those who choose to go meatless. Care to share notes?

I snorted, thinking about the bacon cheeseburger I had for dinner last night. There was no way I could help this man. But still, a cookbook. *That's different.*

Myla gave me a disapproving look. "You shouldn't snort, Mommy," and then she turned back to the technician. "*Yellow* daisy, *please.*"

My thumb hovered over the reply button. *Don't do it. It will just be another failure. Another disappointment. Just shut down the account. Just. Shut. It. Down.*

I hit the reply button and quickly typed,

I added a sad emoji face and hit send.

Never say never. The universe will open doors. I reflected on the poster on the wall at Belmont Hospital of the cat clinging to a tree with the caption, "Hang in there." I was hanging in there.

"Mommy, look. Do you like them?" Myla waved her feet in the air, showing off her newly pedicured toes.

"Very cute, Myla. Now we have to wait for them to dry."

She sighed loudly and said, "Boring."

"Fifteen minutes," said the nail technician. "Then I'll be back to check on you."

Fifteen minutes passed. I stared at my phone. No response from #Blu_Devil. *Fine.* I'm closing my account when I get home.

Myla and I spent the afternoon at the mall. She talked me into taking her to the Brainy Things store, which was full of puzzles, chemistry kits, and slime projects. We left with a bag full of toys. Next, we went to Make-a-Friend, where she picked out a fabric animal carcass and stuffed it with cotton until it was plump and huggable. She chose a yellow dog with big brown eyes.

"I'm going to name him Benny," she told me. "Just like Aunt Evy's dog."

It occurred to me just then that I hadn't heard from Evy for a couple of days, so I texted her.

> Hey! How are you doing?

She responded immediately.

EVY

> Hi! I just woke up.

It was two o'clock in the afternoon.
Me:

> Feeling better?

Evy:

> Yeah, I guess I was just really tired. What are you up to?

Me:

> Mommy and Myla Day at the mall. She's costing me a fortune!

Evy:

> Just don't let her talk you into
> letting her get a tattoo.

I laughed and texted back,

> I'm sure that day is coming. I'm
> just checking on you. See you
> tomorrow morning for our run.

Only three more weeks until the half-marathon. I knew we were both ready for it. We completed twelve miles last Sunday so that extra mile and a half should be easy enough to get through. I was so excited to be doing this with my best friend.

Ding!

I looked at my phone.

"#Blu_Devil messaged you!"

I started to open my account, but Myla pulled on my arm.

"Come on, Mommy. I'm hungry. I need a soft pretzel. I think I'm going to starve to death." Myla dragged me to the food court, where she also talked me into getting her a cinnamon roll. She was a great negotiator. I had high hopes for this girl.

Later at home, Myla snuggled with her new stuffed animal and a warm blanket on the sofa as she watched her favorite princess movie for the hundredth time. I went into the kitchen to make tea and check my MatchUp.com account again. I opened the message from #Blu_Devil.

> Bad charcuterie board? Well, you just didn't build one with the right chef. I know a fix for that.

I messaged back,

> I hope it doesn't end in food poisoning.

Ding! He's online now!

> Hey! Great to see that you're online. I had just about given up on you. I know we haven't gotten to know each other, but I coincidentally have an extra ticket to a cooking class next weekend at No Thyme to Cook. I was supposed to go with my coworker, but she backed out. It's a pasta-making tutorial. Interested?

No Thyme to Cook was the local cooking school that held informal cooking classes for Belmont's culinary-challenged citizens. *Hmmm...pasta.* I *love* homemade pasta. Still, he was a stranger. We hadn't even gone through the awkward niceties of exchanging mundane information about ourselves yet. I didn't have enough information to ascertain if he had a wife with a big in-surance policy and a log splitter lurking somewhere. *Dear God, please don't let him be a LARPer.*

Never say never.

I messaged back,

> Well, today's your lucky day. I'm gearing up for a half-marathon and indulging in all the carbs to fuel my training. Pasta it is!

> Perfect. The class is on Friday night. It starts at 5:30. You'll want to wear comfortable clothes and shoes. We'll be standing for most of it. I'll be the guy in the ball cap.

I decided not to tell Evy about this guy. I held little hope that this would go anywhere. This marked my last hurrah before I returned to my life of spinsterhood. At least there would be pasta.

On Friday night, I dropped the kids off at Jack's and headed to No Thyme to Cook. The owner had transformed an old farmhouse into a cooking school. The outside looked quaint, with white clapboard siding and blue-gray shutters surrounding a sizeable front porch filled with white rocking chairs. On the inside, though, the owner knocked down several walls to create a large room with restaurant-grade tables and appliances.

A small chalkboard outside read, "La pasta è amore. Benvenuti nella nostra cucina!" I pulled up my online translator. "Pasta is love. Welcome to our kitchen!" I wasn't going to argue there. Pasta *is* love. When I walked inside, a woman wearing a chef's hat and a large white apron greeted me.

"Welcome to No Thyme to Cook! I'm Gwyn. What name is your reservation under?"

I looked at her, unsure of what to say. "#Blu_Devil" wouldn't resonate. The reality dawned on me—I didn't even know his real name. Panic set in; I was in over my head. No one was even aware of my whereabouts. I had to make a swift exit. Suddenly, a man approached and intercepted.

"She's here with me." #Blu_Devil stood before me. *Holy hottie—this is #Blu_Devil?*

He smiled at me, held out his hand, and said, "May I?" He took my hand and led me away.

"Great! Thanks, Andy!" Gwyn said and turned to greet someone else walking through the door. He led me to a table on one side of the room. He nervously poured drinks for both of us before settling into the chair opposite mine.

"I know this is horribly awkward," he started. "I mean, what kind of person am I to expect a woman to go out on such short notice with someone she's only ever met once and barely spoken to?"

Met once? I shot him a puzzled look.

"You don't..." he started to say something, but then stopped. Gwyn started the class.

"Chi è pronto per un po' di pasta fatta in casa? Let's cook!"

Just then, a team of kitchen attendants walked through two swinging doors carrying trays of flour, eggs, salt, and water. An attendant set a tray down before us. I caught another glance at him. *So familiar.*

Gwyn addressed the room. "I hope you all came energized tonight because, let me tell you, good pasta is *work.* And don't be afraid to get your hands dirty. This is how they do it in Italy."

She demonstrated how to spread the flour onto the counter's surface and then fold in the beaten egg, adding more flour until it became a hard, malleable lump.

"We're not done yet!" she instructed. "Now we do the kneading."

I looked up to see Andy staring at me. He gave me a small, thoughtful smile and quickly looked away and back to Gwyn, who was still demonstrating.

"You'll want to work this with your table partner," Gwyn instructed. "Both of you, hands together. Pull and then bring it back into the form of a ball."

Andy's warm hand found mine, leading it toward the pasta, but instead of releasing it, he held on.

"See?" he said quietly. "Isn't this better than building a charcuterie board?"

Together, we pulled the pasta apart and then brought it back together. Our heads were down, not looking at each other. We sprinkled more flour on the countertop, rolled out the pasta, and repeated the process. At one point, our large pasta ball slipped past us and almost rolled off the table. Andy caught it just in time. We laughed—he had the best laugh.

People worked earnestly around us at their tables, pulling, kneading, and rolling. Gwyn walked around the room, helping people. One person used too much water, and their pasta was runny. Another made pasta full of lumps. She came over to our table.

"Nice work, Andy. But I wouldn't expect anything less from a *New York Times* food editor."

A what? I quickly looked up at him.

"Damn," he said under his breath. "She blew my cover." He grinned at me.

I am on a date with a New York Times food editor?

I read those columns daily. I got most of my best cooking inspirations from the Food section, including my favorite puttanesca recipe. From *this* guy?

"Is that what you do for a living?" I asked.

"Guilty." He shrugged and then reached over and wiped a sprinkling of flour off my cheek.

"I'm confused. Is that why you wanted to meet me? Because of the charcuterie reference? Because you're into food?"

Andy stopped kneading the dough and took both of my hands in his. He looked me in the eyes and said, "You know what? I hear that Urban Orchard has an amazing selection of charcuterie products. Even if you are building a *non*-charcuterie board."

Wait. It suddenly all came together for me. *Andy from Urban Orchard. Cute guy in the backward baseball cap. Mr. Duke University!*

He smiled when he saw the recognition on my face.

"But you...you had long hair. You looked *different*."

He shrugged again and said, "I cut my hair."

"But why...how did you...why am I here?" Suddenly, the last thing I cared about was the big ball of pasta dough on the table before us. Around us, people began cutting their pasta and preparing it for drying. I just stood there, unsure of what to say.

He looked at me sheepishly. "Ummm...I was behind you at the checkout line that day. I heard you talking to your friend. The checkout clerk told you to try MatchUp.com. I went home that night and created an account to meet you again. I really wanted to find you. But you never showed up online. Weeks passed, and I kept checking, but you were never there. I was getting ready just to give up, but last week, your profile popped up in my feed. I probably sound pathetic."

He came looking for me.

"But the woman. You were there with another woman," I remembered that day vividly now.

"That was my sister in town from Florida," he laughed. *Oh.*

"You look a lot different now, too. I wasn't entirely sure it was you until I saw your handle. #CharcuterieGirl. It all fell into place." Taking my hand, he looked at me shyly. "I hope you don't think I'm some kind of stalker."

Stalker? I had never encountered anything so endearing in my entire life. This guy not only looked for me, he waited for me. Speechless, I shook my head, 'No.'

He sighed with relief and asked, "Do you want to get out of here?"

I looked down at our hands, covered in flour, egg, and pasta dough.

"It's okay," he said. "There's a sink over there." He took me over to the sink, and we washed our hands and headed for the door.

"Leaving so soon, Andy?" Gwyn asked. "We haven't even started on the pasta sauces yet."

He gave her a look. She glanced over at me and gave him a knowing smile. "It's okay," she said. "It's all just flour and egg and water anyway. Have a wonderful evening!"

Outside, the cool night air surrounded us. Autumn began settling into New York. The leaves had started to turn, and although the days were still slightly warm, the evenings took on a crispness and chill. Someone, somewhere, burned a fire, filling the air with the scent of smoky wood.

No Thyme to Cook sat beside a river that ran alongside Belmont. A riverwalk lined the water, now abandoned and clear of the summer's usual crowd of tourists and walkers.

"Up for a walk?" Andy asked. I nodded, still at a loss for words.

"I hope this is okay?" He took my hand again, circling his fingers around mine and pulling me close. How many words had I actually ever exchanged with this guy? Is this safe? It's going to get dark soon. *You don't know him, Emma.* But strangely, I sensed familiarity that I couldn't pinpoint.

"I really didn't fully recognize you," he started to say. "Different now but still beautiful."

"You look different, too. You had that long hair. You were wearing a hoodie. You were talking to my best friend, Evy."

"I remember," he nodded. "You needed to build a charcuterie board, but you couldn't use nuts, meat, or cheese. And gluten-free, if I remember correctly. I'm a food editor. You were in my wheelhouse. I could have helped but felt too shy to talk to you."

"Why?" I asked. He pulled me in closer to him. The air was getting colder, and I shivered a little.

"Because a smart, beautiful woman can render this writer speechless sometimes. Tell me about you," he said.

We walked, and I told him about my kids. Jack. Kiki. OneBank. The horrible divorce.

"I think the best thing that has come out of all this has been meeting my best friend. She has been my rock. My sounding board. When everyone else made me feel alone in the world, she made me feel like I mattered. I don't know what I would do without her."

"Hold on to that friendship," he said. "Friendships like that are worth more than gold." He squeezed my hand and rubbed his thumb over the back of mine, sending a bolt of adrenaline through me.

The sun started to set. We walked in silence for a bit longer, listening to the ducks quacking and splashing in the water. They would be heading south soon. Then he told me about himself.

"I graduated from Duke University with a degree in Business. I immediately took a job with one of the Big Five consulting firms in the city. The partners worked the new associates crazy hours. I had no life back then. It was all about the money and the push to make partner. And it was cutthroat. One day, my best friend at work began spreading rumors about me because he knew they were getting ready to do the promotions to senior associate. I was passed over, and he got the job after all the hard work I had put in. That was when I decided that wasn't the life for me."

"But a food editor? That's a bit of a transition."

"Well, I had a minor in Journalism. I've always liked to write. I was in the middle of New York City, surrounded by every type of restaurant imaginable. So, I started going to restaurants and writing reviews for a local paper. At one point, the *New York Times* food editor contacted me and asked me to freelance. Then, they offered me a full-time job. I guess you can say that I've worked my way up through the ranks to Senior Editor.

I may not make as much money as my old friends at the consulting firm, but I love what I do."

Lights started to go on inside the homes lining the river walk. A half-moon rose over the water. We continued to walk and talk.

"Kids?" I asked him.

"I have a twelve-year-old daughter named Sara. She lives on the West Coast with her mother. She comes here during the summer and some holidays. I really wish I could see her more. I miss her. I mean, with technology, I do get to talk to her often. We video call every Sunday, or she'll call if something comes up that she wants to tell me about."

"That's the thing about divorce," I said. "It steals time away from the people who matter the most to you. But on the flip side, it makes room for new people to come into your life."

He stopped walking and turned to face me.

"Yes," he said. "Even if you have to lurk on an online dating site for a while to wait for them."

He reached over and brushed a strand of hair out of my eyes. He started to say something but then stopped himself. *Is he going to kiss me?* My heart raced.

He paused for a moment and then continued. "Actually, are you hungry? We didn't really get to eat dinner. I know a few good places.".

"I'm sure you do, Mr. *New York Times* food editor!

I'm still up for pasta if you are," I replied, relieved. The moment passed.

"There's a little place right down here on the river," he said. "We can walk to it."

We walked to Mama Scallopinis, a small family-owned establishment crowded with little round tables holding big jugs of table wine. Through the window to the kitchen, I could see pasta drying on racks. The kitchen staff chattered loudly amongst themselves, putting together orders. Savory smells of garlic, tomato, and basil blended into simmering pasta sauces wafted from the kitchen.

"The thing about this place," he told me, "Is that they import these big jugs of wine right from Tuscany. I visited Italy last year to do a news story and noticed this same brand on the restaurant tables. It seems like it wouldn't be any good because if it comes in these big jugs, but tastes better than any bottled wine you would get from California. It's just fresher."

He poured two glasses of wine, and I took a sip. He was right. I reflected on Brian, Mommy Dearest, and the $450 bottle of wine at the upscale restaurant downtown. I would take this table wine over that any day of the week.

A man emerged from the kitchen wearing a food-splattered apron. He placed two paper menus before us and read us the specials. Andy studied the menu for a minute and looked at me. "Mind if I order for us?"

"Go for it!" I nodded.

"We'll start with the pasta de fagioli soup. Then I think we'll each try the ragu. Creme de brulee for dessert." *My favorite.*

"Excellent choice," the waiter said. "Tonight's ragu is a fresh batch cooked by Mama herself."

He handed the menus back to the waiter, and I watched him, thinking back to our first encounter at Urban Orchard. Now I get why he looked so familiar. He saw me staring and grinned. My face blushed warm and I quickly looked away.

"Sorry, didn't mean to stare."

"Stare away," he said, and picked up my hand. He softly traced the back of it with his thumb. "And tell me about that disastrous charcuterie board."

I told him the story of the ill-fated day of the sock drive and Naryan Patel's broken arm. We sipped wine and shared stories. He told me about trips he had taken around the world, doing news stories on different culinary regions. I told him about my OneBank days and the places I traveled when the company was just starting. The waiter brought our food. I devoured the ragu, not even caring that I spilled some on my shirt.

"Here, let me show you something." Andy picked up my fork, did a perfect swirl into the pasta, and then lifted it to my mouth. "Just a little something I learned in Tuscany," he told me.

We talked until all the food was gone and the plates were cleared. The restaurant emptied, and the server stood patiently in the kitchen's doorway, waiting to give us our check.

"I think he wants to go home," I told Andy.

"Yeah, but I suppose we should let the poor guy get out of here." He motioned for the waiter and paid the check.

"Come on, I'll walk you back to the cooking school."

Outside, the air turned very chilly. We held hands and walked in silence, taking in the night. I loved New York in the fall. The half-moon rose higher in the sky, making swirly light patterns on the water.

"I'm parked right over there," I pointed to my SUV.

"I'm around back," he said. We stood looking at each other, unsure of what to say.

"Can I see you again?" He brought his hand to my face and brushed a strand of hair out of my eyes. He stared into them and held my gaze. "I had an amazing time tonight. I don't want to say goodbye to you."

"That would be great." I couldn't help but smile up at him.

"Great!" he said, taking out his cell phone. "Give me your number, and I'll text you so you have my number, too. Is next Saturday good?"

Next Saturday fell on my weekend to have the kids, but I could call in a favor from Evy to help out.

"Saturday would be great. We can work out the details this week."

He put my phone number into his. He grabbed my hand, squeezed it, leaned over, and kissed my cheek.

"What a night," he smiled before turning and walking away.

I made my way to the car, rummaging through the chaos inside my purse in search of my buried keys. *Ugh. I need to clean this thing out.* I turned to see Andy running towards me.

"I forgot something," he said.

"What?"

"This," he replied, breathless.

He gently placed both hands on my face, lifted it towards his, leaned in, and put his soft lips next to mine. He hesitated a moment and then kissed me, slowly at first but then with more intention, pulling me closer. I felt heat spread through every inch of me.

When he stepped away, I glanced down, cheeks flushed, then peeked back up at him with a crooked smile. "So... do we pretend that didn't happen, or are we just skipping straight to the part where we text each other way too much?"

A big smile spread across his face. "I don't think I can forget that just happened." He stepped away, looked into my eyes, and whispered, "Emma, you are beautiful inside and out."

As he turned, I watched him walk away and disappear into the night air. With my head spinning, I got into my car and sat for a few minutes, watching the moonlight dance on the water.

Bewitched.

♥ City Lights ♥

Ding!

ANDY

Good morning, #Charcuterie Girl. Just your friendly neighborhood stalker here.

Me:

Good morning, #Blu_Devil. Kiss me like that again, and I'll be the one stalking you.

Andy:

> Still up for Saturday?

Me:

> Yes! Where are you thinking?

Andy:

> I'm still working out those details.
> Needed to make sure I didn't
> scare you off first. I will text
> you by the middle of this week.
> Have an amazing day, Emma.

Me:

> You too. Looking forward to it.

Later that morning, I entered Evy's condo to pick her up for one of our final training runs. She was in the kitchen, her back to me, tidying up the dishes. I sat at the kitchen table, waiting for her to finish. She hesitated when she turned around to speak and shot me a curious look.

"Why do you have a big dumb grin on your face?"

I shrugged, trying to suppress my smile.

"Emm...what happened? Did something happen? Spill!" She put the dishcloth down and sat across from me, studying me like a curious insect. "Something happened."

"Do you remember the day we went to Urban Orchard to put together the charcuterie board for the sock drive at the kid's school?"

She nodded. "Yeah, I think so."

"I came around a corner, and you were talking to a guy. Do you remember him?"

"Oh yeah! Mr. Duke University. The cute guy with long hair. Why are you still smiling?" She squinted her eyes at me.

"That was #Blu_Devil."

"Blu, who?"

"#Blu_Devil. The guy who messaged me from MatchUp.com the night of the speed dating event."

She thought for a moment, and then her eyes grew huge.

"Seriously? That guy? No way!" She stopped and narrowed her eyes at me, waiting for an explanation. "And you went on a date and didn't tell me? Do you realize how dangerous that is? He could've been a serial killer!"

She smacked me with her dish towel.

I couldn't help but smile. I shook my head. "Not a serial killer. Do you know that he overheard us talking that day at the checkout when the clerk told me about MatchUp.com? He actually went home that night and opened an account to see if I would join. He waited for months."

Her eyes grew wide again. "He tracked you down?"

"He said he didn't know how else to find me again. He said he also went back to Urban Orchard a few times, hoping we would be there. Then he just kept checking his MatchUp.com account to see if I would appear."

She sat for a minute, studying me. "Well, how was it? Where did you go?"

I told her about the cooking class, the walk by the moonlit river, and the quaint little Italian restaurant with the amazing food.

"You know, this is how it's supposed to work, right?" she said thoughtfully. "This sounds like when I met Ben. He waited for me, too."

"Well, I don't know if I would go that far. You two are soulmates."

"Yeah, okay, then wipe that stupid grin off your face. You kissed him, didn't you?"

I didn't answer her.

"You did!" she said. "Wow, I honestly thought there weren't any good ones out there anymore."

"Well, it's only been *one* date. Time will tell. We're

going out again next Saturday. Speaking of which…"

"Yes, I will come over. I miss the kids anyway. This is exciting! I knew something good would happen to one of us. Just a feeling. Where are you going?"

"I'm not sure yet. He said he was still working out the details. Did I tell you he is a senior *New York Times* food editor? He has traveled all over the world doing culinary pieces. And that long hair is gone. He cut it short, which was why I couldn't place him."

"This is such a crazy story," Evy said. "When do I get to meet him? Or should I say meet him *again*?"

"Let's just see how date number two goes, shall we? Alright, let's get out of here. Only seven miles to go today. Feeling energized?" Evy groaned and followed me to the door.

For date number two, Andy texted and said we would go somewhere somewhat formal but to dress comfortably. I consulted my expert in the field of dressing to impress. I met Mona at The Luxe Thrifter.

"Just wow," Mona said as we searched through the clothes racks. "I love every bit of this story. After all this online dating nonsense, maybe your prince charming has been out there all along—lurking in the digital bushes. Ready to *pounce*. Is he cute?"

"Adorable. He has the kindest face. The best smile."

Mona sighed. "Well then, let's find you something to wear. Does he have a brother? A cute gay male friend?"

I groaned.

"What?" she said, looking innocent. "It doesn't hurt to *ask*."

After an hour of trying on outfits, we settled on a simple light blue dress, which Mona said complemented my eyes.

"Sometimes less is more. You don't need much, honey. You could wear a burlap sack and get the men."

She gave me a big hug before we parted ways. "Call me with the after-report," she said. "I want to hear all about it."

When Evy arrived to babysit on Saturday night, I informed her that Andy had texted an address for us to meet downtown. She said she would call me during the date "just in case."

"You don't really know him," she cautioned. "And I'm glad you're meeting him there. It's too soon to give out your address." She walked me to the taxi, waiting outside.

"Have an amazing time," she said as Myla grabbed her arm and pulled her back to the house. She wanted to play with Benny.

The taxi pulled up in front of a building in the down-town business district. It was Saturday night, and the streets were deserted. I exited the car and stared up-wards at a tall building, double-checking the address. *Is this the right place?*

All the street-level businesses, which usually catered to the midday working crowd, had closed for the day. I pulled the building's door handle and walked into a large, dimly lit, deserted reception area.

"Hello?" I said, my voice echoing in the massive foyer. "Anybody here?"

Silence.

What the hell? I started to panic. *Am I in the right building?* I picked up my cell phone to double-check the address that Andy sent me. At that moment, the elevator opened, and a man in a suit stepped out.

"Emma?" he inquired.

"Yes, that's me."

"Excellent," he said. "Right this way." He ushered me into the elevator. *Now is my last chance to turn and run.* "Andy has been expecting you."

I stepped into the elevator, and he pushed the but-ton to the top floor. We rode the elevator all the way up to the rooftop. The doors opened onto the building's terrace. I looked around, unsure of what I was seeing. Somebody had set up a table in the middle of the rooftop, surrounded by lighted torches. In the corner of the terrace, an acoustic singer strummed a guitar and sang softly. Waitstaff bustled about. *Where am I? And more importantly, where is my date?*

I saw him standing by the edge of the terrace, looking out at the city's skyline. He wore a sports jacket and tie. When he turned around and saw me, his face lit up. *Oh my God. That smile. How can this guy just look at me and do this to me?* He approached and took my hand.

"What is all of this?"

"Well, one of the perks of being a food editor is that new restaurants want you to review the ambiance, service, and food before they open."

"But this isn't a restaurant. It's a rooftop."

He laughed, "No, the actual restaurant is on the main floor. I thought we'd have a better view from up here. The owner agreed to do this for me."

He took my hand and walked me over to the terrace edge. "Look at this view."

As the sun set, the city spanned out on the horizon, a scattering of lights and sounds far below. In the distance, the world teemed with life. From up here, it looked like a peaceful painting. Andy and I stood and watched it in silence. His warm hand squeezed mine.

"Sir, your first course is ready." A waiter stood behind

us and motioned us to the table. We sat down, and he brought over two drinks. Another brought out a large wooden board and removed the cover.

"A charcuterie board?" I laughed.

"A charcuterie board for my charcuterie girl."

I didn't know what to say to him. I could only utter, "Thank you."

The musician sang an old Ed Sheeran song. Last week's half-moon was now three-quarters full and rising over the skyline. Andy had orchestrated quite a backdrop.

I moved the food on my plate around with my fork, not looking at him. "I've never been treated so kindly before. This food—this setting—it's all just phenomenal."

His face lit up. "Well, we aim to please. I'll be sure to pass that along to the restaurant owner. He wants a good review." He took my hand. "I'm just glad you're here."

Butterflies again. I started to wonder if I could even eat. My cell phone rang.

"Hey, Ev. Yes, all is good."

"Damn, girl. I can actually *hear* you smiling through the phone," she laughed. "Can't wait to get the scoop. Gotta run. Myla is trying to dress up Benny. He doesn't seem to like it too much." I could hear Benny barking in the background. She hung up.

"Your parole officer?" Andy joked.

"No, it's Evy, my wingman. She always calls when I go on dates to make sure I'm safe. She even makes me use a safe word."

Andy nodded. "I understand. Smart move. I hear a lot of people use the word 'Sasquatch.'"

The waiter came out, cleared away our dishes, and brought out round two. He set down a filet mignon topped with garlic aioli, paired with a baked potato, lemon, and parmesan-crusted Brussels sprouts. My steak knife gently sliced through the tender beef.

"Wow, I've tried a lot of steak over the years, but this one is probably one of the best."

He took out his phone and typed some notes into it. Then he pulled out a camera and took a few pictures. "Sorry, I've got to take a few notes for the article." I watched closely as he skillfully worked his magic.

We spent the rest of the dinner talking about our jobs. I always thought information technology was a boring topic that didn't interest people, but he seemed genuinely intrigued by it.

"So, OneBank was a big success for you. What would you do next if you had the opportunity and could start all over?"

"Well, you need a lot of money to start a technology company, which I'll never have again, working for the government. But if I could? I thought of an idea one night, not that long ago. I was watching TV with my children, and my son wanted to watch something on one of the streaming services. Meanwhile, my daughter was in another room asking me to put a movie on for her on a different TV. Every time I pulled up a streaming service, it prompted me for my password. I was juggling several remotes and getting very frustrated. And then I thought, 'Why can't there be just *one* place to manage all these streaming services and passwords? One application that can store everything and instantly sign you in?' I think I would call it something like Simple Stream."

"Yes! One remote, one sign-in. What a great idea!"

The waiters cleared our plates and brought dessert, wine, and a tray of tiny desserts to sample. *Good thing I've got a race coming up.* I mentally counted the calories in all that dessert. Andy took his fork and scooped up a bite of cheesecake and lifted it to my mouth. The singer serenaded us with another song.

"Dance with me," he said. He took my hand and led me over to the edge of the terrace. The city was now ablaze with tiny lights. The temperature dropped, and I shivered in the night air. He wrapped his arms around my waist and put his forehead next to mine, looking into my eyes as we slowly danced.

After the wait staff left the terrace, just the two of us and the singer remained. He lifted my chin to his face and kissed me sweetly and gently. I lay my head on his chest, taking in all of him and feeling every bit of him next to me.

I don't know how much time passed—or what songs the singer played. I was in another place, dancing and at one with this perfect human being. I checked my watch; the evening had slipped away.

"Do you have to go?" he asked, frowning.

"Yes, I'm sorry. Evy has my kids. I don't want to burden her too much. I think I need to get my ride."

I pulled up my taxi app and requested a driver. The next one was ten minutes away. "Thank you so much for all of this. I meant it when I said it. No one has ever done anything this thoughtful for me."

He took my hands in his. "You don't have to thank me. But you do have to promise to see me again."

"Definitely."

We walked to the elevator, and the door closed. I stood across from him, neither of us speaking. The elevator started to descend. I gave him a small smile—a deceptive gesture, given that my heart was pounding inside of my chest. He was staring at me intently, eyes burning. I held his gaze, unable to look away. *What was happening?*

He rushed to my side of the elevator and pinned my arms against the wall, kissing me so intensely that my knees buckled. With his other hand, he grabbed the small of my back. His body pressed hard against mine.

I didn't resist. He dropped his lips to my neck and then back to my lips, pulling me in closer to him and kissing me harder.

The elevator continued to descend. Without looking away, he pushed the stop button, pausing the elevator mid-course. He released my arms, and my hands encircled his neck, meeting his embrace. We were completely entwined, completely as one. I melted into him.

After a few moments, he stepped back and brought his hand to my face, his fingers gently tracing my cheek. His thumb brushed my lower lip, and he looked into my eyes. He was breathing heavily, looking at me with an expression I had never seen from any other man. This wasn't lust. This was something else. *A connection.*

Pulling back, he smoothed my hair and laid his head against mine. He pushed the elevator button, and it dinged downward again as we stood together, still wrapped in each other. Our breathing slowed. He straightened and took a step back. I was lightheaded, reeling from the encounter.

"*Damn.*" He stared at me, his eyes still blazing.

"I second that," I smiled, holding his stare. The elevator door opened. I could see the taxi waiting outside. He held my hand, unwilling to let go.

"My taxi is here," I said, trying to pull away. He squeezed my hand even harder. After a moment, he sighed and said, "Alright, can I call you tomorrow?"

I narrowed my eyes at him and smiled, "What, are you stalking me?"

He grinned. "Goodbye, Emma."

"Goodbye, Andy."

I walked away, desperately wanting to turn around, but kept going, out into the cold fall night air. I climbed into the taxi, still breathless.

Text to Evy:

> On my way back.

Evy:

> How did it go?

Me:

> Whoa.

Evy:

> I want every single last detail when you get here. All of it. Hurry back. *Friends* is coming on.

Me:

> Be there soon.

Stockholm Syndrome

My eyes peeked open, and I saw the bedroom ceiling fan circling overhead, swirling shadows. The sun filtered through the window blinds, a faint light that would soon grow brighter. My day would have to start, and I would have to move, but right now, I could lie here and dream.

I closed my eyes again as my mind roused in and out of the fog of sleep, memories of last night dancing in and out of my consciousness like snippets of a story I hadn't quite put together yet. Dinner on a rooftop, the New York City skyline, the elevator ride, and *that kiss*. I dreamily pieced it all together and put myself back in those moments. Everything felt warm and perfect and right.

My mind drifted deeper again, and another memory seared through my awareness. I was jolted, wide awake. I sat straight up, and my eyes flew open. *Evy.*

My heart pounded in my chest as I remembered— Evy in my basement bathroom, her ghost-white face lying against the seat of the toilet. Vomit in the bowl. She flushed it quickly. I suspected that I saw blood.

When I got home from my date, I opened the front door and noticed she was missing. The kids were asleep in bed, and a movie flickered on the TV in the family room. Everything felt ordinary until I spotted the basement door open. I headed down and found Benny pacing. Then I noticed the bathroom door wide open, and she was on the floor, gripping the toilet bowl. She looked up at me and quickly straightened herself.

"I'm fine," she said. "My stomach is just a little upset. I didn't want to wake up the kids."

I helped her to her feet and guided her to the kitchen, offering her sips of water until her stomach calmed down. She said she was tired and just wanted to go home.

Fully awake now, I couldn't shake the feeling. *Something was wrong.* I read my cell phone messages from last night.

Text to Evy:

> Are you home? Are you sure you're okay? You scared me.

Evy:

> I'm okay. It's this thyroid medicine. It's upsetting my stomach.

Me:

> Please go back to the doctor next week. They can adjust it or maybe give you something else.

Evy:

> I will. I promise.

Me:

> I'm going to call you in the morning. Call me if you need anything. My phone is right next to my bed.

It was too early to call her. *She's sick again.* Why can't these doctors get her medication right? I was determined. After the race, I will help her get well—maybe find a nutritionist specializing in thyroid conditions. This is probably an easy fix.

Text from Andy:

ANDY

> Good morning!

A link to Aerosmith's *Love in an Elevator* '80s video popped up on my screen. I groaned. *He's such a mess.*

I heard Myla approaching down the hallway. In the doorway, clad in her nightgown, she rubbed her eyes sleepily. Her curly chestnut brown hair, disheveled and wild, framed her face. She climbed into bed to snuggle.

"Did you have fun with Aunt Evy last night?"

"Mmm hmm. I love Aunt Evy. She lets Austin and me eat whatever we want. I tried to dress Benny, but he didn't like it very much. He wouldn't let me put my shirt over his head. Can we get a dog, Mommy?"

I twirled a lock of her long, curly hair around my finger. She looked so much like Jack.

"Maybe someday," I said. "Right now, I'm sure Aunt Evy will let you borrow Benny whenever you want."

She sighed. "Yeah, he's the *best* dog. Will you make some pancakes?" She climbed out of bed and pulled on my arm. "I'm starving to *death*."

"Yes, go wake up your brother for breakfast."

After breakfast, I checked in on Evy.

"Any better this morning?"

"Yes, thank God. I stopped taking the medicine. I think I just needed to clear it all out of my system. I will probably skip running for a few days, though."

"Of course! We're so close to it now. Better to rest up and be ready."

"How was the date?"

"That setup on the rooftop...so romantic. Did I tell you they brought out a charcuterie board?"

Evy laughed. "Seriously?"

"Yes, he said it was a charcuterie board for his charcuterie girl. That's either the cheesiest thing anyone has ever said to me or the most endearing."

"I'd go with endearing. Don't overthink it."

"I'm glad you're feeling better. Seeing you like that was upsetting."

"I think it's just a process of elimination with these medications. We'll check that one off as a big fat *no*. I'll see my doctor next week."

"Good! I will hold you accountable to that."

Ding! Text from Andy:

ANDY

You didn't like the elevator ride?

Oh no! I never responded to him.

"Evy, I've gotta run. Get some rest today!"

"I will. Thanks for checking in on me."

Did I like the elevator ride? *I can't stop thinking about it.*

Text to Andy:

> Seriously—Aerosmith? You
> are so old school.

Andy:

> Good morning, beautiful. When can
> I see you again? I need to do a story
> next weekend about a farm west of
> here. Would you like to go with me?

Me:

> A farm?

Andy:

> We're doing a farm-to-table
> series, and this place gets a lot
> of hype. Thought I would check
> it out. Are you free? It'll be a
> day trip. (Please say yes.)

Next weekend was our last chance to train before
the half-marathon. I should be focusing on that. Evy
and I have missed a lot of runs lately. But I couldn't
help myself. I wanted to see him again.

Me:

> Okay, but don't keep me out too late.

Andy:

> Can I pick you up? Or do you
> want to meet somewhere?

Me:

> 421 Browncroft Boulevard

Andy:

> Excellent. See you on
> Saturday at noon.

Andy arrived on time, pulling up in front of my house at noon on Saturday. I greeted him at the door.

"Beautiful house," he said, looking around. "Big!"

"Yeah, and a big mortgage to go with it," I sighed. "I have no idea how my divorce is going to turn out. But for now, it's home."

"My ex-wife, Jenny, kept the house after we divorced. I insisted. Our split was hard enough on my daughter, Sara. I didn't want to make things any more difficult for her. But then Jenny decided that both of us being on the East Coast was too close for comfort, and she moved away anyway." I could hear the sadness in his voice.

"Are these your kids?" He stood before the pictures hanging in the hallway. "Your son looks just like you. And your daughter is adorable. Beautiful family."

"Thank you." I looked at the pictures of Austin and Myla, wondering what they would think of Andy if they met him. Maybe someday.

"Well," he said, "Ready to go? We're going to Emerson Farms, which is about an hour west of here. It's a beautiful day. Okay to go topless?"

I narrowed my eyes at him, teasing. "I mean...it's a nice day and all...but I'd prefer to keep my shirt on. This is only our third date."

He laughed. "I drive a Jeep. I can put the top back on it if you don't want the wind in your face."

"No, that actually sounds great. Let me grab a hat." I pulled a baseball hat out of my hall closet and tucked my hair inside of it. "Ready!"

I walked with him to his Jeep, and he held the door open for me. "You take over as DJ while I drive. What's your favorite kind of music?"

"I like a little bit of everything, but mostly old school tunes...classic rock. You know...Aerosmith. Stuff like that." He grinned in response.

I tuned the satellite radio to the classic rock station. Fifteen minutes later, we were outside of Belmont's city limits. We turned onto a two-lane country road, where the landscape opened. Sprawling farms and cottage homes replaced the congested planned communities behind us. The mountains loomed in the distance.

Andy sang along to a Journey song on the radio—completely off-key and nowhere near Steve Perry's high notes in *Don't Stop Believing.* It was a bit cringeworthy but also irresistibly adorable. Thinking back over the years, I couldn't remember ever hearing Jack sing—not even once.

Forty-five minutes later, we arrived at Emerson Farms.

"Wow! Look at this place," I said, looking around at the bustling farm.

The farm spread out over several acres and included various barns, a restaurant, and a gift shop. A corn maze stood next to a massive pumpkin patch. Beyond that, fields stretched on in the distance. Men wearing wide-brimmed hats carried people to the corn maze on horse-drawn, hay-covered carts. Children ran through the pumpkin patch—their parents chasing them. Behind the farm, the mountains spanned out in the distance, a watercolor backdrop of yellows, oranges, and reds.

"I can see why it gets so much hype. I don't even know if we'll find a place to park." We circled the parking lot a few times until a spot opened. People milled about everywhere. Andy got out of the Jeep and opened my car door.

"Where first?"

"Let's check out the gift shop."

We entered a charming country store packed with shoppers. In the food section, canning jars filled with jellies, pickles, and relishes, all made on the premises, lined the shelves. Fresh-baked rolls, cakes, and muffins were displayed on a table. A portly gray-haired woman stood behind a candy counter filled with caramels, assorted fudge, and candy apples. She packed a bag with wax soda bottles for a little boy.

I looked around and said, "Oh, cool! A Christmas shop."

A doorway led to a room filled with Christmas trees and holiday decorations. I picked up a snow globe with a miniature farm inside, turned it upside down, and then back over, watching the tiny flakes inside gently fall to the bottom. Through the snow globe, I could see Andy watching me from the other side of the room. I made my way over to him and held it up.

"Let's stop back in here before we leave. Myla and Austin would love this."

"Yes, ma'am. Feel like doing more exploring?

I nodded. "Let's try the corn maze."

We left the store and made our way to the corn maze entrance.

Andy nudged me into the maze. "You go first and get a head start. I'll see if I can find you," He kissed my forehead and said, "See you on the inside."

I walked into the corn maze. The tall stalks towered over the dirt path beneath. Children squealed with laughter somewhere within the maze. I took a left, then a right, walking a few feet before hitting a dead end. I turned around and retraced my steps, this time going right and then left. Long rows followed short ones, but there was no rhyme or reason to any of it.

Completely disoriented, I tried different paths only to find dead ends. I walked and turned corners, but the trail seemed to lead to nowhere. I glanced down at my watch. Twenty minutes had passed, and I still hadn't found my way out. Then I heard someone whisper on the other side of the wall of the stalks, "This way."

"Andy? Is that you?"

All I could hear was the rustling of stalks and distant voices. I rounded a corner, heading toward the sound, only to find no one there. I kept turning corner after corner, but everything looked identical. *I can't believe I'm lost in a corn maze!*

A small child ran past me, his father grabbing his hand.

"Do you know the way out?" I yelped, trying to mask the panic in my voice.

"I was tracking okay, but this little guy keeps running

away, and now I'm lost too. I heard someone say to keep making two lefts and then a right. Good luck."

I made two lefts, then right—another dead end. Panic gripped my chest. The tall, willowy corn branches blew in the wind around me, closing me in. I could almost hear Delores from Belmont General in my mind asking, "How are we feeling right now?" *Well, Delores, I'm claustrophobic,* and *we* are about to have a panic attack. *Help!*

Someone approached from behind. Before I could turn, he placed an arm around my waist, pulling me close and covering my eyes with his other hand. He whispered in my ear.

"Come quietly, and no one gets hurt."

Relief washed over me.

"Andy!"

"Shhhhh! You're being kidnapped. Don't make another sound."

I suppressed a smile. "Fine, I'll go quietly. Just get me out of here."

He pulled a bandana out of his pocket and tied it over my eyes, rendering me sightless. He then took my hand and guided me on a long, twisting path.

"Hmm...I think we're lost," he teased.

"This isn't funny!"

His voice grew serious. "Don't question the motives of your captor," he joked.

He continued to lead me through the maze.

"Left," he instructed me. "Now, right. Keep going straight."

We walked for a few more minutes.

"Are you going to let me go or not? I will scream, you know."

"Shhh...almost there."

We stopped walking. He wrapped his arm around me from behind, leaned down, and kissed my neck, tracing small embraces to my ear and back. I rested my head against him, not wanting to pull away.

"You know, people get put away for kidnapping. Sometimes for years," I murmured.

"Stockholm Syndrome. In time, you'll fall in love with your captor," he whispered in return, still kissing my neck.

He removed the bandana from my eyes and I blinked into the sunlight. The corn maze was a short distance behind us. He had led us through the maze to the other side. I turned.

"Wow!" A field filled with yellow sunflowers spanned out before us.

"Come on, hostage. I'm not done abducting you yet."

He took my hand and led me into the field of tall sunflowers and to a clearing. A checkered blanket lay spread out next to a small picnic basket. *A picnic in a field of sunflowers—he stops at nothing to impress.*

"I see that you don't do well in tight spaces. I hope this is okay."

I punched him in the arm.

He ducked away and said, "I'm serious! Claustrophobia is no joke."

I tried to punch him again, but he caught my arm mid-strike and gently wrapped it around my back.

"Come here," he said, pulling me close and kissing me. My legs stopped cooperating with my brain, and I suddenly felt wobbly—*treacherous legs.*

When I was a teenager, I read in my mother's paperback romance novels about women who swooned, and here I was swooning in a field full of sunflowers, with a hot guy and a picnic basket—and the world in all its Autumn glory. I was Emma Davis, starring in her own romance novel, *Love in Full Bloom.*

He sat down on the blanket and pulled me down beside him. I watched as he unpacked snacks from the basket and arranged them on paper plates.

"Hungry?"

"You set this whole thing up, didn't you? Kidnapping a poor, defenseless, claustrophobic woman in a corn maze." I took the plate from him and pretended to sulk.

"I really am here to do a write-up on farm-to-table dining, but I had this crazy idea last night to make this into a picnic for two. I just really wanted to be alone with you. If at any point you don't feel comfortable, just let me know. This is just date number three, after all."

"Okay, but next time I press charges."

"You know, you can pull the corn maze up on GPS maps to find your way out. I did." He blinked at me innocently.

"That's cheating," I said and threw a cracker at him. We ate in silence for a few minutes. I took in the mountains around us. So many beautiful colors. New York City and its suburbs were so busy and noisy that I quickly forgot that places like this existed.

Andy set his plate aside and lay back, gazing at the puffy clouds drifting across the sky. I stretched out beside him, and he took my hand. We lay there in silence for a long time before I finally spoke.

"Thank you."

He turned and leaned up on one elbow, looking down on me.

"For?"

"Waiting for me."

He grinned at me and joked, "It's not like I had a choice. You were building that unfortunate charcuterie board. I knew I had to track you down to save the world from future culinary disasters."

I closed my eyes, listening to the noise from the farm in the distance. The sun blazed brightly overhead.

When I opened them again, I saw Andy watching me with the sweetest expression.

"Just so you know—you were worth waiting for."

"Come here," I said, and pulled him on top of me. We lay together among the sunflowers, discovering each other. He grabbed the back of his t-shirt and pulled it off, then softly ran his hands down my body while continuing to kiss me.

"You have such a beautiful body," he murmured between kisses.

Beautiful body. Damn. *He really just said that.* I held back tears. *Do not cry.*

His hand traced the outline of me, gently touching every part of me as if he was committing it to memory.

"Daddy! What's that?" A small voice called out as tiny footsteps grew closer, pounding the earth with intention, quickly running towards us. "Daddy! Why doesn't he have a shirt on?"

Panicked, I looked up to see the lost father I had encountered in the maze, still chasing after his toddler. *Oh shit.*

"I'm so sorry," he stuttered. "He ran right out of the maze. I, uh, um...we'll just go. He's a quick one." He looked around at our picnic and Andy's shirt in the flower bed. Smirking, he leaned down and scooped up his child. "So sorry to interrupt. We're out of here."

Andy and I looked at each other and laughed. I threw his shirt at him. "I guess that moment is over."

"For now. I suppose I have an article to research. There's a restaurant here. Let's go check it out."

We packed up the picnic basket and headed back toward the farm. Once at the restaurant, Andy and I sat by a window overlooking the mountain skyline.

"The goal of farm-to-table is to source everything from the farm itself, cutting out the middleman. It's also seasonal, so the menu will change based on what is growing at the time. We're in root vegetable season right now," he explained as I looked over the menu.

The waitress brought a field greens salad topped with feta, apples, and cranberries. The next course included butternut squash soup sprinkled with toasted pumpkin seeds. Chicken pot pie made with leeks and thyme rounded out the meal.

"I'm going to put on weight if I keep dating you," I sighed as the waitress brought homemade apple pie and ice cream.

"I think you worry about your weight too much," he said cautiously. "You're in amazing shape, and besides, I've always thought you were attractive. Try the pie. I need an unbiased opinion. Otherwise, I can't do my job properly."

He dipped his fork into the pie and ice cream and brought it to my lips. "Come on...help a guy out."

I took a bite. The slightly salty, flaky crust surrounded a tart and sweet cinnamon-infused pie filling, perfectly paired with the cold, creamy vanilla ice cream. I grabbed my fork. He watched in amusement as I finished my whole piece in a matter of minutes.

"I'll note that as two thumbs up from the lady critic."

"If I could fit one more bite of food into my body, I'd eat your pie too."

"OK, I'll give this place a decent write-up. Ready to head back?"

I nodded. We had spent the entire afternoon at the farm, and now the sun was just starting to set over the mountains.

"Top up or down?" he asked as we approached his Jeep. The night air was starting to cool.

"I'd prefer to keep it down, but I'm afraid I might get cold."

"Here," he said, pulling a hoodie from the back seat. "Put this on."

I pulled it over my head, taking in his light sweat and aftershave scent. I pulled my hair back into the baseball cap, and we drove away from the farm, listening to a radio cast of classic rock songs. As the sun set, shiny stars dotted the sky. The lights from the city grew brighter and closer. Finally, he pulled into my driveway.

He picked up my hand and held it for a moment

before saying, "Thanks for coming today. Sorry, things got a little crazy with the corn maze. I had counted on you going in first to give myself enough time to set up the picnic, but I didn't think you'd get lost."

"It's okay. You found me. Well, abducted me. Maybe you'll get lucky, and I really will fall in love with my captor." I traced my finger along the edges of his hoodie, not looking up.

He was quiet for a moment and then said, "That is the hope."

Now what? Do I invite him in? Is it too soon? What if he wants to come in and I don't invite him? I don't want to reject him. How many dates is enough? There should be rules!

"I was going to ask you if I can come in, but I don't want to overstep."

Oh. A twinge of disappointment overcame me.

He continued, "I think something is happening between us, and I want to take time to really get to know you. I don't want to ruin things by moving too fast."

I attempted a small smile. "Yeah, I agree," I said when everything inside of me most certainly did *not* agree.

He kissed me again and then wrapped me in a hug. "When can I see you again?"

"The half-marathon is next weekend. Evy and I will be busy all day on Saturday, and then we'll need to rest on Sunday."

He seemed disappointed at first. He frowned as he thought momentarily, then gave me a little smile. "That's okay; it gives me a little time to plan our next date."

At my front door, Andy waited until I found my keys. Once inside, he pulled me into another hug. I wanted him to stay so badly, and I know he did, too.

He kissed me again and said, "I'll call you tomorrow."

"Wait! Your hoodie."

"You hold on to it. I'll get it back from you the next time I see you."

I watched him walk away and get into his Jeep. He pulled out of the driveway and drove away. As I shut the front door, I leaned against it and closed my eyes, taking in the day. I pulled the hoodie to my face and breathed in the scent of him.

When I opened my eyes again, I saw a snow globe sitting on the hallway table. He must have gone back into the gift shop. *He must have slipped it there when I wasn't looking.* I picked it up, carried it upstairs, and put it on my bedside table. I lay in my bed and turned it over, watching the tiny flakes fall onto the little farm inside. I sent Andy a text message.

Me:

> I'm watching the snowfall.

Andy:

> You found your present?

Me:

> So sweet. Thank you.

Andy:

> Anything for my Charcuterie Girl.

I sighed. As the last flakes fell inside the globe, I closed my eyes and drifted off to sleep.

CHAPTER 25

The Race

The Belmont Civic Center's gymnasium bustled with people. Long lines formed with race participants waiting to pick up their race packets. A small makeshift store stood at one corner of the gym with race swag, shirts, hoodies.

"Now what?" Evy asked, looking around the room. "This is a lot of people."

"Packets are arranged by last name. The D and H lines are right over there. I'll see you in a few."

I joined my line, excited. Years passed since I ran a race, and I had forgotten about the excitement and anticipation of it all. Tomorrow is the day. I never thought I'd get back to this place.

"Emma Davis," I said when I reached the front of the

line. A young, athletic guy sitting at the table searched through a bin and said, "Here you go. Number 1502. Good luck tomorrow."

I took the packet and looked around. Evy was still waiting in her line, and I joined her.

"I still can't believe you talked me into this." She picked up her packet and looked through it. She held up her race number. "Where does this go?"

"You'll pin it to the front of your shirt. There's one for your back too. When you pass through the finish line, it will be scanned and then you can later find out where you placed in the race, as well as your run time."

"*If* I finish," she stared at the race pack in dismay.

"We have been training for this for months. You are more than ready. And besides, there's no shame in walking if you get too tired. The goal is to get to the end. How you get there doesn't matter. So now, we have two things left to do. Eat some carbs and stretch. Let's go back to my house. We can call Mona on the way."

❧

When we returned to my house, Mona was waiting for us on my front steps. She wore a pink terrycloth running suit bedazzled with shiny silver sequins and a pair of high-top athletic shoes with leg warmers. Her red wig was pulled back in a ponytail. She was scowling.

"I thought I'd go red today," she told us, fluffing her ponytail. "I'm in a bitchy redhead mood."

"What's wrong?" Evy sat down next to her on the stoop.

"I got stood up last night—again. We were supposed to meet at the movies, but he never showed. I had to sit through the entire rom-com all by myself. At least the ending was good. The boy got the girl. But I'm starting to think love is a fantasy that only happens in movies."

"It's bad out there, for sure," Evy agreed.

"And then there's you," Mona said, pointing at me. "Your dream date was right there, lurking all along. I think I'm just jealous. And hangry. This bitchy redhead needs to eat."

"You've come to the right place," I told her. "Let's go make spaghetti."

Evy and Mona sat at my kitchen island, watching as I heated a pot of water and browned ground beef, onion, and sausage in a pan before adding spices and canned tomatoes.

"Are you two excited about tomorrow?" Mona asked.

"Very!" I replied.

"Nervous!" Evy said.

I remember how nervous I was during the first half-marathon I ran in high school. Overcoming that fear was a game-changer for me and led to years of distance running. Evy just needed a little confidence.

I looked at her and said, "Twenty-four hours from now, that race will be over, and you'll have sore feet, a racing medal, and bragging rights. Trust me, it's a pretty cool feeling getting through that finish line."

"And I will be there to cheer you on!" Mona said excitedly.

"You're coming?"

"Ladies, I wouldn't miss it for the world."

The following day, I met Evy at the civic center. She was at the entrance, clutching her race packet.

"Today's the day! How are you feeling?"

"Anxious. I didn't sleep well last night." She slouched against the wall, looking tired.

"You'll sleep great tonight," I said. "Come on, let's pin our race numbers on and figure out when we start."

"We don't start at the same time as everyone else?"

"No, they put us in corrals based on our running speed and then let each corral go at a different time. I've been timing our runs at a 13-minute mile pace, and that's what I indicated when I registered us. So, we'll be in the 13-minute corral."

"This is so complicated. I thought we'd just show up and run."

"It'll make sense once we start."

The weather could not have been more perfect for a race. On that cool October morning, the sun shone brightly, without a cloud in the sky. Runners milled about near the race entrance. Belmont's *Hit 95* radio station disc jockey, Dallas Kincaid, stood on a stage near the entrance, playing music and periodically making announcements. Kanye West's *Stronger* song blared through the speakers. Evy looked around, taking it all in.

"We're over here," I said, pointing to a cordoned area under the 13-minute sign. We walked over and joined that group of runners.

"Now what?" she asked.

"Now, we wait. In just a minute, the first runners will go."

"Welcome, runners, to Belmont's 10th Annual 10-K and Half Marathon!" The DJ's voice boomed through the speakers. The crowd cheered. "The moment you've been waiting for has come. Corral number one...ready, set, go!"

The DJ held up an air gun and shot it into the sky. A group of runners far ahead of us started to run.

"Those are the fastest runners," I told Evy. "They come from all over for the prize money. They'll be done before we even reach the halfway point." I watched as the corrals opened before us.

Ding!

I pulled my phone from my shorts pocket.
Text from Andy:

ANDY

Thinking about you. Good luck today. DON'T break a leg!

I smiled and tucked my phone into the pocket of my racing shorts.

"Ready?" I looked at Evy.

She shrugged. "Here goes nothing."

Our group started running. As we began, runners crowded each other, and we moved in a pack. Our pace was slow, but the crowd thinned, and we picked up speed.

"How will we know where we are in the race?" Evy asked as we continued along the race path.

"They put up markers. See, there's one right there. We're at mile one. There will also be water stations. Let me know if you need to stop."

We ran past the marker and rounded a corner. Our feet pounded the pavement, and we found our pace, silently running together. The warm sun shone down, and I was filled with happiness. *We worked so hard for this.* We continued, passing mile markers.

When we reached the halfway mark, we saw Mona standing on the sidelines, holding a big sign that read, "*Go, Emma and Evy!*" She squealed with excitement when she saw us and jumped up and down. She shouted out, "Go, go, you amazing bitches!" I blew Mona a kiss as we passed her.

At mile ten, we stopped for a water break. Evy's cheeks flushed red.

"Are you okay? We're almost there."

Sweating profusely, she picked up the corner of her shirt and wiped her brow.

"I'm okay," she said, downing a cup of water. "It just got really hot out here in the sun. Glad we're almost there. Let's keep going."

Our pace resumed, and we continued along. Back in my rhythm, the world fell out around me, and I was inside my head. *So close now. Almost there.* My feet pounded the pavement harder. *I can do this.*

We passed the mile eleven marker. My body exploded with endorphins, and I was overcome with energy. I ran faster, and Evy kept my pace. We passed mile twelve. *So close.*

Oblivious to the runners around me, all I could hear was the sound of my own feet hitting the pavement at a steady, rhythmic pace. I saw the 13.1-mile marker in the distance. My eyes fixated on it. *Go harder.*

I pushed my legs to go faster. I felt as if I was flying. Then I heard Evy's voice just behind me.

"Emma!" she called out.

It's right there. The finish line is just ahead. My feet

hit the cement below harder. *I've waited so long for this.*

"Don't stop now!" I called. I didn't look back. "Push yourself! You've got this!" I saw the finish line in the distance, runners passing through it and being cheered on by loved ones. "See you at the end!"

Suddenly, a commotion erupted behind me as someone yelled, "Runner down!"

I turned and stopped cold. Evy was lying in the middle of the road on her side, a pool of blood forming from a cut on her head.

"Oh my God! Evy!" I ran back to her and turned her over. She lay unconscious, turning pale. I sat in the middle of the road, holding her.

"Ev! Wake up!" I looked around in a panic. "Someone get help!" She lay motionless in my arms.

Within a minute, two paramedics arrived on motorbikes. One took out his walkie-talkie and called for an ambulance. "Stat!" he said. "She's unconscious."

The other paramedic leaned down, checked her pulse, and motioned for me to let her go.

"No!" I said, holding her tighter.

"Ma'am, you need to let her go. We need to check her."

I begrudgingly laid her in his arms and scooted a few feet away, watching as the paramedic took her blood pressure and checked her vitals.

"She's okay. She's coming around."

Just then, Evy opened her eyes, at first a squint, but then they opened wide. She winced in pain.

"What is going on?" she asked, looking around confused.

"You fell and passed out. You hit your head. We're going to take you to the hospital," my voice trembled. She closed her eyes again.

"Are you here at the race with her?" the paramedic asked.

"Yes, I'm her running partner. Can I come along in the ambulance?"

"I was going to suggest that."

The crowd cleared, and an ambulance pulled forward. A paramedic unloaded a gurney and placed Evy on it.

"Probably dehydrated," the paramedic said, hooking up an IV.

"She hasn't been feeling well lately."

"Don't worry," he reassured me, "We'll get her checked out."

Evy did not open her eyes again while riding to Belmont General Hospital. I sat next to her, holding her hand, consumed by guilt. *I'm so selfish. I should have slowed down. I should have stayed with her.*

She awoke again just as we got to the hospital. She was fully awake and lucid when they got her into a room. She had color back on her face.

"I'm so sorry," I said. Despite my best efforts to be

strong, I started to cry. "I should have slowed down. I should have kept your pace."

"You didn't do anything wrong. It was so hot in the sun." She looked down and saw the blood on my shirt from when I held her. Her face suddenly became distraught.

"You cut your head pretty badly," I told her.

An emergency room doctor appeared in the doorway.

"Good afternoon, Ms. Hanover. I understand you took a hard fall today. Mind if I have a look?"

He looked at me and said, "I'm sorry. You will have to leave us for a moment."

"Of course. I'll be right outside."

I moved to the emergency room waiting area, where a mother sat with a feverish toddler curled in her lap. A teenage girl in a field hockey uniform hobbled around on crutches. An older couple sat next to me. The woman kept looking around the room, confused, and asking, "Where are we?" Her partner patiently and lovingly kept reminding her, "We're at the hospital, honey." Minutes later, she would ask again, "Where are we?"

A nurse emerged from the emergency room a short while later.

"Emma Davis?" I stood up. She motioned for me to follow her.

"How is she?"

"She's doing better, but the doctor wants to keep her for observation and have her looked at by the resident physician tonight. Can you possibly get her some things to wear? Some pajamas and a change of clothes for tomorrow?"

"Of course," I said, remembering that my car was still at the civic center. I would need to call a taxi.

"Can I see her?" She led me back to her room.

"Hey," I said. "I'm going to go to your house and get you some things. They are keeping you tonight. I'll be back in a couple of hours."

"Can you keep Benny tonight? He's with the dog sitter. She lives in 4B right across the hall," she said.

I nodded. "You know it. I'll get him."

"Thank you, Emma."

"Don't worry about anything. I'll be back soon."

I turned and left the room, my head reeling at how the day had unfolded. Once back at my car at the Civic Center, I drove to her condo, packed a bag, and picked up Benny to drop him off at my house.

"You be a good boy until I get back." I patted Benny's head. He wagged his tail happily, then curled up on the family room sofa and fell asleep.

Back at the hospital, they moved Evy to her own space. The room was quiet when I entered. I sat in the chair beside her bed and looked around while she slept.

A whiteboard hung on the wall, where someone had scribbled, "Today is Saturday, October 24." "Your nurse tonight is Angela." "Physician on call: Dr. Philips." The equipment monitoring her vitals steadily beeped.

The door opened, and a pretty, dark-haired nurse wearing scrubs walked in. "Hi, I'm Angela. You must be Emma? Evy said you'd bring her some things."

I nodded. "How's she doing?"

"We're monitoring her for a concussion. Dr. Philips will be here in a minute to examine her more fully. Thank you for bringing her clothes. You two have had quite a day."

You have no idea, Angela.

Just then, the doctor opened the door.

"Good evening," he said and looked at me. "Would you mind stepping out while I examine Evy?"

I left the room and moved to the chair outside. I sat very still while they talked, trying to hear the conversation inside. At first, I couldn't quite make out the words. Evy was talking and then quieted. Then the doctor spoke. I sat straight up, my ears straining to hear his words.

"Recurring symptoms."

"Might be out of remission."

"Possibly advanced."

"Oncologist."

Why did he say that to her? Recurring? Oncologist? Evy has never had cancer. *He's mistaken.*

I stood up and looked through the little window of the hospital room. Evy saw me and burst into tears. I sat back down. *Or has she?*

I recalled what I said to her a day ago. *"Twenty-four hours from now, that race will be over, and you'll have sore feet, a racing medal, and bragging rights. Trust me, it's a pretty cool feeling getting through that finish line."*

An omniscient time stamp. The day before, a person's world changes in a blink. The life story that carries on oblivious to the plot twist about to happen. *Does Evy have cancer?*

I had a feeling right then that nothing would ever be the same again.

CHAPTER 26

Secrets

After the doctor and nurse left, I entered Evy's hospital room. She sat quietly in bed, staring at the wall. She twisted a tissue in her hands and wiped away tears. I sat next to her for a minute, neither of us speaking.

"I didn't mean to eavesdrop, but I could hear the doctor talking through the closed door. And what I think I heard scares me." Evy wouldn't look at me. "Are you sick?"

"I think so," she said quietly. "I need to go see a doctor."

"An oncologist?"

She nodded, still not looking at me. "I was pretending it wasn't really happening, you know. Like, if you don't acknowledge something, it isn't real. I guess I can't do that anymore."

"I heard the doctor say you were possibly out of remission. When were you sick?"

"Two years ago. I had non-Hodgkin lymphoma, but they caught it in the early stages."

"Why didn't you tell me? I've known you all this time, and you never once mentioned it."

My voice had a hint of frustration—or maybe it was fear. I remembered the day I researched Evy online and read the posts on her Facebook page where she had written, "Lymphoma Cancer Support. A Silent Killer. Please donate!" And then that period when there were no posts at all. *Now I know why.*

"Please don't be mad at me." Evy sat very still, looking at the wall. I took her hand.

"Look at me." She turned her head, her face full of sadness. "There is no way I could ever be mad at you. You're my best friend. I just don't understand why you never told me."

"This all happened before I met you. After months of treatment, I was starting to recover. My hair grew back. I was in remission. My body was almost feeling normal again. But I still wasn't quite myself. The maintenance medication they gave me slowed my metabolism and made me put on weight. I felt awful about myself. Ben assured me I was fine, and I knew that he meant that. He loved me no matter what."

She put her head in her hands, distraught. "But then

he died. I came to Belmont lonely and scared. I didn't even know how to start over without him. Then there I was one day, sitting behind you in a Healthy Horizons meeting, listening to you mumble to yourself about your miserable life. I thought maybe your life was as bad as mine, and maybe we could both use a friend." She gave me a small smile. "Turns out I was right."

"You could have told me. It wouldn't have made a difference."

She shook her head. "I was afraid you wouldn't want to be my friend if you knew I was recovering from cancer. Most people don't want that sort of trouble. I met a woman in a support group who told me her partner left her when he found out she was sick. People can be awful like that."

People really can. I knew one thing for sure. *Right now, my friend needs me.* I straightened up in my seat.

"Okay, well, you must know I'm not going anywhere. We're going to get to the bottom of this—together. The first thing we need to do is to make sure you're okay after today's fall. You hit your head hard. Once you're cleared to go home, we'll make a game plan."

I pulled something out of my pocket.

"What's that?"

I handed her a shiny medallion attached to a ribbon.

"It's your race medal from today. The race organizer wanted me to make sure you got it. You may not have crossed the finish line, but you still gave it your all. You earned it. And that's the thing, Ev. If you do have cancer again, we need to treat it like that race. Give it everything we've got. It doesn't matter how you get to the finish line; it just matters that you show up and try."

The bravery in my voice was a deception, masking the fear welling inside my body. Everything felt so uncertain.

"I just can't believe it may have come back. And now I may have to go through all that treatment again, only without Ben."

"You will *not* go through it alone. I promise. You have me—and Mona."

There was a soft knock at the door. Nurse Angela entered the room, pushing a cart with food on it.

"Up for some dinner?" she said, giving Evy a hopeful look.

Evy shook her head. "I think I just want to get some sleep."

"Want me to stay for a while?" I asked.

"No, you've had a long day too. You must be exhausted. I'll be okay. I'm just going to rest."

I turned to Angela. "What's the chance she'll go home tomorrow?"

"Very good. The doctor just wanted to keep an eye on her tonight."

"OK, Ev, you get some sleep. I'll go home and take

care of Benny. Call me in the morning when you're ready to go home, and I'll come and get you." She lay her head back and closed her eyes.

"Thank you, Emma," she said as she drifted off to sleep, still holding her race medal.

At home, I couldn't wait to get out of my blood-stained racing clothes. After a quick shower, I grabbed the leash from the table in the foyer to take Benny for a walk.

Early evening had arrived, and the sky turned overcast and gray. I walked along, watching crimson-colored leaves fall from trees and dance in the wind, thinking about all the steps Evy and I had taken around this block together. Remembering back to that first walk when we barely made it around the whole block without feeling winded. All the long talks we had. All those moments when one of us was having a bad day, but just walking those steps and having that friendship made it so much better. I was suddenly overwhelmed with a sense of dread and fear.

What if I lose her? *No, not on my watch*—forgetting that not all outcomes were within my control. I looked to the sky; to the universe. I never subscribed to organized religion because I believed that any God or deity that was good wouldn't care if you worshipped inside the four walls of a church or alone in your bedroom. You just had to show up somehow.

The universe stretched infinitely, and its randomness overwhelmed me. Maybe all things really did happen for a reason. Evy told me she believed she knew Ben over and over, their souls traversing time to reconnect. There were people I met and instantly connected with in my own life, eventually going our separate ways but then picking up again at some point in the future as if no time had passed—conversations that restarted where they ended without missing a beat. *The connections.* There was something to this universe. The mystery of life was figuring it out.

All I knew right then was that I couldn't lose her, not to cancer.

"Come on, boy," I said to Benny. "Let's go home." Rain began to fall.

At home, I heated a plate of leftover spaghetti, sat at the breakfast bar, and opened my laptop. I typed in "Recurring Non-Hodgkin Lymphoma Prognosis."

> The survival rate for recurring non-Hodgkin lymphoma is 48.2%; however, of those patients who do not survive, the cause of death is usually connected to cancer that has spread elsewhere in the body.

I recalled the doctor's words through the hospital door, "Possibly advanced." But what did an emergency room doctor know? I would find Evy a specialist.

Next, I typed in "Non-Hodgkin Lymphoma Symptoms."

> Common non-Hodgkin lymphoma symptoms include swollen or enlarged lymph nodes; flu-like symptoms; fever; fatigue; or lethargy; loss of appetite or vomiting; sudden and dramatic weight loss; night sweats or chills; unexplained pain or swelling; and difficulty breathing.

How many days in recent months had Evy become ill like that? As I added them up, I realized it was almost constant. *She's been sick for a while.*

One final search: "Stages of Lymphoma."

> The lymphoma stage describes how far the cancer has spread, using a numbering system from stage 1 to 4, with additional letters (A, B, E, and S) to provide more detail based on specific factors.
> - **A and B:** The letter 'A' means the patient has not experienced any 'B' symptoms, while 'B' indicates the presence of one or more of the

- following: drenching night sweats, unexplained fever, or sudden weight loss.
- **E and S:** 'E' signifies the cancer has spread to tissues or organs outside the lymphatic system, and 'S' means it has spread to the spleen.
- **Stage 1:** The cancer is located in a single lymph node region or organ.
- **Stage 2:** The cancer affects two or more lymph node regions on the same side of the diaphragm.
- **Stage 3:** The cancer is present in lymph nodes on both sides of the diaphragm, above and below it.
- **Stage 4:** The cancer has spread to one or more organs or tissues outside the lymphatic system, such as the liver, lungs, stomach, pancreas, or bone marrow.

I recalled the time, months ago, when I hadn't heard from her for several days when I found her drenched in sweat and feverish. Evy: constantly sick from her medicine, always too tired to run, vomiting in my basement toilet. *There was blood.* I couldn't read anymore.

I pushed the plate of food away, no longer feeling hungry. In the familiarity of my family room, I curled up on my sectional with a blanket and turned on the television. A *Friends* rerun played, and I wished Evy was there watching it with me. Benny settled in at my feet. I heard canned laughter coming from the TV.

Ding!

Text from Andy:

ANDY

How was the race? Been thinking about you all day.

So tired. I'll just close my eyes for a minute.
And then my world went black.

CHAPTER 27

Hope

When I arrived at Belmont General Hospital the next day, Nurse Angela was still there, helping Evy prepare to leave. She waved me in. "Your patient is all ready to go home," she said.

Evy sat on the side of the bed while Angela helped her with her shoes.

"I've given Evy some discharge papers, and the doctor went over the things to avoid over the next few days. She must avoid screen time, including computers, TVs, and smartphones. Rest for a couple of days and then take short walks. Also, avoid caffeine and alcohol. Evy will likely have a headache for a couple of days. Non-steroidal pain medication should do the trick. Her stitches should dissolve on their own, but we'd like her to schedule an appointment with her family physician in a week to have them checked out to make sure everything is healing properly."

Evy's face was pale and drawn. She looked exhausted. The doctor taped a gauze bandage over her left eye, a glaring reminder of yesterday's fall. Angela helped her into a wheelchair and walked with us to my car. Once inside my car, we pulled out of the hospital parking lot.

"I'm going to stop by my house to get Benny unless you want me to keep him for a few more days. Myla would be thrilled."

Evy thought about it and shook her head, "No, I need to hug my dog. How was he?"

"He was a good boy. I fell asleep in my living room last night and woke up this morning to doggy kisses."

Evy smiled. "Yeah, he likes to do that. Thanks again for taking him."

"No problem at all. Okay, we'll get him. Have you even eaten since yesterday?"

Evy shrugged and said, "I had some Jello. I don't have much of an appetite."

"You need to eat."

After picking up Benny, I took Evy back to her condo and got her settled in. Then I drove to Mama Scallopinis to pick up carryout, thinking about Andy and our first date. *Ugh. I never responded to him. He's going to think I'm blowing him off. So much is happening at once.*

Evy and I sat at her kitchen table, eating linguine with red sauce from to-go cartons. She picked at her food.

"So, it probably doesn't make sense for you to travel back to Washington, DC, to see your old oncologist. I did some research, and there are some highly-rated doctors in the city. And a few at Belmont General. What do you think?"

She stared at her carton of food, twirling a forkful of linguine but not eating it.

"I think I don't want to go through all this again. The tests. The chemo. The radiation. It's just depressing. I don't think I have it in me." She put her fork down. "Sometimes life just pisses me off. Actually, most of the time, life pisses me off!"

Good. Be angry. That's precisely where you need to be right now.

"I understand—let's try to keep things as simple as possible right now. Why don't you see someone local first, and then if you're not happy, we can look around the city? You need to be seen by a doctor soon."

"Okay," she agreed. "Have you said anything to Mona yet?"

I shook my head. "No, this is personal, and I won't say anything to anyone until you decide it's time."

I grabbed my laptop and opened it. "This lady, Dr. Vicki Conyers, works at Belmont General and gets very high marks on RateYourDoctor.com. She specializes in lymphoma. What do you think?"

Evy shrugged her shoulders and nodded. I picked up my phone to make her an appointment.

Ding!

Text from Andy:

ANDY

Is everything okay? Haven't heard from you.

Me:

I have a lot going on right now. I'll fill you in when I can.

Two days later, Evy and I sat in the waiting room outside of Dr. Conyers' office. I looked around the room at the patients in various stages of treatment. An older woman sat across from me, crocheting a blanket. She wore a blue bandana to cover her balding head and a T-shirt that read, "Chemo Gives Me Superpowers."

On the other side of the room, a young girl sat wrapped in a blanket, leaning on her father and looking at the cell phone in his hand. She giggled at the videos of kittens he played for her. She had also lost most of her hair.

Evy sat quietly with her hands in her lap, looking at no one. The door opened.

"Evelyn Hanover?"

"Let's go," Evy said reservedly. I followed her and the medical technician back to a room, where the technician took Evy's weight and typed information into a laptop.

"I'd like my friend, Emma, to have access to my medical information. Is there something we can sign?" The technician left the room and returned with a form for Evy to fill out.

"No more getting information behind closed doors," she said as she handed the completed form to the technician.

A few minutes later, the door opened, and Dr. Conyers entered. The doctor, a middle-aged woman with gray-black hair pulled into a loose bun, was dressed in scrubs like the technicians. Her lightly wrinkled face bore a resigned expression that seemed to have witnessed too much illness. The medical technician quietly closed the door behind us.

"Good afternoon, Evelyn. I'm Dr. Conyers. This is my medical technician, Anna." She peered through her glasses at Evy's bandage and scrunched her face.

"What happened here, Evelyn?" she said as she crossed the room and inspected the bandage. Evy winced when the doctor lifted the bandage to inspect her stitches.

"It's Evy, please. I fell three days ago. My friend Emma and I were running a half-marathon, and I fainted."

"Hmmm...yeah, that doesn't look good. Have you seen your physician for follow-up?"

"No, just the resident doctor in the emergency room. I will make an appointment, though."

Dr. Conyers stood back and studied Evy for a moment.

"So, what brings you here?"

Evy looked at the doctor but didn't speak. As if saying the word 'cancer' made it real again, and she wasn't ready for that yet. *I'll be her voice.* I intervened.

"Hi, Dr. Conyers. I'm Emma. We're here today because the doctor in the ER advised Evy to come here. She has been feeling progressively worse and losing weight over the past several months. She didn't faint during the race; she collapsed. She previously had non-Hodgkin lymphoma but was in remission. The ER doctor fears her symptoms may be returning."

I looked at Evy. She stared at the floor but didn't speak.

"How are you feeling right now, Evy?" the doctor asked.

"Tired," she said without looking up.

"That's understandable. Aside from feeling sick and losing weight, what else can you tell me? When did you start having symptoms again?"

"I moved to Belmont over a year ago from Washington, DC. I was doing well. I had been cancer-free for over a year. But then I started getting tired a lot again. Then, the night sweats and fevers started. Lately, I've had a lot of stomach issues. I can't stop vomiting. Or scratching. My skin has become very itchy."

The doctor read through the notes the technician put into the tablet.

"Are you still on maintenance therapy? I don't see any medications listed here."

Evy shook her head. "I stopped taking it. I was feeling better."

Dr. Conyers placed her hands on the sides of Evy's neck and pressed down. Evy winced.

"Did you have surgery with your last treatment? Were any of your adrenal glands removed?"

Evy shook her head again. "They caught it early. My doctor said the chemo and radiation would be enough."

Dr. Conyers typed notes into her iPad. She turned to Evy.

"Okay, well, unfortunately, you've been through this, so you know what I'm going to say next. We're going to start with a full medical exam, including a biopsy. I also want a full CT and MRI done, as well as a positron emission tomography scan. After that, we should have a better idea of what we're dealing with."

Evy looked like she was about to cry. Sensing this, Dr. Conyers sat down across from her.

"Listen," she said. "Don't be worried quite yet. Your

symptoms mirror a lot of other medical conditions. That's why we run these tests—to rule things out. I'm glad you came in today. We're going to get to the bottom of this."

"Thank you," Evy said quietly. She looked at me, and I nodded in agreement with the doctor.

"Are you married?" Dr. Conyers asked. "Do you have a husband or family in the area?" Evy shook her head.

"She has me," I said. "I'm her best friend."

Dr. Conyers scrolled through the notes.

"I see that she's signed a consent form. Perfect. Anna will work with the two of you to schedule these appointments. I'll need you back here next week for a physical. Anna will give you instructions on how to prepare for that."

She turned to leave the room and said, "Be hopeful, ladies."

Hope.

I remembered a poster hanging on the wall in the Belmont psychiatric ward. It was an Italian proverb that read, "*Hope Is the Last Thing Ever Lost.*"

After Anna helped Evy schedule the imaging scan appointments, I called Mona to join us for lunch—it was time to rally the troops. We met at Sharky's for pizza, where Evy filled Mona in on everything happening.

"Oh, honey," Mona said, tearing up. She held both of Evy's hands in hers. "You fell during the race, and now this. You listen to me. Your friends are right here for you." She pulled out a tissue and dabbed her mascara. "We will kick cancer's butt!"

The waiter brought over a large pizza and set it before us. All three of us just sat and stared at it.

"I knew something was wrong all along," Mona said quietly.

Evy sighed. We were too quiet, and our gloominess wasn't doing her any favors.

"Alright!" I spoke up. "We have a choice. Wallow or win. What's it going to be?"

"Win!" Mona said confidently. We looked at Evy.

"Win," she shrugged. "What choice do I have but to try?"

"What choice do *we* have but to try? We're all in this together. Right now, it's time for some pizza therapy," I said, grabbing a slice of pizza and lifting it to my mouth.

"Hear! Hear!" Mona pitched in, grabbing a slice. I put a piece on Evy's plate. She looked at it for a moment but then started to eat.

Mona hugged her and said, "Good girl."

Later that day, after Jack dropped the kids off at the house, I showed Myla and Austin my race medal.

"That's so cool," Austin said. "Can I wear it?"

"No fair!" Myla argued. "*I* want to wear it." She started to grab it from him, and I stopped her.

"You two can take turns," I said. Myla rolled her eyes at me.

"How was the race, Mom?" Austin asked, running his hand along the grooves of the medal.

"It was hard but worth it. Do you remember when you told me that moving is improving? Look how far I've come."

Austin nodded and smiled. "I remember. I'm proud of you, Mom." *Those words.* My heart swelled.

"Alright," I said, "I'm going downstairs and get on the treadmill for a bit. It's the best thing for sore muscles."

"Can I come downstairs with you?" Myla asked. Having her down there with me was always challenging because she constantly interrupted me while I tried to work out.

"Okay, but you need to find something to do. Go get your crayons. And find some paper to draw on."

Myla sat at a table downstairs and scribbled while I started the treadmill. She talked to herself while she drew.

"Jack Davis. That's Daddy's name!" I looked over to see her squinting at a piece of paper, trying to read the words.

"COR...por...aaaa...t...i...on."

"En...tit...y."

"Juris...d...ick...ton."

"Mommy! Where's my red crayon!"

I took the paper from her. "Myla! What are you drawing on?"

"You said to find some paper. I did. But they all have words on them. I had to draw on the back."

I flipped the page over to find a financial statement for Baylou Enterprises, owned by Jack Davis and Robert Blankenship. It was listed in an offshore account in the Cayman Islands and was worth *seven million dollars.* My heart started to race.

"Where did you get this?" Myla pointed to a large brown box with the words *Holiday Decorations* written in black marker.

"Where did you get that box?" She next pointed to the storage area under the steps.

"Right over there, Mommy," she said. "There are lots of papers in it, but they all have words on them. Can I have some plain paper? Please and thank you."

I pulled the top off the box and saw piles of folders and papers. Another financial statement for Blankenship Pharmaceuticals, worth ten million dollars, was also registered to a Cayman Islands bank. I picked up the box and carried it upstairs to sort through it. There were six businesses totaling over fifty million dollars. I picked up my phone and called Rocco. It went straight to voicemail.

"Rocco, it's Emma. You won't believe this." My hands shook as I spoke. "I found all of it."

CHAPTER 28

Everything All at Once

"This is exactly what we needed," Rocco said the next day as he pulled papers and folders from the box I had carried into Lauren's office. He sorted through the paperwork and arranged papers in neat piles next to sticky notes with company names written on them.

"Baylou Enterprises. Blankenship Pharmaceuticals. J&B Manufacturing. One World Technologies. Strategic Edge Engineering. One Vision Consulting. There are six of them in this box. I wonder if there are more?" Rocco asked as he typed notes into his tablet.

I looked through the papers.

"Do you see any tax statements?"

I shook my head 'no'.

"That's odd. But we can still work with what you found."

Just then, the door opened, and Lauren walked in. She saw the two of us and raised an eyebrow.

"What is all of this?" she asked, settling in at her desk.

"*This* is paperwork that Emma found. Six businesses are registered in the Cayman Islands. Worth over fifty million dollars."

Rocco handed one of the folders to Lauren. She flipped through it and looked at me, shocked.

"Good work, Emma! Where did you get these?"

"In a box labeled 'Holiday Decorations' in a storage closet, I never use. He must have forgotten they were there."

Lauren's eyes narrowed. "Perfect. I knew it. We've got him."

"So now what?" I asked her.

"Now Rocco will research. We will compile all of this into a financial report and provide it to Judge Hawkins. You, my friend, may have just become a very rich lady."

She turned to Rocco. "I want you to drop everything else you're working on. How much time do you need to get this report together?"

"I'll get to work on it right away. I can hopefully have everything researched and compiled in a couple of weeks."

"Perfect. Emma, you're on standby. We'll be heading back to court very soon. We'll be in touch."

I left Lauren's office, my head reeling. *When did he establish all those companies? And why are they in offshore accounts? This is what happened to my OneBank money? No wonder he hid everything from me.* I had been sleeping next to a wolf in sheep's clothing all that time. Oblivious.

I drove to Mama Scallopini's to meet Andy for lunch. When I entered the restaurant, his face brightened into a smile. I tried to smile back, but couldn't. I intended to show up in a good mood, but I couldn't mask my true feelings.

"Everything okay?" I shook my head. The smile on his face disappeared and was replaced with a look of worry. "Did something happen?"

"Yes, everything all at once," I burst into tears. He scooted his chair over next to mine and pulled me into a hug.

"Talk to me," he said.

I blurted out everything quickly. "Evy collapsed. So much blood. I'm a horrible friend. I should have walked, but I ran. Out of remission. Maybe cancer. More tests. And we found out what happened to all my OneBank money! In a holiday decorations box. Cayman Islands!"

Andy pulled me into him and hugged me hard. I sobbed into his shoulder.

"I don't know what you just said. Let's start from the beginning. Tell me about the race. And breathe."

I steadied my breath and began again.

"Wow," he said after I told him everything. "I'm so sorry to hear about Evy. How sick do you think she is?"

"If you want me to be honest? Very sick. And looking back, all the clues were there. I should have paid more attention. I was so focused on us losing weight and running that damn race. The very race that took her down."

Visions of Evy lying in the road were still imprinted in my mind. Tears welled in my eyes again. *Rotten friend.*

"Listen, you couldn't have known. And now that you do know, you can be there for her. She probably feels like she's been carrying around a terrible secret. This might be a relief to her. She knows you'll help her. And your husband's businesses? That's crazy that your daughter found that box. What happens now?"

A waiter placed two salads on the table in front of us.

"Lauren, my attorney, said they will draft a financial statement for the judge. I don't know what will happen after that. Lauren is very good at her job. But I honestly don't care about Jack or the divorce right now. I'm worried about Evy."

He nodded. "I understand."

We ate in silence for a few minutes. I put down my fork and stared at my plate.

"What if she *is* really sick? What if the doctors can't help her?"

Andy scooted his chair back over next to mine. He pulled me into another hug. I hesitated, but he just hugged me harder. I lay my head on his chest. I forgot what it was like to have someone who cared and wanted to help. He felt *safe.* The waiter came out of the kitchen, juggling two plates.

"All you can do is take it one day at a time."

Letting out a sigh, I acknowledged he was right. He pulled out a copy of *The New York Times* and handed me the Food section.

"Here, I brought you this. It's the write-up I did on our trip to the farm. I even included the corn maze."

"Thanks. I'm so happy to hear I made it into your story." I rolled my eyes and wiped away the last of my tears.

"Don't worry, I left out the part about the field of sunflowers." *Oh, what I wouldn't give to be back in that field right now.*

After lunch, Andy walked me to my car. "Where are you headed next?"

"I'm taking Evy to the radiologist. She gets her MRI and other scans today."

"Well, good luck. It's better to know. I hope all goes well with her scans."

⸎⸎

I drove to Evy's condo to pick her up for her appointment. When I arrived, she was sitting in her living room with a bottle of lotion, lathering it on her arms.

"You okay?"

"Yeah, I just can't stop scratching. Everything itches." Her arms were raw and red with nail marks. "It started a couple of weeks ago. It's making me crazy."

Entering the kitchen, I ran two dishcloths under cold water and placed them on her arms.

"Thank you," she said, leaning back and closing her eyes. "That helps so much."

"Maybe you're allergic to something. We can stop by the drug store on the way home and get you some anti-itch cream and an antihistamine."

"I'll try anything at this point."

⸎⸎

Ten minutes later, we arrived at the radiologist's office. In the waiting room, I settled in while she went back for her tests. A rerun of *Fixer Upper* played on the TV on the wall. In the episode, Joanna light-heartedly picked up a sledgehammer to knock down a wall while joking with Chip. They existed in a TV reality world where aged and outdated things could be made shiny and new again with a little work—and some farmhouse flair.

Life should be like that, too, where everything old and in disrepair could be transformed, with a reveal at the end showing everyone happy and smiling. But life doesn't work that way. The reality of life was sickness—cancer—a malignancy that could spread like the threads of a spider's web without a person even knowing.

What I wouldn't give to knock down a wall right now.

An hour later, Evy emerged through the door.

"All set?" We headed to the elevator.

"They said the results should be back in a couple of days." She handed me a piece of paper. "There's an online portal to view the scans. Here's the username and password. I personally don't want to look. I'll wait until next week when we see Dr. Conyers."

I took the paper from her, unsure if I wanted to look either.

"Now what?" We got into my car.

"I don't know. I just don't want to go home right now."

"Got any ideas?"

She thought for a few seconds and said, "Yes, I do know a place."

She gave me an address, and I punched it into my GPS. A short while later, we pulled up in front of an old church in a not-so-nice part of town, replete with dilapidated houses and broken-down cars in the driveways. This was the kind of community where the Bolton Academy parents would orchestrate self-serving compassion in the form of a sock drive. *Warm Feet on the Street.*

Evy looked at her watch and said, "Good, we're right on time."

"For what?"

"Follow me."

After parking the car, I followed Evy into a building next to the church. The air was thick with a cafeteria smell. Men and women bustled around the kitchen while a few set up stations with plates and cutlery. Others arranged tables and chairs.

"Well, hello there, young lady. We weren't expecting you today." An older African American man wearing overalls and a baseball cap walked over and hugged Evy. He had a soup ladle in one hand and a bag of carrots in the other.

"Emma, this is Charles. He runs this kitchen for the Southside Sisters of Mercy."

I shook his hand.

"Evy here is one of our best helpers," he said, smiling at her. "We haven't seen you in a couple of weeks."

Evy helps out in a soup kitchen?

"Things have been a little hectic," she told him. She mindlessly scratched her arms through her shirt's sleeves. "Need help today?"

Charles's face brightened. "Evy, we need help *every* day. Is your friend here joining you?"

I nodded. "Of course! I'm in. Lead the way."

Charles took us back to the kitchen, where we put on aprons and hair nets. Charles put me to work peeling potatoes while Evy cut vegetables. We put everything into a big pot with seasonings, water, and chicken.

"Chicken soup," Charles said, stirring the pot. "It cures the body and the soul."

Next, we baked large loaves of bread and set them on a table to cool before slicing. I stood beside Evy, carefully arranging the slices on a tray.

"You never told me you volunteered here."

"I like coming here. What surprised me the first time I volunteered was the people. You'll see people come in from all walks of life, but most have one thing in common. They don't seem to need much to be happy and are grateful for what they are given." Unlike the wealthy women of Belmont, clad in their designer clothes, with their expensive cars, and exotic trips—yet always inherently miserable.

"It's time!" someone shouted, and the front doors opened to a long line of people waiting outside. Charles handed soup ladles to Evy and me and directed us to the serving stations.

"Good afternoon, Agnes," Evy said as she ladled chicken noodle soup into a bowl for the middle-aged woman standing before her. Agnes looked like she was dressed for a party. She wore a tattered, stained dress, worn-out black shoes, a wide-brimmed hat, and a dirty sable stole. Long strands of yellowing pearls hung around her neck, and she had rings on every finger, most of which were missing their stones.

Beside her, a gray-bearded man extended his bowl for soup.

"Ain't Agnes looking *fine* today, Miss Evy?" He winked at Agnes.

Evy filled his bowl and handed him some bread and butter and a piece of chocolate cake.

"But then again, doesn't Agnes look fine every day?" He chuckled to himself and walked away.

"I think he's sweet on you," Evy told Agnes.

Agnes waved her hand in the air and scrunched her nose. "He don't smell so sweet." Evy suppressed a smile.

A young girl walked up next.

"Well, hello, Ariel!"

Evy put down her soup ladle and hugged the girl. Ariel looked to be about Myla's age. She was thin with a pale face and beautiful brown eyes accentuated by dark circles. Freckles dotted her nose and cheeks. She wore her long brown hair pulled back into a braid. In her hand, she clutched a naked Barbie doll, missing an arm.

"Get going!" A woman stood beside Ariel, scowling. She lashed out at the little girl, slurring her words. "You're holding up the line, Ariel. Move!"

"Yes, Mama," Ariel said.

The pencil-thin woman had needle marks on her forearms. Red sores pocked her face and body, and she appeared to be missing teeth. She wore an oversized hoodie, and her sweatpants slipped halfway down her torso. The woman shoved two bowls in Evy's face and sighed impatiently. Evy grimaced, filled the bowls, and handed them back. The woman walked away, leaving Ariel behind without a thought. Evy piled two big pieces of cake onto a plate.

"Here's one for you and another for your Barbie," Evy said, handing it to her. Ariel's face lit up.

"Thank you, Miss Evy!" she said and skipped away, oblivious to her reality.

I was suddenly overcome with a feeling of sadness. I wondered where she lived. Did she even go to school? I wanted to take her to the Make-a-Friend store in the mall and help her stuff an animal to hug while she slept at night. Buy her a cinnamon roll. Take her for a pedicure where she could get a daisy painted on her toe. My heart felt heavy.

"Did you see it?"

A frail old woman startled me from my thoughts. She stood before me, hands shaking uncontrollably.

"See what?" I said, reaching out, trying to steady her tray for her.

"On the news! President Nixon said it would happen tonight. Can you believe it? A man will walk on the moon!" Her ashen, wrinkled face was alight with innocence and excitement. "And we can watch it on the television!"

"Isn't that something, Audrey?" Evy said. "A rocket will take them over 200,000 miles away."

Evy left her soup station and took Audrey's tray. She put food on it, walked her to a table, helped her with her napkin, and then returned to the soup line.

"She doesn't know what year it is. Last time, she told me that the actor Ronald Reagan was going to tear down the Berlin wall."

She turned back to the line of people waiting to be served. "Marvin! So good to see you. How's Bernice?"

A short, round, bald man stood before her, grinning from ear to ear. His shirt squeezed him tightly, and his pants hung too loosely. He had fastened the heel of his shoe with duct tape. Marvin pointed to a woman sitting at a table a few feet away.

"She's as beautiful as ever. I'm here to get some food for my best girl."

Evy waved to Bernice and filled their soup bowls.

I began to understand why Evy volunteered here. I watched her talk to the people in line and feed them. She seemed to know them all, evidence that she had been here many times. Despite everything happening in her life, she still reached out to help others. Evy was selfless.

We spent the remainder of the afternoon serving people. When the last person left and the doors closed, we helped ourselves to hot soup and bread. We next helped Charles clean the kitchen, putting aside the reality that just hours before, she had been in an MRI tunnel that created detailed images of every part of her body.

Scans writing a story.

A map of things we could not see and did not yet understand.

I wasn't ready to turn that page yet. I wanted to leave the story right where it was. Where for just a bit longer, we didn't have to know.

CHAPTER 29

The Universe

The doctor's words hung in the air like cartoon balloons drifting above us filled with text about to pop and rain down letters—acid rain that stung. Evy squeezed my hand so hard I was afraid she would break my bones.

I watched Dr. Conyers' lips move. She pulled up images on her monitor, her hand pointing to light things on the dark screen, animating a scenario with uncertain conclusions or endings. Her lips pursed in resignation as she described what we were seeing.

"Stage four."

She continued talking, but I couldn't focus. All I could feel was the crush of my fingers in Evy's grip as if I were her lifeline and she was holding on with everything she had—holding on as if she would fall into an abyss and disappear if she let go.

"The biopsy showed non-Hodgkin lymphoma that appears to have originated in the thyroid again, but it has spread. What concerns me are the spots on the liver and pancreas."

She pulled up another image, a monochrome spattering of ink blots on canvas—only the canvas was Evy's body.

Evy stared straight ahead at the computer screen, her face expressionless, but then turned and looked at me, her eyes filled with fear. I swallowed hard, my own fear rising in my throat. Dr. Conyers stopped speaking and looked at us.

"Do you understand what I'm saying?" she asked softly.

I nodded, but Evy just stared at her. I spoke for both of us.

"Now what?"

"This round of cancer appears to be very aggressive. I don't want to waste time on starting treatment. If Evy agrees, we will start with chemotherapy, followed by a course of radiation. Some new drugs on the market are very effective at treating aggressive cancers. However, they don't come without risks. If she doesn't respond to treatment, we will consider surgery as a last resort."

Last resort. *Stop saying words that sound final.*

It was my job to pay attention, filing the information the doctor was telling us into neatly organized mental notes, to retrieve and talk about it later with Evy. But my brain wasn't cooperating. Her words were jumbled. "Combination therapy. Immunotherapy. Stem cell transplant is another option." I stared at her tightened lips, speaking medical jargon in a focused monologue so as not to show emotion.

"I'd like to get started this week. Would that be okay with you?"

Shoulders slumped, Evy nodded. She understood the drill. And she had no other choice. I had to ask the next question even though I didn't want the answer.

"What is the survival rate when it recurs?"

Dr. Conyers' face took on an expression I imagined she had mastered from years of being an oncologist, sitting across the desk from people telling them their fates. She became stoic.

"I won't lie. The spots on the pancreas concern me. That location is going to be hard to treat. But that doesn't mean we're not going to try. At this point, I would say possibly a year or less *if* we can't stop it. If we can, the prognosis is good."

Fuck.

Evy burst into tears. The bones in my hand popped from her grip.

The doctor's face softened. "We will do everything we can to get ahead of this."

Except I knew that the cancer had already gotten ahead of us...and we were chasing a ghost that could not be caught.

Dr. Conyers slid a stack of papers across the desk.

"This is my recommended treatment. I consulted with two other lymphoma specialists, and we feel this will be the best path forward. These papers include a description of the combination of chemotherapy drugs we are going to try and the timing for each of them. For this first round, we will try for six weeks and see how you respond."

Evy read through the documents, wiping away tears.

"What are the side effects?" she asked.

"They should be like what you experienced when you had treatment before, although they may be more severe because this is a stronger drug combination. I will provide anti-nausea medicine, and I can also write a prescription for you for medical marijuana."

My mind wandered back to the night of the speed dating event and the Dudeist Priest who smelled like skunk, wishing we could be back there innocently searching for love in a universe that opened doors. Back before all the doors began slamming shut.

Mona and I accompanied Evy to her first chemo appointment two days later. Evy reclined in a chair in the oncology wing at Belmont General while an IV slowly dripped medication into her veins. At one point, she lay her head back and closed her eyes, drifting off into sleep. Mona and I sat next to her, talking quietly.

"Right now, I wish I were more of a religious person," Mona whispered. "Things are feeling very out of control, and I'd like to know someone or something is in charge."

"You aren't spiritual? You don't believe in anything?" I whispered back. She shook her head, 'No.'

"I grew up in the Bible Belt. My parents were very strict religious people. My mother found my hidden journal when I was sixteen and discovered I was gay. My father became so angry that he sent me away to a camp for homosexuals, where they tried to pray my gay away. And when that didn't work, they resorted to beatings. They sent me home bruised with a label of 'helpless and unholy.' That angered my father even more because he said I didn't try hard enough. So, he beat me, too. That's when I stopped believing in any sort of higher being. No God that was good would put a child through that."

Mona's face was hardened. She stared at the dripping IV as Evy slept quietly in the chair.

I took her hand. "I'm sorry you went through that."

Mona scoffed. "The joke was on them. You can't expect to put a group of gay boys together in a bunkhouse alone every night and assume some sort of miraculous redemption will happen. The things that went on in that room! I met my first true love at that camp—a Mennonite boy named Eli. I remember him telling me about the day he told his mother he was gay. He said she shook her head in disbelief and scolded him. 'How can that be? You're Mennonite.' He responded that the only thing Mennonite about him was that he wished he could have *three* men a night. What did it all matter, anyway? We were all headed for the same fate, and that was to be sent home to angry parents. They couldn't change who we inherently were."

I squeezed her hand. "But you're here now."

"Yes, I was lucky in one respect," Mona said, nodding. "I was always very good at school and got excellent grades. I received a full scholarship to New York University. After high school, I moved away to college. For the first time in my life, I met people who accepted me. That's when I was introduced to the drag lifestyle and created Mona. Those were some of the best friendships I've ever made. I haven't been back to the Midwest since."

"I'm trying to understand the universe, too," I told Mona. "Nothing seems to make sense anymore."

A male nurse wearing light purple scrubs entered the room to check on Evy.

"How's our girl doing?" he asked, checking the IV bag. "Looks like she's done."

He turned and stretched out a hand to Mona. "I'm Nurse Alex. I love that handbag," he said, picking up Mona's Burberry knock-off and admiring it. Mona's face beamed.

At that moment, Evy stirred awake, her eyes heavy with grogginess.

"Hi there, Evy. I'm Nurse Alex. You're just about done here. Your friends can take you home in just a few minutes."

The nurse removed the IV from her arm and placed a bandage over it. He then handed Evy a sheet of paper filled with phone numbers.

"We'll see you back in a week. Here are some contact names in case you experience any serious side effects or need to get in touch with someone on the medical staff. Call these numbers anytime. The doctor's cell is also on here, and you can text her."

He then turned to Mona. "Will we see you back in a week?" Mona smiled and nodded.

"Wonderful! My number is on there, too." Nurse Alex winked at Mona and left the room.

"All set?" I asked Evy. We helped her out of her seat and walked to the car.

"How are you feeling?"

"I'm okay. It usually takes a while before there are any side effects. I'm not looking forward to tonight. Or tomorrow. Honestly, I'm not looking forward to anything at all." Her shoulders slumped, and she walked beside us, staring at the ground.

The ride home was quiet. Mona tried to make small talk, but Evy didn't seem to want to engage.

"The holidays will be here soon. I'm wondering if I should bother putting up a tree for the dogs and myself," Mona mused.

Evy stared out the window, not speaking.

Mona continued, "Last year, Jimmy Chews tried to eat the ornaments because he thought they were dog treats. I'm not dealing with that again! I spent a small fortune at the vet. But still, it won't be the holidays without a tree. Will you be decorating this year, ladies?"

Evy only stared out the window.

"Why don't we stop somewhere for lunch?" I suggested. "Anyone hungry?"

Evy reached down and unlocked her seat belt.

"Pull over! I need to get out."

I barely slowed the car to a stop before Evy swung her door open, got out, and ran into a field by the side of the road. Mona and I looked at each other, unsure of what was happening.

"Is she sick?" Mona asked. I shrugged my shoulders.

"Auuugghhhh!" Evy let out an ear-piercing scream to no one in particular. Her hands formed into fists, and her face contorted into anger. She stood in the middle of the field and screamed again, raging. She looked up at the sky.

"First cancer! Then Ben! Now, cancer again! Fuck you, universe!" she shouted, shaking her fists to the heavens. "Fuck you!"

She dropped to her knees, her shoulders heaving with sobs. Tears streamed down her face.

"We need to help her," I said. "We need to get her back into the car." I started to undo my seatbelt, but Mona stopped me.

"Leave her be." Mona put her hand on mine.

"She's had too much to deal with. She shouldn't be alone."

"Let her go. Yes, she's been through a lot of losses. But it's another thing entirely when you start to grieve your own life," she said quietly as she stared out the window at Evy.

I refastened my seatbelt, feeling helpless. Although deep inside, I knew Mona was right.

Evy's tears eventually stopped, and she quieted as if deep in thought. She looked back up at the sky and started talking. She was having a conversation with God or the universe. Maybe she was negotiating. Maybe she was questioning. Whatever it was, those were words that Mona and I were not meant to hear. Knowing that the best thing we could do to help her at that moment was nothing at all, Mona and I sat in the car and waited.

When she was ready, Evy returned.

"Take me home now."

Mona leaned over, buckled Evy's seatbelt for her, and said, "Sweetie, we always will."

No one spoke for the remainder of the ride back to Evy's condo, as if we collectively understood that just being together was all that was needed—all that we would ever need.

C H A P T E R   3 0

Nor'easter

Voice message from Rocco: *Emma, it's Rocco. I've finished compiling your husband's financial reports. Lauren would like to review everything before we submit it to Judge Hawkins. Are you free this week? Your next court date is coming up soon.*

Voice message from Ms. Williams: *Emma! It's Ms. Williams! I'm sure Austin has told you about our upcoming holiday bazaar at the school. In the spirit of the holidays, we'll be raising money to send lottery scratch-off tickets to the poor in the community. One lucky winner might win enough to buy a turkey! We're going to call it Scratch Snatch. Doesn't that have a lovely ring to it? It will be a silent auction this year, and so exciting! One of our parents is donating a week away at their second home*

in the Poconos! Would you be able to make another char-
cuterie board? Preferably one that doesn't melt. Although
I hear that Mrs. Stone is healing quite nicely. Call me!

Text from Andy:

ANDY

I haven't heard from you.
Is everything okay?

I stood at my bedroom window, watching the first snowflakes of the season fall from the sky. Puffy, white crystals swayed in the wind, painting a white-on-black scene that quieted the world outside. Sometimes winter came early in New York, turning the Halloween jack-o-lanterns on the front steps into frozen white goblins wearing devious smiles.

This year, Chuck Byron forecasted an El Nino year with major snow events that would stretch into spring. But this was a surprise nor'easter no one had expected, quickly turning fall into winter. I considered the months ahead and wondered what life would be like when the first buds appeared again on the trees. How much would have changed?

I had escaped to my room for a few moments to think. Benny followed me and sat at the edge of my bed. He dropped a tennis ball and wagged his tail, waiting to play.

Evy lay asleep in my family room downstairs, curled up in a blanket. After the third round of her chemo treatment, all things fell apart. The much stronger course of medicine caused her to vomit uncontrollably and experience spikes in fevers. Exhausted, she took sips of water and soup only to vomit again. Even the anti-nausea medicine the doctor prescribed wasn't helping.

Earlier in the day, I researched homeopathic remedies online. Ipecac and ginger root. Peppermint. Cinnamon. Vitamin B6 injections. *Tell your loved one to practice muscle relaxation and meditation breathing.* I wondered who wrote those articles and if they had ever watched someone's body start to fall apart from chemotherapy. The advice to "drink plenty of water" wouldn't help when even a sip felt like an acid rainstorm in her stomach. I messaged Dr. Conyers earlier to let her know what was happening. Now, I wait to hear back.

Benny jumped from the bed and nudged my hand, asking me to take him outside. I pulled my winter gear from my closet and quietly dressed, then escaped through the front door with Benny as Evy slept.

Outside, snow blanketed Browncroft Boulevard in a powdery white. Benny and I walked through the quiet while the massive homes lining the street glowed warmly from within, their occupants going about their evenings.

I peered into the windows and saw families at dinner tables. Upstairs, bedrooms glowed from the lights of television and computer screens. An elderly man lay asleep in his recliner by a fire while his cat slept in the crook of his arm—familiar things that made up the days of life.

My cell phone rang, its shrill sound punctuating the quiet of the winter storm.

"Hello?"

"Emma? It's Dr. Conyers. I received your text message. How is she doing?"

"Not well at all. I've been with her all weekend, and she isn't holding anything down. I'm afraid she's becoming dehydrated. This round of chemo was brutal."

"Then we need to get her some fluids intravenously. Would you be able to take her to Belmont General? I'd like to have her admitted."

"Of course," I told her. "I'll take her right over."

When I returned home, Evy was in the bathroom, retching into the toilet. She looked up at me. Her eyes were sunken, and her mouth and lips were dry and starting to chap. I kneeled next to her and helped her up.

"Dr. Conyers just called. She wants to have you admitted into the hospital tonight to get an IV and some fluids."

Evy looked at me with weary eyes. She didn't speak

but only nodded. I quickly packed a small overnight bag and helped her with her coat and shoes.

When I opened the front door, her demeanor instantly changed, her face lighting up like a small child. A smile spread across her face—the first I had seen in days.

"It's so beautiful!" she said, stepping into the snow. "When did this happen?"

"Just a few hours ago. A nor'easter. I think even the meteorologists were surprised by it."

Fat, wet flakes landed on her hair and face. She twirled in the yard like a ballerina, looking up at the sky and laughing. Then she dropped to the ground, her frail, thin body making a snow angel on the ground. She lay in the snow, smiling, while snowflakes rained down on her.

Beauty in chaos.

I helped her back up and brushed her off.

"Come on," I said. "You're going to get wet and catch a cold. That's the last thing you need right now."

An hour later, Evy was in a hospital bed, wrapped in blankets, and hooked to an IV. She lay her head back, watched the snow fall through the window, and then closed her eyes.

"I'm tired, Emm," she said. I held her hand.

"I know you are. Sleep. I'll be back for you tomorrow." She drifted off.

The next morning, I met Rocco and Lauren at the Coventry building. Rocco sat in front of me, holding a stack of folders. He sifted through them.

"Emma, Rocco was able to trace additional information about Jack's overseas businesses. It turns out there were actually eight in total. He currently has over $75 million in investment accounts in the Cayman Islands, all under fake business names."

"Eight? How is that even possible?" I stared at her, incredulously.

Rocco handed me the financial report, and I skimmed through it. Jack had initially invested my OneBank money in the stock market and then transferred the dividends and remaining balances to the eight accounts overseas, where the money was compounding exponentially.

"Something is interesting, though," Lauren said, leaning back in her chair. "No tax records anywhere."

Rocco concurred. "I did significant research, and he hasn't paid a dime."

"What does that mean?"

Lauren snickered. "Foreign accounts are subject to

taxation, and the IRS and U.S. Treasury have strict procedures for reporting overseas assets. U.S. citizens with foreign bank accounts exceeding $10,000 at any point during the calendar year must report these accounts to the Treasury Department. What this means, Emma, is that your soon-to-be ex-husband is in a lot of trouble."

What? I looked over at Rocco.

"Tax evasion," he said flatly.

I flipped through the report again, trying to understand why Jack would have done any of this. He had always been a savvy businessman and kept careful records of everything. *How did he think he would get away with this?*

"There's more," Rocco continued. "For tax fraud and evasion, the law stipulates that individuals convicted may face fines of up to $100,000 and imprisonment for up to five years. For corporations, the maximum fine is $500,000."

I swallowed hard. "*Prison?*"

"You should thank your lucky stars, Emma," Lauren said. "Your name isn't anywhere on those accounts. Be happy he left you penniless."

"Now what?"

Lauren grinned like the Cheshire cat in *Alice in Wonderland*. "I like the element of surprise," she purred. "It will definitely be an interesting day in court."

My head spun. *Should I tell him? He should be*

warned. How could he be so stupid? What about the kids? How could he do this to our family?

And then I recalled what he said to me before he walked out of our lives, in front of our kids. That stone-cold, uncaring look on his face. "Worthless. Sad. Fat, pathetic excuse for a mother. I guess you're not so successful now, are you?"

No, I won't be warning you, Jack. Sleep in the bed you have made for yourself.

Suddenly, the financial report in my hand felt like dirty, toxic contraband I no longer wanted to touch. I dropped it on the desk with a thud.

Lauren continued. "So, if you agree, I'd like to submit these documents to the court in preparation for our next hearing."

I stared at the financial report momentarily, then looked at Lauren and said quietly, "File away."

I left Lauren's office and went to the hospital to check on Evy. The IV fluids seemed to have helped. When I entered the room, she sat awake, talking to the nurse. The color had returned to her face.

"It really snowed last night!" she said, looking out the window. She smiled softly as she ate breakfast from the tray in front of her. Relieved, I hugged her.

"I've been really worried about you."

"It's been hard this time around," she said, spooning Jello into her mouth. "Thank you for bringing me here."

I imagined Ben used to sit by her side, a fact I'm certain she thought about many times over the past several weeks. I was no replacement for him, but was honored to take his place. I noticed tufts of hair on her pillowcase. She was starting to lose her hair. I looked away.

"The doctor wants to keep me another day."

"Okay. You need the fluids. Get some rest."

While en route to Jack's condominium to pick up Myla and Austin, a wave of sadness washed over me as I realized I had missed experiencing the first snowfall of the season with them. There would be many more of these firsts, and it frustrated me. It was amazing how one person's selfish actions could perpetually disrupt so many other people's lives. I pulled up in front of Jack's condo and waited for the kids to come outside. The building door swung open.

"We couldn't play in the snow at Daddy's. The only snow was on top of the building," Myla informed me as she got into the car. "Can I build a snowman when we get home?"

"No, *I* want to make one," Austin argued, as he got in next to her and buckled his seatbelt.

"You can make two. One of each: a snowman and a snowwoman."

Myla giggled. "Snowmen can't be girls, Mommy."

"They can be whatever you want them to be. You can build a snow puppy if you want."

She pondered that for a minute and nodded. "A snow Benny!"

As soon as I pulled into the driveway, the kids jumped out of the car and dashed toward the house, excited to gear up for the snow. As I neared the front door, I heard Myla exclaim, "What is this, Mommy?"

A small white box sat wedged between the storm and front doors. I opened it and pulled out a snow globe with a little village inside. Myla grabbed it from me, turned it upside down, and watched the tiny flakes fall.

"Who left this, Mommy?" she asked.

A note with only three words was placed at the bottom of the box: *"Miss you. – A."*

"Well? Who is it from?" Austin persisted.

"A very sweet friend," I told them. Just then, fat snowflakes started to fall again. I looked at the snow angel still imprinted in the front yard. Myla squealed and ran into the snow, ready to play.

CHAPTER 31

Selfish

Monday, 8:15 a.m. Voice message from Mona: *Emma, it's me. Our girl isn't doing so well. I'm at her place, and she's been up all night vomiting again. She can't keep anything down. I don't know what to do! Should we contact her doctor? Please call me. I'm worried.*

Monday, 9:00 a.m. Text from Andy:

ANDY

> I haven't heard from you. I'd really like to see you, but you aren't calling me back. Did you get the present I left for you?

Mona and I agreed to stay with Evy in the evenings after Dr. Conyers gave her the okay to go home from the hospital. I had no one to watch the kids, so Mona was with her most nights, leaving Jimmy Chews and Bark Twain with a neighbor so she could stay at Evy's condo.

Another week had passed. Evy was in the last week of her six-week course of therapy, but nothing seemed to be improving. She was only getting sicker. I called Mona to check in.

"How bad is it?" I asked. I closed my office door to speak in private.

Mona said, exasperated, "Well, she's kept nothing down. She's been sleeping most of the time, which is a blessing. But she's wasting away. I'm worried about her."

"I will put another call into Dr. Conyers. She may have to go back to the hospital. I can be there with her tonight. I've convinced Jack to take the kids. I hope Kiki doesn't poison them with her cooking."

Mona snorted. "Send snacks."

"We just need to get Evy through the next week, and then she gets a break from treatment. I was planning Thanksgiving dinner at my house next week, but maybe you and I could take dinner to her instead, or make it at her house. Jack gets the kids this holiday, and I will be alone. I can bring the food if you can help me cook?"

"Cooking isn't my forte, but I'll certainly pitch in. She's waking up. Do you want to talk to her?"

"Yes, put her on." I could hear Mona talking to Evy, and then Evy's faint voice on the phone.

"Hey, Emm." Her voice came out hoarse and barely audible.

"How are you?"

"Another rough night. This treatment is nothing like last time. It's been hell."

"I'm so sorry. I'm coming over tonight. Do you want me to call the doctor? The IV fluids seemed to help last time."

After a long pause, Evy responded. "No, I'll get through this. I'm glad you'll be here, though. I think I'm wearing poor Mona out."

I could hear Mona in the background. "Stop it. You know I'm always here for you."

Mona *was* worn out. We all were, but none more exhausted than Evy.

✣

Mona and I stood in Evy's kitchen a week later, preparing Thanksgiving dinner. Over the years, I became an expert at ensuring everyone's holiday was a Hallmark moment, cooking a perfectly browned turkey, and making mashed potatoes that were creamy and buttery with just the right number of lumps. Even my pies were homemade—pumpkin and apple rolled out from freshly made pie dough.

Evy's home smelled like Thanksgiving should, only something felt off. Evy slept in her bed while Mona and I prepped the food. She should have been with us. I missed my kids milling about. I even missed Jack helping pick out the perfect wine for dinner. I couldn't shake the empty feeling. *Where was my family?*

Mona leaned over and put her head in the oven, staring at the turkey.

"Close that!" I protested. "You'll let all the heat out."

"When does that little thing pop up to tell us it's done? The last time I made a turkey, it had a thing that popped up."

"The turkey I'm making doesn't have one of those. Here, peel these."

I steered Mona over to the potatoes, soaking in a water bowl.

"I can't peel those. I'll ruin these nails." Mona flashed her freshly manicured nails at me. "What else can I do?"

I handed her a can of biscuits. She read the instructions and put them on a cookie sheet.

"Voila!" Mona smiled. "Dinner is served."

"You're quite the sous chef," I told her. "Why don't you set the table?"

"That I can do."

Mona busied herself by setting up place settings for three. Benny wandered around the kitchen, sniffing the air. He settled at my feet and looked up at me hopefully.

"You can have some turkey when it's done, buddy." He wagged his tail.

I peeled the potatoes and sighed, lost in thought. *I miss my kids.* Mona stopped setting out dishes and walked over to join me.

"You okay?"

"Yeah, this is just the first Thanksgiving I've ever spent without Austin and Myla. Everything feels off. I'm their *Mom.* I'm supposed to be with them. Not that I'm not grateful to be here with the two of you. I am. I just miss them right now."

Mona grabbed a potato and began to peel it.

"Well, I think you just need to make new traditions for the three of you. I have a coworker who also went through a nasty divorce. Her kids are in college now, but when they were younger, she made a Charlie Brown Thanksgiving every other year when they spent the holiday with their dad."

"A what?"

"A Charlie Brown Thanksgiving. Instead of the usual fixings, she made a dinner of popcorn, jellybeans, pretzels, and toast. Her kids loved it. It was their special thing. That's what you need to do. Start finding your special thing with just them. And don't waste time. My friend also said those years flew by in a blink. Make your special memories now."

For someone without children, Mona always seemed to give the best advice about raising them. Perhaps she reminisced about the childhood she dreamt of but never experienced. She chose to wear her scars proudly rather than hide them.

"I thought you said you couldn't peel the potatoes."

She looked down at her nails. "I don't really like this color anyway. I told the nail tech I wanted holiday savvy. Instead, she gave me holiday *sad*. I mean, who even wears this color anymore? It's so last year. Might as well help you peel!"

My phone dinged, and I picked it up to see a text from Andy:

ANDY

Happy Thanksgiving? I would really like to hear from you.

Sighing, I put it down. Mona peered over my shoulder.

"Prince charming?" she asked. She started cutting the potatoes into big chunks. I took the potatoes and demonstrated how to cut them into smaller pieces.

"If you cut them too big, the mashed potatoes will be too lumpy. And yes, it was him. I just don't seem to have the time for him like I want. I mean, we hit it off *so* great. Everything in my life was going amazingly. And then life just took a turn."

Wracked with guilt, I averted my eyes from Evy's closed bedroom door. She slept quietly on the other side, completely worn down from six weeks of chemotherapy. I struggled with the dichotomy of being frustrated with my own life while she was fighting for hers. There was no balance, and I was mad at my selfishness. As if she could read my thoughts, Mona turned to face me.

"You don't have to feel guilty for wanting happiness for yourself," she said quietly. "It's okay to be a caregiver to someone else, but take care of yourself, too. Text him back."

Evy's bedroom door opened. Mona gasped quietly under her breath. Evy stood before us—tiny, swallowed up by her pajamas. A knit stocking hat was pulled over her head for warmth, yet she still shivered. I grabbed a blanket from the sofa and draped it around her shoulders. Benny licked her hand, nudging her towards the living room.

"It smells so good in here," she said, settling into the sofa. Mona went to the refrigerator and quickly assembled a small plate with cheese and crackers.

"How are you feeling? Here, try to eat something."

Mona passed her the crackers and a cup of tea. Evy wrapped herself tighter in her blanket.

"I'm so tired. I don't think I could have made it through another week of treatment." She leaned her head back and closed her eyes. "What time is it, anyway?"

"It's three o'clock. Dinner should be ready soon." Mona replied, then paused and looked at me. "Will dinner be ready soon? I mean, how do you even *know* without the poppy thing popping up!"

"Poppy thing?" Evy asked, not opening her eyes.

I groaned. "Don't even ask. Let me check the turkey."

I slid the digital meat thermometer into the turkey and shook my head. "125 degrees. We still have a little way to go. Mona, keep chopping."

Mona returned to her cutting board, making perfect squares out of the potatoes. Benny curled up next to Evy as she fell asleep on the sofa.

An hour later, Mona and I had dinner on the table. I nudged Evy awake.

"Wake up, sleeping beauty. Your Thanksgiving dinner awaits."

She blinked, momentarily disoriented, and then smiled. Putting my arm around her tiny waist, I lifted her and helped her to the table. As everyone settled in, I began portioning food on the plates. Evy stopped me.

"Wait. Should we say grace?" she asked.

Mona put her hand up in protest. "I'm not very religious. It's a long story. But yes, we should say something. So let me do it. Let's join hands."

Evy, Mona, and I joined hands. Mona looked around and said, "Now bow your heads."

We bowed heads, and Mona chanted loudly, "Good food! Good meat! Good God, let's eat!"

Evy's face lit up, and she suddenly broke into laughter. I missed that sound so much.

"That's not what I meant, but okay," she said, trying to catch her breath. "Good God, let's eat!"

"That's the spirit!" Mona said, taking her plate.

Evy's warm kitchen was filled with chatter and laughter that evening as we reminisced about the fun adventures we had all been on together and the ones we still hoped to take. The conversation eventually became about what we were all thankful for this holiday.

"I'm thankful for Kiki. Without her ruining my marriage, I never would have met the two of you," I said, raising my glass of sparkling cider.

"I'm thankful for The Luxe Thrifter. Without it, I never would have discovered that gorgeous red ball gown or met my two skydiving, speed dating, and clothes shopping buddies," Mona said.

"I'm thankful for another day to be here still," Evy said. "Another day with the two of you." The table quieted for a moment.

"Amen," I said.

Evy yawned. "I think I'm going to go and lie back down. Thank you for this wonderful meal."

She got up and retreated to her bedroom with Benny in tow. Mona and I surveyed the mess we had made in the kitchen.

"I guess we should clean up," I said, still unable to shake the nagging feeling that something was off. If it had been a typical Thanksgiving, the kids would be fighting over which holiday cartoons to watch because I always told them the Christmas season didn't start until the Thanksgiving turkey was eaten.

Back in the day, I would have filled plastic containers with leftovers in the kitchen while Jack hand-washed the good plates and silverware before carefully placing them back in the dining room credenza. The house would be buzzing with the anticipation of the upcoming holidays. Presents and parties. Visits to the mall to see Santa. But there was none of it this year.

I scraped dishes and prepared plates for Evy to eat later. Mona worked quietly alongside me while we returned Evy's kitchen to its former state. When we checked in on her before we left, she was fast asleep in her bed with Benny.

"Let's go," Mona whispered, and we quietly left her condo. Outside, the late fall air had turned bitterly cold. Mona hugged me.

"Happy Thanksgiving, sweetie," she said. "Your turkey was delicious. Jimmy Chews and Bark Twain will love these leftovers!"

She got into her car and sped away. I drove home silently, missing my kids and hating Jack for making this
world my new reality.

I pulled into my driveway and quickly hit my brakes.
Andy's Jeep sat in my parking spot. I parked next to him
and peered over, suddenly overcome with uneasiness.
Although I had planned to get back to him, I never
responded to his last text messages. Now I felt like an
absolute jerk.

He didn't acknowledge me, his gaze fixed straight
ahead, unmoving. Bracing myself, I stepped out of my
car and cautiously approached him.

"Hi, Andy," I said, attempting a smile.

He rolled his window down, and I took a step back.
My smile left me. His lips pressed together in a thin line
of resignation. He looked frustrated—and hurt.

"I'd like my sweatshirt back," he said.

I peered down at the ground, searching for words—
anything that would change that look on his face.

"Yes, of course. I'll get it. I'm so sorry," I said, and
turned toward my house.

He opened his car door and stopped me in my tracks.
"Do you know how many texts I've sent? How many
times I've tried to call you? You don't respond. Why are
you blowing me off? What did I do?"

How could I explain that every minute of every day
was consumed with taking care of things? That I was

completely out of bandwidth and barely holding on? *I had no words.*

"I'll get your sweatshirt." I turned again towards my house, my heart suddenly thumping in my chest. *How do I fix this?*

"Why are you so selfish?" he blurted as I started to walk away.

I halted abruptly, feeling a rush of heat flood my cheeks as my throat tightened. I faced him. Suddenly, I had everything to say to him.

"*Selfish?* Why am I so *selfish*? Do you know what the last few months of my life have been like? I'm working a full-time job, dealing with a divorce, and taking care of my kids—and I'm trying to help my best friend, who is slowly falling apart in front of me. I think she might be *dying*, Andy. I think I had some other priorities." Selfish. *Unreal!*

"You could have at least responded to me with more than one sentence of text," he said.

I stormed towards my house, opened the front door, and grabbed Andy's hoodie from the coat hook. I threw it at him.

"I'm so sorry if I wasn't *responsive.* I mean, I've been a little busy. It takes some effort to get someone back and forth to chemotherapy treatments. Making sure they are eating and keeping them *alive.* I'm so sorry if I haven't had time for any new *adventures,* but I've been dealing with my own adventures. Adventures that suck! You think I'm selfish? You have no idea what this has been like!"

I quickly turned and choked back tears as I marched towards my house, welling up inside with frustration and anger. I heard Andy's footsteps behind me.

"Emma, wait!"

I turned to him, shook my head, and said, "No!"

I shut the front door and fell against it, sobbing.

"Damn it." I heard him mutter to himself on the other side of the door. Moments passed, and my sobs erupted into a full-on meltdown. Unable to move, I curled into a ball on the floor, pulling myself close as the tears streamed down my face.

"Please. Can I come in?" He knocked on the door. "Emma?"

I couldn't find my voice to respond to him.

A few more moments passed. "Okay, fine. I'll leave you alone."

I listened to the sound of his footsteps receding as he walked away. His Jeep started up, and he pulled out of my driveway. I quickly opened the front door to stop him, only to see the taillights of his Jeep in the distance. *Fuck.*

I shouted into the darkness of my empty house, "I want a do-over! This isn't how things were supposed to be!"

Silence was the only response. Then my cell phone rang and startled me—it was Evy.

"Hey Evy, are you okay?" I said, steadying my voice. She didn't need to hear my troubles right now.

Following a long pause, she responded, "Not really."

"Did something happen? Do I need to come back over? Do I need to take you to the hospital?"

"No," she said quietly. "I'm done."

"What do you mean? Done with what?"

"Treatment. I don't want to do it anymore. I'm done."

I shook my head and paced my hallway. *What was she saying?*

"Ev, Dr. Conyers said there are other options if the chemo doesn't work. She gave you other options." A surge of fear rose within me.

"This last round of chemo was too much. It's all I have in me."

"No, I'm not hearing this. You're *not* done. You're going to keep trying until we have exhausted all options! This isn't all about you, you know. You can't just decide to quit. It's not fair."

"I'm sorry," she said, barely a whisper. "It's too hard."

"Stop thinking only about yourself," I blurted, instantly regretting what I said.

On the other end of the phone, I could hear Evy burst into tears. She was sobbing, unable to speak.

"No, I'm done. I want to go find Ben."

"Ben? There are people here who need you!"

Evy sobbed louder. "I'm sorry, Emm. I'm so sorry. I have to go." She hung up the phone.

"You can't do this!" I yelled into the darkness and fell to the floor, overcome with fear at the realization that she might be giving up—and the overwhelming truth that I couldn't stop it from happening. Tears flowed down my cheeks again. I wasn't sure how much more I could handle.

The front door creaked open, and Andy saw me on the floor. He quickly knelt beside me, pulling me into a tight embrace that left me struggling to catch my breath. He stroked my hair and whispered, "I'm so sorry, Emma."

He rocked me back and forth as I sobbed into his shirt, crying until there were no tears left. All the energy had left my body. I had nothing left to give.

We lay against the wall, immersed in the darkness and silence surrounding us. I looked up at him.

"I've missed you," I whispered.

His expression softened, and a look of genuine love filled his eyes. He leaned down, gently lifting my face toward his.

"I was afraid I would never see you again," he whispered. "You are all I think about anymore. I've been carrying this feeling around since I met you so long ago in that Urban Orchard."

"What feeling?"

He paused, struggling to find his words. "That you are my one."

I melted.

At that moment, my walls broke down, and my inhibitions crumbled, realizing my fear of being without him was greater than my fear of being hurt again by someone I love.

"I think you're my one, too."

Andy stood up and pulled me to my feet. The independent, brave soul inside me did not care that he was scooping me into his arms or that I was chivalrously being carried upstairs to my bedroom. The fighter in me did not fight back when he gently put me on the bed and lay down next to me, kissing me. I wanted to know what it was like to have him love me in every way.

"The timing...I didn't intend for this tonight," he said. "I can go."

I pulled him on top of me. "No. Stay. Stay all night."

He brushed my hair away from my face. "You are so beautiful. Even in grief and sadness. So real. Emma, I think I..."

"Shhhh," I whispered. "Come here."

I pulled his shirt from his back and didn't protest when he slowly undressed me. We lay together, naked and exposed for a little while, just quietly holding each other. Then I pulled him on top of me, and we melted together into each other. At that moment, I finally understood what had been missing for so long in my life. We were physically and mentally together as one.

Outside, snow fell as another winter storm approached. Tomorrow, I would apologize to Evy, be the rock she needed me to be in her life, and be there for her no matter what she decided. But tonight, I needed this man. I curled into his warm body as we drifted off to sleep. For the first time since Jack left me, I no longer felt alone.

CHAPTER 32

Next Steps

"Evy, I'm sorry!" I stood outside of Evy's condo, talking to her door. "I know you're in there! Please open the door." I knocked loudly. "Ev, come on! I know you're mad at me, but please don't do this. I really need to talk to you!"

Silence. I waited a few more moments and then turned and walked toward the elevator. Her door squeaked open, and she stood in her doorway, hand outstretched.

"Look at this," she said. She clenched a fist full of hair in her thin, bony hand. "It's coming out so fast."

Chemo was not her superpower.

"Oh God. Can I come in?" She stepped back and opened the door.

I hugged her. "I didn't mean what I said. You *aren't* selfish. You're the bravest person I know. But I understand, and no matter what you decide, I'll support you."

Evy slumped into a chair and put her head in her hands.

"This is hard," she said, staring at the floor.

"I know it is. I support whatever decision you make. I was just in a bad place last night when you called."

She shook her head. "I shouldn't have done that to you, either. That wasn't fair. I know you are trying to help me."

I pulled up the chair next to her. "So now what?"

"Now, we...keep trying."

"You're sure?"

"Yes. Do you know a good barber?" She ran her fingers through her hair. Thin strands slowly fell to the floor.

"If anyone can pull off bald and beautiful, it's you. When is your next appointment with Dr. Conyers?"

"Next Tuesday. She should have the results by then, and then I guess we can talk about the next steps."

"I'm just happy to hear there will *be* next steps. How are you feeling this morning? Up for some Black Friday shopping?"

She shook her head, 'no'.

"That's okay, I brought plan B."

I pulled two DVDs out of my bag. "*Love Actually*

and *The Holiday.* Let's stay in and binge-watch holiday movies."

"That's more my speed," she said. I pulled Thanksgiving leftovers from the refrigerator while she settled onto the sofa with a pillow and blankets. She fell asleep halfway through the first movie. I sat with her, watching her sleep. My phone dinged—it was Andy.

Andy:

> You're cute when you snore. And I am incredibly grateful to be able to know that fact now.

Me:

> Liar. I do not snore. And if you want me to believe otherwise, you're going to have to come back over and make sure.

Andy:

> Can this be arranged?

Me:

> I'm free on Friday. Does the *New York Times* food editor cook the food or just eat it?

Andy:

> I'm a culinary genius in and out of the kitchen. Your place? I'll bring the cuisine.

Me:

> Deal!

I accompanied Evy to her appointment with Dr. Conyers on Tuesday.

"We didn't see the success we would have liked with this round."

Dr. Conyers' laptop was open, and she pointed to white spots. "The larger tumors have shrunk, and that's great news, but there are new ones over here, " she said, pointing to another area on the screen.

Evy sat next to me, a wisp of her former self. She was engulfed in a hoodie, with what was left of her hair pulled back in a thin ponytail. Her skin and eyes had taken on an orange hue, which Dr. Conyers explained was occurring because of the cancer in her liver.

"There's an experimental drug in early clinical trials; it is proving extremely effective. The pharmaceutical company is seeing great success in its test patients. Evy, I'd like you to be part of that clinical trial if you're up for it."

Evy looked weary. "How long are the treatments?"

"It's a shorter length of time because the medication will be administered every two days instead of weekly. The only caveat is that you will be admitted to the hospital for the duration of the treatment. With any luck, we'll have you back home before Christmas. What do you think?"

Evy paused, looking up to the ceiling as if asking for answers. "When do I start?"

"Right away. You'll be in for about three weeks, so you'll want to pack for an extended stay. We can do the treatment right here in the oncology ward. Does Thursday at 9:00 sound okay?"

Evy nodded. I held her hand.

"I'll take you home and help you pack."

Later that evening, I picked up the kids from daycare. Benny sat in the back seat and leaped on top of Myla when she opened the car door.

"Benny!" Myla squealed and climbed in next to him, hugging him. "Mommy, why is Benny in the car?"

"Benny is going to stay with us for a little while."

Myla clapped happily and then paused. "But won't Aunt Evy miss him?"

"Of course she will, but she can't take care of him right now."

"Why not, Mommy?"

Why not? *How do I tell a small child that someone they love is very sick?*

"Aunt Evy isn't feeling well. And her doctor wants her to stay in the hospital for a few weeks so they can give her some medicine."

"Does she have the flu?" Benny settled into Myla's lap. She scratched him behind the ears.

"No, she has something called cancer."

Austin abruptly looked up from his gaming console. A look of alarm spread across his face.

"Mom," he said. "Do you know Isabella from school? Her grandmother had something called cancer. Her grandmother died."

Myla's eyes grew huge. "Is Aunt Evy going to *die*?"

Now, what do I say? The truth.

"Cancer comes in many forms. It makes some people very sick, but others are just fine. Her doctor is giving her medicine to help her. Sometimes, cancer can't be cured, but lots of times, it can. We are going to be hopeful and help her get better."

Myla scrunched her forehead, looking worried. "Is it contagious? Can I catch it, too?"

"No, it's not contagious. You can't catch it. Don't be scared. Be *hopeful.* Aunt Evy will be in the hospital for a few weeks. What can we do to help?"

"We can make her some get-well cards," Austin suggested.

"She would love that. You can work on them when we get home. Also, can you two help me take care of Benny?"

Myla nodded and lay her head on Benny's back. Then, she laughed when he turned and licked her face.

The following day, Mona and I accompanied Evy to the hospital. Her room in the oncology wing was large and painted a pleasant, hopeful yellow. A big picture window lined one wall, allowing in abundant sunlight. I hung the get-well cards the kids made on the corkboard next to her bed, along with her race medal. I handed Evy the dog Myla made at Make-a-Friend.

"Myla wants you to have this. She said if you care for her dog, she'll take care of yours." Evy smiled and tucked the stuffed dog into the bed next to her. The hospital room door swung open.

"Good morning, ladies," Nurse Alex sauntered in.

He walked over to Evy and took her hand. "I hear the last round didn't go so well, huh? Well, we've mixed up a new cocktail for you. Hopefully, this one will do the trick. And we've housed you in our finest suite. I'll be your primary nurse during your stay. I'm so glad you've brought along your crew for support."

Nurse Alex busied himself with setting up an IV for Evy and taking her vitals.

"Now, this medicine will be strong, but we'll take good care of you and ensure you stay hydrated. Your job will be to rest. Nothing more. Have you eaten this morning? I'm going to suggest a small, light meal. It's best to have a little something in your stomach."

He wheeled over a tray with a carton of yogurt and toast. Evy turned away from it.

"Try to eat a few bites," Nurse Alex suggested. "The doctor will be over in about an hour, and then we'll get started."

He turned and left the room. Mona followed him out.

"I think someone has a crush," I said.

"It would be wonderful if Mona found someone to love," Evy said. She picked at the toast on her plate. "Have you talked to Andy lately?"

"I saw him on Thanksgiving night. He was waiting at my house when I got home." I paused for a moment, "He stayed the night."

"You spent the night with him? Did you two...?" She squinted her eyes at me. "Never mind. You did. You should see the look on your face right now. You look like you got away with something."

I definitely got away with something.

I fluffed the pillow behind her head and spread a blanket over her feet.

"This makes me happy," she said. "Maybe when

I get out of here and start to heal, I'll find somebody again, too."

"I know you will," I said. "It's just a matter of time."

Time.

Leo Tolstoy once wrote, "The two most powerful warriors are patience and time."

Evy's first week of the experimental treatment crawled.

I went by the hospital every day and grew more worried with each visit. She was always asleep in her dark room, and I just silently sat with her, listening to the beeping sound of the equipment monitoring her vitals. I knew sleep was best. She wasn't suffering when she was asleep, but I inwardly wanted her to wake up for a little while and tell me she was okay. Instead, I stared at her tiny body, which appeared to be withering away right before my eyes. When we were overweight so many months ago, we cursed the extra weight on our bodies. Now, I cursed the lack of it.

✲✲✲

Andy arrived at my house Friday afternoon after work, carrying two hefty grocery bags into the kitchen. He pulled out a large bone wrapped in brown paper.

"Know anyone who might be interested in this?"

Benny whimpered at his feet, begging. Andy gave

him the bone, and Benny settled into his bed, tail wagging.

"Now you've got a furry friend for life. So, what is Chef Andy cooking up tonight?"

"Now that's a surprise. But first, you must leave the kitchen. Did I tell you that I'm a reclusive cook? Cooking is an art, and I *must* cook alone."

"You don't want me to help?" I pretended to pout, inwardly grateful that I didn't have to do any of the work. Andy pulled a bottle of wine from the bag.

"Corkscrew?" he asked. I motioned to the utensil drawer.

"Wine glass?" I pulled two glasses from the cabinet.

"Now, follow me."

Andy took my hand and led me to the family room. He patted his hand on the sofa.

"Sit right here."

He tucked a pillow behind my back, stretched my legs out in front of me, and settled beside me. Then he leaned in and kissed me gently.

"No, I do not want you to help me. I want you to relax." He handed me a glass of wine and picked up the remote control. "You need some downtime. I'll be in the kitchen making dinner. Your only job is to chill out. Just yell out if you need a refill."

"Yes, my captor," I teased. "I will do exactly as you say."

"See?" he said as he walked out of the room. "Stockholm Syndrome. I rock at this."

I turned on the TV and flipped through the channels. I heard Andy rummaging through cabinets and drawers in the kitchen, trying to find the right cooking tools. A pan crashed loudly to the floor. Benny barked.

"Sorry!" he called out. "Nothing broke."

A short while later, amazing smells began wafting from the kitchen. Andy poked his head around the corner.

"Got any candles?"

"Pantry," I responded. "And refill, please!"

Andy took my wine glass and returned moments later with a refill.

"Whatever you're cooking smells awesome," I said. "Can I come and look?"

"Absolutely not. I need to clean your kitchen first. Did I also mention that I'm a messy cook? You stay put."

I slowly sipped the wine. *I could get used to this.* A short while later, Andy appeared in the doorway.

"Dinner is served, madam."

He reached out his hand and pulled me up from the couch. "Right this way."

I followed Andy into my kitchen to see that he had lit several candles and placed them on the table, along with a romantic table for two. He even found the good China. He pulled out my chair for me.

"On tonight's menu, we have rosemary-crusted roasted leg of lamb. Baby potatoes with butter and herbs. And lemon and garlic seared broccolini."

"This looks fabulous," I said, looking at the beautifully prepared meal before us.

"I hope so. This is the first time I've made this. I observed them cooking it in the test kitchen last week."

The lamb melted in my mouth. The potatoes were just the right amount of crispiness, and the broccolini had the perfect crunch and lemon zing. I devoured everything on my plate and then put down my fork, unable to eat another bite.

"Wait, there's more," he said, pulling something from the refrigerator. "I put this together last night. Do you like cheesecake?"

He set down a creamy white cheesecake topped with a caramel swirl, sitting on a crunchy graham cracker crust before me. He must have spent hours in his kitchen perfecting this. Without another thought, I put down my glass of wine, went over to his chair, and straddled him.

"Is that a no to the cheesecake?" He laughed.

"That's a no to the cheesecake," I said, kissing him.

After a moment, I jumped up and sat on the kitchen island, kicking a chair out of the way. "Come here," I said. He obliged, and I wrapped my legs around him.

"Thank you for the fabulous dinner."

"Anything for you, gorgeous," he said, lifting my face to his and looking me in the eyes. "But what shall we do about dessert?"

"I have an idea."

We were half-dressed and panting fifteen minutes later, splayed out on my kitchen island.

"You might want to wash this surface before eating on it again. At least that's what the health department would recommend," he said. I laughed out loud.

That night, as Andy and I slept curled next to one another, I fell into a deep sleep. I dreamed Evy and I were on an airplane, staring out an open door. I peered down at the Earth far below.

"I'm going to jump now," she said, turning toward the plane door.

"Wait! Not yet! You don't have a parachute!" I protested, trying to stop her. I reached out my hand to grab hers and held it briefly. She released it.

"It's time to go."

"Stop! You're not ready," I said, reaching for her again.

"I'm not even afraid."

She stood on the threshold of the doorway—a dark shadow of a figure illuminated by the bright sunshine behind her.

"Evy, wait!"

She was gone.

Startled, I sat up in bed, my heart racing. Andy murmured into the darkness, reached over, and pulled me back into him. I lay beside him, staring at the ceiling, remnants of my dream haunting me until I slowly fell asleep. Just before dawn, my cell phone jolted me awake.

"Emma, it's Dr. Conyers. I'm sorry to call you so early. Evy took a turn in the middle of the night. Her white blood cell count is dangerously low. We've moved her into isolation. I've decided to stop treatment until we can get her stabilized. You can check in with me daily for updates or call Nurse Alex. But unfortunately, she can't have any visitors. Her risk of developing infection is too high."

"I understand," I sighed. "I will check in with you every day. Please tell Evy I love her."

"Of course," the doctor said and hung up.

"Everything okay?" Andy asked. I lay in the crook of his arm.

"No, it's not. This time, it most definitely is not."

He pulled me closer.

While I drifted, she fell. We were all falling petals.

CHAPTER 33

Sleighbells Ring, Are You Listening?

"Hold your end up a little higher."

"I'm *trying*. There are so many pine needles." Mona gasped. "And tree sap! My hands are getting so sticky."

"Now I'll walk backward, and you walk with me."

I hit the elevator button with my elbow and stepped backward into it when the door opened. Mona followed, and we pushed the tree into the elevator just before the doors dinged shut.

The tree engulfed the elevator inside, trapping Mona and me on either side of it. I heard her muttering to herself, "I don't know why people bother with real trees anymore. You can order a lovely fake one online, and there's *no mess.* I'll never get these sap stains out of my shirt."

"That's not very Christmas spirit-ish," I said from the other side of the tree.

"Bah humbug!" Mona muttered back through the tree branches.

The elevator door opened, and I called out, "Now, *shove!*" We pushed the tree out of the elevator with all our might and sent it tumbling into the hallway.

"Get the door," I said, grabbing the tree by the trunk. Mona fumbled with her keys and opened Evy's condo door. I dragged the tree inside.

"Now, what do we do with this monstrosity? So much sap!" Mona lamented.

"Now, we decorate it."

I pushed a tub of Christmas decorations I had dropped off earlier over to Mona and removed the lid.

"What's this?" she asked, holding up a construction paper garland chain.

"The kids made it."

"It's adorable," Mona said. "She will love this."

Evy was still in isolation in the hospital, finishing the last week of her treatment. I had not spoken with her. We only texted when she was awake, and that wasn't often. She had no idea that Mona and I were decorating her home for the holidays.

Knock! Knock!

"Who could that be?" Mona asked. Evy's front door opened slowly, and Andy peered his head around the opening.

"Can I come in? I followed the trail of pine needles from outside to the elevator and then here. I see you two have been busy."

Andy walked through the door, carrying another tub of decorations. Mona stopped what she was doing, looked him up and down, and grinned. She turned to me and whispered, "Oh *my!*"

"Where should I put these?" Andy asked, looking around.

Mona almost tripped over her own two feet as she approached Andy, extending her hand. "You must be Andy. You're just...well...my goodness, just *look at you.* So handsome. And look at these arms." Mona put her hands on Andy's biceps and squeezed them.

"You're Mona, right?" he asked, and obediently stood still and looked at me hopelessly while she placed her hands on his chest and felt his pecs. *Guy points.*

"Indeed, I am," she sighed.

"Need any help?" he asked. I nodded and waved him over to the tree.

"Yeah, we need to get this set up. I'll hold the tree up if you can get it set into the base." Andy got down on all fours and crawled over to the tree base. Mona watched him, grinning.

"Stop it," I whispered to her.

"What?" she said innocently and busied herself with the Christmas decorations. She brushed past me as she walked to the kitchen and whispered quietly, "Nice job. Great ass!"

We spent the next hour transforming Evy's condo into a holiday wonderland. After several attempts at getting the tree to stand up straight, we put colorful blinking lights on it and decorated it with a snowman-themed array of ornaments. I added a red and green tablecloth to her kitchen table, set out some candles, and placed the snow globe Andy gave me as the centerpiece.

"She's going to love this," Andy said, pulling me close to him as we looked around the room. "You two are wonderful friends."

Mona watched us from the kitchen, looking wistful.

"I sure hope so," I said. "She needs something happy to look forward to once she gets home."

When we finished, Andy helped me pack the remaining ornaments into the tubs and carried them to my car.

Later at home, I received a message from Rocco.

ROCCO

> Good afternoon, Emma. I hope you're having a nice weekend. Lauren asked me to send you a reminder that we have court on Monday. It's in Room 4B at 10:30. We'll see you there.

Court. Months ago, I couldn't wait for the court date to arrive. Now, a pit of anxiety sat in my stomach. Following Lauren's advice, I stayed silent and cut off most correspondence with Jack. Yet part of me still wanted to warn him. *How was it possible that I could feel pity for that man after he put me through so much?* Karma was a complicated companion.

On Monday, I met Lauren and Rocco at the Manchester County courthouse. Lauren paced the floor like a cat, ready to pounce. She stopped short and smiled when she saw Jack and Kiki enter the courthouse.

I glanced at Kiki's hand, and the social media rumors were confirmed—a big, gleaming rock sparkled on her ring finger. She met my gaze, smirked, and held onto Jack's arm smugly. Standing next to him, Jack's attorney cast a nervous glance toward Lauren. We all entered the courtroom.

"All rise!" The bailiff stood in the front of the room. "Superior Court of the state of New York, County of Manchester, Circuit Court Division, is now in session, the Honorable John Hawkins residing."

We all stood as Judge Hawkins entered and sat in front of the courtroom.

"You may be seated," said the bailiff. He turned to Judge Hawkins and said, "Preliminary divorce hearings are on today's docket." We waited as other couples went before the judge.

"Davis vs. Davis!" the bailiff called out.

"The day of judgment has arrived," Lauren whispered to me and stood. I walked up to the podium behind her. On the opposite side, Jack stood beside his attorney while Kiki sat a few feet away, watching. Judge Hawkins turned his attention to Jack and his attorney.

"Counselor, at our last hearing, your client was required to produce income statements to determine alimony and child support. We received very little information to make any such decision. Given your client's monthly financial obligations, I feel the information you've given is insufficient. Are we missing something?"

James P. Fortney nervously shuffled through the papers on the podium before him. Jack leaned down and whispered something before his attorney addressed the judge.

"No, Your Honor. We have provided tax statements and financial reports for the last two years for J&B Enterprises. You'll see here that we have given the court everything it has requested." His hand shook as he handed the paper to the judge. The judge glanced over the document and dropped it on the desk.

"Is this all?"

"I beg your pardon, Judge?"

"Sir, may I?" Lauren leaned forward. Judge Hawkins paused momentarily, peered over his glasses at Lauren, and nodded.

"Proceed."

"After extensive research of the plaintiff's corporate assets, my team has uncovered significant information I want to disclose today."

Lauren looked back at Rocco and smiled. Rocco gave her a silent nod.

Judge Hawkins looked impatient. "Continue."

Lauren straightened and opened the folder in her hand.

"When my client was still living with the plaintiff, she owned a company called OneBank. OneBank was a successful technology company that sold banking software to community banks nationwide. During their marriage, the plaintiff convinced my client to sell her company so they could start a family under the guise that the proceeds from the sale of OneBank would be put into a business venture with my client's name on it. He falsely claimed the money had been invested in a company that eventually failed. The plaintiff told my client her money was lost in the stock market, and he would start over by establishing a new local consulting company. We assume that would be the J&B Enterprises that is being referenced. Soon after that company was established, he left my client for a younger woman. That woman!"

Lauren turned and pointed at Kiki, drawing the attention of everyone in the courtroom. Kiki glanced desperately at Jack before rising to her feet and calling out, "I plead the Fifth!"

Judge Hawkins sighed in frustration. "I didn't ask you anything. Please be seated."

"I plead the Fifth to that, too," Kiki said.

"I said be seated!" Judge Hawkins bellowed. Kiki slithered down into her seat. Jack's face turned bright red as he looked around the room, flustered.

"May I continue?" Lauren asked.

"*Please,*" the Judge said.

"I would like to present to the court evidence to support the fact that the plaintiff has indeed not been truthful. The money given to him by my client following the sale of her company was invested in the stock market *quite* successfully, I might add. Soon after, he transferred that money and its dividends into several overseas accounts in the Cayman Islands, where the money has grown exponentially, now totaling over $75 million. The money is currently held in eight different companies. Mr. Davis is listed as a joint owner of these companies with an individual named Robert Blankenship. May I list them?"

The judge leaned forward, nodding. Lauren reached into her folder and handed Judge Hawkins a stack of documents.

"Here are the financial statements. One World Technologies. Strategic Edge Engineering. Baylou Enterprises. Blankenship Pharmaceuticals. Davis Corporation. Cayman Financial Group. One Vision Consulting. And Clearwater Investments."

Jack's eyes locked onto mine, his jaw clenched, and his face flushed with anger.

"Your Honor, the plaintiff—" James P. Fortney started to speak, but Judge Hawkins held up his hand to stop him. He turned to Lauren.

"And where are the tax statements for these companies?"

"Well, Your Honor, there are none. You can't have tax statements if you don't file taxes. At least there weren't any tax statements disclosed to the IRS."

The judge turned to Jack, who suddenly looked like

a child caught with his hand in a cookie jar. He stared at the floor. I had never seen Jack look so small.

"Mr. Davis? Is the information provided by the opposing counsel true?"

"My client pleads the Fifth," James P. Fortney asserted.

"Counselor, I am sure you know the implications of tax evasion. I want to open an immediate investigation into this matter. Your client will be detained for questioning. I am posting bail at $100,000. If these allegations are proven, your client is in a world of trouble. Tax evasion is a serious crime that the federal courts do not take lightly. We will get to the bottom of this."

The judge slammed the gavel down, and a police officer stepped into the courtroom, snapping handcuffs onto Jack's wrists. Jack shot me a desperate look, his eyes pleading. With a firm hand on Jack's back, the officer guided him out, and Kiki trailed behind.

Lauren turned to Jack's attorney, smiled, and stiletto-clicked loudly out of the courtroom.

Emma – 1.

Jack – 0.

The shark just won the fight.

CHAPTER 34

The Grand Heist

"Good morning, Dr. Conyers. It's Emma Davis, returning your call."

"Hi, Emma. Thank you for getting back to me so quickly. I know you had planned to come and get Evy today, but we will keep her for a few more days. Her treatment is over, and her white blood cell count has improved, but I still have concerns about infection. She's very weak right now. I'm hopeful that this treatment was successful and that she can get her strength back soon. But for now, we are going to play it safe."

"Can she have visitors?" I couldn't hide my disappointment and frustration. I was hoping for better news.

"Yes, you can visit, but we must limit it to just a few people. When will you be by?"

"This evening, right after work."

"We will let her know that you're coming." Dr. Conyers hung up.

I called Mona to give her the report. "Mona, I know it's short notice. Can you go with me tonight? I've hired a sitter to stay with the kids."

"Yes, of course, I'll go. I've been dying to get out of a mandatory office holiday party tonight. This is the perfect excuse. And, of course, I can't wait to see our girl. I'll meet you in the hospital lobby at 5:30."

Nothing could have prepared us for the moment we opened the door to Evy's hospital room. I choked back a sob when I entered. Mona grabbed my hand. We stood before her, afraid to get closer. Evy lay in her hospital bed, eyes closed. She was covered in blankets, attached to an IV, beeping steadily. Her arms lay on the blankets, wispy sticks attached to bony hands. Cheeks drawn and concave.

"Oh, my word," Mona whispered. "Our poor baby."

Whatever experimental treatment Evy underwent seemed to have the opposite effect of saving her life. She was wasting away. Nurse Alex entered the room, immediately noticing the concerned expressions on our faces.

"I know," he whispered. He checked the fluids in the IV bag. "She's lost a lot of weight. But she's doing better than she looks. She was awake and in good spirits earlier today. I even got her to eat. I'm sure she will be very happy to see you two."

He walked over and placed his hand on Evy's arm. "Evy, guess who is here to see you?" Evy opened her eyes. A smile spread across her face.

"You're here." She stretched her thin arms out as Mona and I engulfed her in a hug.

"We've been so worried about you!" Mona said.

"I got through it," Evy smiled. "The doctor said I'm on the other side now. Nurse Alex has been wonderful."

"Just doing my job! And anyway, you are the tough one. We've got a real fighter here. I'll leave you all to catch up," he said. He squeezed Evy's hand and left us alone in the room with her.

"How are you feeling?" I asked, settling into the chair next to the bed.

"I'm really tired. And I want to go home."

"The doctor said it will be soon. You're still weak. It's easier for them to monitor you in the hospital."

Her expression fell. "It's lonely in here. I miss you two. And Benny. How is he?"

"Myla has been spoiling him rotten. Trust me, he's well cared for."

Evy laid her head back on her pillow and closed her

eyes. A tear fell down her cheek, and she sucked in the air, suddenly sobbing.

"I need to get out of here," she said, her eyes pleading with us.

I took her hand. "Soon enough."

She shook her head. "I can't do this anymore. I need to feel normal again. Even for just a little while. Please take me home."

Mona sat quietly, watching her, and then stood. "I left something important at home," she said. "I'll be right back."

Puzzled, I followed her out and stopped her in the hallway. "Where are you going? You just got here."

"Just trust me," she said and left.

Upon returning to Evy's room, I found she had drifted off to sleep. Settling into the nearby chair, I waited for Mona to return. Exhaustion washed over me, and soon, I also fell asleep.

A short while later, the hospital door swung open, startling us awake.

"I've returned!" Mona said. I opened my eyes to see her wheeling a large suitcase into Evy's hospital room. "I had to slip this past Nurse Alex. That wasn't easy."

"What are you doing?" I asked.

Evy looked around, confused. Mona rolled the suitcase to Evy's bedside and took her hand.

"Okay, Evy. You said you want to feel like yourself

again. Well, you've come to the right person. Look what I've brought!"

Mona flung open her suitcase. An array of wigs, clothing, and makeup was packed inside.

"What are we feeling tonight? Blonde? Brunette? Foxy silver gray? Red? Long hair? Short? I've got it all!"

Evy's face widened into a smile. "Brunette, I think."

Mona pulled two brunette wigs from the suitcase and tried them on Evy.

"What do you think, Emma?"

"Definitely the long hair," I said, watching Mona in amusement. Years of cultivating her Mona persona had turned her into a makeover connoisseur. I watched her work her magic.

"Perfect! Now, what's our mood? Preppy? Bohemian? Grunge? Business casual? 80s yuppie with some shoulder pads?"

Evy smiled at her. "I'll let you decide."

Mona rummaged through the suitcase and pulled out an outfit. "Let's go with some Saturday afternoon casual vibes. A walk in the park kind of day."

She placed a cardigan sweater around Evy's shoulders under the wig and put matching espadrilles on her feet. Next, she pulled a large makeup case out of the suitcase and set it on the table next to Evy.

"Such marvelous cheekbones," Mona said as she applied foundation to Evy's face. "And those eyes! We'll make them just a little bit greener with some eyeshadow."

She rummaged through the makeup case and pulled out a round red tube. "Rouge," she mused. "Every girl needs rouge."

Ten minutes later, Mona took a step back and gave Evy a once-over, nodding in self-approval at her work. She pulled a mirror from the suitcase and put it in Evy's hands. Evy beamed.

"Thank you, Mona," she whispered, staring at her reflection. "Thank you so much."

"Well, all of this wasn't for *nothing*," Mona said. "Let's get you out of here."

I looked up, startled. "What? No, we can't, Mona." I gave her a stern look, but Evy nodded at me.

"Yes, get me out of here. Even if just for a little while." Her eyes were pleading.

I looked at Mona. "How are we going to get her out of here? Nurse Alex is like a bulldog. He'll never let us take her out."

Mona paced the room. "We need a plan," she said. "You call a taxi that is handicap accessible. I'll handle the rest. Now let me see if I can find a wheelchair." She left the room.

"Come on, Emm. Just for a little while." Evy looked at me, full of hope.

I wrapped the cardigan around her tightly and then called for the taxi. Mona returned with a wheelchair.

"The taxi will be here in five," I said. Mona rolled the wheelchair next to Evy's bedside, and we helped Evy into it. I covered her with blankets and secured her IV drip and its battery pack to the chair.

This is crazy. How are we going to pull this off?

I glanced at Mona, feeling desperate. She gave a reassuring nod, silently conveying that everything would be alright.

Ding! I looked at my phone. "It's here," I said. Mona crept over to the door, opened it, and looked both ways. She quickly shut it.

"Nurse Alex is just down the hall," she said. "I'll distract him. When I give the thumbs up, roll Evy out of here as fast as possible. Use the elevator on the other side of the floor. I'll meet you out front."

Adrenaline rushed through me. I felt as if we were pulling off a grand heist, trying to escape with the goods before the police caught up to us. Evy's frail face beamed with excitement and anticipation.

Mona opened the door and walked away. A moment later, she turned a corner with Nurse Alex, giving me a thumbs up as she led him away. I looked at Evy.

"Ready?"

"Go! Go! Go! Go!" Evy squealed.

I opened the door and ran as fast as possible, pushing the wheelchair down a long hall and around a corner to the elevator. The elevator doors opened, and as two people got out, I heard Evy shout, "Get out of our way!"

The couple scrambled into the hallway as we entered the elevator, and the doors shut behind us. I lay against the elevator wall, trying to catch my breath. Evy was laughing.

Outside, the taxi driver helped me get Evy and her wheelchair into the van. A few minutes later, the van door flew open, and Mona jumped into the front seat and looked back at us.

"You made it!" she said.

"We're going to get in trouble for this," I warned her.

"Nonsense," she replied. "I took care of it. I left a note."

"What did it say?"

"It said, 'We'll bring her back.'" She turned around and put on her seatbelt.

"Where to, ladies?" the driver asked. I looked at Evy.

"The Repub," Evy said. "It's buy-one, get-one margaritas and half-price tacos. Let's celebrate the punch that landed you in the Belmont Fat Girl's Hall of Fame."

"The Fat Girl's Hall of *what?*" Mona asked from the front seat.

"442 Pratt Street," I told the driver.

We arrived, and I helped Evy into her wheelchair before rolling her into the noisy bar. The college crowd was in full swing, with students packing the place. We found a seat near the small stage, and I went to the bar to grab three sodas. When I returned, I saw Evy resting, her head leaning back against the wheelchair, eyes closed.

"Are you okay?"

"Yes, just tired. This is more energy than I've exerted in so long. But I wouldn't change anything right now. I'd rather feel tired and alive than tucked away in a hospital room somewhere."

"Well, you let us know when you're ready to go. We can stay as long as you feel up to it."

Mona looked around. "Exactly why are we in a college bar?"

I explained, "Evy and I met at the church across the street at a Healthy Horizons meeting. We decided to go for a drink afterward, and this is where we ended up. This is where we first became friends."

"Oh," Mona said, nodding her head and looking around. "I understand. The beginning of a great story."

A squeal filled the room as a mic dropped on stage. Two college kids fumbled with karaoke equipment.

"That's the night I found out that Emma is a horrible singer," Evy whispered to Mona.

I stood up and walked onto the small stage, addressing one of the students setting up the equipment. "I have a special request," I said to him. I asked to see the playlist and pointed to a song.

He nodded and said, "It's all yours. Just give me a second to queue the music."

He handed me the mic. I turned and addressed the room.

"I'd like to dedicate this song to my friend." I pointed to Evy. The room quieted slightly as all eyes turned to her. The DJ queued *You're My Best Friend* by Queen. I followed along, not caring that people winced at my singing. I sang loud and proud for all the room to hear.

Evy stared up at me, beaming. At that moment, she looked like her old self, full of life and light. Mona sat in the chair next to her, crying quietly and dabbing her mascara with a bar napkin.

The entire room of college students joined the chorus. When the song ended, I took a bow, and the crowd cheered. I stepped off the stage, made my way over to Evy's wheelchair, and wrapped her in a hug.

"Thank you so much," she said to me.

"Anything for my best friend," I told her. Overwhelmed by emotion, a bittersweet joy and sorrow came over me. At that exact moment, I wished time would stand still.

"I'm ready to go back now."

"You're sure?"

"I'm sure."

Mona and I wrapped Evy in her blankets, and I called the taxi driver to take us back to the hospital. Evy fell asleep on the ride, and we quietly wheeled her up to her room, removing the clothing and wig. Mona gently wiped the makeup from her face. Evy's eyes peeked open as we tucked her into her bed.

"Thank you. I love you both so much," she said. She reached out and held our hands before closing her eyes again. We sat with her as she drifted off to sleep.

Mona looked at me and whispered, "Mission success."

I glanced over at the suitcase in the corner and smiled.

CHAPTER 35

Illusion

Two days later, with Evy still under observation at the hospital, I tried to lose myself in work. After the weekly staff meeting, I left the conference room and returned to my office. As I closed the door behind me, my eyes landed on my cell phone, its screen blinking rapidly. Three missed calls.

11:10 a.m. *Missed phone call from 512-467-8200.*
11:30 a.m. *Missed phone call from 512-467-8200.*
11:45 a.m. *Missed phone call from 512-467-8200.*

"Good morning, Emma. It's Nurse Alex. Can you please call me right away? It's important. 512-467-8200.

If I don't answer, please tell the nurse attending the front desk to find me."

I quickly hit the reply button.

"Belmont Hospital Oncology Ward. Nurse Alex speaking. How can I help you?"

"It's Emma Davis. You called me?"

"I'm afraid I have some concerning news, Emma." He hesitated and then continued, "Evy became unconscious last evening. She is stabilized, but right now we are monitoring her to determine if she should be moved to the ICU."

I fell into my chair, my head shaking in stunned disbelief. *No, he's mistaken. I was just with her two days ago.*

"What happened? What is the doctor saying?"

"Dr. Conyers has requested we call in the hospice team for support. I'm arranging that right now."

"Hospice? But that sometimes means..." My voice trailed off. "Can I come to sit with her?"

"Yes, of course. The sooner, the better."

I reflected on how, just two nights ago, we helped Evy escape. A deep, overwhelming guilt settled over me.

"Oh my God, we did this!"

I rose to my feet and began pacing my office. "We never should have done what we did! We never should have taken her out of there!" *Idiots.*

"Emma, no, wait. That is not true at all," Nurse Alex's voice softened. "Leaving a hospital room for a few hours does not send someone into a coma. Her illness is very progressed. You and Mona didn't do anything wrong. If anything, you made her happy for a little while. That was a blessing."

"I don't believe you!" I blurted into the phone.

"Emma, stop. Listen to me. There is a medical term for this. It's called terminal lucidity. It happens when a patient gets a burst of energy. They rally for a little while. It's quite common. Do *not* blame yourself. You didn't do anything to hurt her." *Wrong. I blame myself for all of it.*

"Thank you, Alex," I said. "I just need to let my team know that I'll be out for the rest of the day. I'll be there soon."

"We'll see you shortly," he said, hanging up the phone. I stood before my credenza, staring at the pictures. Front and center sat the photo of Evy, Mona, and me in our jumpsuits after skydiving. That was the day she taught me to be brave.

∂♪♪

I arrived at the hospital within an hour. The ride up the elevator to the oncology ward was long, as I remembered Evy's smile from when we escaped the hospital two nights prior. I could still hear the squeal of her laughter as I raced her down the hallway. The look of excitement and joy on her face when the elevator door closed. She was so relieved to be leaving that hospital room behind. How could she have slipped into a coma so quickly? *She looked so alive.*

I entered Evy's room, noticing Mona's suitcase still in the corner, with her clothing and wig tossed carelessly on a side table. In the shadows next to Evy's bed, I saw someone beside her, adjusting her blankets. Hearing my arrival, she turned to face me.

"Can I help you?" An older woman stood before me; her face graced with gentle wrinkles. She wore her long gray hair tied neatly back, and a pair of glasses rested on the tip of her nose. She had the warm, comforting presence of a loving grandmother.

"It's Emma. I'm here to check on Evy," I said.

The lady's face brightened. "Of course. Alex said you would be coming by. I'm Cathy, Evy's hospice coordinator."

I approached Evy, who appeared to be peacefully sleeping. Long, snake-like tubes and an IV extended from her body, connecting her to various equipment. The room was filled with the hum of machinery and the mechanical whirring of the IV drip. The image on the heartbeat monitor repetitively straightened and spiked.

"Is she breathing on her own?" I held Evy's hand. Her mottled red and purple skin felt cold to the touch. I recoiled slightly and placed it back on the bed.

"No, I just arrived about an hour ago, but Nurse Alex told me that she was struggling with her breathing in the middle of the night, so she's now hooked up to a ventilator."

I stared down at the mask engulfing Evy's face. "I just don't understand how this could happen. She was right here talking to me two days ago."

I sank into the chair next to her bed. Cathy stopped adjusting Evy's sheets and pulled a chair beside me.

"From the medical reports I've been provided, it appears that Evy went through a very potent round of chemotherapy. We never know how a patient will respond. This took a toll on her. But from what Nurse Alex has told me, she's a fighter. Our goal now is to keep her comfortable. I'm here to help Evy and all of you."

I held Evy's hand again. "Why is her hand so cold? Why does it look like that?"

"Her organs are struggling to function," Cathy explained. "Her circulation is poor. But keep holding her hand. She can feel it."

I took both of Evy's hands in mine, hoping that somehow, somewhere in her mind, she knew I was by her side. Cathy pulled a stack of papers from her backpack and put them on the table beside me.

"This is information on hospice—an overview of our services. And although it's not the most comfortable read, I've included some information on end-of-life progression. She will hopefully come around, but it's better to be informed so you understand what could happen."

Evy suddenly sucked in the air and started to choke. I jumped to my feet.

"Is she waking up?"

"No, this is common. And she's okay. She's just struggling to breathe. I encourage you to read through the information I've given you. I know this is frightening, but my team and I will help you. I'm here if you have any questions. Here is my card."

Cathy pulled a card from her backpack and handed it to me. "You can call me at any time. I need to work with the front desk on the hospice paperwork. I'll be back in the morning."

I sat silently as she packed her belongings and left. Then, I kept watch beside Evy. The steady beating of her heart monitor filled the room. My eyes closed briefly, trying to shut out the sound, but it grew louder and more insistent. I squeezed her hand tighter.

"Evy, I don't know if you can hear me. I hope you know I'm here with you. I wish you would open your eyes, but I understand if you can't right now."

The machines whirred and beeped in response. I hung my head and stared at the floor, trying to steady my voice.

"I mean, I don't even know how we got here. This

is craziness. When I met you, all we wanted was to be thin. To love ourselves again. To start over. I would give anything to trade places with you. If I could, I would take on every bit of pain you felt losing Ben and fighting that God-awful cancer. If you hang in here with me, I promise to help you find love and happiness again. Please don't give up."

The heart rate monitor rose and fell. Her raspy breath, steady but strained, told a story of exhaustion. Outside her door, people spoke in hushed voices.

I scoffed at myself, shaking my head in frustration. "I didn't need to lose weight. What I needed was *you*. This—our friendship—is what has mattered. You might be very sick, but you saved my life. And I can't imagine a world without you *in* my life!" My throat tightened as I tried to hold back tears.

"Don't forget, Evy! Never forget—all our adventures together. That stupid charcuterie board. Our disastrous dates. The nights we spent at home binge-watching *Friends*. The hundreds of miles you walked with me. You used to say, 'I rescue you, you rescue me,' but I can't rescue you right now, and it is killing me! Please open your eyes! Please wake up!"

Evy lay still, not moving. Unable to hold back my tears anymore, I sobbed, holding her hand. "I love you so very much. Thank you for being my friend."

All at once, the room felt like it was closing in on me.

The whirring and beeping of the machines roared in my ears. My vision blurred. My lungs felt like they couldn't get air. I grabbed my coat and ran down the long hallway to the elevator. I rode down to the bottom floor and ran out to the street. I was immediately enveloped in bitterly cold air.

I need to move.

I walked in no particular direction. The festive holiday lights outside the stores shone brightly. A man in a Santa suit stood by a Salvation Army bucket, ringing a bell. Christmas music blared from someone's car stereo.

Stop the holidays. My best friend might be dying. She may never see the Christmas tree we put in her living room. She may never know another Christmas morning.

I need to run.

I rushed by people on the sidewalks, pushing them aside. I had no idea where to go, so I ran until my legs ached and my lungs felt like they would collapse from the winter air. Out of breath, I stopped short and turned. Our Lady of Mass Consumption stood before me.

Freezing and exhausted, I entered the empty church, its warmth blanketing me from the bitter cold outside. Silence filled the sanctuary. I returned to the pew where I first met Evy and sat in the stillness, attempting to slow my racing heart. My voice echoed through the darkness.

"God? Higher being? Universe? I have something I need to say to you. I don't understand you. I don't understand how you can take a lovely soul like Evy and put her through so much. You make good people suffer, and there's no rhyme or reason. She's sick with cancer. She lost her husband. Why would you give her so much pain to handle? Why am I selfishly thriving, and she is lying in a hospital room, possibly dying? You should have chosen me! Why can't you help me fix this?"

Hot tears welled in my eyes and spilled down my cheeks.

"Control is an illusion," a voice said behind me, startling me. I saw a figure a few feet away in the room's shadows.

I thought I was alone.

"Who are you?" I said out loud into the dark room.

"I'm Sister Margaret. I work here. I come here when I need solace and have questions. I overheard you."

I nodded and replied bitterly, "My best friend might be dying. She slipped into a coma last night. I don't know how to help her. I'm so angry that I can't."

"I'm so sorry to hear that. I know this must be hard for you." She was quiet for another moment, searching for words. "God. The universe. Your higher power. Whatever you believe in. They are all a mystery. I've spent my whole life trying to understand why things happen like they do. Sometimes, none of it is fair, but I do think all of it is intentional. I've concluded that control isn't real; it's merely an illusion we tell ourselves.

Perhaps we weren't meant to know how or why, but simply to have faith that we are all playing a part in a bigger plan."

A bigger plan.

Was it a coincidence that Evy sat behind me that day in the Healthy Horizons meeting? Or that Andy was in Urban Orchard the same day I ventured inside with Evy to build a charcuterie board? What about that warm summer night so many years ago when Evy pulled up in her rusty old Honda Accord to a party in college where she met and fell in love with her soulmate? She told me that she would find Ben again. I now believed she would.

"I get it, but it's just hard," I said. "I don't know what I would do without her."

"Your friend has given you strength. Now is the time to own it."

I sat quietly for a few moments, pondering what she said. I turned to express gratitude to the woman, but she was gone.

As I rose from the wooden pew, the quiet of the empty church surrounded me. My eyes drifted to the third row on the left—Evy's spot. The place where, all those months ago, she came into my world when I needed her most. I suddenly wished I could go back, hear that belly laugh, and do it all once again.

When I stepped outside, a chill overcame me. Snow

rained down as I reached for my coat and realized I had left it inside the sanctuary. I also needed to find the nun and thank her. I retrieved my jacket and encountered a church employee on my way out.

"Excuse me," I said to the man. "I was just here a few minutes ago talking with a nun. She said she works here. Sister Margaret. Could you tell me where I can find her?"

The man looked confused. "I'm not sure who you're referring to, ma'am," he said. "We have no sisters or convents associated with this church. I can direct you to Father Wohlrab's office?"

I shook my head. "No, she was just here, in the sanctuary. She was talking to me."

He shrugged his shoulders in response. "Are you sure you have the right place?"

"I'm sure, but thank you anyway."

Turning away, I left the church, confused. *Am I crazy?* As I pulled my phone out of my pocket to call a taxi, I stopped short on the sidewalk. Reading the blinking message, I froze in place.

Missed phone call from 512-467-8200.

That number. That's the hospital. *Why are they calling me?* My hands shook as I fumbled to punch the numbers into my phone.

"Belmont Hospital Oncology Ward. Nurse Alex speaking. How can I help you?"

"Nurse Alex, it's Emma. I just saw the missed call."

"Emma, I am so very sorry to tell you this." He was silent for a long moment. "Evy has passed."

"What? When?" I choked back a sob.

"Right after you left. I saw you running down the hall, so I checked on her. When I opened the door to her room, I thought she was coming around. Her eyes opened momentarily, and I heard her whisper, 'I love you too,' but then her heart rate monitor flatlined. She went into cardiac arrest. The team did everything they could to try and revive her." He paused momentarily and said, "Please know that she went peacefully."

I stared at my phone, barely able to get the words out. "Can I see her?"

"Of course, honey. I'm so very sorry."

"I'm on my way."

The weight of his words bore down upon me, knocking the breath out of me. I leaned against the city building wall and squeezed my eyes shut. My universe cracked wide open at that moment as stars crashed from the sky and the sun went dark. It was the deafening sound of everything splintering all at once. For the first time, I understood the unbearable weight of a heart breaking over something forever lost.

I listened to the distant sound of the Salvation Army man ringing a bell.

She will never see another Christmas morning.

A chill overcame me, leaving me shivering uncontrollably. I shut off my phone and began the long, cold walk back to the hospital.

My beautiful Evy is gone.

CHAPTER 36

The Last Things Said

Evy's memorial service was held in early January on a bright, sunny, cold day. At the funeral director's request, I arrived early at the facility to assist with setting up the reception room. He met me at the front door and ushered me in from the cold.

"Good afternoon, Emma. I'm Marcus. Let me take your coat." I followed Marcus through the funeral home to the reception room.

"It certainly is a beautiful day for her service. As you can see, we've received an overwhelming number of flower arrangements, and I want to make sure we've displayed them to your liking."

The reception room was lined wall to wall with floral displays. I would have expected nothing less. A large picture of Evy stood on a pedestal at the front of the room next to the podium. Next to it, a memorial table covered with photos and memoirs was lined up on another wall. Her college degrees. Awards she received. Pictures from yearbooks. Her race medal from the half marathon. A picture of Evy and Ben hugging Benny. Andy helped me go through her condo to find all these pieces that told her life story.

"The flowers look beautiful," I said. "In fact, I think it all looks just perfect. This is exactly how she would have wanted it."

Marcus nodded at me and smiled. "We will open the doors in about thirty minutes, and the service will start at 2:00 p.m. This will allow you time to greet guests. And then, I'll open with a few words at the podium and turn it over to you. Then, we will allow the guests to pay their last respects. I'll be in my office down the hall if you need anything until then."

Marcus left the room, and I sat in a chair, mentally preparing myself. The door opened, and Andy peeked his head around the doorway.

"Want some company before things get started?" I sighed with relief. Nodding, I beckoned him over.

"How are you holding up?" he asked, settling in beside me.

"I'm running on adrenaline right now."

I looked at the picture of Evy next to the podium. It

was one of the photos I took in the park when we set up our online dating profiles. That day felt like a million years ago.

"This is a lot of flowers," he said, looking around the room. "A lot of people must have loved her."

"I know I did," I said. Andy squeezed my hand.

"Who has your children today?"

"Jack. He said he would take them out to do something fun. He was actually kind to me when I told him about Evy. Maybe he's not the soul-less monster I thought he had turned into when he met Kiki. Maybe there's hope for him."

Just then, the door to the reception room opened again, and Mona walked in. She was adorned in an elegant floor-length black gown, accessorized with black and gold jewelry, and wore a sleek wig.

"My goodness!" She looked around at all the flowers. "What a display!"

She sat down on the other side of me and grabbed my hand. "Are you ready?"

I nodded. "Ready as I can be, I guess."

"I've brought someone with me. He's parking the car." Moments later, Nurse Alex walked in and joined us.

"Evy had a feeling about you two," I told her. A big grin spread across her face.

Marcus poked his head in. "Guests are starting to arrive. Are you okay to begin early?"

"Of course. Bring them in."

I stood at the reception room's doorway as a steady stream of people trailed in. Charles from the Southside Sisters of Mercy soup kitchen was the first through the door, followed by Agnes, wearing her Sunday best. Marvin and Bernice followed.

A group of Evy's former students and fellow teachers from Maryland traveled to Belmont in a carpool, as did a team from Golden Paws Rescue in Washington, DC. Ben's former workmates also arrived.

A couple who introduced themselves as Ben's parents, along with his siblings and their families, showed up. Colleagues from the University of Belmont. Old friends from her high school and college days. Evy had touched many people's lives; they were all there to pay their respects.

The reception room was packed by two o'clock, with people spilling out into the hallway. Marcus went to the podium, welcomed everyone, and then turned it over to me. I stared at the large crowd before me and spoke, trying to calm the quiver in my voice.

"Thank you all for coming today. As you all may know, Evy was predeceased by her parents and her husband, Ben, but looking around the room today, I now realize that Evy was part of a much larger family that included all of you. She would have been thrilled to see this outpouring of love."

Mona sat in the front row with Nurse Alex. Andy sat on the other side of her, looking up at me. He gave me a subtle nod, silently urging me to continue.

"But love is what Evy was all about. At least, that's what she always showed me. I first met her when I was at one of the lowest points in my life, when I was feeling very alone and scared. She immediately befriended me and taught me that life isn't perfect, but adversity can still be beautiful. She showed me that joy can still be found even in our lowest places. She had just lost Ben when I met her and was struggling with her own sadness, but she showed me laughter through tears."

Ben's parents nodded in agreement as if that was exactly how they remembered their daughter-in-law.

"Evy and I definitely had our adventures! We trained for and ran a half-marathon together. She talked me into jumping out of an airplane. She told me I was the worst singer she had ever heard and banned me from karaoke bars for life. We both loved binge-watching old TV shows. We shared a terrible taste in boxed wine. And in search of love, we went in together, full of hope, despite all the setbacks we encountered. My favorite thing about her, though, was her adventurous spirit. Every time I turned a corner, Evy was there making a new friend."

Mona started to cry. Nurse Alex pulled out a tissue from his pocket and dabbed her tears.

"She never gave up on anything—including me. She helped me turn my self-pity into self-love and helped me grow as a person because of it. I wouldn't be the person that I am today without her friendship. Looking around the room, I know that all of you have a story to tell. I wish she were here today, knowing how many lives she touched. But she's now somewhere in our crazy universe, chasing down her soulmate, Ben. To Evy, I salute you. I love you. And I will never forget you. Thank you for being my friend."

The room fell quiet. Andy peered up at me and whispered, "I love you." My heart fluttered.

"Would anyone else like to speak today?"

Charles from the Southside Sisters of Mercy stood and walked to the podium. He regaled the room with tales of Evy's adventures in the soup kitchen, including when she accidentally added cayenne pepper to the fried chicken instead of paprika. "Now that was some hot chicken!" he chuckled.

High school friends talked about their formative years when Evy would sneak out of her parents' house late at night and steal their car. She never got caught. Others shared tales about life in the dorm rooms with Evy in college, including a disastrous frat party where she showed up dressed as a nun because someone told her it was a Halloween party. She was the only one in costume.

Her students shared stories about Evy's love of literature and theater. One of her former students was just finishing writing her first novel. She addressed the room.

"Ms. Hanover shared a quote with me once that changed my life. American novelist Toni Morrison wrote it after she received the Nobel Peace Prize. She said, 'Wordwork is sublime because it is generative; it secures our difference, our human difference—the way in which we are like no other life. We die. That may be the meaning of life. But we do language. That may be the measure of our lives.' I will dedicate my first novel to the woman who taught me how to write about the beauty in life."

Ben's mother shared a story about the first time he brought Evy home, saying she knew immediately that Evy would be his future wife. "Ben changed so much after meeting Evy that summer. I could tell he was head over heels. And, for some reason, he even started calling his 'cah' a 'car', and he tossed out his boat shoes and stopped wearing polo shirts," she added with a laugh, giving a little shrug.

The room quieted after everyone had spoken. Marcus approached me. "Ready to wrap things up?" I nodded.

Marcus thanked everyone for coming, and I stood at the doorway and wished everyone well as they departed. I was thankful to be part of this proper send-off for my beautiful friend.

When everyone had left, Andy helped me put boxes of memorabilia into my SUV.

"That was really nice," he said, opening my door.

"It was," I nodded.

"Doing okay?" He grabbed my hand and looked me in the eyes. "I know this has all been a lot for you."

I shrugged. "I just miss her. So much. I feel like this empty feeling will never go away." I tried to push away the gnawing ache inside my stomach.

"Maybe you could use a break. I'm going to be researching a story in California in two weeks. 'The Avocado Craze—A Deep Dive into California's Avocado Industry'. I was hoping I could convince you to tag along. Just for two nights. Think about it?"

I offered him a faint smile and nodded. As he began to walk away, I caught his hand and gently tugged him back. He turned to meet my gaze.

"What's up?"

I looked up at him. "I just wanted to tell you something." I held my breath momentarily, feeling as if my heart was teetering on the brink of a tall cliff. *Be brave, Emma. Just say it.* I exhaled slowly, "I want you to know I love you, too."

We held each other's stare momentarily before his lips curved into a small smile – just like the one he wore when I met him for the first time so long ago. He put his hands on my face, looked into my eyes, and said, "Finally."

"I'm sorry it took me so long to say it."

His thumb gently brushed my cheek. He continued to hold my gaze. "It doesn't matter. You said it now. That means everything to me. Come here."

Andy pulled me into his arms, holding me so tightly I could hardly breathe—and yet, for the first time in a long time, I felt as if I finally could.

I drove away from the funeral home and headed to Jack's condo in the city, eager to pick up Myla and Austin. When I arrived, the building door flung open, and Myla raced past the doorman, dashed out of the building, and jumped into the back seat. Austin followed close behind.

"Finally!" Myla said, exasperated. "What took you so long, Mommy?"

"I'm sorry I'm late. What's wrong? Didn't you have fun last night?"

"No, it wasn't fun at all," Myla sighed. "It was boring."

"Why? I thought Daddy and Miss Kiki were going to take you out for pizza and bowling."

Austin shook his head. "All we did was watch TV. Dad barely talked to us. And Miss Kiki isn't there anymore." His voice went flat. "She's gone."

"What do you mean 'gone'?"

Myla dramatically flung up her hands as if fed up with the situation. "Daddy said she's left and isn't returning. She took all her clothes with her. Now Daddy's sad. I guess now he's going to have to find himself a new Coochie." She shrugged and fastened her seatbelt.

Gone?

Pulling away from the building, I saw Jack in my car's rearview mirror. My foot hit the brake momentarily as I exchanged a look with him in its reflection. He stood in the doorway of his building, looking defeated, shoulders sagging. A feeling of pity briefly came over me. *How could I still feel anything for this man?* He held my gaze for a moment before giving me a brief wave, turning, and walking back into his building. Alone.

C H A P T E R   3 7

Vanished

oice message from Rocco: *"Emma! Lauren and I need you to call us back right away. I was preparing the final financial statements for court next week. Something has happened. I have terrible news."*

I immediately returned his call, "Rocco, it's Emma. I got your message. What is going on?"

"You're not going to believe this. Apparently, Jack's business partner, Robert Blankenship, emptied the overseas accounts when Jack's fiancée tipped him off that they were under investigation for tax evasion. They ran off together. There's no trace of them or the money anywhere."

I sat down hard on my kitchen barstool, speechless. *Kiki ran off with him and took all the money?*

"I'm broke?" *I will be working for the Federal Center for Fiscal Enforcement until the day I die.*

"Judge Hawkins has opened a criminal investigation. The police are on their way to Jack's condo as we speak. He will be held without bond this time. Even though that money is gone, he's still in serious trouble."

"I can't believe this! How can they just take the money and run?"

"People do things like this and are sometimes never found again. I'm sure they've fled to a country with a no-extradition treaty. Lauren is beside herself. None of us could have predicted this."

"But my divorce. Now what?" *I'm going to lose the house. The kids will have to go to a new school. This changes everything.*

My stomach twisted into a knot, now faced with so much uncertainty. I needed to talk to Evy, but remembered I couldn't. *I miss her so much.*

"Your name isn't anywhere on those accounts. You can still proceed with the divorce, and Lauren said she would advise it. You'll want to get as far away from this situation as possible."

Still reeling from the news, I put my head in my hands.

That ruthless little tart.

My OneBank money–everything I worked for.

Vanished.

CHAPTER 38

Free

"All rise!" The bailiff stood in the front of the room. "Superior Court of New York, County of Manchester, Circuit Court Division, is now in session, the Honorable John Hawkins residing."

We all stood as Judge Hawkins entered and sat in front of the courtroom.

"You may be seated," said the bailiff. He turned to Judge Hawkins and said, "Final divorce hearings are on today's docket."

I sat with Lauren, waiting to be called.

"Davis vs. Davis!" the bailiff called out.

"Let's go," Lauren said. The two of us stood before Judge Hawkins. Lauren approached the bench.

"Your Honor, given the circumstances of my client's

situation and the fact that Mr. Davis is incarcerated, we are requesting that my client's request for full custody of the two children and retention of the marital home be granted. I contacted his attorney and was informed Mr. Davis has chosen not to be present today."

The judge peered over his glasses at me as if studying me.

"Ms. Davis, in the absence of your husband's appearance, I am granting your divorce and will honor your request for full custody and retention of your home. I've signed the Final Decree of Divorce, which will be sent to the clerk for final signature. Good luck, Ms. Davis. You've been through a lot. Please take care of yourself and your children."

"Thank you, sir," I said.

Lauren took my elbow and led me to the hallway outside.

"That's it?" I asked her.

"That's it," she replied, hugging me. "Congratulations, Emma. You're free."

Ironic

oice message from 212-563-3000: Good after-noon, Emma. My name is Jacob Tennenbaum. I am contacting you regarding your late friend, Evelyn Hanover. I was wondering if I could set up a meeting with you to discuss some important information. Please call my office at 212-563-3000 and ask to speak with my receptionist, Brittany. She will assist with setting up a time and provide directions to our office. I look for-ward to meeting with you.

Spring arrived late in Belmont that year. After the cold nor'easter winter, the air warmed, and the ground thawed. Andy, the kids, and I walked along Browncroft Boulevard, admiring the newly sprouted peach blos-soms on the trees. Benny ran beside our newly acquired golden retriever rescue puppy. Myla insisted we name her in honor of Evy.

"Mommy, can we take Benny and Evy to the park later? I want to teach the puppy how to catch a frisbee."

I shook my head. "Sorry, kiddo. I have a meeting to go to."

Myla scowled. "You *always* have meetings!"

"I could take them," Andy suggested.

"You sure?"

"Yeah, of course. Go to your meeting. She can teach me how to play frisbee, too."

Myla nodded happily and skipped ahead of us. The dogs followed her, barking.

Later that day, I drove into the city. I entered Jacob Tennenbaum, Esquire's law office, at 2:00 p.m. A far contrast from Lauren's plush office, the wood-paneled walls in the old building were covered with photos of Jacob Tennenbaum working out in the community.

In one photo, he was pictured painting an old, rundown home during a Christmas in April event. In another, he served people experiencing homelessness at a Thanksgiving feast. He even volunteered at the Belmont Boys and Girls Club. He seemed exactly like someone Evy would have hired as her attorney. I sat on an old leather sofa and looked through a magazine, waiting to speak to him.

The door opened, and a middle-aged man stepped into the room. His slightly gray hair was tied back in a ponytail, and he was dressed in khaki pants paired with a denim shirt, its sleeves casually rolled up. *This guy is a lawyer?* He extended his hand.

"Emma?"

I nodded and shook it.

"So good to meet you. Please, follow me." He guided me to a small conference room and gestured for me to sit. Moments later, he returned with a stack of papers in his hand.

"Emma, first, I want to say I am so sorry to learn of Evy's passing. She was wonderful, and I feel honored to represent her today."

"I miss her horribly," I replied. The pit in my stomach never seemed to ease every time I thought about her. "Why was I asked to be here today?"

"Evy entrusted me to handle her estate. She met with me quite a while ago when she feared her cancer might be returning. She said she wanted to get her affairs in order, just in case."

How long ago was that? My heart ached thinking about how alone she must have felt with her secret. She knew this day was coming.

"Evy may have disclosed at some point that her

husband ran a very successful financial management company. When he passed, he left stock options in that company and a very sizeable insurance policy in her name. Your friend had quite a large estate. Millions, actually."

Millions? Evy never told me she was worth millions.

"She has left all of it to you," he said.

My heart stopped. I stared at him, speechless.

"Except for yearly stipends to the Golden Paws Animal Rescue and Southside Sisters of Mercy soup kitchen, she wanted you to have everything. She has left you over fifteen million dollars."

Fifteen million dollars? I couldn't speak. *Fifteen?*

"I know this must come as a shock." He pulled a sealed envelope from his folder and handed it to me. "She also wanted you to have this and asked that I not give it to you until I disclosed the inheritance. She wanted you to read it alone. Do you have an attorney or a financial advisor that I can work with on the legal aspects of this inheritance?"

My head was reeling. I took the envelope. It was strange to know that she once held this same envelope in her hands, unsure of her future. I clutched it harder, feeling our connection.

"Yes, I do, a very good one. Please reach out to Lauren C. Livingston. I will give you the number for Rocco, her paralegal." I scribbled Rocco's phone number on his notepad.

"Thank you. I'll contact Ms. Livingston right away. I'll contact you once I can sort through the details with your attorney."

He led me to the front of the office. "Best of luck, Emma."

After leaving his building, I walked along the city sidewalks in a daze. Fifteen million dollars? *Evy rescued me one last time.* I found a nearby park and settled on a bench beneath the shade of a tree. Pulling out the envelope, I carefully opened it and read the letter tucked inside.

Dear Emma,

Tomorrow, I will be going in for my next round of chemotherapy. I don't know how this experimental treatment will turn out. To be honest, I'm scared. But I promised you I would keep trying. I'm writing this letter in case things don't go well, and I will send it to my lawyer tomorrow. Hopefully, this letter will never be put into your hands. If it does, I have some things I need you to know.

First, I can't believe I died. I was really hoping to stick around long enough to find love again... watch your children grow up with you...see my students succeed in life...and maybe knock a few more items off my bucket list. But I guess we have no control over when we move on. Life is the ultimate adventure, though, isn't it? Live it like it is. I hope you face all the scary things in your life with the same bravery you felt when you jumped out of that airplane. You are stronger than you know.

Second, never ever sing karaoke in front of Andy. I hope he is your true love, so don't scare him off with your singing. Soulmates traverse time to find each other, and he found you one afternoon in an Urban Orchard. He knew it when he saw you. I can still remember the look on his face. You never know what waits around every corner, which leads me to my next point.

I've thought about it for a long time and have come to a conclusion. We don't get just one soulmate in life. We can have many. Soulmates come in all forms and sizes. And you, my friend, are one of mine. Whether this was our first encounter or one of many, we just fit together.

I have loved being your best friend, and I am sorry to have to say goodbye. You made my world a better place. I will miss all the things connected to you, but I know I will see you again someday.

Please take care of Mona. She is a beautiful soul who deserves to find happiness and love. Your friendship will see her through. Also, please take care of my Benny. I am leaving him in Myla's care. She will make a great dog mom to him.

You should know by now I've left all my money to you. I know you'll do great things with it. OneBank was just the first success of many. I wish I could be there to see it, but I know you will excel. Do something great! But why wouldn't you? Look at you today. You went from being a mumbling mess when I first met you to the self-confident heroine of her own story. You've overcome so many obstacles. Can I just tell you how proud I am of you?

And just one last thing. I love you.

Until I see you again...

Evy

I folded the letter and pressed it against my heart. I sat alone in the park for a long time, lost in thoughts of her. Life continued around me—children laughing and playing on the playground, a young mother nursing her baby on a nearby bench, and an elderly couple strolling past, hand in hand.

My phone beeped and startled me.

Andy:

ANDY

I think I've worn the kids out. Okay if I make dinner for all of us tonight?

Me:

That would be amazing.
I am heading back now.

Back at my car, I got in and rolled the windows down, feeling the warm spring air on my face as I returned home. Still, deep in thought, I turned a corner at a stoplight. The Belmont McDonald's stood before me on the other side of the street. I paused, feeling Evy's presence.

"Okay, my friend," I said out loud, looking to the sky. "Okay, then."

I pulled into the drive-through line.

"Welcome to McDonald's. What can I get for you today?"

"I'd like some fries." I paused for a moment. "*Hot ones—with salt.*"

On the ride home, *Ironic* by Alanis Morrisette played on the '90s station on satellite radio. Loud and off-key, I sang along.

The End

About the Author

JA Wright earned a Master's degree in Writing from Johns Hopkins University and a Bachelor's degree in English from Frostburg State University, as well as a Master's degree in Information Technology Program Management from National Defense University. A proud member of the Women's Fiction Writers Association, she balances her passion for writing with a career in Information Technology leadership. In her spare time, she enjoys cooking, boating, and playing frisbee with her hyper border collie. A lifelong Marylander, she grew up along the shores of the Chesapeake Bay and continues to live in Maryland with her fiancé, son, and crazy dog. *Charcuterie Girl* is her debut novel.

www.ingramcontent.com/pod-product-compliance
Lightning Source LLC
Chambersburg PA
CBHW030335010826
48973CB00004B/1009